HIS MISTLETOE BRIDE

He studied her with a silent, predatory watchfulness that penetrated her to the bone. And even though his body remained as still as a marble statue, his eyes burned like flame, with a scorching sensuality that leapt across the space between them.

She drew in a tattered breath. She might be innocent in the ways of men—especially men like Lucas Stanton—but she thought she knew what that particular look meant. It frightened and excited her all at once. For an instant, she could think of nothing else, see nothing else but the hot gleam in his eye.

Her eyes grew wide as Lucas swooped down to kiss her. But when his lips met hers she squeezed her eyelids closed, overcome by the shock of his touch and the temptation that trembled through her. Her heart pounded with something akin to fright, yet she could not resist his lure—hot and sweet, hinting of champagne and something forbidden. . . .

Books by Vanessa Kelly

MASTERING THE MARQUESS

SEX AND THE SINGLE EARL

MY FAVORITE COUNTESS

HIS MISTLETOE BRIDE

AN INVITATION TO SIN
(with Jo Beverley, Sally MacKenzie, and Kaitlin O'Riley)

Published by Kensington Publishing Corporation

His
Mistletoe
Bride

VANESSA
KELLY

ZEBRA BOOKS
KENSINGTON PUBLISHING CORP.
http://www.kensingtonbooks.com

ZEBRA BOOKS are published by

Kensington Publishing Corp.
119 West 40th Street
New York, NY 10018

All Kensington titles, imprints and distributed lines are available at special quantity discounts for bulk purchases for sales promotion, premiums, fund-raising, educational or institutional use.

Special book excerpts or customized printings can also be created to fit specific needs. For details, write or phone the office of the Kensington Special Sales Manager: Attn. Special Sales Department. Kensington Publishing Corp., 119 West 40th Street, New York, NY 10018. Phone: 1-800-221-2647.

Zebra and the Z logo Reg. U.S. Pat. & TM Off.

ISBN-13: 978-1-4201-1484-3
ISBN-10: 1-4201-1484-0

First Printing: October 2012

10 9 8 7 6 5 4 3 2 1

Printed in the United States of America

I dedicate this book to my stepmother,
Anne.

From the beginning,
you have been my biggest fan and supporter.
Thanks for being so wonderful to me and to my dad.
Love you!

Prologue

Phoebe Linville would never see home again.

She braced herself against the roll of the sailing packet, clutching the damp wood of the ship's railing in a hard grip. The church spires and red brick buildings of Philadelphia receded into the early morning mist drifting across the whitecaps of the Delaware River. A cool October morning with a salty bite to the air, hinting at the impending change of seasons.

A perfect day to start a new life.

Excitement quickened her breath. For months her energies had been focused on this moment, despite George's strongly worded attempts to change her mind. She wouldn't miss his strident lectures, but she would miss her sister-in-law, and her nieces and nephews. And now that she was leaving, Phoebe would even miss George. Although their relationship had been fraught with tension for so many years, her half brother loved her and always sought to keep her footsteps on the righteous path. To George, her decision to reject a life in America was a profound betrayal of their father's family and their Quaker roots.

But God had shown her another path to take.

England.

Phoebe could hardly believe she would soon be in that distant land, and with the grandfather whose letters had assured her of his welcome. England, the land of Chaucer and Spenser, a place of legend steeped in tales of fairy queens and ancient kings, whose knights swept through the land in their quests for glory.

Not that Phoebe had ever read those tales for herself. Such frivolity had no place in a Quaker household, even given her father's rather lax adherence to tradition. But her mother, still loyal in her heart to the old country, had whispered bedtime stories of fairies and sprites that roamed the copses of that green and gentle land. Father, bless him, had never once objected to the stories knowing that Mamma, even though long estranged from her English relations, had needed the comfort of telling them as much as Phoebe had needed the excitement of hearing them.

And now that same family was calling Phoebe home. After years of silence, her grandfather, whom she had never met, had finally acknowledged his only grandchild.

A decisive footstep sounded behind her, breaking her thoughts.

"Child, thee should come below now. It is much too cold and damp to be standing out here for so long."

Phoebe turned to her friend with a smile. Mrs. Tanner stood a few feet away, arms crossed, shaking her head with motherly concern, her plain gray cloak flapping in the freshening breeze off the water.

"Thee must not ruin thy dress with the wet, Phoebe, and I do not think the sun will burn through this fog. Come below. There is nothing more to see."

Phoebe glanced over at the shoreline, barely visible in the mist. The views of the city were long gone and only woods and the occasional farmer's field remained. The river grew wider with each passing mile, spilling into the expansive bay leading to the Atlantic.

Still, she couldn't bring herself to turn away. "I know. But soon there will be nothing to see but water, and . . ." Her throat suddenly tightened as she thought of all she had left behind, travails as well as joys. Her past seemed to be flowing away, much as the water rippled and flowed under the ship, its churning wake eventually disappearing in the formless expanse of the river.

"And thee will never see family or home again," her friend said, finishing the sentence.

Phoebe nodded. As eager as she was for this adventure, leaving her nieces and nephews had been wrenching. She had helped care for them since the day they entered the world, and saying good-bye as they clutched their little arms about her waist had scoured her with grief. Since her father's death five years ago, those children had been the most important part of her life, and she would miss them terribly.

Mrs. Tanner gave her arm a compassionate squeeze. "This need not be a permanent leave-taking, Phoebe. I will only stay in London for a few months, then I will be returning to New Jersey. Thee is always welcome to return home with me."

Phoebe studied the other woman's solemn expression. After Mamma's death, Mrs. Tanner, an old family friend, had stepped into the role of mother as best she could. It had been Mrs. Tanner who had cared for her in the aftermath of her father's death, and it had been Mrs. Tanner who supported Phoebe when the letter arrived from her grandfather several months ago, begging her to come to England. When George initially thundered out his refusal in a very un-Quakerlike manner, the redoubtable woman had stood up to him, offering to escort Phoebe to England herself. After that, George had been forced to agree.

"But you wanted me to do this," Phoebe protested. "You were the only one who did. Why do you question it now?"

"I do not question it. I question thee. Does thee begin to doubt the purpose of thy journey?"

Phoebe closed her eyes, trying to tamp down her impatience. As George had so often pointed out, lack of patience was her greatest failing, often prompting her to make rash decisions or, worse, lose her temper. For a Quaker, that was a distressing failing, indeed.

Taking a breath, she worked to recapture the sense of rightness that washed over her whenever she read her grandfather's letters. She mentally envisioned the first one, scrawled on the crackling sheets of parchment. Desperation had fairly leached from the pages in a broken man's plea for his sole grandchild to come to him.

Unbidden, one of her father's favorite sayings from William Penn's writings flashed through her mind.

Right is right, even if everyone is against it; and wrong is wrong, even if everyone is for it.

The blinding certainty that had seized her on reading her grandfather's words snapped once more into place, along with a surge of relief that eased her sadness.

She opened her eyes and met Mrs. Tanner's gaze. "I want to be with my grandfather and my mother's family. I need to find out if they want me to be a part of them, as my mother always wished me to be."

The older woman nodded. "I am glad. But thee must always be aware of the challenges that face thee. Although thy dear mother tried to prepare thee for life among the English, they will find thee . . . different."

Different.

A loathsome word, so often applied to Phoebe and her mother, Elspeth Linville. Neither had ever fit in, and their Quaker community had not let them forget it. Although they were never cast out, they had endured a subtle shunning because of her mother's refusal to conform to some tenets of the faith. Phoebe's sense of separation had only increased after the death of her mother and then, years later, of her father. Under her half brother's tutelage, she had struggled to meet the rigid expectations of her community. Failure, unfortunately, remained as likely a result as success.

Phoebe squared her shoulders and met Mrs. Tanner's gaze. Her life lay ahead in England, not behind in America. Her Quaker relatives did not approve of her decision, but Father had always taught her to think for herself. After all, he had married her mother—Anglican faith and all—so it behooved Phoebe to give her English relations a chance, too.

"When have I not been different?" she asked. "Heaven knows I did not fit in with our village. I am hopeful my new family will accept me as I am, faults and all."

Mrs. Tanner grimaced. "I understand, but thee must also remember that London is a very worldly place. While I do not know the Stantons, they are aristocrats and move in circles not remotely familiar to thee."

"But I grew up in Philadelphia," Phoebe argued. "We did not move to Haddonfield until after Mother's death. I am not entirely a rustic."

"Thee *will* be to such as the English, but it should be of no consequence if thee continues to walk in righteous paths. That is my concern. Not what they think of thee, but what *thee* thinks of them."

Mrs. Tanner's lips pursed, as if she had tasted vinegar. Phoebe repressed the temptation to fidget, waiting her friend out.

"Phoebe," the older woman finally said, "much temptation will be cast before thee. Fine dresses and jewels. Parties and balls, with vainglorious men who will court thee with compliments and frivolous language. There will be an endless round of entertainments, and gossip from morn till night with nary a moment in the day for solitude and silent reflection. Thy English family is rich, and will lead a life of gaiety and excess, no matter what thee might think of it."

Phoebe tried to look properly horrified. Her mother had told her many times about her debut into the ton, and her years in London as one of society's most popular debutants. Although her mother had sworn she did not miss that life, Phoebe had never failed to notice the wistful gleam in her eyes and the soft smile on her lips when Mamma recounted those stories. To Phoebe, that world had sounded magical.

But she also recognized what duty and faith demanded of her. "I will do my best to resist temptation," she said, trying very hard to mean it.

Mrs. Tanner peered at her anxiously. "Given the difficulties with thy brother, I have always wanted thee to know thy English family and to have the chance to make a life with them. But I also hope thee will remain true to the heart of our beliefs. The temptation to conform will be strong, but understand that thee must be a child of God first, and a child of the world second. It is to be hoped thy grandfather understands this truth."

Phoebe nodded, trying not to feel too gloomy. She had hoped to spend at least a little time in London with the entire Stanton family. She did want to fit in and belong somewhere, to someone, but if it meant compromising her beliefs, she did not know what she would do.

She shook her head, annoyed with herself. It mattered not where Grandfather lived—country or city. Nor that he was an aristocrat and a member of the fabled ton. If he wanted to retreat to his country estate for the rest of his days, so be it. Lord Merritt—Grandfather—already loved her, as his affectionate correspondence had confirmed beyond all doubt. That kind of warmth had for many years been missing from Phoebe's life, and she yearned for it with a hunger that grew with each passing day.

"All that matters is being with my grandfather," she said. "As for the rest of the Stantons, Lord Merritt wishes me to meet them, but he wrote that we will leave for his estate in Kent shortly after my arrival." She wrinkled her nose. "I suspect I will have very little opportunity to face temptation, much less throw myself into a life of sin."

As well, the fact that she was already twenty-three years of age and still unmarried made it a great deal more likely that her future lay in a life of quiet spinsterhood, rather than in one of gay dissipation in London.

Mrs. Tanner hesitated, but finally nodded. "Thank Providence for that. I will remain in England with my relations for at least two months. Thee must not hesitate to ask for advice and support, even refuge, if thee should ever need it."

Touched, Phoebe went up on her toes and pressed a kiss to her friend's cheek. "I promise I will."

But she knew in her heart she would never again stand in need of the older woman's support. She had a grandfather now and a new family, one who would claim her as their kin. Those long years ago, Grandfather had rejected his only daughter for marrying a Quaker merchant from America. That marriage had caused a bitter estrangement that had lasted a lifetime.

At last, those terrible wounds would be healed. Within the month, God willing and the Atlantic winds prevailing, Phoebe would be in the arms of her grandfather, ready to embark on a new life.

Chapter 1

London
November 1817

A quiet knock sounded on Phoebe's bedroom door. Straining to open her eyes, she tried to clear the fog of exhaustion and lingering illness from her brain. When the maid entered the room, holding a tea tray in her sturdy hands, Phoebe pulled herself upright and stifled a yawn.

"Good morning, ah . . ."

"It's Agatha, miss. Mrs. Poole asks, please, that you step downstairs to the drawing room. She sent me to help you dress."

"What time is it?"

"It's gone on nine o'clock, miss," Agatha said as she deposited the tray on a dressing table.

Phoebe gaped at her, and then her brain lurched into function. She struggled out from under the covers, thumping onto the floor to search for her slippers.

"Why did she not send to wake me earlier? The morning is half over!"

As soon as they arrived in London last night, Phoebe had wanted to dash off a note to her grandfather's town house. But their hostess, Mrs. Poole, had deemed it too late. Almost dead on her feet from the grueling journey up from the coast, Phoebe had capitulated. With the maid's help, she had crawled into the blessedly clean and comfortable bed in the small guest room before falling into a heavy sleep, only awakening just now to Agatha's knock.

Not that she felt much better for her night's rest—not after the nightmare voyage from America. The winds had pushed against them the entire way, lengthening the crossing to almost seven weeks instead of three. Storm after storm pummeled them, and sickness had hit both crew and passengers hard. Phoebe had held out longer than most, but finally succumbed the week before they docked. Even now, her legs still wobbled and her temples throbbed with a headache.

She stumbled to the washbasin and splashed water on her face.

Agatha opened Phoebe's trunk and started sifting through it, her pleasant face registering dismay. "Lord, miss. Who packed your clothes? Everything's a right mess."

Phoebe grimaced. She'd been too ill to properly repack her trunk before leaving the ship. Fortunately, she did have one clean dress for her visit to Grandfather. She had hung it in the wardrobe, the only unpacking she had managed before dropping into bed.

"Take the one from the wardrobe," she said as she stepped behind the screen to pull off her night rail.

A few moments later, Agatha joined her behind the screen, gown in hand. She didn't look any more impressed than she had when she looked through Phoebe's trunk.

"Miss, this dress is clean but it could use a good press. It'll only take me a few minutes, if you don't mind waiting."

"It does not matter. I am sure my grandfather will not care, and I must be on my way as soon as possible."

"I'm afraid not, miss, seeing as one of your relatives is

waiting for you downstairs. That's why Mrs. Poole sent me to wake you."

Phoebe gaped at the maid. "My grandfather is here?" She felt breathless, even though her stays were barely laced up. "Mrs. Tanner must have sent a note around."

"It ain't your grandfather, miss, I can tell you that," Agatha said, turning her around to finish lacing the stays. "The man downstairs is no more than forty, and a fine-looking fellow he is, too. And he's dressed like a proper lord."

Phoebe's mind went blank. Her grandfather had never mentioned anyone like that in his letters. "Did he say who he was?"

"I'm sure, but Mrs. Poole didn't tell me. Miss, let me help you with your gown, and then you can have a nice cup of tea while I fix your hair."

Anxiety surged in a hot rush through her veins, making her dizzy. Why had Grandfather not come himself to fetch her? Was he ill?

Taking a deep breath, Phoebe forced her head to clear. "No. I have to see this man right away."

Agatha took her by the arm and steered her to the dressing table. "He'll wait. If you don't have something to drink, you'll keel right over. Now, have your tea while I brush your hair."

A half cup of tea later, Agatha grimaced and finally let Phoebe rise from the dressing table. "You won't be winning any prizes with that hair, miss, but I'll take you down."

The maid led her downstairs and through a simply ornamented entrance hall to the door of the drawing room. "There, miss. They're waiting for you."

Phoebe nodded, suddenly so nervous her knees shook. She silently ordered the starch back into her muscles and opened the door. What she saw brought her up short.

Mrs. Tanner sat in a low chair by the fireplace. A very tall, broad-shouldered man stood opposite her, on the other side of the chimneypiece. He was very handsome—quite the handsomest man Phoebe had ever seen. And when his attention, narrowed and intense, jumped to her, it struck her with an almost physical force.

Alarm skittered along her nerves. Absurdly, she had the impulse to back out of the room as quickly as she could.

Silly. Why be afraid of someone you have never met?

But as they stared at each other, she sensed some ill-defined peril, and she instinctively knew something dreadful was upon her.

Mrs. Tanner rose from her seat, momentarily splintering the tension. "Phoebe, please come in. This is a member of thy grandfather's family, Major Lucas Stanton, come to welcome thee to London."

Phoebe slowly entered the room, trying to shake the notion that she was approaching something awful and irrevocable. The guarded expression on Mrs. Tanner's face did nothing to dispel that impression.

Major Stanton took a step forward, looming—and looming seemed the only correct description—over her. He was broad across the chest and shoulders, and every part of him looked hard and muscular. Phoebe did not make a habit of dissecting the male figure, but he wore a well-tailored, dark coat, pale, skin-tight breeches, and tall leather boots, all of which showed off every line of his impressive physique. Just looking at that brawny, masculine strength made her body hum with tension.

Cheeks flushing, she fixed her gaze on his face. She found it disconcerting, too, since his hard-cut, impassive features served as a stark contrast to eyes the color of a stormy sea. The emotions she thought she perceived in their depths struck her as dangerous as the gales that had bedeviled her trip across the Atlantic.

"Major Stanton," said Mrs. Tanner, "this is Miss Phoebe Linville."

Phoebe stared up at him a moment longer, transfixed by his slashing cheekbones and the granite line of his jaw. All the men she knew were farmers and shopkeepers, simple men who dressed plainly and looked nothing like this man. Next to them, he resembled . . . well, she did not know what. But she knew she had never met anyone like him, though they had yet to exchange even a simple greeting.

His gaze, somber and wary, turned to one of puzzlement, jolting her into motion. The poor man must think she was a wordless half-wit.

Though Quakers generally made it a point not to bow or curtsy before those of higher station, she dipped low, ignoring Mrs. Tanner's *tsk* of disapproval. Why risk offending the first relative coming to greet her? "Major Stanton, thank you for coming to meet me. It was kind of you to do so," she said, offering her hand in greeting.

His big hand closed around hers and he lifted it to his lips, brushing a lingering kiss across her sensitive skin. The breath seized in her throat. Quaker men did *not* go around kissing hands, much less making a show of it.

Fortunately, he returned her hand, and her lungs recommenced function.

"Phoebe," said Mrs. Tanner, sounding horrified, "please sit."

Her friend nudged her to a sturdy, brown-colored sofa next to the fireplace. With a severe nod, Mrs. Tanner indicated to the major that he should take the seat facing them. He did not bother to repress a low sigh as he carefully settled on a small caned chair that gave an alarming creak in response. The sofa would have been a more appropriate choice for his large frame, but Mrs. Tanner clearly intended to punish him for his forward behavior.

"Major Stanton, how is my grandfather?" Phoebe asked impulsively. "Did he ask you to fetch me?"

The swift glance he exchanged with Mrs. Tanner brought Phoebe's anxiety rushing back. Its choke hold tightened when the older woman reached over and took her hand in a comforting clasp.

"Phoebe, thee must prepare for unfortunate news. But I ask thee to remember that the Father's hand is in all things, and that He will watch over thee always."

Fear swept through her. "What are you talking about?"

When Mrs. Tanner hesitated, Phoebe shook off her restraining hand and jumped up. The major rose immediately.

"Please, sir," she implored. "Take me to my grandfather."

Compassion softened the grim lines of his face. He struck her as a man not much given to that tender emotion, so whatever the cause, it must be dire.

He stepped closer, reaching out to take her hand in a gentle grip. "Miss Linville, you must sit." He had a firm, deep voice that held a compelling note of authority. As it washed over her, she had to resist the impulse to automatically obey. He smiled, as if to soothe her, and one finger stroked lightly over the back of her hand. "I'm certain you should have a cup of tea before we have any further discussion."

Unnerved by his touch, she pulled her hand away. "I do not want a cup of tea. I want you to tell me about my grandfather."

He ran a thoughtful gaze over her face, as if taking her measure. "Very well. Miss Linville, it grieves me to inform you that your grandfather—my great-uncle, Lord Merritt—died from an infection some weeks ago. I didn't write to you, since my letter would not have arrived prior to your departure. I hope you will believe I would have spared you this trip, if it was at all possible."

A strange buzzing noise arose in her ears, then her knees buckled and she sank onto the sofa. Her heart throbbed in her chest, straining against the shock. For a terrible moment, she could not draw a breath.

Mrs. Tanner gasped her name and Major Stanton let out a low curse. Swiftly, he came down on one knee before her and gripped her shoulders, holding her steady. Until he touched her, Phoebe had not realized she needed someone to keep her upright.

"Hold her while I get some water," exclaimed Mrs. Tanner as she rushed from the room.

"Steady on, Miss Linville," Major Stanton murmured in her ear. "Just lean against me."

Coming up onto the sofa, he eased her into his embrace, resting her head against his broad chest. As if controlled by some unseen force, her eyelids fluttered shut as, for the first time in her life, she found herself in the arms of a man other than her brother or father. Her morals registered a faint objection, but her body wanted nothing other than to collapse against that solid wall, her cheek nestling comfortably against the soft wool fabric of his coat. Tumult swirled in her brain, but his gentle embrace staved off the screeching panic that hovered at the edge of thought.

The door opened. Footsteps hurried across the floorboards as Mrs. Tanner rustled up to them with a glass of water in her hand. "Major, thee must allow me to tend to Miss Linville. Please let her sit up."

Phoebe flinched at the note of censure in her friend's voice. Mrs. Tanner had every right to be offended because Phoebe had no business clinging to a man, no matter what the circumstances. But she could not help shrinking farther into his embrace. Her stunned brain had latched on to the idea that as long as she remained in his arms she would be safe, that all the hurtful things in the world could not harm her.

Ridiculous, whispered the voice of reason. She started to pull away, but Major Stanton gently adjusted his hold to keep her close. Phoebe had to bite down on the whimper of relief that almost escaped her lips.

"I assure you, Mrs. Tanner," he said, "I will release my cousin as soon as I know she won't keel over in a dead faint."

Phoebe frowned. She never fainted. And now that her wits were slowly returning, she felt the first flush of humiliation that she had allowed a perfect stranger to hold her so intimately. Pushing herself upright, she began to withdraw from his arms.

For a second he resisted, keeping her fast in his embrace. And, for a second, she did not want him to let go.

Finally, he allowed it.

"Thank you, Major," she managed, feeling oddly winded. The strange emotions swirling through her resulted, no doubt, from shock. They could not possibly have anything to do with the man who had captured her in an embrace that somehow felt more like a *possession* than support.

The major's smoky gaze narrowed with skepticism, likely fostered by the squeaky tremor in her voice, but he moved back to his chair.

Mrs. Tanner took his place and handed her the glass of water. Phoebe gave her a faltering smile, sipping slowly as she tried to bring her rioting emotions under control. She wanted to weep with grief for her grandfather, but she kept her tears in check. When she could be private again, she would give way to the sadness wrenching her heart. But at this moment she needed to understand what would happen next. And however unprepared she was, she had decisions to make, ones that already caused her heart to sink.

She sat up straight, meeting Major Stanton's gaze with as much equanimity as she could muster. His expression revealed nothing other than a calm readiness to respond to whatever he might be called upon to do. Phoebe knew nothing of military men or matters, but she could well believe that this hard-eyed man across from her could handle any situation without turning a hair. Even one as awkward and dreadful as this.

Although he did study her with a caution suggesting he thought she might faint after all.

"I assure you, Major," she said, "I will not faint. I am yet recovering from an illness contracted on shipboard and have not regained my full strength."

"I'm sorry to hear that," he said. "Perhaps you should retire to your room. We could finish this discussion later if you find it too distressing."

Irritation began to edge out her shock. "I would have to be a fool not to be distressed by such news. That does not mean I am incapable of having a rational conversation."

Mrs. Tanner sighed, but the major appeared unoffended by her sharp words. In fact, he seemed to bite back a smile, which Phoebe found more than a little surprising.

And annoying.

"If you are satisfied I will not keel over, perhaps you might tell me what happened to my grandfather," she said in a tight voice.

The glint of humor in his eyes vanished. "Of course. Lord Merritt died nine weeks ago. As I said, I knew a letter would not reach you in time to prevent your sailing. Your grandfather would not have wanted that, in any event."

She bit her lip to hold back a sudden welling of tears. All these weeks had passed and she had assumed her grandfather was alive. All these weeks she had thought of him, imagining what he looked like, what he would say to her when they finally met. She had imagined a future of memories, built on the foundation of their shared loved for Elspeth Linville, her dear mother and Lord Merritt's only daughter. In the worst of the voyage, when she lay ill in her bunk, the image of her grandfather's joy at their reunion had kept her spirits buoyant.

But all that time, her grandfather had been dead. She had been alone for weeks. All hope of home, of family—of *her* family—had been extinguished forever.

She sat quietly, blinking her eyes and refusing to cry in front of the handsome stranger who had shattered her world.

He and Mrs. Tanner waited patiently until she regained her voice. "I am grieved to be robbed of the chance to have known my grandfather. I wanted to be with him more than all else."

Major Stanton nodded. "He shared that desire. My great-uncle was most concerned for your well-being after his death.

The Stantons are your family now, and Lord Merritt's express wish was that you remain here with them. With us," he corrected with a slight frown.

She stared at him, not comprehending. "Are you saying my grandfather wished me to remain in England with strangers who could only be considered distant relations?"

His brows arched with an arrogant tilt. "Your family will not be strangers for long, Miss Linville, and your mother was never considered a distant relation. I am charged by General Stanton, the head of the family, to bring you to him and Lady Stanton as soon as can be arranged. I assure you there is no safer place for you than under his protection."

Mrs. Tanner made a sharp intervention. "That will not be necessary, Major Stanton. Miss Linville will never be without protection. Her father's family in New Jersey will be eager for her to return, and I will escort her back to her home. Her *real* home."

Phoebe looked at her friend's determined expression, and the despair she had been holding off finally gripped her. Of course she must return to America. Her brother would wish it, and even though she loathed the idea of spending the rest of her life as his dependent, there was no other choice. No matter what her grandfather had wished for her, she could not throw herself on the mercy of total strangers, London aristocrats who knew nothing of her and her way of life.

Major Stanton's eyes narrowed with a look of stubborn determination. "I think we can agree, Mrs. Tanner, that Lord Merritt's last wishes for his granddaughter should take precedence over those of a half brother. And from what Lord Merritt communicated to me before he died, there is little Mr. Linville could offer his sister that could not be bettered by her family in England."

Phoebe opened her mouth in automatic defense of George, but Mrs. Tanner squeezed her arm in warning. "Phoebe is not without resources," she said. "Her father left her a modest income—"

"Modest being the operative word," he replied sarcastically.

Mrs. Tanner's lips thinned. "Her brother is well able to take care of her. Phoebe will live in peace and comfort, well removed from the frivolous life that would no doubt be forced upon her by thy relatives."

The major bristled at the insult, but Phoebe jumped in before he could respond. "Major, I thank you for your concern, but my friend is correct. There is no longer any reason for me to remain in England. I will be happy to visit with the Stantons, but I will be returning to America with Mrs. Tanner."

Just saying the words opened a well of desperation inside, but she clamped down hard. She would only shame herself and offend God by railing against what could not be changed. If only it did not feel so much like her own life was coming to an end, along with her grandfather's.

Major Stanton switched his focus from Mrs. Tanner to Phoebe and she stiffened, resenting his skeptical examination. He seemed to be peering right past her pitiful defenses to what she struggled to hide. "Is that what you really want? To return to America?"

She started to say yes, but could not bring the lie to her lips. Her father had always taught her to reject falsehood, but neither could she bring herself to tell the truth. Not to this man. "I do have a life in America, sir."

"Is that so?" he asked. "What exactly will you do?"

She recalled her dreary existence in her brother's household, and latched on to the one thing that gave it meaning. "I will help care for my brother's children."

"Ah. So, you will be the spinster aunt, dwindling into obscurity. Is that truly all the life you wish for?"

Her right hand balled into a fist as resentment brought a hot flush to her cheeks. Sharp words sprang to her tongue, but she bit them back. Major Stanton clearly possessed a knack for making the most gentle of souls—which did not include her—lose his temper.

Relaxing her hand, she tried to remember that he was genuinely concerned for her, however poorly he might express it. "I must trust that eventually my path will become clear. In truth, sir, it matters little what I might desire. I have no choice but to return to my family. I know God will provide for my safety and comfort."

There. The decision was made. She had accepted her fate with good grace, and would prepare to return home. She glanced at Mrs. Tanner, seeking support. All she wanted now was to retreat to her room and mourn her grandfather—and the death of all her dreams—in peace.

Mrs. Tanner gave her a tiny nod. "Thee has made a generous offer," she said, addressing the major, "but Phoebe already has a family who will protect her. Now that her grandfather is dead, it makes little sense for her to remain in London"—she raised her eyebrows in a pointed fashion—"with strangers."

Major Stanton leaned forward to dispute the point, but Mrs. Tanner held up a restraining hand. "Besides, she is young and it would be a mistake to assume she will never marry. Thee cannot know such a thing."

Mortified, Phoebe dropped her gaze to the floor. Her, marry? Not likely. Only two men had ever offered, each much older than she. Much to her brother's dismay, Phoebe had refused to marry either one. Even worse, at least from George's point of view, her unconventional upbringing had tainted her in the eyes of almost every man in their Quaker fellowship.

A fraught silence hung in the room, one that neither her friend nor the major seemed inclined to break. Finally, Phoebe lifted her head and met his gaze. He studied her calmly, as if she were a slightly vexing puzzle to be solved. Then he seemed to reach a decision.

"Mrs. Tanner, I would be grateful if you would give me a few minutes alone with my cousin."

Phoebe gaped at him, alarm making her heart flutter. The last thing she wanted was to be left alone with this intimidating, hard-eyed soldier. A man who would no doubt start handing down orders the minute they were alone.

She made a slight, frantic shake of her head in her chaperone's direction. Unfortunately, Mrs. Tanner's attention was directed entirely at Major Stanton. "I wonder why thee would need to see my friend alone, sir."

The contours of Major Stanton's face remained unchanged, but Phoebe sensed impatience in every line of his muscular physique.

"I mean no disrespect, Mrs. Tanner. I give you my word that your charge is safe with me. But my uncle left private instructions for Miss Linville and I'm loath to discuss them with anyone but her."

His compelling gaze locked with Mrs. Tanner's as they took each other's measure, not as enemies but surely not as friends. Then he seemed to let go of some troubling notion that had stood like a bulwark in his mind, and his face relaxed into a smile. A charming smile, Phoebe noted with surprise, one so engaging and warm she felt something inside her give way, too.

Mrs. Tanner, as mature as she was, was obviously not immune to such masculine charm, either. She cast a glance at Phoebe and then inclined her head in a surprisingly gracious nod. "Very well. I see no harm in leaving thee alone with Miss Linville for a few minutes. But I would ask thee to remember that she has suffered a terrible shock. Nor has she recovered completely from the illness that struck her on the crossing."

Phoebe rolled her eyes. They had all suffered on board the ship, and Mrs. Tanner even worse than the rest of them. In fact, Phoebe had nursed her and several other women and children through the depths of the sickness before falling ill herself. Still, Mrs. Tanner, like most of the people in Phoebe's life, too often insisted on treating her as little better than a helpless child.

Major Stanton placed his hand over his heart, as if making a vow. "You have my word that I will do my best not to upset Miss Linville. Her well-being is more important to me than anything else."

"But, surely—" Phoebe began.

His intent gaze shifted to her again, silencing the protest on her lips. Some invisible force arced between them, and Phoebe's breath snagged in her throat. How could eyes that studied her with such cool regard make her feel so . . . hot? As if he wanted something from her that was both unknown and forbidden.

That he did want something she felt certain. And some inner sense told her that even if she was not prepared to give it, Major Stanton was the kind of man who would take it anyway.

Chapter 2

The door closed, leaving Phoebe alone with her newly found relative. She supposed they were cousins of a sort, although she could hardly think of him that way. A cousin was a comfortable sort of creature—family, but without all the loving complications and tender hardships imposed by mothers and fathers, or even half brothers and sisters-in-law.

But there was nothing easy about Major Stanton. Too big and too worldly, he had an arrogant cast to his handsome face and soldier's body. And despite his polished manners and fine clothes, she sensed a restless temper in him—one tightly leashed, but never far from the surface.

She recognized that restless temper because it lived inside her, too. It was a feeling she had fought all her life to repress. But she suspected the major had it in abundance, and it unnerved her.

"Thank you for agreeing to speak privately," he said, not sounding intimidating at the moment.

Her fluttering nerves settled a bit. "You left me little choice, Major. I am surprised Mrs. Tanner succumbed so readily to your town manners and worldly charm."

His jaw slackened, and she felt a guilty tingle of satisfaction. Then his eyes sparked with amusement. "You surprise me, Miss Linville. And here I was thinking you nothing more than a meek little Quaker from the country."

She bit the inside of her lip, resisting the temptation to bristle at his playful jab. "I may have been raised in a Quaker household," she finally said, "but you will find I am no rustic from New Jersey. My father was a well-educated man, and my mother had several Seasons in London before she married. Between them, I believe my education to be as accomplished as that of any English girl of good family."

"Probably better," he said, his eyes retaining a hint of laughter. "But I stand corrected. I will not make the same mistake twice."

She nodded, then asked him the question that had been preying on her mind for some minutes. "Major, before you tell me what my grandfather wished me to hear, could you explain why he asked you to impart this information? What is your exact relation to him, and to me?"

He looked rueful. "It seems I owe you yet another apology. I should have explained that right off."

Phoebe liked that he apologized to her so freely, unlike many men—even some Quakers. Major Stanton appeared not to have any such false pride, and it made him seem less overwhelming, at least for now.

"I am your cousin, Miss Linville, although removed by several degrees. Our grandfathers share a grandfather on the Stanton side."

He paused, and a black scowl fleetingly crossed his features. She shivered as the engaging man who sat before her became once more the grim, hard-eyed stranger of their initial encounter. What had caused the change?

"As you know," he continued in a carefully neutral voice, "your grandfather, Lord Merritt, had only two children, your mother and her brother, Robert. Your Uncle Robert died two years ago, leaving your grandfather without a direct heir."

She nodded. "He wrote several months after that sad event,

asking me to travel to England. I was all that remained of his immediate family, and he believed it was right to return home to him."

Home. The word floated through her mind, teasing her with its elusive promise of security.

She clamped her lips shut, holding back the swell of grief. If only she had ignored her brother's attempts to hold her back, which had delayed her departure for months. She should have taken the packet to England as soon as she received her grandfather's first letter.

Major Stanton nodded. "He told me that. He also told me he regretted nothing more than his estrangement from your mother, which he blamed entirely on himself. His greatest wish was to see you before he died, and your name was the last word he spoke on this earth."

A confusing tangle of emotions welled up in Phoebe's chest, squeezing so hard she hunched her shoulders against it. She fought it, drawing in deep, shuddering breaths. When a few unwelcome tears leaked from her eyes, Major Stanton rose from his seat and moved to sit next to her. Startled, she edged away until she hit the arm of the sofa. It could not be appropriate for him to sit so close with no companion or chaperone in the room.

"I'm sorry," he murmured in a kind voice. "I regret distressing you, but I thought you would want to know exactly how Lord Merritt felt about you, and about your mother."

He extracted a handkerchief from some mysterious inner pocket and handed it to her. She took it with a grateful, half-suppressed sob and carefully blotted her cheeks. The snowy white fabric felt soft against her skin, and so much finer than the prosaic cotton squares she usually carried in her pocket. His had a cool, silky texture, and it reminded her of a beautiful old scarf her mother had once owned.

She dabbed her cheeks one more time but when she tried to return his handkerchief, he pressed it into her hands.

"I thank you for telling me," she said, touched by his compassion. "You must excuse me. It is simply the effects of that wretched voyage that make me act so foolishly."

He reached over and took her hand. She jumped at the contact.

"I don't think you're foolish, Miss Linville," he said. "What you did in leaving the only home you have ever known took fortitude and courage, and I honor you for it."

She stared at him, her limbs fighting a strange weakness. Not weakness from illness, but weak from the touch of his calloused hand and from the way his large frame loomed over her. Sitting next to him, only inches apart, made her feel as delicate as a hummingbird. She felt drawn to him, as if she could rely on him to solve all her problems. It was not a feeling she liked.

"I thank you," she said, extracting her hand. "Please continue. You were about to tell me the exact nature of your relationship with my grandfather."

That amused gleam returned to his eye. She silently vowed to ignore it.

Ignore it but for the fact that her cheeks flamed with heat. His ability to unsettle her made no sense. It could not possibly have anything to do with his powerful body and handsome face, or the way he studied her so intently. She was immune to that, and had always been. A man like Major Stanton could not be attractive to her. He was a soldier and she had been raised as a Quaker. Despite his kindness, he was a hard man who earned his living in the hardest of ways.

"I am your grandfather's heir," he finally said. "I am the eighth Earl of Merritt through the next direct line of male heirs in the Stanton family."

She blinked, momentarily confused, and then realized he

must have introduced himself as Major Stanton so as to mitigate the shock of Grandfather's death. "That was kind of you to think of me with such compassion, Major . . . Lord Merritt." She dredged up a grateful smile.

He did not return it. In fact, he looked like a man about to deliver more bad news.

"What else?" she asked in a hollow voice.

He grimaced, enough to make her heart sink. *Dear Father in heaven.* How much worse would this day get?

She straightened her spine. Whatever it was, she would confront it directly and do her best to accept it with good faith. Unfortunately, faith had a nasty habit of abandoning her, and her grandfather's death might just have delivered it a mortal blow.

"You must tell me," she said, clenching her fists within the folds of her gown.

He cast her another of his assessing looks before pulling a letter from his inner pocket.

"Lord Merritt wrote this on his deathbed. I thought to speak with you about his wishes before showing it to you, but perhaps there's no point in attempting to blunt the impact of his words."

He wore a look of grim resignation as he handed over the envelope, and it struck her how unpleasant this duty must be for him. He was trying to be gentle with her, even though that particular quality did not seem to come easily.

With shaking fingers, Phoebe unfolded the letter and spread it in her lap. The spidery crawl of words proved difficult to read, so she brought the thick piece of vellum close to her face. As she absorbed the words, the air grew heavy in her lungs and the blood in her veins surged in a sickening rush. Aghast, she read it three times. But each time the meaning refused to change, no matter how hard she tried to wrestle the words into another, less bizarre import.

Now she understood the tension that lay over the major like an ill-fitting coat.

"Why would my grandfather want me to marry you?" she exclaimed. "I never even knew you existed before today."

A muscle flexed in his jaw, and she belatedly realized how horrified she sounded, as if she could imagine nothing worse than marriage to him. She realized with a start that she was shrinking away from him, as if frightened.

Hastily, she jerked back to an upright position. Unfortunately, her correction came a moment too late.

"Miss Linville," he said in a carefully controlled voice, "I promise you there's no need to cower from me. I'm not some ogre come to snatch you away from your friends."

She closed her eyes, humiliated. But keeping her eyes closed would not lessen her embarrassment or make the situation disappear. "I know." She opened her eyes to meet his probing gaze. "It is just that—"

"I understand. And I will try to explain Lord Merritt's wishes as best I can. You must believe he had only your best interests at heart."

Her mind reeled from one frantic thought to the other. "You must realize the entire notion is ridiculous. Was my grandfather still in his right mind when he wrote this?"

One of his brows flew up into a haughty arch she was beginning to recognize. She had offended him, and how could she blame him? He was a man who likely had women throwing themselves at his feet, not reacting with horror to the very idea of marriage to him. Not to mention the fact that she was questioning her grandfather's sanity.

"I can assure you," he answered with a little growl that sent a shiver down her spine, "Lord Merritt was indeed in his right mind. I watched him write this, and his intent could not be clearer. In fact, we discussed it at length, and came to some conclusions as to what would be best for you when Lord Merritt was gone."

They had discussed it? Two men she had never met, deciding the entire course of her life? The very reason she had left America was to escape the restraint her half brother and her community had tried to impose on her. She would *not* be dictated to.

She waved the paper at him. "This letter is beyond anything! It is . . ."

"Insistent?" he cut in dryly.

More like desperate. As if only the prospect of her accepting Major Stanton's hand could ease the torments of the old man's deathbed. Her grandfather's letter verily begged her to marry him.

The major returned her gaze with eyes the color of the Atlantic after a northern gale, and just as turbulent. His attitude, however, remained cool and controlled. Phoebe wondered what *could* make this powerful man lose his impressive control.

She had the idea she did not want to find out.

He finally answered her in the patient kind of voice one might use with a slow-witted child. "Your grandfather believed you needed the protection of your family. Your *real* family. He was greatly distressed by the circumstances of your life in America. It was apparent to him through your letters that you were unhappy. Lord Merritt could not tolerate the idea of his only grandchild living a life of dreary obscurity as a dependent."

Phoebe bit her lip, irritated she had revealed so much of her unhappiness to Grandfather. But he had been so open in his own letters and had encouraged her to be equally frank.

Major Stanton leaned forward to capture her attention. "As the new Earl of Merritt and as a member of your family, I agreed with your grandfather's assessment. Nothing you have said today changes my opinion. It would be best for you to remain in England, with us."

Still clutching his handkerchief, Phoebe raised a hand to her mouth as she wracked her brain for an appropriate response.

A whisper of exotic spices drifted up her nostrils, bracing and utterly masculine. The square of fabric she clutched carried the scent of the man looming over her, and she found it oddly comforting.

Then she met his hard gaze again and humiliation came rushing back. That she hated her life in her brother's household was partly her own fault. If she were a better person—a better Quaker—she would no doubt accept her lot in life with a cheerful heart. But Phoebe was rebellious like her mother, as George had so often reminded her. That her grandfather had exposed her moral weakness to a perfect stranger stung her to the quick.

"Forgive me, sir. But I fail to see what business it is of yours. You have never met me before today, and surely our connection is too remote to make an appreciable difference."

"I disagree. In any event, I gave Lord Merritt my solemn word that I would provide for you and protect you, whether you wished to marry me or not."

What did he expect her to say to that astonishing statement? She struggled to answer. "That is not necessary, nor would it be right. Surely, you must see the best solution is for me to return to America."

His brow furrowed in a scowl, and Phoebe held back a sigh. She was heartily sick of the men in her life—she supposed the major now counted as being in her life—disapproving of her decisions. And she was weary of other people rearranging her life as if she were nothing more than a table setting.

Even if this particular arrangement coincided with her wish to remain in England. "Major, I—"

As he reached out and took her hand, she spluttered into silence. Carefully, he pried her fingers apart and removed his handkerchief, folding it back into a tidy square and placing it in her lap before recapturing her hand.

She stared at him, dumbfounded. The aggressive cast of his face had gentled. He cradled her hand in his, resting them both on his knee. Heat seemed to arc from his palm into hers, and she could hardly breathe.

"Miss Linville, I will not try to force you to do anything contrary to your wishes, nor will anyone else in the family. But I made a promise to a dying man, and I intend to honor that promise. I would also ask you to remember that he had only your safekeeping at heart. He loved you very much, and wanted only the best for you."

He leveled an engaging smile at her, one so enticing she could do nothing for a few moments but blink at him.

"And having finally met you," he continued, "I can understand why he felt so protective of you."

She frowned, not sure of his meaning. "But, surely, you do not wish to marry me, do you? The very notion is . . . is absurd."

He shrugged, as if it were of little consequence. "Not to a dying man riddled with guilt and fear for his granddaughter. You cannot cavalierly disregard his wishes."

Phoebe had the sensation someone had cast her adrift in a bubble, and she could no longer fathom which way was down or up. "Major Stanton, do you actually wish to marry me?"

His eyes gleamed with a teasing calculation. "I don't frighten you, do I? Yes, I look like a grizzled old soldier, but I promise I'm actually a very mild fellow."

Startled, she stared at him. How could he make a joke of it? "I suspect that is not true," she said with as much dignity as she could muster. Carefully, she pulled her hand from his grip.

His answering laugh, low and masculine, wrapped around her, deflecting her anger in some inexplicable way. "You needn't worry. I'm not asking you to marry me. I simply suggest you consider the wishes of a fine man who desired your happiness more than anything on earth."

She eyed him with suspicion. Her grandfather's instructions left little room for doubt as to what those wishes entailed. "Then what do *you* wish of me?"

"The root of Lord Merritt's desire was to see you safe with your family. He always meant to keep you here in England. An old-fashioned man, he naturally saw the most efficient way to do that was through marriage. He planned to take up residence in London and introduce you to society, in the hopes you would find an acceptable husband. Unfortunately, fate intervened. When he knew he wouldn't live long enough to complete his plan, he settled on the next best alternative. Me."

He softened that last word with a self-deprecating smile, but Phoebe was not fooled. The major struck her as a man who would go to great lengths to uphold his honor, and pledging a deathbed promise would count as an enormous debt of honor.

"Any discussion of your marriage to me or anyone else is premature," he continued. "But I did agree to secure your safety, and to provide for all your needs in the same way your grandfather would have done. And that is exactly what I intend to do."

He made her sound like an unwelcome obligation, which she probably was.

"I do not need taking care of," she snapped.

"Your grandfather didn't agree, and neither do I."

"Thank you for your consideration, sir," she ground out, "but it is not necessary."

He winced. "That wasn't very adroit of me, was it? I apologize. Aunt Georgie frequently tells me I have the subtlety of a charging bull."

Phoebe had no idea who Aunt Georgie was, not that it mattered. "Even so—"

He cut her off by touching a finger to her lips. She jerked at the slight warmth, her eyes rounding with astonishment. "Miss Linville, don't you at least want to meet your family before you make any decisions? They will not reject you, I can assure you."

She did her best to ignore her tingling lips and peered into his face, trying to find truth. Her insides twisted into a knot of doubt and worry. "Are you sure?"

That distracting and much too enticing gleam was back in his eyes. "Am I sure they won't reject you? Without a doubt."

"Oh," she breathed, finally letting the notion of meeting her mother's family settle in her mind. "Then if I am not to return to America—"

The triumphant gleam in his eye brought her up short. She held up a hand.

"Not that I am agreeing to anything, but if I do not return to America right away, what am I to do? I cannot remain with Mrs. Poole forever, and Mrs. Tanner will soon be leaving to visit her relatives in the north."

Even as she voiced her concerns, all the difficulties of her position struck her with blinding force. How could she throw herself on the mercy of a family she had never met, and who would likely think of her as their odd and inconvenient distant relation? The thought that she might be a burden to them made her cringe.

She took a deep breath for courage. "No, Major. I do thank you for your kindness, but I think it best if I return to America. I am sure Mrs. Tanner will help me make the arrangements." Better to return to the family she knew than risk an ugly, inevitable rejection.

He studied her. "Are you so eager to return?"

She stared into his face—each rugged, handsome line imbued with determination—and felt her fragile, wavering resolution begin to finally crumble. It was wrong of her, but the thought of returning to her former life filled her with a depressing melancholy.

"No," she whispered. "I am not."

"Then it's settled. You won't be going back," he said as calmly as if they'd been discussing the price of eggs.

She bristled, torn between shame that he should see her weakness and anger that he could treat her distressing situation so lightly.

"And how are we to manage this?" she said tartly. "Thee has yet to provide me with an answer."

His eyebrows shot up at her verbal lapse, and she almost groaned. Her mother had always insisted she speak the finest King's English, and Phoebe only lapsed into rhythms of Quaker speech when she was upset or lost her temper. It was an annoying and sharply ironic habit.

"Well," he said, trying not to laugh, "I actually do have an answer. Her name is Lady Stanton, and she's very eager to meet you."

Chapter 3

Phoebe Linville stared up at him, her sherry-colored eyes huge and full of worry. Those eyes and her lush pink mouth were the only color in her drawn face. Lucas hadn't expected such an enticing mouth on a poorly dressed, skinny little Quaker. It was incongruous and gave him all kinds of thoughts he had no business thinking, especially given the awkward circumstances.

His cautious, duty-bound marriage proposal had certainly horrified her, and he'd sounded the retreat almost immediately. He'd made a solemn vow to the old earl that he would take care of Miss Linville, but he'd also made it clear to the wily bastard that marriage was very much an open question. Merritt had been desperate to settle the girl's fate, so the old man had grudgingly accepted the compromise—with the proviso that Lucas would consider a proposal if the girl was amenable to it. To placate and honor a dying man, Lucas had agreed.

From the looks of it, though, Phoebe was not remotely agreeable to the suggestion. Apparently, she found the idea of marrying a complete stranger as disconcerting as he found the notion of marrying a Quaker rustic from America.

When Phoebe had walked into Mrs. Poole's drawing room, Lucas's fears had been confirmed. She was barely of average height, too slender, and poorly dressed in the most appalling sack of a dress. Her thick dark hair was pulled up in an untidy and unattractive knot. The thought that such a poor dab of a thing could survive either the wolf pack of the ton or marriage to him was demented.

But the ensuing encounter had surprised him. Though initially stunned in the face of distressing news, she had revealed an inner fire. Closer inspection hinted at quite a lovely figure under her drab, old-fashioned gown. Obviously, her frail appearance resulted from her recent illness. Rest, some good English food, and Aunt Georgie's mothering would soon set that to rights.

Recovering from the additional shocks *he* had delivered, however, would take more time.

Now, as she stared up at him, Phoebe's lips parted and her pretty pink tongue quickly swiped between them. A throb of heat flashed to his groin, and he had to clamp down hard on a surprising and ridiculous surge of lust. He did so by imagining his friends' laughter should he ever reveal he actually considered taking a homespun Quaker girl as his wife.

"Who is Lady Stanton and what is her relation to me?" Phoebe asked uncertainly. "Why would she be willing to accept me into her household, sight unseen?"

She had a soft, pleasing voice, which partly offset her direct manner of speaking. He found it an intriguing combination.

"Lady Stanton is married to General Sir Arthur Stanton, who is my uncle and the second son of the second son of Robert Stanton, the fifth Earl of Merritt. My grandfather was the first son of that particular line, while your grandfather was the direct descendant of Robert, through his oldest son. Since your grandfather died without issue, the title descended through Robert's second son to me."

The girl's eyes glazed over, a combination of fatigue and

her attempt to parse the complicated web of relations that made up the Stanton family.

"You needn't worry about it," he said. "You simply need to know that you are indeed related to the family through your mother and more than welcome in General and Lady Stanton's home. As the head of the family, my uncle in fact insisted on it."

He didn't bother to add that the General had ordered him to bring Miss Linville home immediately, and not leave her in the company of *those damned religious fanatics*.

"I am grateful that Lady Stanton wants to meet me," Phoebe said, her voice catching a little.

The glimpse of yearning the girl was trying to hide tugged at his heart, and he gave her a reassuring smile. "She has given me strict instructions to bring you home with me this very afternoon."

Startled by that bit of news, she shot up from the sofa, stumbling into the table. When she swayed a bit, Lucas quickly stood to help her. His fingers closed around her slender wrist, her delicate bones feeling fragile under the thick wool of her sleeves.

"Phoebe," he said, deliberately using her first name, "sit down before you fall down. Mrs. Tanner will have my head if anything happens to you." It was time the girl understood she *was* family, and that he would take care of her.

She blushed, the deep pink flying high on her delicate cheekbones. The reaction made her look young and vulnerable. Instinct rustled within him, and it took a considerable effort not to pull her into a protective embrace.

As she cautiously settled back down on the sofa, he couldn't help noticing the swell of her breasts, pressing against her plain bodice. She had an alluring shape—too slender, but with some distinctly appealing curves. Not for the first time since he'd entered the room, Lucas could almost see the advantage to taking Phoebe as his wife. She was pretty and modest, but with a touch of fire. He'd also wager that as a gently bred Quaker, she couldn't tell a lie to save her life.

The exact opposite of Esme Newton, his first and last love.

"I could not possibly leave this afternoon," she protested. "As pleased as I am at Lady Stanton's generous offer, thee must recognize how inappropriate my sudden departure from this household would be. Mrs. Tanner would be distressed."

He smiled, amused by her quaint speech. The ton might label her a bumpkin, but the longer he conversed with her, the more her manner appealed to him. She meant exactly what she said, a quality he had found in abundance among the soldiers in his former command, but was sorely lacking in his new life as a peer.

Even so, the girl obviously required careful handling. Although full of mettle, she was suffering from exhaustion and shock. Push her too hard and she might break.

"Of course not," he replied calmly. "It's understandable that you wish to remain with your friend until she departs for her trip up north. She leaves in a few days, does she not? That should give you ample time to get your bearings. And there's no reason you can't meet the General and Lady Stanton before then. Become acquainted with them first before moving in."

He gave her his most persuasive smile, the one that had landed many a beautiful woman in his bed. Phoebe, however, seemed unimpressed. He was either losing his touch or innocent Quaker ladies were immune to his brand of charm.

Time to pull out the big guns.

"Phoebe, I understand your hesitation, but your mother's estrangement was a source of genuine sorrow for all of us, and your presence would heal that breach."

That was an exaggeration. He had only been vaguely aware of his distant cousin's existence until the old earl imposed responsibility for her onto him. But Aunt Georgie and the General were both keen to have her, and since Phoebe's weak spot was clearly her obvious longing to be reunited with her mother's family, he had every intention of exploiting it.

For her own good, naturally. Why should she return to a wretched life in America when she could live in comfort with the Stantons?

The yearning in her eyes told him he'd hit the mark.

"Lady Stanton was very fond of your mother," he added, turning the screws. "Did you know that? She sponsored her first Season in London."

"No," Phoebe breathed. "Mother never told me that. I think it was difficult for her to speak of the family she had left behind in England."

But Lucas wagered by the look on Phoebe's face that Elspeth Linville had told her enough to whet her daughter's interest.

"Lady Stanton will tell you all about it," he assured her. "I will call on you tomorrow afternoon and escort you to Stanton House. Shall we say at three o'clock?"

She looked so young and innocent as she pulled her lower lip between her small white teeth. Another bolt of sexual heat lanced through him. Phoebe Linville was a great deal more interesting than he first thought, and it suddenly seemed imperative to keep her in London—both because he had promised her grandfather, and because she might be what he was looking for after all.

She met his gaze. Her eyes seemed to show everything she felt, a characteristic both appealing and useful. "What if they do not like me?"

He reached over and took her hand, feeling a small surge of triumph when she didn't pull away.

"That would be impossible. But I give you my word that if you eventually deem yourself ill suited for life in London, I will escort you back to America myself."

Her eyes opened wide with wonder. "You would do that?"

"I would, indeed."

Her lips parted in a genuine smile, one so entrancing it stunned him. If she were to come out from behind that Quaker disguise, she'd have all the rakes of London tumbling at her feet.

Lucas knew with a disagreeable certainty he wouldn't like that one bit.

"Thank you, Major," she exclaimed with relief. "I will not forget your kindness or how selflessly you have acted toward me."

"It is my honor to help you."

"In that case, I would be most happy to meet Lady Stanton. And I am sure tomorrow will be acceptable to Mrs. Tanner."

As she beamed at Lucas, his satisfaction grew. She was sweet, innocent, and mostly biddable, and he had little doubt he could eventually bend her to his will—gently, of course. He had no wish to break her spirit, which even a hardened soldier like him could perceive to be a delicate thing.

Yes, Phoebe Linville was nothing like Esme. The more he thought about it, the more he realized she just might be the correct antidote to the woman who had once meant the world to him, but who had demolished his life.

Chapter 4

The carriage jolted through a rut, bouncing Phoebe as she made a grab for the leather strap. Major Stanton—or Lord Merritt, as she must now think of him—smiled at her from the other bench, his solid frame undisturbed as they rumbled over London's cobblestone streets.

Not that she could possibly hurt herself. That seemed impossible in the velvet and leather cocoon of Lord Merritt's town coach. Phoebe had never ridden in such a luxurious vehicle, and she had to resist the urge to stroke the rich burgundy fabric on which she sat. She *was* trying hard to feel guilty about enjoying such earthly pleasures, but could not muster up the appropriate concentration.

"I hope you slept well last night, Phoebe," said Lord Merritt. "I imagine London is quite a bit noisier than you're used to."

"Yes, but I am sure I will get used to it." She hoped so, anyway. London was a veritable din of competing sounds, many of them unpleasant. She had grown up with silence, both that of the country and the Silence practiced by Friends. Rarely had she chafed against the quiet peace of the countryside, but in many a Meeting or in silent family prayer, her thoughts had wandered and her body had betrayed her with a bad case of the fidgets.

"True silence is the rest of the mind," George would intone, quoting William Penn in a doom-laden voice. "It is to the spirit what sleep is to the body, nourishment and refreshment."

Phoebe had never understood that particular epigram until now.

Lord Merritt's eyes held amusement, as if he could see right through her false cheer. He had a disconcerting ability to read her expression or guess her thoughts. Not that one needed a great deal of perception to deduce she had passed a restless night, given her pale complexion and fatigue-smudged eyes. Appalled by her appearance, Phoebe had donned her best gown and allowed Agatha to ornament her just-washed curls with a pretty blue ribbon.

She had even pinched some color into her cheeks, loathing the idea of appearing before Lord Merritt or her London relatives looking like a poor country miss. Both Mrs. Tanner and Mrs. Poole had looked shocked when she entered the drawing room, but Lord Merritt had given her such an approving smile that Phoebe had silently vowed to spend an extra fifteen minutes before bedtime meditating upon the sins of vanity and false pride.

He had that same smile on his face right now as his gaze roamed over her body and came to rest on her face. She sat very straight against the velvet squabs, determined not to squirm like an undisciplined schoolgirl.

"You'll get used to the noise," he said. "Soon enough, you won't even notice it."

"I shall look forward to that day with great anticipation."

He answered with a low, husky laugh that made her skin prickle with heat. She gave him a small smile and looked pointedly out the window, determined to control her disturbing response to him. Surely, it was all the confusion and distress of the last few days that made her react in such an odd fashion.

Grandfather's death *had* been a terrible blow, but the man

sitting across from her had transformed despair to hope. Only one more obstacle lay ahead, and all questions would finally be answered. Would the Stanton family truly be willing to take her in, an impoverished, unknown relation? She hoped so, because the prospect of going back to her dreary life in America filled her with gloom.

Taking a deep breath, she pressed her hand against her stomach. Lord Merritt eyed her, then launched into a colorful commentary on the various landmarks they passed on their trip to Mayfair. Despite her nerves, she began to enjoy herself. He had a knack for description, and he seemed to know a great deal about history and architecture. She had not thought a military man would be so knowledgeable about the city passing by the carriage window.

She studied him as he lounged across from her, casually pointing out scenes of interest. Initially, she had thought him arrogant and intimidating, but he had consistently surprised her with his well-informed mind and his no-nonsense compassion. He did still make her nervous, because she was not used to men like him. He was a soldier, and a wealthy and powerful aristocrat. Tough, handsome, and, as far as she could tell, possessed of an outrageously confident character. He was as far from being a Quaker as she could imagine.

She would certainly ignore Grandfather's instructions to marry him. Why Lord Merritt had agreed to those instructions was a question that kept her awake much of the night. She had finally concluded that the answer was exactly as he had stated—he felt obligated to honor Grandfather's dying wish. Why else would a wealthy and handsome peer marry a plain Quaker spinster with barely a penny to her name?

Lord Merritt interrupted his monologue to stare at her. "Is something wrong, Phoebe?"

"Ah . . . not at all, sir. Why do you ask?"

"You have an odd look on your face. Are you not well?"

She held back a sigh. Why must everyone assume she

was always on the verge of some kind of collapse? "Not in the least."

He nodded wisely and gave her gloved hands a reassuring pat. "I expect all this jostling about is making you rather sick to your stomach. Not to worry, we're almost at Stanton House."

Not for the first time, Phoebe wished she could swear. Some of the interesting words she had heard the sailors use on the sea voyage would do quite nicely.

Instead, she conjured up a smile. "You are too kind, Lord Merritt."

He looked dubious, but their timely arrival cut short any further expressions of concern.

Dismissing her irritation, Phoebe drew in a nervous breath and waited for the steps of the carriage to be let down. Lord Merritt unfolded his long legs, ducked his head, and stepped to the pavement. He then carefully guided her to the pavement as she gazed, mouth open, at the building in front of them.

She clutched his muscular arm and stared up at the huge, imposing town house. The short trip through London's streets had not made her sick, but taking in all the gleaming marble, polished windowpanes, and glittering brass fixtures made her feel more than a little dizzy.

"Don't be nervous," he murmured. "Everyone will love you."

"Lord Merritt, you cannot know that," she said, hating the quaver in her voice. She had never thought of herself as a coward, but right now she wished she could turn tail and run.

"I wish you would stop calling me *Lord Merritt* in that gloomy voice," he said as he led her to the front door of Stanton House. "It makes me think you're likely to box my ears."

She cast him an uncertain look. His eyes laughed back at her, and a reluctant smile tugged at her mouth. Under other circumstances, she might have been tempted to scowl at him, but his methods worked. Her nerves began to settle.

Until he knocked and the gleaming white door flew open. Phoebe's mouth dried up at the sight of a brawny footman dressed in colorful and very ornate livery. Just taking in all his magnificence made her feel exactly like a poor country cousin.

The very trimming of the vain world would clothe all the naked one.

The Quaker epigram popped into her head, steadying her. Having to memorize all those quotations had always seemed pointless, but for once the tedious work served a useful purpose. All men and women were equal before God, and that included the Stantons.

She lifted her chin and gave the footman a bright smile. He slowly blinked, rather like a large owl, then bowed and stepped back.

Lord Merritt squeezed her elbow. "Ready?"

"I am."

He ushered her across the threshold into a spacious and beautiful entrance hall with a grand staircase that rose in a graceful spiral to the upper floors. Several enormous paintings of men and women in the elaborate costumes of days gone by rose almost from the floor to the wainscoting. Portraits of Stanton ancestors, she assumed. Her ancestors, too. She could not help staring at them, hoping to see a resemblance to her mother.

A dignified older man dressed in sober black garb approached from an alcove under the staircase. "Lord Merritt," he said, "it is a pleasure to see you."

"Tolliver, you're looking fit as a fiddle," Lord Merritt replied with an easy grin. "This is Miss Linville, General and Lady Stanton's young relation. She'll be coming to live with you one day soon, and I expect you to look after her. Cousin Phoebe, this is Tolliver, my uncle's butler. He's been with the family as long as I can remember, and knows exactly where all the bodies are buried."

Phoebe blinked, but not even by a twitch of his white brows did the butler acknowledge Lord Merritt's jest. Instead, with a precise and formal dignity, he gave her a welcoming bow. "Miss Linville, I am at your service. You must be sure to let me know if I can help you in any way."

She had no idea how to respond to such a gracious salutation delivered by a servant in the employ of an aristocrat, since the few servants in her brother's household were generally treated on equal footing with the family. Surely, it would be rude not to acknowledge it.

"Thank you, Mr. Tolliver," she said, dipping into a shallow curtsy.

The butler's eyes widened in shock.

Drat.

Lord Merritt's big shoulders shook with suppressed laughter. Likely it would not be the last time she amused him with her social blundering.

"Don't worry," he whispered as the butler turned to slide back a set of pocket doors. "He'll recover from the shock soon enough. Besides, you look very fetching today, especially with that ribbon in your hair. Tolliver could never resist a pretty girl. Come to think of it, neither can I."

He murmured that last bit right in her ear. After casting him a reproachful glance—which only made him grin—she fixed a smile on her face and allowed him to lead her into a tall-ceilinged, light-filled drawing room. Despite her annoyance, she dug her fingers into his arm, holding on as if he were safe harbor in a stormy sea.

Four people stood to greet them. The petite, dignified woman with snowy white hair was obviously Lady Stanton, and the tall, slightly stoop-shouldered old gentleman with the fierce eyebrows must be General Stanton.

The other man and woman, decades younger, caught Phoebe by surprise. They were both tall and strikingly handsome. The golden-haired man bore a strong family resemblance to Lord Merritt. The woman by his side had a wealth of glossy black hair, and a face and figure that would draw the eye of every man she met. Although the man looked proud and a little aloof, the woman studied her with a friendly and open curiosity.

The older woman spoke first as she moved to Phoebe, hand extended. "My dear child," she exclaimed with a warm smile, "I can't tell you how happy we are to finally have you with us in London."

Phoebe glanced up at Lord Merritt. He gave her a slight nod. She dropped into a proper curtsy, certain this time that she was doing it right.

"Aunt Georgie," said Lord Merritt, "this is Miss Phoebe Linville."

Lady Stanton pulled her into a soft, lavender-tinged embrace. "Welcome to England, my child. We have waited so long for this day."

Phoebe clutched her, the unexpected tightness in her throat making it difficult to answer. "Thank you, Lady Stanton. I am most happy to be here."

Lady Stanton gave a brisk click of the tongue. "No titles, my dear. You are to call me Aunt Georgina, or Aunt Georgie, as this rascal of a nephew calls me. We do not stand on formality within the family, and you are quite obviously a Stanton, just like your dear mother."

"Told you so, little doubter," murmured Lord Merritt.

Phoebe ignored him. "Thank you, Aunt . . . Aunt Georgie," she stammered.

The older woman smiled. "Come meet your uncle. He's been most eager to welcome you."

Phoebe doubted that, given the stern expression on her uncle's craggy features. Even his iron gray eyebrows seemed to bristle with a fierce life of their own. But to her surprise, he took her hand and gave it a fatherly pat.

"Well, Miss Phoebe, it's about time we meet. Can't think what that old scoundrel Merritt was about, leaving you to languish away in that colonial backwater. Should have brought you home the minute your father passed away. Most irregular."

Phoebe froze, uncertain how to answer. Part of her was offended for her grandfather's sake, but another part could not help thinking he was correct.

"Really, Arthur," Aunt Georgie said, "I hardly think now is the time to rattle old family skeletons. Phoebe, greet your uncle, and then I will introduce you to your new cousins."

Phoebe began to drop into another curtsy, but the old man pulled her into an embrace so vigorous it made her squeak.

"We're all happy to have you here, gel," he murmured in her ear. His bushy sideburns tickled her cheek, just like her father's had when he hugged her as a little girl. "We hope you'll stay with us for a very long time."

Her vision suddenly blurred, and she automatically hugged him back. His greeting may have been gruff—and rather insulting to poor Grandfather—but it had been a long time since anyone had embraced her with such genuine enthusiasm. She clung to him, feeling a rush of gratitude.

Aunt Georgie's soft touch on her shoulder brought Phoebe back to an awareness of her surroundings. Blushing, she drew back, giving her uncle a shy smile. His eyes gleamed with a suspicious brightness and he cleared his throat with a loud cough.

"That's enough of that nonsense, miss," he exclaimed. "You say hello to your cousins. We'll have a comfortable chat later, after you've had a rest. You look done to a cow's thumb, which is not to be wondered after all you've been through."

She gave him a wry smile before turning to meet her other relatives.

"Phoebe," said Aunt Georgie, "this is my nephew, the Marquess of Silverton, and his wife, Lady Silverton."

She stared up at the awe-inspiring couple. They were both tall and graceful, and dressed, as even she could tell, in the height of fashion. Although they both regarded her kindly, never had she felt more like an awkward country bumpkin.

"Lady Silverton," she managed, "I'm very happy to meet you."

The tall woman gave her a welcoming smile and took her hand. "Dear Phoebe, we don't stand on formality when amongst ourselves. You must call me Meredith. And don't be afraid to call my husband by his given name, which is Stephen." She threw him a laughing glance. "Or Silverton, if that's more comfortable for you. He can be rather intimidating, and even I sometimes have to fight the urge to curtsy before him."

Lord Silverton made a scoffing sound, but Phoebe could well believe it. She eyed him, wondering how she could ever be comfortable in the company of someone so magnificent. But then he smiled, and the effect was dazzling. When he smiled, Lord Silverton was quite the most handsome man she had ever met.

Except for Lord Merritt, of course, who was at this moment standing back from their little circle, looking irritated, to be exact.

Before she could puzzle that out, Silverton took her hand and dropped a brief kiss on it. The familiarity of it made her blush, but she supposed she had better get used to it since men in London seemed rather fond of the habit.

"My wife has been longing to meet you," he said in a deep voice that echoed Lord Merritt's tones. The family resemblance between the two men struck her anew. "Like you, she is a country woman, and misses that life very much. She's eager to speak with you about the Christmas holidays, and entreat you to spend time with us and our children at Belfield Abbey, our estate in Kent."

"I . . . I would like to speak with her about that very much," Phoebe stammered, not sure what to say. She'd barely met these people and already they were issuing Christmas invitations. Since Christmas was not something Quakers generally celebrated, she had little idea what was involved.

Lord Merritt pointedly cleared his throat, and Phoebe jerked her gaze to him. Had she done something wrong? She looked back at Lord Silverton, who was clearly waiting for an answer.

"Forgive me—" Phoebe cast about for an appropriate form of address, and then settled on one that seemed most appropriate for the circumstances. "—Cousin Stephen. Your offer is most generous, but my plans are not yet fixed, other than hoping to spend time with my aunt and uncle. As Lord Merritt will tell you—"

"Phoebe," Lord Merritt interrupted, "I told you to stop calling me that. If you can bring yourself to use Silverton's first name, then I should think you'd be able to use mine, too. It's Lucas, by the way, in case you've forgotten it."

Phoebe gaped at him. She had known him only a short time, but despite his sometimes imperious manner, he had treated her as carefully as a piece of fragile stemware. But now he not only sounded angry, he looked it. His mouth had thinned into a hard line and his eyes had transformed to a cold, silvery gray.

But he was not glaring at her. The target of his ire was Lord Silverton.

"She might be more inclined to do that if you didn't bark at her as if you're her commanding officer," the marquess replied in a tone that came perilously close to a sneer.

In a flash, the atmosphere in the room grew tense as hostility swirled between the two men. Meredith gave a disgusted snort and Aunt Georgie threw her husband a long-suffering, pleading look.

Uncle Arthur took the hint. "That will be quite enough of that nonsense. You should both have the manners not to act like ruffians in front of your new cousin. And," he said, scowling fiercely at both men, "in front of my wife."

Meredith elbowed her husband. "And in front of *your* wife," she muttered.

Both men had the grace to look embarrassed.

"Forgive me, Aunt Georgie," said Lord Silverton with a little bow.

Lord Merritt—*Lucas*—simply smiled at his aunt and shrugged his big shoulders. After narrowing her eyes at him, the older woman murmured something to Meredith, who crossed to a corner of the room and tugged on an ornate bellpull. The tension in the room gradually eased as everyone moved to a grouping of pretty blue and yellow silk chairs. Phoebe stood transfixed, still stunned by the snarling little interlude, but shook herself free of it when Lucas came up to her.

"Did I do something wrong?" she whispered anxiously.

He sighed. "Of course not, my dear girl. It's just some old Stanton history, best forgotten. Come sit down. Meredith has rung for tea, and I'm sure you could use a cup."

She peered at him, startled both by the affectionate term and the bleak glance he cast in Silverton's direction. Obviously, the old history had *not* been forgotten—at least not by the two cousins—and she could not help but be curious. For now, though, it seemed as if everyone had decided to ignore the incident, so she had no choice but to follow suit.

Aunt Georgie, seated on the luxuriously stuffed yellow sofa, patted the space next to her in invitation. Phoebe gingerly lowered herself, painfully aware of the delicate and expensive silk fabric. Much as she had in the carriage, she had to resist the temptation to stroke it. She knew it would feel cool and smoothly textured beneath her fingers, and she mentally winced with guilt at what her brother or Mrs. Tanner might think to see her in such rich surroundings.

Actually, she knew exactly what George would say, and none of it would be good.

"Phoebe," her aunt said, "tell us about your journey. You

must have been very nervous to leave your family and embark on such a voyage."

"Damned irregular," muttered Uncle Arthur, and his wife cast him a warning glance. The old man subsided into his chair, but that didn't stop him from scowling when Phoebe related the difficulties of the passage and how so many had fallen sick.

"Oh, dear," exclaimed Meredith. "There's nothing worse than nausea for weeks on end. I suffered that for several months earlier this year when I was with child. And to be trapped for weeks on a ship with no respite . . ." She shuddered. "How awful."

Phoebe smiled, already drawn to her cousin's warmth and sympathetic nature. "I was fortunate not to succumb until a week before we arrived in England. The worst was watching the children fall ill. We worried that several would not survive the voyage."

Everyone made the appropriate noises of concern, and the conversation continued until the butler and a footman arrived with a tea service. That seemed to be her uncle's cue to rise to his feet.

"Well," he said in a hearty voice, "I expect you ladies will want to talk about my new niece's move to Stanton House, as well as shopping and all the other silly details you'll need to decide upon for her coming-out."

Phoebe's anxiety spiked. "We will?" Her voice cracked on a high note.

Lucas gave her an encouraging smile. "Don't worry, Phoebe. You're in good hands with Aunt Georgie and Meredith. Just let them take care of everything. Life will be much easier if you do, I promise."

"But . . . but," she spluttered.

"Capital," boomed Uncle Arthur. "I think the lads and I should repair to my library for a brandy. You ladies certainly won't want us underfoot while you perfect your battle plans."

Phoebe's alarm turned to panic when Lucas stood as well. She had no desire to talk about clothes or her move or her coming-out, nor did she feel ready to face any Stanton, no matter how kind, without Lucas there to lend support. She had barely made up her mind to stay in London, much less make such detailed plans.

"Lucas, I do not think . . ." Well, she did not know what to think, and her features must have shown it.

His voice gentled. "It's all right, Phoebe. I need to run a few errands, and then I'll return to take you home." He looked at his aunt. "In about an hour, shall we say?"

"No need for you to leave," said his uncle. "The girl obviously doesn't want you to go, either."

That brought a hot blush to Phoebe's cheeks. She was not a child, and she had better stop clinging to Lucas as if she were.

Uncle Arthur gestured to Lucas. "Why don't you join us in the library? It's been weeks since you and Silverton saw each other, what with the time you've been spending down in Kent at the manor."

Lucas gave his uncle a polite bow. "Forgive me, sir, but I have an appointment I must attend. Another time, I promise."

His gaze turned wary and slid over to Lord Silverton, who looked down his nose at Lucas in a haughty manner. Just like that, the tension that had gripped the room earlier returned. Aunt Georgie let out a tiny sigh.

"If that's the case," the marquess said in a cold voice, "you needn't trouble yourself to return. Meredith and I will escort Phoebe home."

Lucas studied his cousin. Even though he barely moved, a noticeable change came over him. Suddenly, he looked every inch the soldier, and a dangerous one at that. He did not need a uniform or a rifle for Phoebe to recognize the ruthless nature lurking beneath the polished exterior.

"Phoebe is my responsibility," he said. "I will return for her in an hour and take her home."

"Perhaps I can engage a hackney for my return to Mrs. Poole's house," Phoebe ventured. "I do not want to cause any inconvenience."

"It's no inconvenience," Lucas said in a hard voice. "And you will remain here until I return to pick you up. Do you understand?"

Speechless, she stared at him.

"There's no need to go ordering your poor cousin about like she's some raw recruit," Uncle Arthur barked. "You'll frighten her."

Phoebe sighed. Her relatives must think her a poor dab of a girl, indeed. Not that she liked the way Lucas snarled at her, but she was not ready to hide under the sofa just yet.

Lucas raised his eyebrows in a skeptical arch. "Did I frighten you?"

"No. I simply do not wish to inconvenience you."

Lord Silverton parted his lips in something that only remotely resembled a smile. "So, it's settled then. *We'll* take Phoebe home and *you* can run along to your important appointment."

Lucas hissed out a breath, and Phoebe almost choked on the realization that the two men were staring at each other with hatred. It swirled so thickly around them that it almost made her ill, as did the notion they were using her as a means to express it.

"Oh, for God's sake," Meredith exclaimed. She got up and dodged around the tea table, inserting herself between the two men. "Lucas," she said, turning her back on her husband, "your sense of responsibility toward Phoebe is commendable, but you can't be so selfish as to keep her all to yourself." She sounded cheerful, but no one in the room could miss the warning in her voice. "We'll take Phoebe home when she's ready to go, and you can call on her later to finalize the arrangements for her move to Stanton House."

As tall as Meredith was, Lucas still loomed over her, looking very intimidating. But Meredith simply stared up into his face, a little smile playing around her lips.

After a tense moment, he let out a grudging laugh. Much to Phoebe's surprise, he bent to drop a quick kiss on Meredith's cheek. Lord Silverton's eyes narrowed but he remained silent.

"I stand corrected. Forgive me for being such a selfish brute." He cast a hard glance at Lord Silverton. "This woman is too good for you. I hope you know that."

"I do," his cousin replied. "But that's hardly any of your business."

Meredith turned to her husband and began to scold him in a quiet but no less vehement tone.

"Phoebe," Lucas said as he came to make his farewells, "I'll see you tonight."

She simply nodded, too distressed to say anything. Lucas bowed his good-byes and left the room. A few moments later, the other men repaired to the library, leaving Phoebe, Meredith, and Aunt Georgie to sit in pensive silence.

"Well," Meredith finally said, "that was almost as awful as the last time they saw each other."

"No, dear," Aunt Georgie replied calmly. "It was much better. This time they didn't try to hit each other, which I take as a sign of great progress."

Chapter 5

Aunt Georgie sipped her tea, apparently unperturbed by the drama her nephews had inflicted on the family. Phoebe looked from her to Meredith, searching for some clue as to how to react.

Should she ignore what had transpired? Perhaps that would be the conduct expected of a lady of the ton, but she found herself too disturbed by the incident to pretend. After all, her future and her security were now in the hands of this family. She needed to be able to trust that they were kind and honorable people.

"Do they always act like that around each other?" she asked cautiously.

Meredith rolled her eyes. "Sadly, Aunt Georgina is right. It's usually much worse. Last Easter they actually got into a fistfight, in the middle of my sister's dining room. I had to fall into a fit of hysterics to get them to stop."

Horrified, Phoebe clapped a hand to her cheek. "How awful for you!"

Meredith laughed. "Not really. I've never fallen into hysterics in my life, and Silverton knows it. But I was pregnant at the time, so it worked like a charm. Even he was fooled, and poor Lucas turned as white as a ghost."

Aunt Georgie grimaced and set her teacup down. "As effective as Meredith's intervention was, however, the damage was done. That fight brought years of bad blood to the fore. Instead of making their apologies to each other, and to the rest of us, Stephen blamed Meredith's reaction on Lucas. Lucas then stalked out of the room and galloped off on his horse like a character from a melodrama. Ever since, they can barely stand to be in the same room. Only the combined pressure from the rest of us keeps them from repeating that unfortunate episode."

Phoebe blindly reached for her cup and took a large gulp of tea to moisten her suddenly dry mouth. To know Lucas could act so violently was disturbing, to say the least. As for Lord Silverton, he did not seem the kind of man to engage in fisticuffs in front of his relatives.

A wave of trepidation swept over her as she realized how different life would be with the Stantons, and how much more complicated. She had certainly experienced times of strain and unhappiness in her brother's household, even injured feelings, but no member of the family would ever speak to each other in the violent tones she had heard only moments ago.

And her brother, George, would die of shame if he ever lifted a hand in anger against any man. That kind of action was unthinkable among Quakers.

"Have they always been like that with each other?" she asked, trying to understand.

Aunt Georgie's faded blue eyes filled with sadness. "They used to be the best of friends. When Stephen and Lucas were growing up, no two boys could have been closer. Stephen was a few years older and he always watched out for Lucas, who hero-worshipped him. Even when they went on to Eton and Oxford, they remained close."

Meredith nodded. "Silverton rarely talks about Lucas, but once or twice, before he had the chance to think about it, he mentioned some youthful scrap or adventure of theirs." She smiled at her aunt. "I take it there were quite a few back in their university days."

"You have no idea. I always say they were the reason the General's hair turned gray at such an early age. They were sent down from Oxford several times until Stephen began to mature and take his responsibilities more seriously."

"Then what happened?" Phoebe asked. "How could they go from being so close to . . ."

Aunt Georgie grimaced. "Hatred? Only the oldest and most foolish reason known to man. They fell out over a woman."

Phoebe's mind went blank for a moment. Then, startled, she stared at Meredith.

Meredith threw up her hands. "No, it wasn't me. But that makes it all the more ridiculous for Silverton to hold a grudge. He adores me and our twins, so why he should remain angry at Lucas over such an old dispute defies reason." She blew out a frustrated breath. "Sometimes the stubborn man needs a good slap. They both do."

Phoebe's eyes widened. Her Stanton relatives did seem to be a combative lot. Fitting in with them threatened to be a considerable challenge, one she was not sure she wished to take up.

Meredith took one look at her face and broke into laughter. "I'm joking, Phoebe. Forgive me. I assure you, no Stanton would ever raise a hand to anyone, except in self-defense."

"Except for Lucas and your husband, apparently," Phoebe could not help adding.

Meredith sighed. "Yes, except for them, but they're just being stupid. The strange thing is, if Lucas ever needed Silverton's help—I mean, *really* needed it—Silverton would climb mountains to do it."

"And Lucas would do the same," Aunt Georgie said. "That's why this entire situation is so absurd. But it's been going on for so long I don't think either of them knows how to get around it."

Phoebe nodded. That she understood. If an injury was left untended it always festered, and that included injuries to the spirit.

"Who was the woman?" she asked. "Does Lucas still love this person?"

Meredith and Aunt Georgie exchanged glances, and Phoebe wanted to bite her tongue. What matter if Lucas loved another woman? Even though he had in essence asked Phoebe to marry him, she had no intention of doing so. After what she had seen today, she could hardly believe they would suit, and she found his anger and barely repressed aggression disconcerting, to say the least.

"No, dear," Aunt Georgie replied. "This tawdry little situation happened many years ago. Silverton was twenty-three. Lucas had just turned twenty-one and had recently taken up his commission in the Dragoon Guards. They remained the greatest of friends, but life was beginning to pull them in different directions. Silverton was a marquess and had many responsibilities, while Lucas was embarking on what he perceived as a grand adventure."

The old woman's eyes warmed with memories. "They were both determined to make their mark in the world. And," she added ruefully, "both were rather spoiled and too proud for their own good."

"How very surprising," Meredith said dryly.

Phoebe could not hold back a giggle.

"Well," said Aunt Georgie, "they were both only sons, and much cherished by their families. Not to mention that both were ridiculously handsome from an early age. Women practically threw themselves at their feet."

"They still do," commented Meredith, taking her aunt's teacup and refilling it.

"But Lord Silverton is a married man," Phoebe exclaimed, scandalized. "How can women still pursue him?"

"You have a lot to learn about the ton, my dear cousin.

Many of our acquaintances would never let something as trivial as marriage vows hold them back."

Phoebe grimaced. The more she heard about the London aristocracy, the less she wanted to have anything to do with them. What she did want, though, was to hear more about Lucas and his cousin.

"Who was the woman who caused so much trouble?" she prodded.

"The woman in question was Esme Newton. She was a diamond of the first water," replied Aunt Georgie.

Phoebe cast a puzzled look at Meredith, who nodded in understanding.

"That means she was a great beauty, Phoebe. Apparently, Esme held that distinction for three Seasons. And she was very well aware of it, from what I've been told."

Aunt Georgie patted Meredith's hand. "She didn't hold a candle to you, my love, and Silverton knows that."

"I'm sure," she responded in a dry tone. She glanced at Phoebe and grinned. "As you can imagine, this is not a topic Silverton and I are fond of discussing."

"I can imagine. But I still cannot understand how it occurred. How did this woman cause such a drastic falling out between cousins who revered each other so greatly? Surely they valued their friendship and family bond more than a woman, no matter how beautiful."

Aunt Georgie and Meredith stared at her as if she had a large beetle perched on her nose.

"You don't know very much about men, do you, Phoebe?" asked Meredith.

She shrugged. There was no point denying the truth.

"Silverton fell madly in love with Esme," Aunt Georgie explained. "She was his first real love, which made it all the worse. He intended to marry her, and the only reason he delayed in asking was that his mother objected to the alliance."

She glanced over at Meredith. "Back then, Silverton actually thought he had to listen to his mother."

The two women shared a laugh—Phoebe had no idea about what—and then Meredith took up the tale.

"Esme encouraged Silverton's addresses, but she was also a terrible flirt. My husband was a great prize on the marriage mart, and Esme enjoyed keeping him on a string. She thought it added greatly to her consequence."

Phoebe wrinkled her nose. "She sounds horrible."

Aunt Georgie sighed. "Merely silly and spoiled. But poor Silverton was so head over heels in love that he allowed her to lead him around by the nose. He simply didn't know what to do with her. Unfortunately, Lucas did."

That did not sound good. "What did he do?"

"I don't think Lucas initially meant to pursue her, but Esme thought it would be great sport to have two of the most eligible men in London—cousins, no less—at her beck and call. If she could make both men fall in love with her, it would be quite a feather in her cap."

Phoebe shook her head, mystified at such cruel manipulation. But why did Lucas allow himself to become her pawn?

"How could Lucas do that to his cousin?" she blurted out. "How could he be so coldhearted?"

Aunt Georgie shook her head. "If Esme had just been flirting, Lucas would have seen through it. But she actually did develop strong feelings for him, even though I expect she never intended to. He was so very handsome and dashing in his uniform, and he has always had so much charm. What started as a lighthearted flirtation quickly developed into something more. Lucas was convinced Esme loved *him*, not Silverton. Under those circumstances, he felt justified in pursuing her. That error was compounded by the fact that Silverton had delayed his proposal, leading Lucas to believe his cousin wasn't serious about Esme."

"How unfortunate," Phoebe said softly.

"Indeed. In any event, Lucas did pursue Esme, and quite masterfully. Despite the fact he was two years younger than Silverton, he had a great deal of boldness. He courted Esme with a single-minded purpose that left no one in doubt as to what he wanted."

Phoebe discovered she was clenching her hands into fists. Startled, she opened them, smoothing her damp palms against her skirt.

"Why did they not marry?" she asked, feeling rather bleak about the whole thing. She could well imagine Lucas had never stopped loving this woman, no matter what anyone said.

"Esme never had any intention of marrying Lucas," Aunt Georgie said bitterly. "Once he formally proposed, she realized her mistake. Silverton was always the prize for her. After all, he was a wealthy peer whereas Lucas, while possessing a handsome income, was a soldier just starting his career. So, Esme rebuffed him. Quite thoroughly, I suspect, if his subsequent reaction was any indication."

Phoebe pressed a hand to her chest, heartsick. From the first, she had sensed that Lucas lived according to a strict code of honor, and to be treated so dishonestly by the woman he loved would have inflicted a terrible blow on his pride.

"Lucas must have been devastated," she said.

"He was furious," Meredith replied. "He blamed Silverton, claiming he deliberately turned Esme against him. That particular conversation did not end well."

Aunt Georgie nodded. "That incident ended in a fight in this house, in your uncle's library. If it had been allowed to run its course, it might have ended there. My husband, wise in the ways of proud young men, initially made no attempt to stop it. Unfortunately, Silverton's mother—a very foolish woman— heard the commotion. She burst into the library and promptly fell into hysterics, forcing the General to end the fight."

"How could that be a bad thing?" Phoebe protested.

"Because they needed to get the poison out of their systems," Meredith explained. "Silverton accused Lucas of acting dishonorably, and Lucas then felt he had no choice but to challenge him to a duel."

Phoebe gazed at her with horror. "You mean they actually tried to kill each other?"

Aunt Georgie shook her head. "It never would have come to that. But young men are notorious for lack of common sense, so your uncle again was forced to intervene. He absolutely forbade them to duel, and shipped Lucas off the next day to join his regiment in the Peninsula."

Phoebe slumped in her chair. "Thank God."

"Quite. Almost two years passed before they saw each other again, and by that time they both realized they could not inflict such heartbreak on their families. They came to some kind of arrangement to never speak of the incident again. That, however, does not mean they ever forgave each other."

Phoebe reached over to touch her aunt's hand. "That must be very difficult for you. I am so sorry."

The older woman gave her a lovely smile. "In reality, we were all able to ignore it for a very long time. Lucas has spent the last twelve years in the army, and made a point of rarely being home. And even when he was in London, he and Silverton avoided each other."

"Unfortunately," Meredith interjected, "your grandfather's death changed all that. It forced Lucas to sell his commission and come home to take up the earldom. He and Silverton can no longer avoid each other, and both appear to be very good at holding on to grudges."

Aunt Georgie gave a delicate shrug. "Silverton and Lucas will scrape along somehow. If they don't, we'll eventually have to force them. But right now, we have more important matters to attend to. Namely, what's to be done about Phoebe."

Phoebe jerked a bit, sloshing some of her tea into the saucer. She carefully set the cup down onto the tray.

"I understood I was coming to stay with you, at least for a little while," she said, trying not to sound anxious.

The older woman gave her a blinding smile. "Of course you will, Phoebe. Your room has already been prepared, and you can stay as long as you want. I'm talking about your future here in England, and what you might be envisioning."

Phoebe hesitated, not sure what to say. "I . . . I do not know. My grandfather's death was such a shock, and I have not had a chance to think much beyond that."

Both women nodded sympathetically but still regarded her with expectant looks on their faces.

She took a breath and forged ahead. "Lucas suggests that I stay at least until the spring. He said if I then wished to return to America, he would escort me back himself."

Aunt Georgie's eyes narrowed. "He offered that, did he?"

Phoebe nodded, confused by her aunt's displeasure. Was she angry that Lucas might wish her to return to America? She did not relish the prospect either, but one could hardly expect the Stantons to support her for the rest of her life.

Her aunt drummed her fingers on the arm of the sofa, looking as if she were sifting through some weighty matter. Meredith simply smiled and poured herself another cup of tea.

"Phoebe," Aunt Georgie said rather abruptly, "did Lucas show you a letter from your grandfather?"

Phoebe's stomach dropped. "He told you about that?"

"Of course he did. The poor man hadn't a clue how to deal with it. He was worried you might drop into a dead faint as soon as you read it."

Phoebe winced. "I almost did."

The other two women laughed.

"Don't be embarrassed," Aunt Georgie said. "Your grandfather wrote to me before he died, too. He was tormented with worry for you and pleaded for my help. I have no doubt his letter and the request it contained was a shock, but it was his way of looking after you."

"But the idea of marrying a stranger is ridiculous," she protested. "And I am sure Lucas has no desire to marry me. He only asked because my grandfather made him."

Aunt Georgie's eyebrows arched. "So, he did ask you?"

"Yes. No. I . . . I am not really sure. It was a very confusing conversation." She took a deep breath. "In any event, he only raised the issue because he made Grandfather a deathbed promise. Lucas obviously felt he had no other choice."

"Are you sure about that?" Aunt Georgie asked softly.

Phoebe started to answer, then closed her lips. Most of the night she had lain awake, trying to convince herself that Lucas was *not* serious. But now, as she peered at the calm and confident face of the woman sitting next to her, she could not be sure. Was it possible he did really wish to marry her? Whatever for?

She dug both hands into the silk fabric beneath her fingers, trying to steady herself. Her head spun, and all the shocks of the last few days suddenly seemed too much.

Aunt Georgie took her hand in a comforting clasp. "My dear, forgive me. This all must seem overwhelming. It was foolish of me to even mention the letter."

Phoebe gripped her hand, desperate for something to hold on to. "I do not know what to think. I hardly even know what to feel. Nothing is as I thought it would be."

The older woman gave her a quick hug. "The situation is dreadfully awkward, but you are not to think of the letter or anything else that might distress you right now. You needn't make any decisions for quite some time. You have come from America to visit with your family, and that is all anyone need know. No one will breathe a word about your grandfather's letter."

Phoebe glanced warily at Meredith, who dramatically drew a finger across her mouth as if sealing it shut. She choked out a breathless laugh, relieved that no one would force her to confront all the fraught questions about her future, or about Lucas.

"Now, let's get down to the most important business," Aunt Georgie said.

Phoebe frowned. "What would that be?"

Meredith laughed. "Why, shopping for your new wardrobe, of course. That's the most important thing of all."

Chapter 6

Phoebe stared at her reflection in the mirror. It was a frequent activity these days, but not one she enjoyed. Especially when trying on yet another of the expensive new dresses Aunt Georgie insisted she must have for her introduction into the ton.

Like the one she had on now. The tawny color suited her complexion and the silk gleamed with a soft shine, but the bodice . . .

"My dear, what are you trying to hide? Please turn around so I can see your gown," Aunt Georgie prompted.

Her aunt sat on a low divan in the corner of the dressing room. Meredith sat next to her. For a week, Phoebe had resisted their combined efforts to order a ball gown for her, but she had finally given in. For the last hour, a very fashionable dressmaker had fussed and measured, poking away at Phoebe until she felt ready to scream.

She supposed the impulse reflected a sad lack of gratitude on her part. Since her move to Stanton House, all her relatives had been kinder than she could have imagined. Still, Phoebe was reluctant to throw herself wholeheartedly into her new life, fearing she would embarrass herself and her new family once she ventured out into polite society. Better to remain quietly at Stanton House, making only the occasional excursion to one of the nearby parks, until she could fathom whether she could truly be comfortable with all the changes that faced her with each new dawn.

But today, Meredith and her aunt had put their beautifully shod feet collectively down, insisting she must add appropriate evening wear to her wardrobe. Nettled, Phoebe had told them she could not afford any more shopping and that there was nothing wrong with the clothes she already owned.

Her aunt, sitting at the writing desk in her private sitting room, had given Phoebe an understanding smile. "I appreciate your scruples, but if your grandfather had lived you would have allowed him to pay your bills, correct?"

"Um, yes," she'd answered. But even if her grandfather had lived, Phoebe had never imagined a life of such luxury. Mrs. Tanner had warned her, and she had been right. Buying new clothes when not needed was an extravagance, and one that made her debt of obligation to her aunt and uncle all the greater.

But Mrs. Tanner had never encountered Aunt Georgie.

"We've all been waiting for you to come home for such a long time, and we're so happy to have you with us," Aunt Georgie had said in a gentle, plaintive voice. "Besides, the clothes you wear now would make you stand out, and the General would be most distressed if anyone thought we were treating you as a poor relation. You don't want that to happen, do you?"

Sighing, Phoebe had capitulated. Before she could even catch her breath, Aunt Georgie and Meredith had whisked her off to the fashionable shops of Bruton Street.

And into the shocking dress she was currently wearing.

"Phoebe," Meredith said, "you must turn around so we can see whether this dress suits you."

Phoebe gave one more fruitless tug on the bodice. "I still do not understand why I need evening gowns in the first place. I have no desire to gallivant around town, especially since I am still in mourning. Surely no one expects to see me at social functions, do they?"

Gallivant was one of Uncle Arthur's favorite words, and Phoebe had unconsciously adopted it along with some of his other colorful expressions. One of the greatest surprises in her move to Stanton House had been the easy way she and her uncle had fallen in with each other. She appreciated that he was a plainspoken and serious man, even if a bit rough in his speech. He, in turn, had deemed her *a sensible girl*, not one who wasted her energy on fripperies, parties, and balls. She did not bother to explain that for now, she much preferred spending her days in his library, reading by the fire or talking to him about his travels on the Continent as a young man.

She also loved it when Lucas came to visit Uncle Arthur. The men never asked her to leave, and Lucas always made an effort to draw her into the conversation. Sometimes he made her blush with his teasing, but he also treated her with great gentleness. He seemed to sense whenever she was ruffled or unhappy, and had a knack for making her feel secure, even safe. That he could do so surprised her, given that his manner could be arrogant, even fierce, when something displeased him.

Unfortunately, not even Lucas could protect her from today's indignities.

Scowling at her reflection, Phoebe gave her bodice another useless tug. Meredith stood and moved behind her, gently placing her hands on Phoebe's shoulders and turning her around.

"You're only in half mourning," Meredith said as she skillfully rearranged the whisper-thin material across Phoebe's bosom. "Your grandfather has been dead for over two months, so it's entirely appropriate for you to go out into company, as long as you don't dance. And this gown is both tasteful and discreet. Just the perfect thing for a young lady in your situation."

Phoebe almost choked on Meredith's description of the

gown. Half her chest was exposed. If she did not succumb to a fatal chill, she would likely die of mortification the first time she went into public.

Without thinking, she slipped her hand up to the bodice, ready to yank it up. Meredith caught her fingers.

"You'll ruin the fabric," she warned.

"But I feel . . . naked."

Aunt Georgie laughed. "I'm not surprised, given what you normally wear. But I assure you, that dress is modest by ton standards. It's the perfect thing for your appearance at Lady Framingham's ball next week."

"Aunt Georgina is right," Meredith said. "Half the women at the ball will be falling out of their gowns. One or two of them quite literally." She smoothed down the bodice over her own generous chest and sighed. "Just look at me. After having twins, I practically have to strap myself in whenever I put on evening attire, or I'd give my husband a fit."

"But everything seems to fit you perfectly." Despairing, Phoebe gestured at her overflowing chest. "Unlike me. I'm skinny everywhere but up here. I look top heavy, like some sort of puffed-up bird."

Aunt Georgie smiled. "The dressmaker can alter the gown to fit perfectly. And you have a lovely figure. Most girls would give their eyeteeth to look like you. Most importantly, I'm sure any man in his right mind would agree. Lucas, for instance. He seems quite taken with you."

Not again. Phoebe did not want to have this conversation, not when she knew her cheeks turned red as fire at the very mention of his name. "I am sure he is not."

"I'm sure he is," Aunt Georgie gently insisted. "We hardly used to see Lucas from one week to the next, but now he practically haunts the General's library. He's visited every day since you've arrived."

Phoebe blushed even harder. "He is acting out of simple kindness to a newcomer, nothing more."

Meredith laughed. "Kindness has nothing to do with it. Can't you tell?"

That was the problem. She could not. The men she had grown up with were nothing like Lucas, or anyone else in London, for that matter.

Flummoxed, she could only stare back at her aunt and cousin, uncertain what they wanted from her.

"Phoebe," Aunt Georgie said, "have you given any more thought to your uncle's letter?"

"Of course not."

That was not strictly true, but she had tried very hard *not* to think about it. Sometimes, late at night, she did turn the contents of that letter over in her mind. And no matter how absurd her grandfather's plea, there was an insidious kernel of attraction to the idea of being married to Lucas. When she was alone, with Stanton House silent and still around her, Phoebe allowed herself to dream about her own family and home, with a man who truly loved her—a man as strong and protective as Lucas.

"Only because you do not know what else to do with your life," she said, absently voicing her thoughts.

When Aunt Georgie arched her brows, Phoebe repressed a groan. Why in heaven's name had she blurted *that* out? The idea that a man like Lucas would want to marry a countrified Quaker was simply too absurd to contemplate.

It took a bit of a struggle, but she managed to return her aunt's perceptive gaze with a bland smile. After a few moments, the older woman nodded, as if some question had been answered.

"I think that dress will do very nicely for the ball," she said, surprising Phoebe by dropping the subject. "And the dusky rose cambric will be perfect for tomorrow night."

Phoebe rolled her eyes. She had forgotten about the party to be held at Stanton House to introduce her to a select circle of family friends. Well, not forgotten, exactly, but done everything she could to drive it from her mind. Her aunt had assured her she need not worry at all. Even the General had said she would enjoy herself, since there was not a bird-witted female or an overscented dandy in the bunch.

"I agree," said Meredith. "The rose cambric will be the perfect thing for a Christmas party in the country, too. But Phoebe will also need some warmer gowns. Belfield Abbey can be drafty in the wintertime."

Phoebe perked up. "Is that where we will be spending Christmas?"

Although her Quaker relations had never celebrated the holiday, her mother had sometimes told her of Christmas festivities in England. Not often, but enough to whet Phoebe's interest.

Meredith smiled at her. "Yes. It's only a short trip from London, and it's also very close to your grandfather's"—she wrinkled her nose and corrected herself—"the new Lord Merritt's estate in Kent. Lucas will be traveling down there at the beginning of December. The property, unfortunately, was badly neglected during the last few years of your poor grandfather's life. We thought it would be best if the rest of us were close by, in case Lucas needs our help."

Phoebe gnawed on her lower lip. "But Lucas will not wish to go to Belfield Abbey, will he? Given the way things are . . ." she trailed off, making a helpless gesture with her hand. Lucas would no doubt do everything in his power to avoid seeing Silverton.

Which meant Phoebe would not be seeing him on a regular basis, if at all, which bothered her more than it should.

Her aunt's eyes twinkled with mischief. "I wouldn't worry about that. Meredith and I believe this estrangement has gone on long enough. Christmas is a time of both forgiveness and rebirth, and we are determined that Silverton and Lucas *will* forgive each other."

"If we have to murder them to make them do it," Meredith added.

Phoebe gaped, and her cousin laughed.

"Metaphorically speaking, of course. But it's more than time to let the old grudges go. And things are different now, especially for Lucas."

"But they can barely sit together in the same room," Phoebe protested. "What has changed, and why Lucas, specifically?"

Her aunt and cousin exchanged a swift glance, and a whisper of caution drifted through Phoebe's mind.

"Never mind," Aunt Georgie replied. "Everything will work out just as it should. What we need to do now is have you fitted for a nice, warm pelisse. I know you don't ride, but you will certainly want to take walks around Belfield Abbey, and I'm sure Lucas will want you to see his estate, too. In fact, I believe he'll insist upon it."

"He will be too busy," Phoebe said. Lucas would no more want the lot of them trooping over to his estate than he would want to visit Belfield Abbey.

"Don't count on it," Meredith said.

Phoebe peered at her suspiciously. She had a strong sense that Meredith and Aunt Georgie were speaking in some kind of family code, but she had not the slightest idea how to decipher it.

She opened her mouth to question them but Meredith cut her off, calling for the dressmaker to rejoin them. After that, Meredith avoided her eye as she chattered away about fabrics and trim and fur muffs. Aunt Georgie, meanwhile, sat quietly in the corner, looking as satisfied as a mouse with a piece of cheese.

Oh, yes, they were hiding something, and Phoebe had the feeling that if she knew what it was she would not like it one bit.

Chapter 7

Lucas gratefully entered the warmth of Stanton House. London on a dark November night didn't match the biting cold of the Pyrenees in the winter but it was dreary enough, with the damp fog penetrating even the wool of his greatcoat. Still, he'd gladly exchange the mansions of Mayfair for a soldier's camp in the high mountain passes of Spain. For one thing, he'd be spared the social inanities that awaited him in his aunt's drawing room. For another, he wouldn't have to see the bane of his existence, his cousin Silverton.

Tolliver made a dignified approach across the entrance hall. "Good evening, Lord Merritt. May I take your coat and hat?"

Lucas forced a smile. He was here tonight for Phoebe and no one else. He'd stay out of his cousin's way, and hope Silverton had the sense to do the same.

He glanced up the imposing central staircase. "They've all gone in, I suppose?"

He hoped so, since he could then slip into the party without a fuss and hope to slip out later, just as easily. God, he hated these evenings. They always provoked a vague, restless sensation, his muscles twitching with the need for action. Fourteen years of soldiering were to blame. Ever since he resigned his commission, everything else in life had bored him by comparison.

Except for his new estate. That wasn't boring. It was a nightmare, and another responsibility in a long list of responsibilities he'd never wanted.

"Yes, my lord," said Tolliver. "The General and her ladyship will be happy to receive you in the yellow saloon."

Ah. It was a formal affair. Poor Phoebe. His little cousin wouldn't know what hit her when confronted with all the trappings of the haute ton, but Aunt Georgie was obviously intent on sending a message.

She's a Stanton. She's one of us. Accept her, or else.

Smiling at her tactics, Lucas climbed the stairs two at a time. He gave his waistcoat a tug, then stepped into the saloon, taking a moment to study the lay of the land. Best to know the territory one's friends and enemies had staked out before entering the battlefield.

Aunt Georgie held court at the far end of the room, surrounded by four of the most influential dragons of the ton. Close by, the General chatted with some of his retired military friends and Silverton, which meant Lucas would be avoiding that corner of the room. The rest of the guests drifted about the elegant space, or gathered in small, chattering groups.

But where the hell was Phoebe?

There. Tucked away in a window alcove, trying to attract as little notice as possible. She sat with Meredith, who was conversing with her half sister, Annabel. Robert, Annabel's husband and grandson to General and Lady Stanton, stood behind them, a look of boredom already apparent on his youthful face.

Lucas had to repress a laugh. Robert hated these evenings almost as much as he did. In fact, the lad had grown quite adept at getting out of them since he had married Annabel. The fact that the whole family had turned out in force underscored the importance of the event.

Since no one had noticed him yet, he took a moment to

study Phoebe. He'd seen a good deal of her these last few weeks, going to Stanton House most days ostensibly to visit his uncle. His intent lay elsewhere, of course, which General Stanton had certainly deduced, although he'd had the good sense not to mention it to Phoebe.

Much to Lucas's unending surprise, the girl intrigued him. She had from the moment they met. Phoebe had a sweet, winsome beauty and a gentle manner, but underneath her calm exterior there lived an intelligent mind and a quick wit.

Not that anyone saw the wit very often. Phoebe approached life in a serious fashion. That partly stemmed from her dreary Quaker upbringing, but Lucas also suspected other forces at play. What caused her to engage with life in such cautious manner, he had yet to discern. But he would. Unless his instincts had failed him, she was developing an attachment to him. It manifested in the shy but eager smile that lit up her face whenever he walked into the room, and in the way she focused her attention on him. Not in a flattering, obsequious way, but with a quiet intensity that seemed to be entirely unconscious on her part.

Considering his plans for her, that pleased him a great deal.

As he watched her, her head came up and she turned his way. Their gazes locked. A pink blush tinged her cheeks and her lips parted in a luminous smile. He felt the impact of that smile reverberate through bone and muscle like a hammer blow.

Startled, he shook it off. Never again would a woman exercise control over him, even one as gentle and honest as Phoebe. That, however, didn't mean he couldn't enjoy her attentions, or revel in the fact that she appeared as fascinated with him as he was with her. He realized what was happening between them, even if she was too innocent to recognize the signs.

With a little luck, she wouldn't be innocent much longer.

Given the way she looked tonight, he could hardly wait. Aunt Georgie and Meredith had transformed Phoebe into a stunner, with her gown clinging to soft, enticing curves, and glossy dark locks artfully arranged in a riotous tumble around her neck and shoulders. She was a prize, and he hoped to claim her as soon as he could.

"Good evening, ladies," he said as he came up to the small group. "Annabel, it's a pleasure to see you in town, but I can't say the same for your husband. How you tolerate him is a mystery no Stanton has been able to solve."

Annabel giggled as he bent to kiss her cheek, but Robert snorted. "It's because I'm such a pleasant, well-mannered fellow. Unlike some people, who can't be bothered to show up for a family dinner even when his favorite cousin has just arrived in town."

Lucas raised his eyebrows in mock enquiry. "Yes, I certainly did miss seeing Annabel, but the thought of dining with you was too much for my delicate stomach."

Annabel tried to look severe, an impossible feat for one so elfin. "Lucas, you are a terrible tease. But we were beginning to wonder if you would bother to put in an appearance tonight."

Meredith threw her sister a warning glance, but remained silent. Lucas couldn't help but appreciate her discretion. He would never abandon Phoebe during her first outing, but dinner had been out of the question. The last time he and Silverton had shared a table the meal had ended in a brawl, as Annabel well knew because it was her damn table.

"Forgive me," he said politely. "I was engaged earlier in the evening, but I would never miss Phoebe's first party."

Phoebe narrowed her eyes at him. She obviously knew the reason for his late arrival, and it seemed to bother her, too.

Mentally, he shrugged. On this particular matter she would soon learn to respect his wishes, as had every other Stanton. She might not like it, but his careful avoidance of Silverton when at all possible made life easier for everyone.

To distract her from the topic he loathed more than any other, Lucas took her slender hand and carried it to his mouth, causing her to blush. "Phoebe, I hardly recognized you.

Surely my aunt has arranged for you to be kidnapped, and another woman substituted in your place. Where is my shy little Quaker? Who is this fashionable, self-assured woman sitting in her place?"

As anticipated, Phoebe starched right up. She worked hard to subdue her temper, but he sometimes enjoyed prodding it to the surface. He liked the passion in her, and liked even more the prospect of unleashing that passion when her body lay naked under his.

Meredith leapt to defend her charge, much like a tabby might defend her only kitten. "Phoebe looks very pretty and just as she should, and you well know it."

He laughed. "I do. In fact, pretty doesn't do her justice. Stunning is the more appropriate term. Phoebe, I always knew you were hiding your light under a basket. I'm happy to see you letting it shine for all to see."

She gave an adorable little grimace, looking torn between pleasure and embarrassment. "I am pleased to pass your inspection, *Lord Merritt*," she replied, giving his name a sarcastic emphasis. "But I cannot help feeling rather odd. As kind as Aunt Georgie's guests have all been, I rather think they anticipate something unexpected from me. Like falling into a religious fit, or speaking in tongues."

She was trying to make a joke of it, but he could sense her discomfort. Phoebe hated standing out. Her upbringing should have armored her against the censure of the broader world—since her people normally didn't give a damn about the opinions of non-Quakers—but he'd learned that she had felt no more at home in that rigid little world than she did among London's elite. She was neither fish nor fowl, and her usual tactic was to fade into the wallpaper and hope no one noticed her.

Lucas hooked an arm around a chair and pulled it next to her. "Once they get to know you, your religious beliefs won't make a whit of difference."

She looked so sweet and vulnerable, trying to act as if none of it really mattered, that he could barely resist the temptation to pull her into his arms and comfort her. Now *that* would give the gossips something to chatter about.

"Lord," said Robert, waving a negligent hand. "I don't know what all the fuss is about. You don't even speak like a Quaker, Phoebe. Why, you're nothing like those sour-looking crows in black, always preaching at some poor fellow. Cursed rum touches, I say."

Annabel's mouth dropped open and Meredith shook her head. Lucas, however, choked back a laugh. No Stanton gathering would be complete without Robert making at least one baffle-headed remark.

Phoebe's decisive chin jerked up a notch. Lucas quite liked that chin, with its small, defiant cleft. While not usually an attractive characteristic on a woman, it lent her an air of exoticism that steadfastly contradicted her attempts to play down her beauty.

"And how does thee imagine a Quaker speaks?" she asked politely.

Robert's eyes rounded with dismay. "Rather like that, actually."

Annabel glared at her husband but Meredith now looked ready to laugh, probably at the haughty lift to Phoebe's slender eyebrows. Taking in Phoebe's expression, Lucas could understand how such a meek little thing could survive a crossing of the storm-tossed Atlantic, then venture into a strange land to start a new life.

Robert stared at Phoebe with alarm. "Good Lord, Cuz, never meant to offend you. It's just that . . ." He broke off when a smile played around the corners of Phoebe's mouth.

"Whew," he exhaled. "Thought you were having me on. It's just that you don't really talk like any Quaker I've ever met. Not that I've met all that many, and I'm sure they'd be just as nice as you. Except for those outfits, of course. They're beastly and no getting around it."

"Their clothing makes it easier to get dressed in the morning," Phoebe said, "but I do take your point. I do not normally speak like that. My brother and his family certainly do, but my father did not, nor did my mother. She was determined that I speak what she called *proper King's English*."

She glanced at Lucas, offering him a shy smile. "Some people seem to expect me to deliver an evangelical lecture over dinner, and I cannot disabuse them of the notion. I suppose I must simply look and act too *plain*."

"Nonsense, Phoebe," said Annabel, obviously misunderstanding the Quaker meaning of the term. "You're the prettiest girl in the room and you have the loveliest manners, too."

Robert looked thoughtful, which usually boded ill. "Well, Phoebe is a dashed pretty girl, Belle, but to be fair, there ain't that many girls in the room to begin with. You and Meredith don't qualify anymore—"

Meredith reached over the back of the sofa and pinched him, but Robert simply grinned and carried on.

"As for the rest, given how old most of the guests are, it'll be a miracle if one of them doesn't keel over dead into the punch bowl by the end of the night."

Annabel rounded horrified eyes at her husband. "Do not let Grandpapa hear you say that. He's certainly as old as most of the guests tonight. And you know how sensitive he is about his age."

Robert cast an alarmed eye in his grandfather's direction. If there was one thing calculated to reduce him to silence, it was the fear of the old man's wrath.

"Yes," said Meredith. "Let us not upset the General. Although," she added, trying to repress a laugh, "Lady Bellingham does look to be nodding off as we speak. I do hope she doesn't begin snoring like she did at the Wellbourne's musicale last week. She was so loud she drowned everything out, including Cissy Patterson's performance on the harp. And you know Cissy. Any little thing pitches her into hysterics."

Phoebe blinked, clearly not knowing how to respond to that piece of information.

"Poor Phoebe," Lucas said. "We are all so gay to dissipation."

She laughed. "I do not mind in the least. While it is true that several of the guests are rather deaf, which does make conversation a challenge, one cannot fault their kindness or courtesy."

Robert gave a dramatic sigh. "I'm ready to hang myself, just to break the boredom."

"I'm sure your hanging would greatly enliven the evening," Meredith said in a tart voice. "Enough nonsense, Robert. I'd like to hear how the new Lord Merritt is faring with his estate. I believe you have quite a mountain of work ahead of you, do you not, Lucas?"

Now Lucas had to repress a sigh. The state of his holdings was another topic he'd rather avoid, but he couldn't be rude to Meredith. If Silverton had asked the question, he would have rebuffed him, but Meredith had treated him with nothing but warmth and generosity from the day he'd met her.

"I'm sorry to say the home farms are in a deplorable state, which is my greatest concern. The house needs significant repair, and the stable looks ready to collapse any minute, as does the dairy. The orchards are in better condition, which is the only blessing in the lot."

Phoebe listened to him with eager concentration. "The estate in Kent is quite large, is it not?"

"Large enough. There is also a small hunting lodge in Lincolnshire, but Mistletoe Manor is the primary seat of the earldom."

Phoebe scrunched up her nose. "Mistletoe Manor? It's lovely, but rather an odd name."

"You have no idea." Whichever ancestor had applied that demented label to the once-dignified Elizabethan manor deserved to be whipped. The name was bad enough, Lucas mused, but the manor staff—most of them descended from families who had served the Merritts for generations—cherished a bizarre obsession with everything the name implied. Why, even the housekeeper—

Robert's laugh interrupted his gloomy thoughts. "I'd

forgotten about that. From what Grandfather told me, the Merritts make quite a fuss about Christmas, do they not? All Yule logs and boar's head and Lord of Misrule, if I'm not mistaken." He winked at Lucas. "I suppose I know where we'll all be spending the holiday, ain't that right, Belle?"

Annabel rolled her eyes at her husband. "Not unless we're invited, and I certainly can't imagine why Lucas would want to invite *you*."

"I would love to see the manor, Lucas," Phoebe broke in, her eyes shining. "I would be so happy to see where my mother grew up."

Lucas smiled. Phoebe would see Mistletoe Manor soon enough, but not until he had it in decent enough shape that it wouldn't instantly frighten her off. She needed time to get used to what he had planned for her, and taking her to a broken-down estate didn't enter into those plans.

"Belfield Abbey is only a short distance from Mistletoe Manor," Meredith said. "I'm sure something can be arranged after we settle in."

Lucas shot her a frown. "Phoebe is going to Belfield Abbey for the holidays?"

"Everybody is," said Annabel. "At least for part of the time. Isn't that right, Meredith?"

"Yes," Meredith replied, watching Lucas carefully. "There will be plenty of opportunities to visit, if you will have us."

Their gazes locked, and an uncomfortable silence fell over their group. Lucas could feel his jaw twitch, but he fought to keep his face impassive. Christ! The entire family camped out at Belfield Abbey for weeks, right on his bloody doorstep? It was bad enough he had to grapple with all the problems foisted on him by his dilapidated inheritance. Now he would also be expected to dance attendance at every inane holiday gathering *and* put up with Silverton to boot.

Phoebe reached over and touched his hand. "Forgive me. I had no right to ask for an invitation in so rude a manner. You have many pressing matters to attend to on the estate, and I will be happy to wait until you are ready to receive guests." She smiled, but her dark eyes held a wounded dignity.

Lucas mentally winced. Phoebe was the last person he wanted to feel bad about this. Aunt Georgie and Meredith and all the other interfering women in his family were up to something with their Christmas plans, and he didn't like it. He wagered Silverton would be equally annoyed.

As if his thoughts had conjured up the devil himself, Silverton's voice broke in. "This looks to be a very lively group," he said in a sardonic voice.

Annabel plastered a bright smile on her face. "We were discussing Christmas plans, and how much fun it will be to visit Mistletoe Manor while we're all down at the abbey."

"Yes, won't it just," Silverton replied in his most bored voice.

Meredith flashed her husband a look that could slice through stone, and even Lucas had to feel a degree of sympathy for him. But he ignored the unwelcome emotion and focused on Phoebe. "Of course you must visit," he said, taking her hand. "You must regard Mistletoe Manor as much your home as it is mine. You will always be welcome there."

She earnestly searched his face, then cast her gaze to their still-joined hands. "Thank you," she murmured in a shy voice.

Silverton muttered something under his breath. Ignoring him, Lucas released Phoebe's hand and rose to his feet. "Ladies, if you'll excuse me, I must pay my respects to my aunt and uncle." He smiled down at Phoebe. "I'll speak with you again before I leave, all right?"

She nodded, but her gaze flicked warily between him and Silverton.

He turned and glanced at his cousin, who studied him with an alert, suspicious gaze. Scowling, Lucas brushed past him and strode away.

Chapter 8

Clearly eager to escape a lecture from his wife, Cousin Stephen murmured an apology before dragging Robert off to the other side of the drawing room. Phoebe could not help noticing he made a wide berth around Lucas, casting him a dark glance.

Lucas was equally to blame for the ridiculous male feud, but Phoebe could never stay angry with him for long. And he *had* overcome his loathing of Stanton family events to appear at her modest debut. She was grateful for his support, and for the fact that he never seemed to care about her dress or her manner of speech. Lucas listened to her—really listened— and made her think her opinions mattered.

But tonight he *did* seem to care about her appearance. In fact, when their gazes first met, he had looked at her in a way that scorched the air between them, robbing her of breath and heating her from the inside out. She had not expected his reaction, and it had turned her brain to mush and muddled her insides with an unfamiliar, shivery sort of feeling.

But then Cousin Stephen had approached and Lucas's eyes had taken on the flat, gray cast of a winter sky. A cold facade had snapped into place, and he retreated into the persona of the arrogant aristocrat. That version of Lucas chilled her to the marrow, and she knew with depressing certainty that his animosity for Cousin Stephen held a greater sway over his emotions than anything he might feel for her. His precipitous escape confirmed that.

Meredith muttered a surprisingly rude oath as she glared daggers at her husband's retreating back. Phoebe blinked in surprise, while Annabel let out a laugh.

"That certainly says it all," Annabel finally managed. "I suppose I was foolish to hope that Silverton and Lucas might be trying to patch things up."

Meredith sighed. "If anything, it's worse. Perhaps it's because they can no longer avoid each other. Before Lucas returned to England, they could pretend the other didn't exist."

"It's just too ridiculous," Annabel huffed. "Grown men acting like children, and on such an important night, too."

"Oh, no," Phoebe protested. "Everything has been perfectly . . ." she trailed off, unable to lie.

"Exactly," Meredith replied. "We know how gruesome it must be for you to be caught in the middle. You can be sure my husband will receive a piece of my mind when we return home. If only there was someone to do the same to Lucas."

"I think the situation is much more upsetting for my aunt and uncle," Phoebe said. "As for someone talking to Lucas, I do not think it would do any good. Uncle Arthur tried to discuss it with him just the other day. Lucas did not take it well."

Not well was an understatement. Phoebe had been reading quietly in the corner of the library while her uncle and Lucas were discussing new farming techniques. When Uncle Arthur had suggested that Lucas consult with Silverton, who had already implemented some of the new techniques at Belfield Abbey, Lucas had snapped at him. A sharp exchange followed, with the older man exhorting his nephew to stop acting the fool. Lucas's expression had grown cold and haughty. Barely holding his temper in check, he had clipped out a terse apology and excused himself from the room. Pausing briefly as he passed her, he had brushed a gentle hand across her cheek but then turned and stalked out. Her uncle had flicked a glance at her, then shrugged and returned to his correspondence.

Yet another example of Lucas's contradictory behavior, the episode had left her shaken. She knew him to be a kind and gentle man, but the anger that flared all too quickly when he was crossed troubled her. Perhaps it was a legacy of his soldiering days, and she worried that it had become an indelible and disturbing part of his character.

Meredith studied her. "Perhaps it depends on the person speaking to him. With the General, I can imagine how that conversation played out. But have you spoken to him about it, Phoebe? I suspect he might listen to you."

Surprise jolted her. "Why would you ever think that?"

"It's obvious Lucas wants you to think well of him. From what I've observed, he goes out of his way to please you, which is not something I've seen him do with a woman before other than Aunt Georgina." Meredith's eyes twinkled. "And I'm quite certain Lucas's feelings for you are very different from the ones he holds for our aunt."

Annabel nodded. "That's what Grandmamma told me, too. She said he's very protective of you, and even on short notice I can see he likes you very much."

Phoebe's heart gave a hard thump, and her gaze involuntarily jumped across the room to where Lucas talked with his aunt. As she studied his commanding figure, so handsome in his severely elegant evening attire, a sudden pang of longing tightened her chest. He had become so familiar in such a short period of time that she could barely imagine a world without him. How in heaven's name had she allowed that to happen?

As if she had tapped him on the shoulder, he glanced over, raising his eyebrows in a questioning arch. Her breath caught as a lazy smile curled up the corners of his mouth, and her body flushed with a heat that made her squirm.

Phoebe clenched her jaw. She distrusted that disconcerting

heat. Surely no properly modest woman should feel that way, especially toward a man whose intentions were unclear.

Yanking her gaze away, she found Meredith and Annabel exchanging satisfied glances.

"Told you," Meredith said to her sister.

Phoebe's heart sank. "Told her what?"

"We'll talk about it later, when we have more privacy. But we must return to our present topic of conversation, which is how to resolve the estrangement between Silverton and Lucas."

"Is that what we were doing?" Phoebe asked cautiously.

"Of course," Annabel piped in. "Grandmamma says the silly situation has gone on long enough. Everyone in the family is heartily sick of it."

"I can certainly understand that, but how has the situation changed?" Phoebe asked.

"Nothing has changed between *them*, so the rest of us have to change the circumstances," said Meredith. "That's why we're all going to Belfield Abbey for Christmas. The more we throw Lucas and Silverton together, the greater the chance they'll reconcile."

"Or perhaps murder each other," Annabel said cheerfully. "Either way, at least the problem will be solved."

Phoebe grimaced. "Unfortunately, murder would appear to be the likelier outcome."

Meredith's eyes crinkled with amusement. "I do believe there's cause for hope. Silverton has confessed to growing weary of the estrangement, and I think he would be relieved to see it end."

Surprised, Phoebe raised her eyebrows. "Did he actually tell you that?"

"Well, not at first," Meredith said, "but with a little prompting—"

Annabel snorted. "I can well imagine the type of prompting you employed. The bedroom type, no doubt."

"Whatever works, dear. I'm sure you've resorted to similar measures, on occasion."

Phoebe blushed. For two such refined women, Meredith and Annabel could be remarkably candid when discussing the private relations between men and women. She did not really mind, though. Despite her embarrassment, she found such honesty refreshing. Not to mention those conversations provided her with information she sorely lacked.

"In any event," Meredith continued, "Silverton eventually confided that he was tired of the fighting. He even confessed to regretting some of the things he said to Lucas all those years ago. I was astounded, since he rarely admits fault."

"Just like a man," Annabel murmured.

Doubtful, Phoebe shook her head. "I still do not understand how the family removing to Belfield Abbey for Christmas will solve the problem. Will not Lucas simply retreat to his estate? You cannot force him to be with us."

When Meredith and Annabel exchanged another of their knowing glances, Phoebe had to resist the urge to roll her eyes. "Whatever it is, please tell me and get it over with."

Meredith eyed her before answering. "Well, dear, if Lucas wants to see you, then he'll have to come to Belfield Abbey."

Phoebe wrinkled her brow, then enlightenment struck with blinding force. "Absolutely not," she said emphatically. "You are quite mistaken, I assure you."

Meredith tilted her head to study her. "About what, dear?" she asked in a deceptively mild voice.

"About whatever it is you believe might be happening between me and Cousin Lucas. He does not have any feelings for me beyond what is entirely appropriate."

Whatever *that* meant. When it came to Lucas, Phoebe could no longer be sure how they were supposed to feel about each other. From the beginning, her grandfather's letter had influenced every aspect of their relationship, even though neither of them had spoken of it past that first day. But how could she ever be sure of anything Lucas said to her regarding matters of the heart, knowing the burden Grandfather had imposed on him? What the Stantons perceived as affection could, in reality, be nothing more than a debt of honor promised to a dying man.

Frustrated, she tried to explain. "Even if he did return my—"

When Annabel beamed an encouraging smile, Phoebe almost choked on her unthinking admission.

"—which he does not," she continued grimly, "I still fail to see what that has to do with Cousin Stephen."

"Because if Lucas were to be happily married, then he would no longer have any reason to hold on to his anger," Meredith replied. "My husband is getting close to putting the past behind him. He's happy now, you see, and that's made it hard for him to hold on to the grudges of the past, even one that runs as deep as this one." Her eyes went soft and misty. "The twins had much to do with that, of course. Neither of us ever thought we could be this happy."

Phoebe stared at Meredith, and saw a contented joy that made her chest ache. Would she ever experience such happiness in her own life? Could Lucas ever love her the way Cousin Stephen clearly loved Meredith?

Annabel picked up the conversation. "If Lucas married you, then he would be happy, too, and realize it was a waste of energy to continue feuding with Silverton." She gave an excited little bounce in her seat. "Really, it makes perfect sense. Grandmamma is brilliant to have come up with such an excellent scheme."

Aghast, Phoebe stared at them. Their logic was so incredibly flawed it made her head spin. "Does everyone in the family think that way?" she finally managed in a faint voice.

Meredith squeezed her hand. "There's no need to be embarrassed. The men don't have a clue. Once it became clear how Lucas felt about you—and that happened much sooner than we anticipated—Aunt Georgie and I discussed the situation. Then we told Annabel. That, however, is as far as it goes. You needn't worry anyone else will ever find out."

"But I have no true idea how Lucas feels about me," Phoebe burst out in a voice louder than she intended. And, truthfully, she was not entirely sure how *she* felt about him. So much about him mystified her.

Meredith cast a swift glance around the room. "Hush, dear. It was foolish of me to raise the issue tonight in such company. Forgive me. I let my irritation with those silly men get the best of me."

Striving for calm, Phoebe nodded. As upsetting as the discussion was, it stemmed from the best of intentions. The Stantons loved Lucas and they had already come to love her, as they had assured her of so often. They only wanted Lucas to be happy and they wanted peace in the family. Laudable goals. If only they knew how unrealistic they were.

Annabel gave her a sympathetic grimace. "You needn't worry. Nobody will try to make you do anything you don't want to do. It's just that . . ." Her words trailed off.

"What?" Phoebe asked.

"Don't you want to get married some day? Have a family of your own?"

Frowning, Phoebe stared down at her lap. In the last few days, she had actually allowed herself to imagine what life with Lucas might be like. How she would be safe and secure with him. The appeal of that image pulled at her with an irresistible yearning that grew stronger every time she saw him.

But then she thought of everything that stood between them—her grandfather's deathbed pleas, their differing backgrounds and beliefs in life—and doubt rose up in a swamping wave.

"I . . . I cannot say," she stammered. Irritated, she firmed her voice. "It matters not. Lucas has given no indication of his true feelings for me, and I have not yet decided whether I will remain in England or return to America in the spring."

Annabel opened her mouth, but Meredith gave her sister a warning look. Then she rose to her feet, urging Phoebe up, too. "Come, dear. I know Lady Bellingham would like to speak to you. If she's awake, that is."

Grateful for the retreat, Phoebe took her arm. As Meredith chattered amiable social nonsense, Phoebe wrestled her turmoil into a quiet space in her mind. Later, in the privacy of her bedroom, she would unpack her feelings and examine them. For now she owed it to her family to behave with appropriate consideration for the occasion.

She had almost succeeded until they passed by Lucas, deep in conversation with Uncle Arthur and a few other male guests. His gaze, alert and suspicious, locked on her, following her across the room. Panic flared in her chest, along with the conviction that he knew *exactly* what they had been talking about.

Though she fought to hide it, her composure crumbled to dust.

Chapter 9

Lucas watched Phoebe weave her way through the crowds at the Royal Academy, her hand tucked securely through Annabel's arm. She frequently craned her neck to watch the other spectators as they gossiped, flirted, and otherwise acted out the inane comedies and dramas that passed for life in the ton, her innocent, open curiosity heightening all his protective instincts.

Not that any harm would come to her in this setting, but Lucas didn't trust the young bucks and rogues prowling the galleries of Somerset House looking for bored matrons and pretty girls to charm into bed. And Phoebe looked more than pretty in the wine red pelisse that hugged her enticing curves and served as canvas for her creamy complexion, expressive brown eyes, and dusky curls. He stood in one of London's premier temples to the arts, but none of the paintings could hold a candle to Phoebe's luminous, gentle beauty.

Lucas narrowed his eyes as a beau with ridiculously padded shoulders backed into her, pretending he hadn't seen her in his rapt contemplation of one of the paintings. With an extravagant bow, he apologized. Phoebe gave him a sweet smile and chatted with him for a moment before turning back to Annabel. Unfortunately, the beau failed to take the hint, eyeing her shapely backside as he waited for her to turn around again.

Clenching his fist, Lucas moved to intervene. He was brought up short by a firm tug on his sleeve, keeping him in place.

Christ. He'd been so intent on watching Phoebe he'd forgotten Aunt Georgie was holding his arm.

"You are not in the Peninsula and no one will ravish Phoebe in the middle of an art exhibition," his aunt admonished. "There's really no need to sound the call to battle or pull me off my feet."

He gave her a sheepish grin. She was right, but that didn't mean he wouldn't pummel any man who even glanced at Phoebe with a hint of lust in his eye. And since men looked at her like that whenever she went out, Lucas had to spend a great deal of time controlling an annoying combination of protective and violent impulses. Even on the battlefield he'd rarely let his emotions get the best of him, but a little Quaker miss from New Jersey was testing him in ways he hadn't thought possible.

That annoyed the hell out of him, too.

"Forgive me, Aunt. But I'm not sure Phoebe is used to these types of crowds. She's looking out of her depth, if you ask me."

"Really, Lucas? You're the one who seems out of his depth. And don't bother directing fierce looks my way. They don't work on me, remember? Even the General has never been able to intimidate me, and he's had a great deal more practice."

Lucas had to laugh. "I surrender. But Phoebe is a babe in the woods, and you know it. She might not even realize a man was flirting with her, or worse."

It was *the worse* that kept him awake some nights. Who knew what type of trouble she would get into if she wasn't carefully supervised? Phoebe knew nothing of the wolves prowling through the ton, sniffing out their next victim.

Decent men would perceive her innocence and treat her with respect, but there were those who would like nothing more than to take advantage of her sweet, unblemished nature. Now that she was making the rounds, she was even more vulnerable. He couldn't keep watch on her twenty-four hours a day, so the sooner they all repaired to the country, the better.

Besides, he'd wasted enough time in London, all while his new estate continued to collapse into decay without him.

He glanced back at Phoebe, only to see the overdressed beau still trying to gain her notice by peering over her shoulder as if he, too, were a great fan of Benjamin West. He stood so close his gloved hand dangled a mere inch from Phoebe's bottom.

Fortunately, before Lucas had to break heads Annabel came to alert. She turned around and gave the idiot a lethal-eyed stare before guiding Phoebe out of harm's way.

Aunt Georgie laughed. "Annabel clearly has the matter in hand. You must stop worrying, and cease slavering over Phoebe like some mad dog when she goes out in public. It makes her nervous."

He bristled. "I never slaver. I'm simply watching out for her, as I promised her grandfather. Phoebe is my obligation as much as she is yours. More so, since her care was handed directly to me."

With barely the twitch of an eyebrow, his aunt managed to look both imperious and offended. At one time, it quelled him, that look. Not anymore. Once a man had been to war, not much did.

"Lucas, is that all she is to you? An obligation?"

He grimaced. His intentions toward Phoebe had only recently firmed, but he supposed his aunt deserved an honest answer.

"No, Aunt Georgie. But I don't think she's ready to hear that yet."

His aunt visibly relaxed. "I'm relieved to hear so, and I

agree with your assessment. As much as I think a match between you and Phoebe might be a very good thing, I'm not sure you're ready for her yet, either."

He cast her a startled glance. "You know I would take care of her every need."

She nudged his arm, urging him to follow in Phoebe and Annabel's wake. "It's not just a matter of providing for her material needs. Phoebe is a sensitive, tenderhearted creature. Since her father died, she's been very much in need of nurturing and support. She is not like the other young women of the ton, and cannot be treated as such."

"I'm not a fool," he said tersely. "I haven't failed to notice that."

"You may have noticed, but will you be able to respond appropriately?"

He rolled his eyes. "Hell and damnation, Aunt Georgie. I have no idea what you're talking about."

His oath earned him a glare from a passing matron, the purple plumes of her high-crowned bonnet quivering with indignation. He winked at her, and her mouth dropped open.

"Language, dear," Aunt Georgie admonished.

He grinned. She didn't give a hoot about such things and he knew it.

"Dreadful boy," she said, her lips twitching. Then she grew serious. "Are you sure you don't understand?"

He had to resist the urge to yank at his suddenly too tight cravat. "Aunt Georgie, I will discuss many topics with you, but physical intimacy with Phoebe is not one of them."

She cast her eyes to the ornate, arched ceiling, obviously praying for patience. "I'm talking about *emotional* intimacy, you foolish man. Phoebe is a spiritual, loving person and, unless I miss my guess, she carries a great deal of hurt from the death of her dear parents and her brother's disapproving nature. You must be gentle and kind. Always."

"I know that, and I am," he responded gruffly. He'd sensed

that vulnerability in Phoebe from the first, perceiving her need for a sheltering strength to keep her safe from the cruel twists of fate. He understood that better than anyone, and he would provide that shelter.

And not just because of a promise made to a dying man. She was exactly the kind of wife he wanted—sweet, trusting, and honest. During his years in the military, marriage had never crossed his mind. But inheriting the earldom had changed everything, including his desire to remain single. If marry he must, then he must have a woman as loyal and loving as Phoebe.

Esme had taught him that lesson.

They strolled along in silence. The art lovers and gossips milled around them in a cheerful chaos, some actually studying the paintings, others staring at the fashionably dressed crowd. Lucas glanced ahead, eyeing Phoebe's slim figure, searching for signs of tension in her back or shoulders.

As if she sensed his regard, she glanced over her shoulder. Her gaze darted from his face to Aunt Georgie's, and a quizzical little crease puckered her brow.

Lucas gave her a reassuring smile. Although her mouth lifted in a shy smile in return, it didn't quite reach her eyes. Then Annabel said something to her and Phoebe turned back to respond.

His aunt let out a quiet sigh. "You do know that you make her anxious, Lucas."

Stunned, he jerked his head to stare down at her. "Has she told you that?"

"No, dear. Phoebe is very loyal. And it's not that she's afraid of you. It's more your . . . manner. Your way of dealing with the world. It makes her uneasy."

The tight knot in his stomach eased a fraction. Still, he didn't like the idea that he gave Phoebe any cause for concern.

"I'm a soldier, with a soldier's manner. I won't apologize

for that, but I would never hurt her in any way. Never," he said with quiet emphasis.

His aunt passed in front of an allegorical painting of the battle of the Titans. She took her time studying it while he tried to quell his irritation.

"Phoebe has a very spiritual nature, Lucas. After all, she was raised as a Quaker," she finally said.

His impatience spiked. "I am well aware of that fact. Surely Phoebe doesn't expect me to ride off to battle, pistols blazing. And when would I have time for warfare, my dear aunt, what with all my present obligations to keep me busy?" This time, bitterness slipped into his voice.

Another slow nod from his aunt. "Yes, you are an earl now, with all the obligations and privileges the position entails. But in your heart you are still a soldier, and Phoebe senses that. A very significant part of you has not left the battlefield."

He let out a ghost of a laugh. No one who had lived through war could ever completely turn his back on it. And part of him didn't want to. Not the killing, of course, but the purpose and clarity that came with knowing what must be done, and then doing it. No messy relationships or extravagant emotions, no broken promises or betrayals that could turn a man's life into a complicated hell.

Lucas shrugged. "She'll have to accept me as I am, and know that she will never have anything to fear from me."

Aunt Georgie huffed at him. "I have no doubt she will eventually understand, if you would bother to make the effort."

He gave her an incredulous look, but she just laughed. "Yes, dear. The General tells me you've been very good. But Phoebe doesn't have any idea how you feel about her." She frowned. "Come to think of it, neither do I. Other than the fact that you obviously find her attractive as a potential wife."

Blast it. Did she really expect him to make some dramatic declaration of love? He'd been done with that sort of nonsense for years.

"I am well aware of Phoebe's qualities, and I will always cherish her. I'm convinced she will make me a fine wife," he said in a cool voice. With any luck, his tone would end this gruesome discussion.

"How romantic. I'm sure you will sweep her right off her feet," his aunt caustically replied.

If he wasn't in public, he'd gladly utter a string of curses that would turn the air blue. Better than anyone, Aunt Georgie knew he would never put himself in thrall to a woman again. That didn't mean he wouldn't do right by Phoebe, or even care for her. Hell, he already did.

"I thought you wanted this," he exclaimed. "I promised I would protect Phoebe, and you want her to stay in England. This is the best way to achieve both goals. Besides, I do need a wife. One I can actually respect, and who's nothing like—"

He clipped back the words. He didn't even want to utter Esme's name. And unlike Esme, Phoebe was sweet and innocent, and he would see to it she remained that way.

"I do want it," Aunt Georgie replied, "and it pleases me that you wish to protect her. But remember. Phoebe may be vulnerable and innocent but she is not weak. Once her principles are engaged, she will stand firm. You cannot manipulate her into thinking you care for her when you do not."

He ground his teeth. "Of course I care for her. A great deal. I have every intention of making Phoebe happy, I promise you."

"I'm glad to hear it, but Phoebe needs convincing, not I."

"What would you suggest?" he asked, exasperated.

"You might try actually wooing her instead of merely holing up with her and the General in the library. As much as I love your uncle, he can hardly be called an inducement to romance."

He gave a reluctant laugh. True, he'd been very careful with Phoebe these last few weeks, but perhaps the time had come to exert pressure. "You make a valid point. I will adapt my strategy accordingly."

She arched her imperious brows. "She is not a battle to be won, Lucas. It would be wise if you remembered that."

He was hard put not to roll his eyes again.

His aunt gave him a little grin. "Don't fall into a huff, my boy. I'm simply offering you the voice of experience." She nudged him in Phoebe's direction. "Well, get to it."

Phoebe studied the vibrant and thoroughly outrageous painting. While it depicted a classical theme, one could hardly call it proper given the fleshy goddesses whose diaphanous garments revealed more than they concealed. Her brother, George, would have been scandalized, which rather increased her enjoyment than diminished it.

Frowning, she leaned forward and peered at a detail she had only just spotted. *Goodness.* Was that really a woman's—

"You seem much taken with that painting, Phoebe. Any particular reason why?"

She gave a guilty start and looked up into Lucas's face. His eyes glittered with amusement, and she had a sinking feeling he knew exactly what had drawn her attention. Her cheeks flooding with heat, she took the coward's way out.

"Not particularly. All the paintings are lovely, are they not?" she said in a bright voice. "I have already discovered several by Benjamin West, which was the reason I asked my aunt to allow me to visit Somerset House. Mr. West was originally from Philadelphia. Did you know that, Lucas?"

His lips pressed into a thin line as he fought to hold back laughter at her ineffectual evasion. Inwardly she winced, knowing full well she sounded the definition of a hen-witted female.

She cast a quick glance past him. At least Aunt Georgie had

not seen her peering at that painting, since she had taken Annabel's arm and moved to the other side of the gallery.

Lucas placed her hand in the crook of his elbow. "I did not know that, Phoebe. Perhaps you could show me some of Mr. West's paintings."

His mouth twitched and his eyes still held that telltale gleam.

She sighed. "Very well, although I know you are humoring me. And I also know it was very bad of me to be looking so closely at that indecent painting. But I have never seen anything like it, and you cannot blame me for being curious."

"My sweet, there's nothing wrong with curiosity. Besides, you're bound to see more scandalous sights if you remain in London. I've attended balls where more than one lady's wardrobe malfunctioned in the most spectacular way. Not everyone would think that's a bad thing, either," he mused.

Her jaw slackened. She could not decide if she was more shocked by his casual acceptance of vulgar behavior, or by the fact that he called her *my sweet*.

Too flustered to respond, she let him guide her at a measured pace around the room. Fortunately, the din from the crowd minimized the need for conversation. She studiously gazed at all the paintings, trying to ignore the way he studied her. Even more importantly, she tried to ignore the way his very masculine presence made the breath shallow in her lungs and her legs go wobbly. She had to resist the urge to clutch his arm and lean against him, but that would only heighten the alarming sensations flooding through her body.

"Phoebe," he prodded in a deep, quiet tone.

"Yes?"

When he didn't answer, she looked up at him. His smoky gaze snagged hers, and her knees knocked against each other. Lucas affected her in the strangest way, and the fact that he was so much taller and broader than she was prompted some rather naughty and wholly embarrassing thoughts.

His lips curled in a roguish smile. "You're looking lovely today, did you know that? Your new bonnet is charming. In fact, everything about you is charming."

His extravagant praise made her pause. Why had he taken to complimenting her so effusively these last few days? He had never cared about her clothes and appearance before. She could not be sure she liked it. It made her too aware of him when her nerves were already stretched tight.

"Thank you," she said cautiously.

"I don't think I've seen that brooch before." He touched the cameo on her shoulder. "There's a larger, similar portrait of your grandfather as a young man at the manor."

She touched it, letting her fingers rest there for a few seconds. For years, she had fancied she could draw strength from the cherished heirloom. It somehow connected her to the family she had never known, serving as a lifeline to something precious in the lonely days after her father's death.

"It was my mother's most prized possession." She flicked him a tentative glance, hoping he would understand. "I know that seems odd, given they remained estranged to her death."

"Your grandfather had a portrait of your mother, from her first Season. He kept it in his study, where he could always see it." He made a subtle movement, bringing her closer to his side. Phoebe knew she should resist, but thinking of her parents left her with an aching heart, and Lucas offered comfort.

"I didn't know your grandfather that well," he said. "I saw him very little, during those years in the Peninsula. But I spent a fair amount of time at his side in the months before his death, and I know he deeply regretted the parting with your mother. He truly loved her."

A joy that felt more like sadness closed her throat. Taking a deep breath, she focused on a large canvas of a farmer's field on a bright summer's day. The colors swam in a haze of tears, forcing her to blink them away. "Then why do you suppose he never wrote to her?"

He gently turned her so her back was to the canvas and his body shielded her from any curious onlookers. "Pride, I suppose. From what Uncle Arthur has told me, the earl was never one to admit a mistake. But the fact that your grandfather wanted you with him should tell you how much he loved your mother, even if it came too late."

He tipped her chin up, brushing a finger along her jaw before dropping his hand down. Such a small gesture, but she trembled nonetheless. "I know he would have loved you, too," he said. "Those last months, all he cared about was your future. He worried about you, Phoebe. That's why he asked me to take care of you."

His eyes probed hers, intense and watchful. She inhaled a tangled mix of emotions—longing, anxiety, and something that had the power to completely devastate her if she let it. Her mind skittered away from it, frightened that Lucas might see it in her eyes.

She cleared her throat. "Thank you, Lucas. But as I have told you before, I do not need taking care of."

His eyes got that flinty look. Not a good sign. "Phoebe, what do you want from life?"

The abrupt question surprised her. She peered up at him, wondering if he really expected an answer.

His patient, watchful silence indicated he did. Shifting uneasily, she glanced around the room. Aunt Georgie and Annabel were sitting on a bench in the center of the room, talking to a woman in a purple-plumed hat. The rest of the room was a whirl of noise and motion, everyone too busy to notice her or Lucas. She felt separated from the rest of the world, encased in an odd little bubble with him.

She raised her eyes back to his face. "I wish not to be a burden to my family or friends."

His eyebrows shot up. "That's it?" he asked incredulously. "That's the sum total of your worldly ambitions?"

She shrugged. What else could she tell him? That she

wanted what everyone wanted—home, family, love? How could she say that to him, knowing the burden her grandfather had placed upon him? He would surely take it as a reminder of his obligation to her—or what he believed his obligation to be. She no more wanted to be a burden to him than to her brother, George, or to the Stanton family.

He muttered something under his breath. Taking her arm, he started them back on their round of the room. "And how does this grand desire of yours translate into practicalities?" he asked, his voice hinting of sarcasm.

She cast him a scowl. "I did have a life before I came to England. It might not mean much to you, but it had purpose and meaning for me."

"Ah, so we're back to that. Do you really wish to return to a life of drudgery in your brother's household?"

"It was *not* drudgery," she replied stiffly.

He snorted. "You're avoiding the question."

"I believe we have discussed this before, Lucas. You already know I do not wish to return to that life," she said with as much dignity as she could muster. "Not if I have a choice. But nor can I spend all my days living off General Stanton's generosity."

Except the thought of leaving her uncle's household made her positively ill. She felt at home at Stanton House, more at ease with life than any time since the death of her father. But that sense of belonging did not make it right, nor did it justify a life of idleness at the expense of her aunt and uncle.

"But apparently you could spend the rest of your days living off your brother's generosity," he said with a charming smile. "I think there's a flaw in your logic, sweetheart."

She stared at him. How was it possible he could both annoy and flatter her at the same time? His condescending attitude deserved a set down, and yet her treacherous heart melted with pleasure at his teasing affection.

She took refuge in the irritation. "I do not have to be a dependent. There are other things I could do."

"Really? Like what?" he asked with great interest.

"I am very well educated. I taught my nieces and nephews. Surely I could teach other children, as a governess."

His amusement evaporated. "The hell you will."

Disconcerted, she looked away. "I will not spend the rest of my life as a dependent."

His finger tapped her chin again, provoking her to look at him. A tiny gasp escaped her when she beheld the stern, proud expression on his face.

"You are the granddaughter of an earl, and a Stanton. You were raised by a gentleman in genteel circumstances, and a life of servitude will never be in the cards for you. Do you understand?"

His tightly repressed anger hollowed out her stomach, but she would not allow him to intimidate her. She thrust out her chin. "I will do whatever I believe is right."

He bent his head, coming nose to nose. "Phoebe, I will not repeat myself. You will not again speak of this madcap idea of being a governess, do you understand?"

As she glared back at him, she heard a titter from beside her. Glancing to her right, she saw two young women watching them with avid interest. She groaned inside. The last thing she wished for was to make a spectacle, but the determined look on Lucas's face showed he held no similar compunctions.

"Very well," she grumbled, desperate to end the discussion.

"Very well, what?"

She rolled her eyes. "I understand I must give up any notion of being a governess."

He studied her for a moment before nodding his head. "Good. And I suggest you never mention it around the General, in particular. I guarantee you wouldn't like the reaction."

She sighed, deflated. "I promise. But what am I to do with myself? I cannot go on like this forever, no matter what you and my aunt and uncle might think. It is not right, Lucas, and such an aimless existence would not make me happy."

As tempting as it was to disregard the future, her life with the Stantons could only be a temporary respite. Even Lucas must think the same, since he had raised it in the first place. Given that, what choice did she have but to return to America, to George and his family? At least there she had her brother's children to love.

But anguish speared through her just at the thought of leaving England . . . and Lucas. Her chest grew tight and she found it hard to pull in air.

"Phoebe, look at me."

His voice was quiet but carried a commanding tone. She looked up. His eyes were gentle with understanding, but that only made her throat tighten more.

"There's no need for you to worry about anything until after Christmas," he said. "Everything will be sorted out in due course. I promise."

She wanted desperately to believe him. His gaze heated as she studied him, and a coil of that all too familiar yearning spun out from the center of her body to her limbs.

"You do trust me, don't you?" His voice went low and husky.

Repressing a shiver, she nodded.

"Then let it go for now, and try to enjoy yourself," he said. "You've more than earned it."

"I will try," she whispered.

"Good. Now let's collect Aunt Georgie and Annabel. I'm taking you to Gunter's for ices. Have you ever had one?"

She shook her head.

"I thought not," he said with a grin. "Consider it all part of the plan to enjoy yourself as best you can. Whether you want to or not."

Then he took her hand and settled her against his side, as if she had always belonged there and always would.

Chapter 10

Lucas glanced at the casement clock in the corner of his uncle's library, impatient for the women to join them. Tonight was Phoebe's first ball and an important one at that, since Lady Framingham's semiannual extravaganza marked the official close of the Little Season. Tonight would herald Phoebe's formal introduction into London society.

But how long did it take to put on a gown and dress one's hair, especially with a whole bloody regiment of lady's maids to assist?

Uncle Arthur cleared his throat, bringing Lucas back to the stilted conversation in the library.

"Forgive me, sir," Lucas said. "What did you say?"

From behind his imposing desk, his uncle studied him with an ironic eye. "I didn't say anything. It was your cousin Silverton who addressed you, but you were so deep in thought you failed to hear him."

Lucas repressed a grimace. His cousin was the reason for his foul mood. Aunt Georgie had decreed that the Marquess and Marchioness of Silverton would accompany them to the ball, to illustrate the full weight of the family's support behind Phoebe. Although Lucas could appreciate the strategy, it meant spending even more time in Silverton's company.

On a rational level, he knew how ridiculous their feud had become, and how tiresome for the family. Some days, when he was especially weary of hating Silverton, he even thought about asking his forgiveness for stealing Esme away. There were even times when the words came to the tip of his tongue, but something always held him back. Perhaps it was the understanding that Lucas could never forgive *himself* for betraying the man who'd been his best friend. He had rightfully earned Silverton's enmity and he wasn't about to give it up, especially since his cousin had never given any indication he would accept an apology. Better to go on as they were rather than risk exacerbating the ugly drama that had nearly blown the family apart all those years ago.

"If his lordship would repeat the question," Lucas said in a bored voice, "I will do my best to answer it."

Lounging in an armchair on the other side of his uncle's desk, Silverton simply smiled. But Lucas knew him better than almost anyone, and read the meaning in his expression. Inside, his cousin seethed.

"I wondered when you would be returning to Mistletoe Manor," Silverton replied in an equally bored tone.

Lucas snorted. "Does it matter? I hardly think you'll be visiting."

Silverton's eyes narrowed to frosty blue slits. "For some reason I cannot fathom, Meredith has a desire to see the manor, and I would not care to deny her the pleasure of a visit. If it would not inconvenience you too greatly, that is," he finished with heavy sarcasm.

Lucas almost groaned. He loathed the idea of Meredith and the other Stanton women traipsing around his ramshackle manor house. Especially Phoebe, who would likely run screaming in the other direction, or burst into tears at what her grandfather had let the house become. He hated disappointing her but neither did he want to offend Meredith.

"Meredith will always be welcome at Mistletoe Manor. I

would suggest, however, that she wait until after Christmas. I hope to have the house ready for visitors by Twelfth Night."

Even then it would be evident how bad the situation was, especially to Silverton, who had the finest holdings in Kent. The last thing Lucas needed was the family taking on the Merritt estate as their next project. He had enough obstacles to overcome without their well-meaning but usually ill-fated interference.

To his surprise, Silverton nodded. "I understand the old earl left matters in regrettable shape. The estate has some of the best orchards in Kent, not to mention one of the finest examples of an Elizabethan manor house in the county. I sincerely hope you'll be able to restore it to its former glory."

Oddly enough, his cousin sounded sincere. Lucas couldn't remember the last time they'd had a civil conversation. In their youth, they would babble away for hours about everything under the sun, but those days were long gone.

"Perhaps Silverton and I can ride over one afternoon and take a look," said Uncle Arthur. "Your cousin and I have been managing estates for years, while you're still new to the game. Doesn't hurt to ask for help, you know."

What a bloody awful idea. Lucas didn't need Silverton poking around the place. Mistletoe Manor was a wreck, and the idea of comparing it to Belfield Abbey—and Silverton *would* compare them—made Lucas's insides go tight.

But his cousin did not appear entranced by the idea, either. In fact, in that imperious way of his, Silverton looked downright appalled.

Fortunately, the library door opened and Aunt Georgie and Meredith walked into the room. His aunt looked dignified and elegant, and Meredith's pink net gown set off her statuesque beauty to great effect. Silverton's face lit up when he beheld his wife, and Lucas had to repress a flash of envy.

Not that he desired Meredith. He'd learned firsthand the harsh lesson to never covet another man's woman. But he did envy what they obviously shared—happiness with each other and their children, and a deep contentment with life. Lucas doubted he would ever possess anything similar, and perhaps he didn't even deserve it.

"Good evening, Lucas."

He jerked around. Phoebe had slipped so quietly into the room he'd failed to notice. But he noticed now, and what he saw rendered him speechless.

A diamond of the first water.

Her gown, gauzy and clingy, was the color of an autumn leaf just beginning to fade. Her glossy black curls were piled on her head, revealing her slender neck and pretty ears. A few artfully arranged tendrils curled down around the sides of her face, drawing attention to her delicate features. Her big brown eyes shone with excitement, and her lips, pink and luscious, curved into a shy smile.

But what set him back on his heels was what the dress revealed. The quaint little rustic had been consigned to distant memory, and in her place stood a lush, sweetly curved temptress. The gown barely skimmed her shoulders, and the neckline dipped down over plump white breasts that would drive any man under the age of eighty insane with lust. Yes, she wore long gloves that covered most of her arms, but that was nothing in comparison to all the tempting flesh laid bare for any man to see.

Phoebe's smile faltered under his bemused gaze, replaced by an uncertain look. She bit her lower lip as she cast a doubtful glance in Aunt Georgie's direction.

"Lucas, does your cousin not look lovely?" His aunt's voice held a note of reprimand, prompting him to recollect himself. He forced a smile as he stepped forward to take Phoebe's gloved hand.

"Without question." His voice deepened to a rumble, and that had him mentally wincing. "I have no doubt Phoebe will be the belle of the ball."

He also didn't doubt he would be spending the evening protecting her from rakes and wolves, while doing his best to keep his own hands off her luscious body. Never in his wildest dreams had he imagined Phoebe like this, nor considered how greatly it might affect him.

She wrinkled her nose at him. "It is very kind of you to say so, but I cannot help feeling uncomfortable. I feel so . . ." Blushing, she let her voice trail off.

"Exposed?" he finished dryly.

She nodded.

Meredith laughed. "Lucas, don't be such a prude. Half the women at the ball will be wearing dresses a great deal more revealing. Phoebe looks just as she should."

Silently, he disagreed. One of the things he truly appreciated about Phoebe was that she was *not* like most of the women he knew.

Aunt Georgie gave Phoebe a reassuring smile. "There is nothing in your appearance that will cause any kind of remark, other than the fact that you look perfect."

Phoebe sighed. "I will defer to your collective wisdom, but I know I will have to resist the temptation to spend the evening yanking up my bodice."

Everyone laughed but Lucas.

Aunt Georgie turned to smile at him. "Lucas, I believe you have something to give your cousin, do you not?"

Right.

He'd been so knocked back by the new Phoebe that he'd forgotten what came next. It had been his aunt's idea, but with a little luck he'd be the one to benefit from Phoebe's gratitude.

Reaching for the velvet pouch he'd left on the end table, he carefully tipped out the contents into his hand. "This was your grandmother's," he said, holding up the ruby and diamond necklace.

While not large, the stones were of the best quality and superbly cut. The finely wrought setting perfectly suited Phoebe's delicate beauty.

Phoebe sucked in a breath. "That belonged to my grandmother?" Her voice sounded curiously strained.

"Yes. By tradition, this necklace has been worn by the countesses of Merritt since the early seventeenth century. Your grandfather gave it to your grandmother, and now I'd like to give it to you."

He undid the clasp and prepared to put the gleaming strand around her unadorned neck. The only jewels Phoebe wore were simple garnet drop earrings. He and Aunt Georgie had planned it that way so she could wear the necklace. Such an occasion demanded a special gift, and it didn't hurt that the giving would also signal his intentions, both to Phoebe and to the rest of the family.

But as he stepped forward to place the gemstones on her neck, Phoebe backed away. She held up one hand, and damned if she didn't look ready to fly into a panic.

Lucas stopped short and frowned. "What's wrong?"

She shook her head. "I cannot wear it."

"Why not?"

"It is much too ornate for me," she responded in a tight voice.

He tamped down his impatience with the inconvenient re-assertion of her Quaker modesty. She would parade herself in a revealing gown and yet balk at wearing a cherished family heirloom? God preserve him from female logic.

Meredith cast him a swift glance and moved to stand beside Phoebe. "My dear, the necklace is perfectly appropriate, I assure you. And it's your grandmother's, too, so you shouldn't feel any hesitation in wearing it."

Phoebe's chin jerked up in defiance. "And yet, I do."

She returned her gaze to Lucas. Her features had settled into a calm mask, but her eyes held a volatile mix of emotions, including a pain he didn't understand. "I thank you for your generosity, Cousin," she said in a formal voice. "But I cannot accept your gift."

Lucas could barely restrain his frustration. "Why the devil not?"

Uncle Arthur bristled. "Watch your language around the ladies. Especially your aunt."

Aunt Georgie rolled her eyes. She heard worse from her husband every day. Nonetheless, the entire situation had turned into a fiasco, made more humiliating by the fact that Silverton was shaking his head with disbelief.

Lucas switched his gaze back to Phoebe. From the neck down she was the most tempting woman he'd ever seen. But from the neck up she was all rigid, disapproving Quaker.

"I am not comfortable with excessive ornamentation," she said stiffly. "Naturally, I am grateful for your generosity, but I would ask you to respect my wishes."

That was too much for Uncle Arthur. "Good Lord, child. Those are the Merritt jewels and the Earl of Merritt wishes you to wear them. What possible objection could you have? Don't want to offend your cousin, do you?"

Phoebe's eyes widened, and Lucas bit back a curse. Yes, he was angry she had chosen this moment to exercise her ridiculous scruples, but he didn't want his uncle reprimanding her in front of half the family.

"Arthur, you are not helping," warned Aunt Georgie.

"Well, dammit, my lady," her husband protested. "The gel isn't making any sense, and I'd like to know why."

"Perhaps this isn't the best time to discuss the issue," Meredith broke in. "After all, we don't want to be late for Phoebe's first ball."

"Very wise, my love," Silverton said. "I vote for tabling this debate until later." He cast an ironic glance toward Lucas. "Preferably when the rest of us aren't around."

Lucas felt his temper rise, but this time he couldn't keep it in check. "I don't give a damn what you think," he growled at his cousin. "But I do give a damn about what Phoebe thinks."

He turned back to her. She stood her ground, unbending and cold. She'd shut him out, and that infuriated him.

"No, Lucas," his aunt said firmly. "Now is not the time."

He kept his eyes fastened on Phoebe's pale face. She locked her gaze on his waistcoat.

"Aside from the excessive ornamentation of the piece," she

finally said, "it would be most improper for me to accept it, especially from thee. As thee said, the necklace is handed down through the generations, from one countess of Merritt to the next. I am not the countess of Merritt and, therefore, I cannot take it."

And from the tone of her voice, she never would be.

Lucas must have made a sound, because she finally looked at his face, her eyes gone hard with moral condemnation. That look tore through him like cannon shot. He'd always found her Quaker philosophy quaint and rather charming, but now he realized how he'd misjudged. Under that lovely facade lived a puritan, and a cold, contemptuous one at that.

Her contempt was leveled right at him. Why? Because he wasn't a Quaker? Was it his career in the military that condemned him in her eyes? He didn't know, and right now he didn't care. Clearly, Phoebe was not the woman he'd thought she was.

With a curt nod, he retreated. "As you wish. Forgive me for offending you."

He slipped the necklace back into the velvet pouch and dropped it carelessly onto the end table. Phoebe bit her lip, and a look of anguish flashed across her features. That gave him pause, but he shoved aside his concern. She'd made her feelings known, and he wouldn't trouble her again. She was Aunt Georgie's and Uncle Arthur's problem now. He'd done his best by her, and she'd rejected him.

In front of the whole damn family, and Silverton, no less.

"Well," said his aunt in an aggrieved voice, "isn't this a delightful way to start the evening? Lady Framingham will be *so* happy to see us."

Chapter 11

Phoebe studied the immense stone lions guarding the doors of Lady Framingham's ballroom. With their fierce expressions and arched backs, the beasts looked ready to pounce on any unsuspecting dancers who wandered too close. Right now, she rather wished one of them would come to life and swallow her in a single gulp.

Repressing a sigh, she perched on one of the delicate chairs grouped against the wall, pretending to listen to Meredith and Annabel as they chatted away. According to them, Lady Framingham's ball was an unqualified success. Jammed with guests attired in beautiful fashions and glittering jewels, the ballroom shimmered in the light of a thousand candles. A good-natured din filled the cavernous space, so loud one could barely hear the orchestra at the other end of the immense gold and crimson room. All were having, or seemed to be having, a wonderful time.

Unfortunately, Phoebe hated every moment. It was too loud, too hot, and at least half the guests were so inebriated she marveled they did not pitch over onto their faces. She could not think of one thing she liked about Lady Framingham's ball.

Except for the lions. Their fierce scowls matched exactly how she felt.

A hand touched her arm and she jumped.

"Forgive me for startling you," Meredith apologized, "but I don't think you heard Annabel's question."

The sisters stared at her with concern. Meredith had steadfastly remained by her side from the moment they entered Framingham House, which had been when Lucas abandoned them. A few minutes later Annabel had arrived, and the two women had swept Phoebe away to a relatively quiet corner of the ballroom.

She mustered up a smile. "Forgive me." She leaned across Meredith to address Annabel. "What did you wish to know?"

The young woman studied her with a grim expression. "It doesn't matter. What does matter is that you're having an absolutely awful time, aren't you?"

Phoebe opened her mouth, then clamped it shut. Never had she experienced so many impulses to lie as she had since arriving in London. Perhaps she should move back to America, since her new life seemed to be having an unfortunate effect on her morals.

And her temper, if her behavior in her uncle's library was any indication. She did not even regret her rude remarks to Lucas, which surely illustrated how far her conduct had slipped.

Meredith scoffed at her sister. "Of course she's having an awful time. How could she not, given how badly Lucas is behaving? I'd like to box his ears."

Phoebe choked down a laugh that felt more like a sob. The image rather horrified her, but right now she was trying to repress the same impulse.

As one, the three women turned their eyes to Lucas, who was dancing with yet another beautiful woman. He and his partner were engaged in a waltz, and to Phoebe's eyes he was holding the woman scandalously close. Given that the lady's flimsy bodice barely covered her ample charms, it was a wonder her bosoms did not pop right out and land on Lucas's waistcoat. He certainly had not been jesting when he told her many of the women at the ball would be more than half naked.

He seemed determined to dance with most of them before the evening was out. And was enjoying every minute of it, too, by the appreciative smile on his face.

They watched grimly as Lucas swung the lady—Phoebe used the term very loosely—through another turn. His partner gazed up at him with sultry eyes and nestled even closer as he swept her down the room.

Phoebe clenched her jaw as anger jostled aside the anguish from that ugly scene in Uncle Arthur's library.

"Why is he acting so badly?" Annabel asked in a mystified voice. "Lucas has always enjoyed a flirtation, but I've never seen him quite like this. Especially not since—" She glanced at Phoebe. "Well, not for a while, anyway."

Meredith sighed. "He's in a pet because Phoebe wouldn't accept his gift. It was so unfortunate he decided to present it to her in front of half the family. Men are such idiots."

Phoebe ducked her head, cheeks burning as she recalled Lucas's offhanded manner in presenting her with the precious family heirloom. How could he treat her—and the gift—in so careless a fashion? She knew from her mother's relation of family history the importance of that necklace. The Merritt rubies were only given to the wives of the earls—as a token of true love and esteem—and never handed down from mother to daughter.

Was Lucas signaling his desire to marry her by his presentation? She had not even been able to tell. And if he was, how could he do it in a way that would be sure to embarrass her? To do something so private and meaningful, paraded in front of half the family, and with no warning given to her first. He could not love her and yet treat her with so little respect.

Caught off guard, she had taken refuge in the one excuse

that popped into her head, and in doing so, she had clearly offended him. She winced as she recalled the angry glitter in his eyes. Nay. *Offended* was too neutral a term for how Lucas felt about her now.

Annabel gazed at her in shock. "You mean the Merritt ruby necklace? The one the earls give to their brides?"

Phoebe nodded, feeling bleak. "The very same."

Annabel shook her head. "Heavens. Then why is he acting like . . ."

"Like a ruthless flirt?" Meredith finished in a sarcastic voice. "Because he was too dense to realize how embarrassing the situation would be for Phoebe. I was surprised Aunt Georgie didn't try to stop him, but she told me she thought it was a lovely gesture of support. The entire family standing behind her, that sort of thing."

Phoebe grimaced. Her aunt had already made an abject apology to her before they came upstairs to the ballroom, and that was almost worse than anything.

Well, not worse than having to watch Lucas flirt with one woman after another. He had refused to look at her on the way over in the carriage, and now he ignored her. Obviously, he had not been asking her to marry him when he offered the necklace. He was likely assuaging his guilt that she had received no bequests from her grandfather, while Lucas had inherited everything. Perhaps he thought the necklace counted as some part of his imagined obligation to her.

She took a steadying breath. "You must not worry about me. You have all treated me with a great deal of love and respect. No one owes me anything."

Meredith gave her a puzzled look. "You do understand what the necklace means, don't you?"

Before she could answer, the waltz came to an end. Phoebe's gaze fixed on the spot where Lucas and his buxom partner had swung to a halt not far from where they sat. His glance flicked in Phoebe's direction and the breath seized in her lungs.

But instantly he was smiling again into the laughing face of the woman on his arm. She took his elbow, plastering herself against his side as they strolled off the dance floor toward the refreshment table.

Jerking her gaze away, Phoebe swallowed a tight ball of misery in her throat. "If you do not mind, I would prefer we not discuss this topic."

Meredith cast a disgusted glance in Lucas's direction. "Of course, dear. But I don't want you to worry. I promise everything will work out just as it should."

Phoebe gave her a polite smile, though her heart ached. Nothing would be fine. Not as long as she remained in London, reminded on a daily basis that she was falling in love with a man who neither respected her nor deserved what she wished to give him. The sooner she returned to America, the better.

"Meredith, look," cried Annabel. "There's Sophie and Simon. I was beginning to think they weren't coming."

Phoebe exhaled a sigh of relief, grateful for the distraction from her foolish woes. Fixing a smile on her face, she rose with Meredith and Annabel to greet the Earl and Countess of Trask. Phoebe had met them a few days ago at a small dinner party the countess had hosted, and had liked them immediately. Especially Sophie, Lady Trask. Only a year or two older than Phoebe, she was a cheerful young woman who wore spectacles and did not seem to worry if the ton thought her fashionable or not. Lord Trask had been a tad forbidding, but he so obviously adored his wife and their little daughter that Phoebe had soon been able to see past his stern exterior to the kind, honorable man beneath.

A man much like Lucas, or so she had thought.

Her smile began to slip, but she pinned it back in place as Sophie swooped in to hug her sister-in-law.

"Annabel, how are you? And where is that scapegrace brother of mine? I can't believe he has abandoned you already."

Annabel laughed. "No, he's sulking over there in the corner with Silverton. We sent him away so we could talk."

Sophie gave Meredith and Phoebe quick hugs, murmuring a friendly greeting. "Talk about the menfolk, I presume. What an excellent idea." She turned to her husband and made a shooing gesture with her hand, rattling the gold bangles on her slender arm. "Be off with you, Simon. I'm sure you'd much rather hole up in the card room all evening, or talk business with Silverton."

Lord Trask had just finished making his bows to them, but now he studied his wife with a severe expression on his handsome features. "Sophie, I want you to sit down and not move from that chair until I get you something cold to drink. If you're not here when I get back, I will hunt you down and haul you right back home."

Sophie started to bluster, but Annabel was already dragging another chair over into their little group. Meredith guided Sophie into it, inspecting her with a worried eye.

"Are you feeling unwell? Perhaps you shouldn't have come tonight. It's always such a dreadful crush at Lady Framingham's affairs."

Sophie rolled her eyes as she settled into the chair. "I'm breeding, not sick. And I still have another three months to go, according to Dr. Blackmore. There's no need to worry, and there's no need for me to sit at home like a bump on a log."

She scowled up at her husband, but Phoebe could see the affection lurking in her gaze. It made her heart contract with an odd little ache. Would she ever marry as happily as the Stanton women had? Would she ever marry at all?

"No one expects you to sit home all the time," Lord Trask replied, "but you were feeling a little light-headed earlier. Given your propensity to trip over your own feet, I have no desire to see you combine that little habit with a fainting spell."

Phoebe blinked at the earl's plain speaking, but Sophie spluttered out a laugh. "Simon, you beast! You know I only trip over my feet when I'm not wearing my glasses. I promise I will keep them firmly on my nose tonight."

Lord Trask looked skeptical, and his wife wrinkled her nose at him. "Truly, I'm fine. Now, please go away. I promise I won't stir from this seat until you get back."

He gave her a faint smile as he touched her cheek. "I'll hold you to that."

"Don't worry, Simon," said Annabel. "We'll sit on her if we have to, and hold her down."

With a grin, Lord Trask sketched a bow and melted off into the crowd.

"Now," Sophie said, rubbing her hands with relish, "what are we talking about? Anything interesting? Any scandals breaking out that I don't know about?"

Meredith slid her glance in Phoebe's direction, and her heart clutched.

"Oh, nothing worth speaking about," Meredith said evasively.

Sophie frowned. "Really? That's disappointing. I was hoping—" She stopped, pushed her spectacles up on her nose, and leaned forward to peer at something across the room.

"What in heaven's name is Lucas doing with Mrs. Dorkington in that window alcove? I realize she's a widow, but he shouldn't let her drape herself all over him like that. Goodness! What will Grandmamma think?"

They all followed the direction of her gaze. There, in an alcove across from them, stood Lucas, one arm propped against the wall as he loomed over the buxom woman he had been dancing with. The woman had one hand on his chest, standing very close as she giggled up into his face. Bile rose in Phoebe's throat, and she had to swallow hard to force it down.

"Drat the man," muttered Meredith. "This time I really will slap him."

Annabel let out a little groan. "Oh, Grandmamma won't

like this one little bit." She cast a swift glance around. "And it looks like other people are starting to notice, too."

Phoebe ran a swift gaze around their nearest neighbors. Sure enough, more than a few were watching Lucas and Mrs. Dorkington, some with tolerant amusement, others with disapproving frowns.

Her heart sank. How could Lucas make such a spectacle of himself? She understood his anger, but did he have to punish them all?

"What's gotten into him?" Sophie asked. "I thought . . ." She glanced at Phoebe, then back to Meredith. "You know."

"We seem to have hit a few bumps in the road. There was an unfortunate scene at Stanton House this evening, and Lucas is quite annoyed with Phoebe. Not," Meredith hastened to add, "that it was any fault of hers. Quite the opposite, in fact. But Lucas has obviously chosen to express his dissatisfaction in typical male fashion."

As one, Meredith, Sophie, and Annabel turned and glared across the room at Lucas. He happened to glance over just at that moment, and caught the full force of their irate gazes head-on. His jaw dropped and Phoebe could swear he turned red. Then he frowned and turned back to Mrs. Dorkington. Phoebe did notice, however, that he removed his hand from the wall and took a step back from the widow.

Mrs. Dorkington, apparently, did not approve, since she tried to snuggle up to Lucas again. He evaded her attempt with a laugh and took her arm, escorting her back in the direction of the refreshment table and out of his cousins' line of sight.

"Men," said Sophie, her voice dripping with contempt. Awkwardly, she pulled her chair half round to close off their group in a semicircle.

"You mustn't be too upset, Phoebe," she said. "Lucas is behaving like a spoiled little boy, but it doesn't really mean anything."

Phoebe repressed a groan. "I am not upset in the least," she answered, as calmly as she could. "Lucas is free to spend his time with whomever he wishes. I am just sorry his family should see him behaving so badly."

There. She sounded quite convincing.

"I can see you don't care a whit," Sophie replied in a dry voice. "Believe it or not, we've all been in your shoes. Not Annabel, of course. I'll say one thing for my brother Robert. He's always had a great deal of common sense when it comes to women."

Annabel grinned, and the other two women smiled as if they knew the answer to some vexing puzzle. Only Phoebe felt completely at sea, which was not surprising given her lack of experience with the male of the species. And in spite of her reluctance to talk about Lucas—or even think about him— her curiosity was caught.

"What do you mean?" she asked.

Sophie glanced around to make sure no one was eavesdropping, then leaned in to their little circle. "Simon acted almost as badly as Lucas on the very night we became engaged. He arrived at a ball on the arm of the most notorious widow of the ton, and spent quite a bit of time flirting with her that evening. Needless to say, I was furious."

Phoebe's eyes widened. "I cannot believe it. His manners are so distinguished."

"Believe it. We had quite a dustup later, as you can imagine. It turned out to be quite an interesting evening."

To Phoebe's surprise, the countess turned red and began vigorously fanning herself.

"I can just imagine," interjected Meredith. "Silverton did the same thing to me before we were married. I was very annoyed at the time."

Phoebe let out a little squeak of dismay. Not Lord Silverton, too! Were all her illusions to be shattered tonight? "How is that possible? He is devoted to you. Are all men so faithless before they are married?"

"Oh, some men are quite faithless even after they're married," said Annabel in a cheerful voice. "But you mustn't think any of our husbands are. They're all hopelessly in love with us."

Phoebe let out a frustrated sigh. Sometimes it seemed her London cousins spoke in a foreign tongue. "Why are you telling me this?"

"Because," said Meredith, "Lucas's idiotic behavior doesn't really mean anything. I know it feels horrible to you now, but it's what men do when they're upset with the women they really want. Sometimes they don't know how to express it any other way."

Phoebe gaped at her but before she could protest, Sophie picked up the thread of the conversation. "And sometimes they don't even know they're doing it."

Phoebe gave her head a shake, but it still did not clear the fog. "Doing what?"

"Flirting. Most men and women in the ton flirt as easily as they breathe." Sophie tapped her chin with her fan, as if ruminating. "Although Lucas seems to know exactly what he's doing, which I find interesting. He must like you very much indeed."

Phoebe straightened her spine. "I am sure he does not. By any rational measure, his behavior would give the lie to that."

Annabel waved her protest away. "Rational has nothing to do with it. Of course you should punish Lucas for being so rude, but Sophie's right. It means nothing."

Phoebe stared down at her hands, gripped tightly in her lap. How could such behavior not mean something when it hurt so much?

She eased her hands open, smoothing the wrinkles out of her new silk gloves. Looking up, she let her gaze roam over the expectant faces of the other women. "Right is right, even if everyone is against it. And wrong is wrong, even if everyone is for it."

Meredith sighed and gave her a sympathetic pat on the arm, while Sophie looked morose.

Annabel, however, tilted her head with interest. "Is that a quote? Who said it?"

"William Penn," Phoebe murmured, still caught in her struggle to understand Lucas's behavior.

Annabel nodded. "It's very apt. I'm sure any number of men I know could benefit from Mr. Penn's wisdom."

"What I still fail to understand, however . . ." Sophie began. Then she cut herself off with a little gasp.

Meredith peered at her. "What's wrong?"

Sophie closed her eyes and visibly swallowed as she pressed a gloved hand to her lips.

"It's . . . it's just my stomach," she said in a thin voice. "It happens. I'll be all right in a minute."

"You don't look all right," Meredith replied. "Do you want me to take you to the retiring room?"

Sophie shook her head. "No, I just want to sit here."

"Is there anything I can do?" Phoebe asked. The sickly cast to Sophie's face sent ripples of alarm racing along her nerves.

Meredith cast an impatient look around the room. "Blast him, where has Simon gone to?"

Annabel jumped up. "Don't worry, I'll find him."

Phoebe also rose from her chair. "We will find him more quickly if we both look. This room is so large, it would be quite easy to miss him."

Annabel nodded and headed up the near side of the room.

"I don't know," Meredith said. "Phoebe, you barely know a soul here, and it's not a good idea to wander about without a chaperone. Perhaps it would be best if you stayed with us."

Phoebe hesitated. The room was huge and crowded and noisy, and she really had no idea where to look for the earl. Did it make sense for her to wander about by herself? She bit her lip in frustration. Why had Lucas chosen tonight of all nights to abandon her?

Then Sophie grimaced and pressed a hand to her stomach, and Phoebe knew she had to do something. "I am quite sure. If I cannot find Lord Trask, then I will look for Silverton or Lucas."

"Just be careful," warned Meredith as she rubbed Sophie's back. "And don't leave the ballroom."

Phoebe nodded and started to weave her way around the edge of the dance floor. It was slow going as she dodged her way around guests clustering in tight little knots. Every minute or so, she stopped and went up on tiptoe, straining for a glimpse of Lord Trask. After ten minutes she was only a third of the way down the room, making her stomach twist with frustration.

Glancing at a bronzed clock on a side table, she was startled to note the late hour. Soon the guests would be called down to supper, and she would have an awful time trying to fight the crowd back to the top of the room. Sweat began to prickle between her shoulder blades as her breathing grew tight. She was not used to large crowds and this gathering was not only large, it was packed into a space not big enough to hold it. A bubble of panic began to build in her chest as two drunk men jostled her, pushing her into a column. She hissed when her elbow connected with a sharp jab against the marble.

Forcing herself to take a deep breath, she leaned against the column to compose herself. She knew it was foolish to be anxious—after all, she was in the house of one of the most respected leaders of the ton, not wandering about in the streets. But not once had she gone out on her own since arriving in London. Lucas or one of her relatives—or even a maid—had always been with her, and right now she felt very much alone.

She let out a snort of disgust at her descent into self-pity. Sophie was ill and she needed her husband. What matter that the crowd pressed so closely or that she was on her own? She would be sure to find one of her party sooner or later, and then all would be well.

Stepping out from behind the column, she collided with a tall, heavyset man. Cold, unnerving eyes stared down at her, and she had to resist the temptation to shrink against the pillar.

Instead, she squared her shoulders and dipped him a slight curtsy. "Please forgive my clumsiness, sir. I did not see you."

The man studied her for a few seconds, then a cruel smile curled his lips. She had never seen a smile like that before, and it sounded warning bells in her head.

"What friendly god has dropped you into my lap?" he asked in a voice dripping with smug calculation. "Not that it matters, but I do believe this dreary affair has just become a great deal more interesting."

Chapter 12

The stranger blocked Phoebe in against the pillar and the wall, not only preventing her escape but obscuring her from the view of most everyone in the ballroom. His gaze traveled slowly down her body, then up again, lingering on her chest before returning to her face. By the time he finished, she was grinding her teeth.

"You are quite the little morsel to be wandering around a ballroom all by yourself, aren't you?" he purred.

"I do not wander, sir. I am looking for someone."

He propped a shoulder against the pillar and gave her a wolfish smile. "I see. Could this person you're looking for be a man?"

Phoebe's hackles rose at the implication. "I am looking for Lord—"

"Then look no further," he teased. "I am a lord, and unlike the one you seek, I would never be so rude as to leave you on your own."

He leaned in and this time she did shrink away, edging back behind the pillar. He did not follow, but his eyes tracked her with an avaricious gleam. "There's no need to be nervous," he said with a chuckle. "We're in the middle of a ballroom, after all."

He glanced over his shoulder, as if checking to see who

might be watching. Phoebe took the opportunity to stand on her tiptoes, hoping to see a member of her party. Unfortunately, she saw no one she knew, and the crowd was now so dense it would be almost impossible to make her way back to Meredith at the head of the room. Lady Framingham's guests were packed in as tightly as a herd of cattle driven through narrow streets to market.

Again she met the stranger's gaze and again she was struck by his cold eyes and the dissipated lines of his face.

"Such a mad crush," he sighed, "and so typical of Lady Framingham. The woman never knows where to draw the line. I cannot in good conscience allow you to disappear into this crowd. Heaven only knows what could happen."

"I thank you, but there is no cause for concern. I would be most grateful if you would let me by."

He gave her an oily smile. "The guests will be going down to supper in a few minutes, and the room will begin to thin. Do me the honor of waiting with me and then I will escort you down myself."

Impatience flared under her growing sense of unease. Sophie was ill, and this rude man kept her from completing her task. She could only hope Annabel had been more successful in finding Lord Trask. "Thank you, but no. I will be joining my friends for supper."

Now he affected a wounded look. "You grieve me. I would not have thought it possible for so beautiful a woman to be so cruel."

He surprised her by stepping forward and making her a flourishing bow. Phoebe scrambled back, again banging her elbow against the pillar. She bit off the oath that sprang too readily to her lips.

"If I cannot persuade you to join me for supper," the stranger said, "then perhaps you would take pity on your already devoted admirer and grant me a dance."

Really, the man was a complete fool. "I do not dance tonight."

He gave a soft laugh that sent a chill rushing up her spine. "You are the stubborn one, aren't you? I like that. A challenge always whets a man's appetite."

She blinked at the outrageous comment, a combination of nerves and frustration tangling her tongue.

"If you won't dance, perhaps you'd like a glass of champagne." His gaze, openly greedy now, slid over her face and chest.

"Again, no," she ground out. "I would ask you once more to let me by. My party will begin to wonder where I am."

He raised his eyebrows. "I think not, or they would have found you by now."

Angry and a bit frightened, Phoebe tried to slide by him. He blocked her path.

"Sir," she exclaimed, "I insist you move aside."

When he reached out to touch her, she jerked away, fetching up directly against the pillar.

He chuckled. "Your resistance is quite entrancing and wholly feigned, I suspect. I'm tempted to do something outrageous. Like kiss you."

This time, Phoebe did gasp in shock. She debated slapping him, although the very thought of acting so violently made her queasy. Unfortunately, the awful man was lowering his head as if he really was going to kiss her. She raised a hand, preparing to defend herself, when a welcome voice interrupted her.

"There you are, Miss Linville. Never thought to find you tucked away in the corner at the far end of the ballroom. Silly of me not to have thought of it in the first place. Girls always seem to end up in corners at mad crushes, whether you expect them to or not."

Phoebe almost collapsed with relief as Mr. Nigel Dash slipped smoothly around her tormentor to stand by her side. She grabbed his arm, swaying toward him. With a concerned look on his kind face, he steadied her.

"Mr. Dash," she blurted out. "I am so happy to see you. I was searching for Lord Trask, and I got caught up with this . . . this . . ."

From the angry expression in Mr. Dash's eyes, her explanation was not necessary. Startled, Phoebe peered at him. She had only met him a few times, but he had impressed her with his gentleness. However, right now he glared at the man still blocking them, clearly furious enough to do something they might all regret. If she wished to avoid a scene, it appeared she must act quickly.

"This gentleman noticed I was unattended," she said. "He graciously offered to escort me to dinner. I was in the process of explaining that I was looking for my party, Mr. Dash, when you arrived."

She finished by pinching the inside of his elbow, just to make sure he understood.

He flashed her a startled glance, then wry understanding filled his gaze. "How kind of Lord Castle," he said in a dry voice. "But you needn't worry, my lord. I'll see Miss Linville back to her party."

Lord Castle leisurely inspected Mr. Dash through a quizzing glass that had just appeared in his hand. "Always ready to lend fair maidens and aging dragons a helping hand, eh, Dash? What would the debs and old matrons do without you?"

Mr. Dash ignored him. "Are you ready to return to your party, Miss Linville?"

"Yes," she said, fervently. "I most certainly am."

Unbelievably, Lord Castle held up a restraining hand. "Before you whisk away the most interesting woman in the room, Dash," he said, "perhaps you could give me a formal introduction. That way I could ask the lady to dance without fear of offending the proper authorities."

Under her fingertips, Phoebe felt the muscles in Mr. Dash's

arm grow rigid. Lord Castle must be entirely the wrong sort of person if he balked at a formal introduction.

Now what would they do? The impertinent man simply would *not* leave her alone.

Just then, Lucas appeared out of the crowd, and he looked ready to breathe fire.

"Sorry, Castle," he growled, inserting himself into the middle of their group. "You'll dance with her when hell freezes over."

It had taken Lucas ten agonizing minutes to make his way through the damnable crowd and across the ballroom. He'd been avoiding Phoebe all evening, but he'd kept an eye on her from a distance. As long as she remained with her cousins she had nothing to fear from the rakes who prowled the overheated rooms of the ton, hunting their next willing—or unwilling—victims. Though still angry with her, and himself, for that ridiculous scene in his uncle's library, that didn't lessen his obligations. She might be a starched-up little Quaker, but she was also unbearably innocent and far too likely to fall into harm's way if he didn't prevent it.

Unfortunately, he'd lost track of her when he allowed himself to be lured into Sarah Dorkington's bosomy clutches. The widow had been after him for months, but his unforgivable lapse had led to Phoebe's entrapment in Castle's much more dangerous snare.

When Lucas had first spotted her, backing behind a pillar in apparent retreat, rage had burst through him like an exploding shell. She'd fallen prey to the most vicious rake in London, a man Lucas knew all too well. If it hadn't been for Nigel's timely arrival, Lucas would have plowed his way through the crowd without a care for havoc or injury. Still, he'd jostled more than a few complaining dancers as he forged straight across the packed floor.

Now, as Phoebe stared up at him, her big eyes full of relief, he had to struggle to contain another flare of anger, both with himself and with Castle. It was his fault she'd tumbled into trouble. After tonight, he'd make damn certain she never found herself in this or any kind of danger again.

Castle's lips peeled back in a cruel smile. "Ah, it only needed this to make the evening more delightful. Major Stanton, as crude and vulgar as always. Or, should I say, *Lord Merritt*. Really sir, your language in front of the lady is appalling. Perhaps you forget this is a ballroom, not a battlefield."

Without answering, Lucas removed Phoebe's hand from Nigel's arm. He tugged gently on her gloved fingers, prepared for her to resist, but she came willingly and plastered herself to his side. A slight tremor rippled through her body as she settled against him, and a tiny sigh of relief escaped her lips.

That little sigh made his heart throb with guilt. Castle had frightened her, and Lucas had to fight to repress the impulse to beat the bastard to a pulp.

He smiled down into Phoebe's face, giving her a quick, reassuring wink. Her eyes brightened and her mouth quirked up into a rueful smile. With a defiant tilt of her elegant chin, she stared at Castle, a stern expression settling on her pretty features. As delicate as she was, Phoebe had done her best to stand up to the vicious viscount, but the thought of her alone with someone of his ilk raised icy prickles on the back of Lucas's neck.

"Are you ready to go down to supper, Phoebe?" he asked, his voice gone gruff. "Aunt Georgie and the others will be waiting for us."

"You cannot imagine how ready I am," she said in a voice so enthusiastic he had to choke back a laugh. And the surprise on Castle's face almost made the whole nasty situation worth it.

Unfortunately, as Lucas prepared to guide Phoebe into

the flow of people heading to the supper room, Castle put up a restraining hand. "Merritt, you can't run away now. Not before properly introducing me. I take it this young lady is General and Lady Stanton's mysterious relative from America."

The bastard unleashed a particularly nasty smile. Lucas recognized that smile, and it boded ill.

"I should have guessed, of course," Castle drawled on, still blocking their way. "She does have the quaintest accent. Quite charming, really, if one goes in for that sort of rustic style."

Lucas weighed his options. He could either plant Castle a facer now, thus precipitating a scandal, or deal with him later when the ladies weren't present.

Before he had a chance to decide, Phoebe interrupted with an irritated huff. "For heaven's sake," she said. "If an introduction will end this absurd scene, then, yes, I am Phoebe Linville, niece to General and Lady Stanton. You, I take it, are Lord Castle. I wish I could say it has been a pleasure to meet you, but that would be a lie, and I never lie."

Castle's face went slack, and Lucas didn't bother to hold back his grin. Even Nigel, who had impeccable discipline, couldn't repress a snort of laughter.

Magnificently unaware of the impact of her words, Phoebe carried on. "Now that we are introduced, I ask you once and for all to move aside so we can join our party. I have suffered quite enough of your unwelcome attentions for one evening, and I do hope you will have the courtesy to spare me a repeat if we ever have the misfortune to meet again."

By the time she finished her little speech, Castle stopped looking stunned and started looking furious. He took a menacing step forward.

"I wouldn't if I were you, old man," Nigel interjected in a sharp voice. "Ladies present, and all that."

"A lady?" Castle sneered. "I very much doubt that. After all, I found her wandering about the ballroom unescorted.

And Miss Linville seemed more than happy to receive my attentions."

Against his side, Lucas could feel Phoebe quiver with outrage. "That is most untrue, and thee knows it! Thee should not tell such awful lies."

Castle's eyebrows practically shot up into his hairline. "*Thee?* Good God, Merritt. I had discounted the rumor, but I see now it's true. A Quaker! How delightfully odd. The Stantons do have a habit of taking in all kinds of strays, don't they? Whatever next, I wonder? A trained monkey?"

Phoebe went rigid beside him, and Lucas ruefully shook his head. He could almost feel sorry for Castle, too stupid to understand the hellfire he would shortly rain down on him.

"I suppose you're looking for something different in a woman," Castle said with deliberate malice. "But a religious fanatic from America . . . how quaint! Esme would be so amused, if she knew."

Phoebe threw Lucas a startled glance. Suddenly feeling old beyond his years, he repressed a curse. Would he never be free of the legacy of bitterness Esme had left in her wake?

"Lucas, we must go," Phoebe whispered. "Aunt Georgie is waiting."

He heard the worry in her voice, and her need for him to step away from the looming confrontation. But he couldn't. Not from Castle. He owed the man nothing but his contempt, and he had no bonds of family to hold him back.

"In a minute," he replied in a soft voice.

Nigel rolled his eyes and sighed, then moved to take Phoebe from him. But when Nigel tried to draw her away, she resisted.

Ignoring her flustered protest, Lucas stepped forward, mere inches away from Castle. The other man had breadth across the chest and shoulders, but Lucas still topped him by a good three inches. He had no problem using his height and size to make his point.

"You'll apologize to the lady, Castle," he said quietly.

The viscount let out an ugly laugh. "Or, what? You'll challenge me to a duel?"

Lucas stared at him, not bothering to voice the obvious.

Castle snorted. "Really, Merritt. I fear all those years in combat have addled your brain. If I wouldn't fight you over Esme, I'm certainly not going to fight you over this chit." His lips curled into a sneer. "Why would I bother?"

Lucas gave him a lethal smile. "Because no one insults my fiancée without paying the price."

Chapter 13

Phoebe stared at Lucas as the floor seemed to tilt under her feet. The heat of the room stifled her, but the dazed woolliness in her head resulted from the stunning announcement Lucas had just calmly delivered.

Lord Castle gaped at Lucas. "Miss Linville is your fiancée?"

His disbelief certainly echoed hers. She wondered if Lucas was drunk. There seemed no other explanation for his astonishing behavior, especially after the scene in the library. Flushed, she raised a hand to her perspiring forehead, feeling dizzy.

Her movement brought Lucas's head around and their eyes met. He frowned, his worried gaze sweeping over her, searching for the cause of her distress. His eyes were clear, and he appeared as somber and sober as a magistrate. With another stab of shock, she realized he *was* serious. About everything.

He gave her a fleeting smile of reassurance, then directed another challenging stare at the viscount. That stare was so cold and so eerily calm that a whisper of premonition shivered down her spine. Phoebe had never witnessed a man in a killing mood, but she imagined he would look much as Lucas did right now.

Lord Castle broke the suffocating tension by jerking his attention to Phoebe and letting out a sardonic laugh. "Well, this is wonderful, to be sure." He bowed to her, clearly intending mockery rather than respect. "My dear Miss Linville, allow me to offer you my congratulations. Your engagement will surely be the talk of the town, and I mean that in the best possible way."

Lucas narrowed his eyes to frozen gray slits, while Phoebe almost groaned. Shaking off her paralysis, she grabbed his sleeve. "We must go. We are attracting attention."

A quick glance around her confirmed it. Several men and women had paused to watch, evidently anticipating an amusing scene, or even a brawl.

Lucas gently removed her hand. "I'm still waiting for Lord Castle to apologize to you."

Phoebe wanted to shake him. "I do not need an apology. The wrong Lord Castle has committed is against himself."

Lucas glanced down at her. As he studied her face, his eyes flared with an admiring heat that made her heart thump and the blood rush to her cheeks. His mouth kicked up in a different sort of smile, one that seemed to curl around her with a lick of fire.

Lord, her wits had gone begging if he could affect her so greatly in such embarrassing circumstances.

"You may not need an apology, love," he said, "but I do on your behalf. And we're not leaving until I get it."

Perhaps she was losing not just her mind, but also her hearing. Lucas could *not* be making a declaration in the middle of a ballroom filled with strangers. It was simply too outrageous a notion to contemplate.

Lord Castle barked out an ugly laugh. "Really, Merritt, you and your *fiancée* are more amusing than the acrobats at Astley's. Perhaps you should consider joining the circus."

Something snapped in Phoebe's head. She stepped in front of Lucas and glared up at the viscount. "You, sir, are a poltroon, a braggart, and a . . . a loose fish," she stormed.

Lucas, Lord Castle, and Mr. Dash froze in unison. Uncle

Arthur often used those same words to great effect, and Phoebe had every intention of adding them to her vocabulary from now on. "You have bothered us long enough, Lord Castle. I insist you take yourself off before I really have something to say about it."

She seized Lucas again, trying to drag him away, but he refused to budge.

"Phoebe," he said, the warning clear.

Her frustration spiraled, exploding through her body. Some great force outside her control took hold, and she jabbed Lucas in the arm as hard as she could.

"No! There will be no apologies, no arguments, and certainly no talk of duels, which we all know is where this conversation is headed. I insist thee takes me to Aunt Georgie, Lucas. Or help me find Lord Trask, whose poor wife is waiting for him."

"Best do what she says, old man," Mr. Dash cut in, casting a quick glance over his shoulder. "We're starting to attract quite an audience."

Phoebe glanced around, and some of her anger dissipated. She had been so caught up she had failed to notice how large the group of spectators had grown. It included a few haughty matrons she recognized as Aunt Georgie's oldest friends. They looked on with horror, while the rest of the fashionable guests openly snickered.

Phoebe closed her eyes briefly as a humiliating flush crawled up her face.

"Yes, old man," mocked Lord Castle. "Best do what she says. After all, you do have a habit of allowing the ladies to lead you around by the nose, don't you?"

Lucas growled and took a step forward. Fury, so palpable it seemed a living thing, swirled between the two men.

"Viscount Castle," he said, "you will oblige me by naming—"

"No," Phoebe yelled, pushing Lucas hard in the chest.

Tears of anger and panic blinded her. "If thee says one more word, I will not marry thee and I will never speak to thee again. I will not tolerate violence, especially in my name, no matter what thy stupid masculine honor might dictate." She stabbed her finger through the folds of his cravat. "Is that perfectly clear?"

Lucas opened his eyes wide with surprise, and something else. Was it . . . laughter?

Her temper surged on a scarlet wave. She spun on her heel, gave Lord Castle a furious shove, and stomped off. The other guests scattered before her, their laughter rippling in her wake.

Phoebe rushed out, humiliation closing her throat and tears obscuring her vision. Almost tripping over her feet, she hurried down a hallway that led away from the ballroom, avoiding the stream of guests snaking down the large staircase to the supper room. The idea of facing her relatives right now—facing anyone—was unbearable.

Her heart raced, and she had to stop to catch her breath. Sucking in air, she leaned one hand against the wall of the corridor. As she struggled to calm herself, an unwelcome fact seeped into her brain—her behavior had been almost as wretched as the men's. She had lost her temper, raised her voice, and stormed across the ballroom.

And she had actually shoved both Lucas and Lord Castle. Phoebe always knew she had a volatile temper, but with her father's guidance and support she had learned to hold it under tight rein. Tonight, however, when she most needed control, it had come roaring forth.

She was surely the worst Quaker one could imagine.

Sighing, she rested her forehead against the smooth papered wall, pondering her next move. She could not skulk in the corridor forever, nor could she go back into the ballroom.

Besides, who knew what Lucas and Lord Castle were doing at this very moment? They might be brawling, or flinging challenges at each other. What if they had already left the ball, each one determined to go off and kill the other?

She jerked her head up, stricken by the image of Lucas prostrate on the ground, a bloody hole in his chest. She had to stop them. *Stop him*. Find Meredith and Silverton right now and—

A hand touched her shoulder and she spun with a strangled shriek. Lucas stood before her, looking worried and irate. With her, if his countenance was any indication.

She pressed a hand to where her heart pounded against her breastbone. "Thee startled me."

"I'm sorry. I didn't mean to." He did not sound sorry at all.

His tone, along with her slip into *plain speech*, nudged her anger back to the surface. "Well, *you* did," she snapped, forcing her way past her unwelcome habit. "But at least you had the good sense to leave the room before you and Lord Castle got into a brawl." She narrowed her eyes at him. "You did manage to avoid that, I hope."

He scowled. "Do you take me for a complete idiot?"

She fisted her hands on her hips and stared. He settled his arms across his brawny chest but then his lips twitched, as if he held back a smile.

"Apparently, you do," he said. "Phoebe, I'm—"

"Did you challenge him to a duel?"

His jaw flexed and he cast a quick glance around. "This is no place to discuss the matter. Let me take you down to supper."

She gave her head an angry shake. "I will not go anywhere with you until you answer my question."

He rubbed an impatient hand over his face. "Very well. But I'm not going to stand out here in the corridor arguing with you."

He grasped her arm and pulled her down the length of the

hall. She was about to object to being hauled about like a sack of grain when he stopped, opened a door, and gently shoved her into a room.

She shook him off. He gave a short laugh and closed the door. Leaning against it, he gave her a hot, heavy-lidded look that sent an inconvenient prickle of excitement racing across her skin.

Really, the man was insufferably arrogant, considering what had just happened. And she had every intention of giving him a proper set down once she figured out where to start.

She moved to the center of a very pretty sitting room that looked to be in regular use. Comfortable chairs and a sofa were casually arranged before a cozy fire in an iron grate, and a crystal lamp on a side table shed a soft glow over the room. Quiet settled over them, as they were far enough from the public rooms for the chatter of voices to fade. The steady ticking of a clock somewhere in a dim corner and the crackling fire provided a soothing counterpoint to her rattled nerves.

After a few moments she felt steady enough to turn around and face him. When she did, her precarious sense of control slipped again.

He studied her with a silent, predatory watchfulness that penetrated her to the bone. And even though his body remained as still as a marble statue, his eyes burned like flame, with a scorching sensuality that leapt across the space between them.

She drew in a tattered breath. She might be innocent in the ways of men—especially men like Lucas Stanton—but she thought she knew what that particular look meant. It frightened and excited her all at once. For an instant, she could think of nothing else, see nothing else but the hot gleam in his eye and the seductive curve of his hard, sensual mouth.

Then reality came flooding back and she remembered his declaration of marital intent, and what had prompted it. It was surely the result of anger and wounded pride, rather than real desire or true affection.

She crossed her arms at her waist, trying to close herself off from the alluring energy that shimmered around him.

"Please answer my question," she said in a quiet voice. "Did you, in fact, challenge Lord Castle to a duel?"

He pushed away from the door and strolled over. She had to resist the urge to retreat, to pull back from the visceral reaction that curled through her body as he neared. She would *not* let him see the depth of his affect on her.

With a hint of a smile, he brushed a careful hand across her cheek. She had to clench her teeth against the urge to nestle into it like a sleepy puppy.

"You don't have to be upset, sweetheart," he murmured. "Nothing bad is going to happen."

Even though her knees quaked at the husky note in his voice, she schooled her face to blandness. "I am not upset. I am simply concerned."

"*Thee* is upset," he said, playing with a lock of hair that drifted down from her temple. Her eyelids fluttered and closed as his fingers brushed down her cheek and over her jawbone. "They always give you away, your *thees*."

Her eyes snapped open at the hint of laughter in his voice. Deliberately, she pushed his hand away. "*You* will please answer my question. Did you or did you not challenge Lord Castle to a duel?"

When he did not reply, her dignity deserted her. She grabbed the lapels of his coat and yanked them. Hard. She heard a little ripping noise, but ignored it. "I swear, Lucas, if you did, I will . . . I will be very, very angry with you."

His large hands engulfed her fists. The tender expression in his sea smoke eyes made her legs go knock-kneed.

"You're quite fierce for a Quaker, Phoebe. It's been a revelation. But I assure you Castle won't be a problem," he said, releasing her hands.

She stared up at him, too suspicious to let it go. "What exactly does that mean?"

His lips quirked up in a roguish smile and he wrapped an arm around her shoulders, drawing her in. He did it slowly, as if he expected her to bolt from his embrace. "It means exactly what I said. Don't worry. I promise everything will be fine."

Suddenly, the strain of the evening overwhelmed her, and her limbs began to tremble. She allowed him to pull her close, leaning into him as if it were the most natural thing in the world.

"I cannot believe I lost my temper," she whispered, muffling her voice against the slippery satin of his waistcoat. Her shame came flooding back. "I have not acted like that since I was a child."

He rested his chin on top of her head, cradling her. It was wrong of her to allow it, but she craved the comfort and warmth he offered.

"You shocked me and everyone else in the room, I suspect," he mused. "I doubt poor Nigel will ever recover. Who would have thought Miss Phoebe Linville, of all people, could be such a firebrand?"

Sighing, she pulled out of his arms. He frowned but let her go—reluctantly, she thought.

"Are you sure you're all right?" he asked in a puzzled voice.

She swallowed a groan. Were all men this dense? Did he even remember how they had all acted out there in the ballroom? And her temper was rising again, which told her something important. Since meeting Lucas, she was apparently losing every shred of self-discipline she ever possessed.

"The evening started with that horrible fight in the library, then I was pestered by the rudest man I have ever met, and then you appeared and threatened that same man to a duel, *after* announcing to the whole world that I was your fiancée." She windmilled her arms in frustration, forcing him to step back a pace. "How could I possibly be all right?"

One corner of his mouth kicked up. "Not quite the whole world, love."

She froze. That word fell so easily from his lips, but she had no idea if he really meant it. What she did know was that his easy affection made her stomach flutter and her body long to be in his arms once more.

Mentally, she shook herself. He was trying to distract her, that was all.

"Lucas," she said sternly, "you may not have noticed at the time, but we did attract quite a great deal of attention. And Lord Castle will be sure to spread as much ugly gossip about us as he can. The man is a . . . a . . ."

"Poltroon?"

She crossed her arms under her chest and scowled at him. His gaze dropped to her bosom, and his amused little grin disappeared. Some other expression took its place, one so full of heated appraisal it sent a disconcerting ripple of excitement flowing through her veins.

"Lucas, you must stop doing that," she said through clenched teeth.

He looked up, then widened his eyes with feigned innocence. "Stop what?"

She blew out a breath. "Never mind. We were speaking of Lord Castle and the trouble he will cause when he starts spreading rumors about our supposed engagement."

He shrugged. "It's not a rumor. And I'll make sure Castle doesn't become a problem."

Phoebe stared at him. Had she banged her head getting out of the carriage tonight and failed to notice? She had assumed Lucas's public declaration had been meant to put Lord Castle in his place. But she now realized that was a ridiculous assumption. No one tossed out marriage proposals with such cavalier abandon, at least not a man like Lucas.

Her mind flashed back to the scene in General Stanton's library. Had Lucas, in fact, been asking her to marry him after all? Her foolish heart had longed for it, but her common sense had intervened to reject the notion. Who asked a woman to marry him in front of a roomful of people?

Her mouth opened, a thousand questions poised on her lips. Only two mattered, though. Did Lucas truly intend to marry her? And, if so, did he love her?

But her tongue seemed to cleave to the roof of her mouth. Silently cursing her lack of courage, she fell back to her more immediate concern.

"Lucas, you have not yet answered my question. Did you or did you not challenge Lord Castle to a duel?"

His face turned to stone. "He impugned your honor."

Frustrated, she shook her head. "My honor is my own. No man can impugn it without my consent."

That made him scoff. "Phoebe, please do me a favor and stay clear of things you don't understand."

Oh, she understood very well. Men willingly fought and even killed over inconsequential matters, and they liked nothing better than justifying their actions in the name of honor.

Man's honor. Not God's honor.

"Truth often suffers more by the heat of its defenders, than from the arguments of its opposers," she said in a severe voice.

He peered at her as if she had just sprouted wings from her forehead. "What the hell does that mean?"

Phoebe grimaced. She had thought Mr. Penn's quote to be more than apt, but Lucas obviously did not agree. Perhaps she could make him up a small book of quotations to give him for a Christmas present. He could certainly benefit from them.

Frustrated, she spread her hands wide. "Why are you so upset by this ridiculous matter? It makes no sense."

"It makes perfect sense to me," he growled.

She recognized his flinty expression. He wore it whenever he encountered Silverton, or was forced to speak with him. Understanding finally dawned. "This is not about me," she said slowly. "This is about Esme Newton."

His expression went positively glacial, but she would not be put off. "You have no right to be offended, Lucas. You have used me as an excuse to resurrect an old grievance, one that has little to do with me. It was not kind of you."

"Christ," he muttered. He paced over to the fireplace, then across to the door. His hand reached for the knob, and for a horrible moment she thought he intended to storm out.

But he drew back and she could breathe again. Turning to face her, he remained by the door. A casual observer would have thought him calm, but she saw stormy visions of the past roiling in his gaze.

"Phoebe, you couldn't possibly understand."

She clasped her hands in front of her, sending up a silent prayer. If they were to have any future together, Lucas must learn to trust her. "Then tell me so I will."

He blew out a tense breath. "Very well. Castle was one of Esme's flirts, although that term doesn't precisely capture it. He knew how I felt about her and he knew how she felt about me, yet he pursued her anyway."

"Ah. Just as you pursued the same woman against your cousin's wishes."

He frowned and his gaze dropped to the carpet. "I suppose. I regarded it differently at the time."

She remained silent for a few moments, letting him grapple with his conscience. "And Esme allowed this?" she finally prompted.

Lucas glanced up with a bitter smile. "To my complete astonishment, she did."

Phoebe could not help rolling her eyes. "Is there no man she did not flirt with?"

That elicited a short laugh from him. "Esme loved the attention. She even loved that men fought over her, although I don't think she understood how ugly it all would get until the end."

"Until Silverton."

He nodded slowly. She ached for him, but kept silent as he worked it through.

"Esme loved having us all on her string, although I didn't realize at the time how manipulative she was. I truly thought she loved me." He shrugged, as if it didn't matter. "Maybe she even did, in her own fashion. She said it often enough, at least in the beginning. Before Castle. And before Silverton," he finished softly.

"Why did she not marry Lord Castle?"

He snorted. "Because he wasn't a lord back then, just a second son. He didn't inherit until a few years ago. In any event, a viscount would never be a match for Silverton. But when my cousin eventually spurned her, she had to settle for a moderately wealthy Scottish earl, who then took her to Edinburgh."

His voice was laced with contempt, but she could not tell if he reserved it for Esme Newton or for himself.

Hesitantly, she moved toward him. "Lucas, this woman has caused you nothing but anger and grief."

He remained motionless against the door, looking impossibly remote. "I do understand that, my dear."

She took another step closer, silently willing him to let her in. "She was not worthy of you or Cousin Stephen. Nor is her memory worth the continued estrangement between you."

Phoebe had an impression that he flinched. His eyes, though, remained cold, freezing her out.

Pulling in a shaky breath, she stepped right up to him. "Do you still love her?"

His head jerked back. "God, no."

"Are you sure?" she whispered.

The ice in his eyes finally melted. "Looking back, I don't think I ever loved her. I believe *obsession* is a better way to describe it."

"That offers me little comfort, Lucas."

He reached for her then, his hands drifting over her bare shoulders. His touch—tender and light—made her tremble.

"You needn't worry, sweetheart," he murmured in a voice so dark and tempting she almost melted against him. "Rest assured I won't allow her memory to come between us or our marriage."

His words thumped her back to earth. It was time to stop hiding behind her fears, and confront him directly. "Lucas, I do not even know if there is anything between us. And you have not even asked me to marry you yet, much less told me you love me."

Something flickered across his features, and a chill shivered through her.

"You do not love me, do you?" she asked, trying to pull away.

His grip firmed on her shoulders even as his eyes narrowed. "I want no other woman but you, Phoebe. Never doubt it."

"Wanting is not loving," she challenged. "I will not accept wanting."

A muscle ticked in his jaw, as if he was holding something back. "Phoebe, I'm extremely fond of you, which you surely know. I will cherish you and our marriage. But you must understand that I am not given to extravagant declarations. I'm not a boy anymore, given to such foolishness."

She swallowed, her mouth tasting dry and bitter. For once, anger seemed a reliable ally. "You are very fond of your horses, too, but I do not expect you to marry them."

He stared at her for an endless moment before he let out a crack of laughter. "Christ, Phoebe! Where do you come up with these ridiculous ideas? My sweet, I never wanted to kiss my horses either, but I *do* want to kiss you."

And between one breath and the next, he did.

Chapter 14

Phoebe's eyes grew wide as Lucas swooped down to kiss her. But when his lips met hers she squeezed her eyelids closed, overcome by the shock of his touch and the temptation that trembled through her. His mouth took hers in a silken slide, softly at first, as if granting her time to adjust. She had never felt a man's kiss on her mouth. Her heart pounded with something akin to fright, yet she could not resist his lure—hot and sweet, hinting of champagne and something forbidden.

And it was not just any man who kissed her. It was Lucas, and she knew now that she had been waiting for the touch of his lips for a very long time.

His mouth was gentle, exploring her as if she were a newly discovered landscape. Mentally, she stumbled in that landscape, searching for a way forward and knowing it could only come through him. From the feel of his calloused hands wrapped around her bare arms, his fingers caressing her skin, and from the breathtaking heat of his mouth. Every unique sensation drew her forward, unmooring her from every experience that had come before.

Who knew a kiss could be so . . . transporting?

She spread her hands flat on his chest, sinking her fingers into the rich fabric of his waistcoat. Seeking the beat of his heart, she found it, fast and steady under her palms. Her pulse, though, fluttered everywhere throughout her body—behind her breastbone, in her throat and wrists, even behind her knees.

And as Lucas deepened the kiss, those knees grew dreadfully weak.

She clutched at him, whimpering under the tender onslaught of his lips. He answered with a deep, masculine rumble as his hands moved from her arms to slide around her back. He splayed them wide, holding her in a firm clasp. It protected her, that embrace, making her feel safe and cherished. In the circle of his arms, with his mouth igniting a slow fire in her blood, Phoebe could almost believe anything was possible. Even that Lucas might love her.

Her body melted against him. She tipped her head back, searching for more, something deeper, hoping he would know what it was.

He did, for his tongue came between her closed lips, tracing along the seam. Phoebe jerked in surprise and her mouth opened on a startled gasp. His tongue stroked into her mouth—just for a second—and then retreated with a quick, feathering taste to the corner of her lips. Her eyes snapped open. She stared at him—at his mouth, mere inches from hers and seductive and damp from their kiss—and his gaze, dark and smoky with desire, bored into her.

The intimacy shook her to the soul.

"Was that your first kiss, Phoebe?"

His deep voice whispered through her, doing the strangest things to her body. She had a sudden, shocking urge to rub against him, like a cat who wished to be petted.

Phoebe found herself very much wishing that Lucas *would* pet her. "Yes," she managed to croak.

That pleased him, if the arrogant smile tugging at his lips was any indication. She decided on the spot that Lucas had the most entrancing mouth she had ever seen.

"Did you like it?" His husky tone sounded much like a purr, one made by a very big, very wicked cat. She had not imagined a man could make a noise like that, and it seemed to drain all reason from her brain.

"Um . . . I," she stuttered. She *had* liked it. But should a lady even consider admitting that sort of pleasure? It occurred to her that her education was vitally lacking in this very important area.

He laughed, and she felt an answering vibration at every point where their bodies connected. "Let me rephrase, my sweet. Do you want me to do it again?"

She frowned. Was this a trick, or a test in some way? Even though she had imagined more than once Lucas kissing her, she had never thought to be required to do more than stand there. That is what women did under the circumstances, or so she had always assumed.

"Do you want to kiss me again?" she said hesitantly.

His eyes went heavy-lidded and slumberous. "Actually, I'd very much like it if *you* would kiss *me*.

Her mind stuttered as she tried to read his expression. Desire she saw most clearly, but something else lurked in his gaze, too. Shadows darkened his eyes and she sensed a need in him beyond that of mouth touching mouth, skin touching skin. It seemed Lucas wanted more—a declaration, perhaps. She had already rejected him once tonight and she wondered if he sought proof she would not do it again.

Carefully, she placed her hands on his shoulders and went up on her tiptoes. Stretching up another inch, she shyly pressed her trembling lips to his firm mouth.

He froze under her shy touch and for an awkward few seconds Phoebe thought she had done it wrong. Then his lips moved beneath hers and his tongue swept into her mouth, drawing her into a deep, devouring kiss. As she fell against him, hardly able to stand, he took her hands and fastened them around his neck. She clung to him as a bulwark against the sensations spinning through her body. Nothing could have prepared her for the aggressive thrust of his tongue, tasting her with a delicious, intoxicating greed.

Vibrant emotions stunned her. They shimmered through her mind like bright clouds, overriding caution and modesty, tawdry concerns that crumbled before the power of what he shared with her. She had never experienced anything like Lucas and his kisses—so much warmth engulfing her, making her forget who and where she was.

At that vague thought, a warning bell sounded faintly in her mind. Her concentration suddenly expanded to include the awareness that they leaned against a door in Lady Framingham's mansion, just one floor away from a room where hundreds of guests sat down to supper.

Guests that included Aunt Georgie.

Her eyes flew open and she started to draw back, but Lucas gently bit her lower lip, sucking it into his mouth. She groaned as something pulled low in her belly, and she collapsed against him.

He held her close, breathing a husky laugh against her lips before his tongue returned to ravish her mouth. His arms tightened around her shoulders, drawing her up to the very tip of her toes and mashing her against his chest. It should have hurt, he was that muscular and hard. Instead, her nipples contracted with a sharp pleasure, pulling her farther into a spiraling sensation of need.

Phoebe sighed into his mouth, giving herself over to his ardent demands. Her limbs grew heavy and the place between her legs ached with a pleasurable tension. That ache made her long to do forbidden things, like squirm against him to increase the pressure of his muscled body against hers.

An instant later she froze in horror with the realization that she *was* squirming against him. Even worse, a part of him—a very big and hard part—pressed into her belly with a good deal of insistence. And that should have horrified her, too, but instead she felt another bizarre urge to wriggle against it.

That, she felt sure, would be a very bad thing to do.

With a soft nuzzle of her mouth, Lucas broke the kiss. His gaze traveled over her face, her neck, her breasts, like a lingering caress.

"Do you want me to stop?" he asked.

She drew in a shaky breath. The very sound of his voice made her insides quake with longing. When he looked at her like that, she could not seem to process one rational thought. She should come up with a sensible answer, but had no idea what that might be.

"Do you want to?" she asked.

He gave a soft laugh. Without answering, he bent and slipped one arm behind her knees, hoisting her up high against his chest. She squeaked out a protest, but he simply dropped a fast, hard kiss on her mouth as he strode across the room to the sofa.

"Lucas," she gasped. "I very much enjoy being with you, but we do have a few more things to settle between us. And Aunt G—"

"Hush," he murmured. "We'll go down soon enough. And we can talk in a minute."

She eyed him doubtfully as he sank onto the sofa, still cradling her in his arms. Suddenly, he grimaced and reached under her bottom to arrange something. She blushed when she realized what it was. "Ah, I do not think this is a very good idea. I have not even accepted your proposal of marriage. If, that is, you even made a proposal."

His eyes flared hot, then he dipped his head to her neck. His tongue flicked out to lick the pulse throbbing at the base of her neck. She jumped, but he held her in place.

"You know very well that I proposed," he murmured, kissing her throat. She moaned at the contrast between the smooth feel of his lips and the rasp of his faintly bristled chin.

"Well . . . I have not yet accepted it," she managed in a quaking voice.

She absolutely could not think while he nibbled little kisses back down her neck to where it met the junction of her shoulder. Then he nipped her there, and thought fled her brain. Her head, too heavy to hold upright, fell back against his shoulder.

"Don't worry, Phoebe," he murmured. "I promise everything will be fine."

She could only sigh as he kissed and tongued his way over her shoulder to the top of her tiny sleeve. Beneath her, the hard length of his erection nudged her bottom, sending a shivery sort of spasm pulsing between her legs.

Phoebe gasped, so surprised by the sensation she hardly noticed Lucas nudging down her tiny cap sleeve to completely bare her shoulder. The gauzy bodice sagged low across her breasts, only just covering her nipples. In fact, when she glanced down at herself, she could see them almost peeking out over the top of her lace trimming.

"Lucas, I do not—"

His glance flicked back up to her face and he swooped in to give her another one of those quick but devastating kisses. Then he looked back down at her breasts while his fingers skimmed over the top of her bodice.

"God, Phoebe. You are so beautiful," he said in a tight voice. "I can't wait to see all of you."

That almost shocked her into silence. Almost.

"Truly?"

No man had ever told her she was beautiful, or even pretty—not that Quaker men made a habit of paying fulsome compliments.

Lucas's mouth lifted into a wry smile. "Trust me, love. You ravish me."

She heard the smile in his voice, and that eased the knot of anxiety in her stomach.

His gaze remained fixed on her breasts, seemingly entranced as he traced his fingers over her skin. "So white and soft," he whispered.

He sounded fascinated, and that drew her with him. Equally entranced, she watched as his index finger pushed below her lace, just brushing against the rosy circle of her nipple. She bit her lip as tingles raced through her flesh and the tip pulled into a tight, aching bead.

His breath hissed out and he shook his head. "Damnation, woman. You're going to kill me."

Lifting his head, he took her lips in a kiss so encompassing it burned away all but the knowledge of him. She saw, tasted, and breathed only Lucas. Only his touch mattered, only what happened in the circle of his arms held any meaning.

Which was why, no doubt, Aunt Georgie had to clear her throat three times before Phoebe even registered that she and Lucas were no longer the only people in the room.

Chapter 15

A gloomy silence fell over the coach, discouraging any attempt at conversation. Lucas repressed the impulse to growl at everyone and instead studied the dejected slump of Phoebe's shoulders as she huddled forlornly in the opposite corner. She hadn't said a word since they left the scene of the crime, and refused to even look at him. That, combined with her obvious distress at being discovered in a compromising position—by her aunt and cousin, no less—set Lucas on the knife's edge, ready to snap at the first person who dared reprimand her or add to her humiliation in any way.

Finally, Meredith let out an aggravated sigh. "I swear, Lady Framingham's house must be cursed. I for one intend to come down with a migraine before I ever set foot in the place again."

"Indeed," Aunt Georgie intoned in a voice of doom. "It would appear that Lady Framingham's affairs lead to an alarming collapse in the manners of my nieces and nephews."

Phoebe retreated farther into her corner, which shredded Lucas's heart with remorse. Fortunately, Meredith lightened the moment by letting out a surprising burst of laughter. "Well, it *was* horrible when Silverton and I disgraced ourselves at that ball a few years ago, but everything turned out for the best."

She patted Phoebe's arm. "Don't worry, my dear. Aunt Georgie is very adept at deflecting scandal, as is the General. I'm sure people will forget all about it in no time."

"I find myself loath to contradict you," Aunt Georgie said, "but Mrs. Brackett witnessed the entire scene in the ballroom and made a point of searching me out and telling me all about it. Quite loudly, as you will recall."

Meredith scrunched up her nose. "I was trying to forget that."

"Mrs. Brackett is an old biddy and a terminal gossip," Lucas growled. "Nobody with an ounce of sense listens to her."

"Very true," Aunt Georgie responded in a sarcastic tone. "But they will listen to Lady Harpwell and Mrs. Cherry, both of whom saw you propel Phoebe into that sitting room. I can't even imagine what you were thinking when you did that, my boy. Thank God, Meredith and I interrupted you when we did."

Lucas clamped down on the retort that sprang to his lips. No matter the provocation, he would not rip up at his aunt, but what she failed to understand was that he would have stopped long before matters progressed to a true state of danger. Phoebe had been so beautiful in her disheveled glory, and so responsive, that he had been hard-pressed not to flip up her skirts and take her on the spot. But he would never treat her so shabbily, and he was perfectly capable of resisting temptation—for her sake, if no other. And he was damned certain he could have spirited her away from the ball with a lot less fuss and commotion than his interfering relatives.

Phoebe stirred. With a tragic but determined expression, she faced Aunt Georgie. "My dear aunt," she said quietly, "this was my fault, and I beg your forgiveness for betraying your trust, and for bringing shame onto the family. If you feel it necessary to send me back to America, I will not object."

Lucas stared across the small space separating them, stunned she could even suggest it. Phoebe would leave England, and him, over his corpse. "Phoebe, you have nothing to apologize for. There will be no scandal, I assure you. I'll handle everything."

He leaned forward, compelled to touch her, but Aunt Georgie laid a remarkably strong restraining grip on his arm. "Not another word from you, Lucas. I hold you entirely responsible for this debacle, which you can be sure I will communicate to the General as soon as we arrive at Stanton House."

Irritated, Lucas tried to stare her down, but she just cocked an imperious eyebrow at him. "Well, that has me trembling in my boots," he said dryly, settling back into his seat.

His aunt gave his arm a small, affectionate squeeze, even though her expression remained stern. "It should. I shudder to think what your uncle might say to you."

He grimaced, torn between laughter that she thought he would tremble before his uncle's bluster and irritation that she treated him like the greenest of lads. She was right about one thing, though. He had made a hash of everything, and Phoebe would undoubtedly suffer the brunt of his mistakes.

He glanced from Aunt Georgie to Phoebe, who searched his face with a worried gaze. As if to comfort him, she dredged up an encouraging smile, one so sweet and forgiving it made him feel like the greatest cad in the world.

Christ. That she believed *he* needed comfort only served to illustrate her generous nature, and he couldn't believe he'd ever thought her rigid or judgmental. Well, he'd damn well spend the rest of his life making it up to her. And no one would ever hurt her again.

"Phoebe," his aunt said, "Lucas is correct about one thing. The Stanton family is certainly used to handling situations like this. Far worse, in fact. I have no doubt we'll be able to brush through with only a modicum of trouble."

Phoebe gave her aunt a grateful smile, looking relieved. Lucas knew she failed to understand that there was only one way out of this mess, and that was for them to get leg-shackled. Everyone had already realized that except her. Phoebe remained a babe in the woods when it came to understanding how the ton would blow up this incident into the biggest scandal of the Season. All the elements were in place, including the fact that she was an outsider, and a Quaker to boot. The only sure way to protect her was through marriage to him.

The sooner, the better, too. Lucas wanted her away from the London gossips and from his family, who couldn't seem to keep their interfering noses out of his business.

Most of all, he wanted Phoebe to himself, in his arms and in his bed, without any more damn interruptions.

When the carriage came to a halt in front of Stanton House, he handed the ladies out in silence, giving Phoebe's hand an extra squeeze as she stepped down. She sighed and tugged her hand from his grasp. That sliced through him, and he knew it would take time and careful handling to restore her trust in him. Time, unfortunately, was the one thing they didn't have.

They clustered for a moment in the entrance hall as the butler and a footman relieved them of their outerwear. Aunt Georgie gave Phoebe a little push toward the stairs. "Go up to my sitting room with Meredith, my dear," she said. "I'll be up in a few minutes."

Phoebe nodded. She threw Lucas a fleeting glance, dipped a sad little curtsy, and fled up the stairs. Meredith shook her head and gave him a wry, understanding look, and then followed her cousin.

"Come, Lucas," said Aunt Georgie. "Silverton and Robert should have arrived home by now with Annabel, and are no doubt waiting with your uncle. It's time you faced the firing squad."

Phoebe stood in the window alcove in her aunt's sitting room, peering out at the night-shrouded garden. Darkness obscured everything but she looked anyway, pretending to be fascinated by the clipped hedges and leafless rosebushes barely visible under the thin November moon. She burned with humiliation, not yet ready to face Annabel and Meredith, who sat together on the chaise longue in front of the chimneypiece.

She heard the rustle of silk skirts behind her and sighed, wishing she could put off this conversation forever. How could she ever begin to explain her behavior when she could barely fathom it herself? But when Lucas had kissed her so passionately, she had returned his embrace with every ounce of longing in her soul, forgetting all her unanswered questions. Only now, when he was no longer seducing her into the warmth of his arms, did she realize he had not answered a single one.

And he had not told her he loved her.

Meredith's hand rested on her shoulder, gently urging her to turn around. "Come and sit down, Phoebe. You can't hide in the alcove forever. I know because I tried it once myself."

Phoebe cocked an eyebrow in silent enquiry, and Meredith responded with a generous smile. "Once I stood in this room much as you are now, waiting for the wrath of the Stanton family to fall on my head. It didn't, of course, and nothing bad will happen to you, either."

"What did you do?" she asked, allowing Meredith to draw her over to the chaise.

"She and Silverton were very bad indeed," Annabel chipped in, springing up from the chaise to allow Phoebe to take her place. Phoebe sank down, suddenly aware of how very exhausted she felt. Would this dreadful night never come to an end?

"I cannot imagine that Meredith was caught kissing in the anteroom," she muttered. Her cheeks flushed with shame at the mental picture of Meredith and Aunt Georgie standing in the doorway of the little room, their mouths agape. After that, everything was rather a blur, including their ignominious exit. They had not managed to escape without observation, and Phoebe had all too clearly heard giggles and whispers from more than a few guests lingering in the hallway and on the stairs.

"Oh, it was much worse than that," Annabel insisted. "Meredith waltzed with Silverton without first receiving permission from the patronesses of Almack's."

Phoebe stared at her. "You must be joking."

"Sadly, no," Meredith replied.

Phoebe shook her head. "London is the oddest place one could ever imagine."

"It is, but the point is that it all worked out for me, as it will for you."

"How?" Phoebe almost dreaded the answer.

"Eventually I married Silverton."

Her stomach took a sickening drop. "Are you saying my only course of action is to marry Lucas? When he does not even love me?"

"Are you sure about that?" Annabel asked. "His actions speak otherwise."

Phoebe shook her head. "He does not."

Meredith sat down next to her and took her hand. "Why do you think that?"

"Because he said so," she answered miserably.

The sisters exchanged a startled glance. "What exactly did he say?" Meredith asked in a wary voice.

"He said he was not a boy, and he no longer engaged in such foolishness."

Meredith groaned. "What an idiot. Let me guess. You asked him about Esme, didn't you?"

Phoebe nodded.

"It's a good thing that woman lives in Scotland, or I would have to murder her," Meredith groused. "She has been the cause of a great deal of trouble in this family." With a firm look in her eye, she took Phoebe by the shoulders, forcing her to meet her gaze. "Phoebe, listen to me. Lucas suffered a devastating hurt as a young man, and he's only now letting it go. And he's letting it go because of *you*. He may not yet be able to say he loves you and, frankly, most men choke on the word. But I'm convinced his affection for you is genuine and strong."

Phoebe knew what they wanted her to say, but she hesitated, still worried Lucas wished to marry her for all the wrong reasons.

After several long moments, Meredith sighed and removed her hands. "I don't think I'm convincing you, am I?"

Phoebe gave a helpless shrug. "Never marry but for love, but see that thee lovest what is lovely."

"Another quote from Mr. Penn, I presume," Meredith said, wrinkling her nose.

"And a pretty one, too. But not very useful in our current situation," Aunt Georgie interjected.

They all looked around as the older woman entered through the door from her bedroom. Blushing, Phoebe jumped up from the chaise.

Her aunt gave her a faint smile. "Sit, my child. Meredith, be so kind as to allow me to sit next to your cousin."

When Meredith rose from the chaise, Aunt Georgie took Phoebe's hand and drew her down beside her.

"Phoebe, the time for beating around the bush is past. We must speak frankly—woman to woman—about Lucas and your future."

Her aunt's words set the nerves in Phoebe's stomach dancing with anxiety. "How . . . how is Lucas? I hope my uncle was not too harsh with him."

Aunt Georgie gave a snort. "The General gave him a rare trimming. That I expected, just as I expected Lucas wouldn't take it very well. For a moment, I thought they would come to blows."

The wry smile on her aunt's face told Phoebe how unlikely that was, but the idea that Lucas and Uncle Arthur had violently argued sickened her. This terrible drama and discord was her fault.

Well, to be fair, Lucas must also share the blame. Both for that scene in the ballroom and afterward, when he dragged her into the anteroom and kissed her. But she should have been strong enough to resist the temptation he posed. Now, because of her weakness, another breach had opened in the Stanton family.

"What happened next?" she asked, fearing the answer.

"Something surprising. Silverton stepped up and defended Lucas."

That stunned them all into silence for several moments.

"Truly?" Phoebe finally managed.

Aunt Georgie nodded.

Meredith uttered a disbelieving laugh. "Will wonders never cease?"

Aunt Georgie grinned. "Silverton made a strong case on his behalf, stating that Lucas had no choice but to defend you against the insults of Lord Castle."

Phoebe ground her teeth at that, but let the matter drop. In the scheme of things, the issue of the viscount's insults no longer seemed very important. "What are they doing now?"

Aunt Georgie turned serious again. "I left them to discuss the details of what must happen next, as should we. We must come to a decision, Phoebe, and there is only one course of action, at least the only one to keep you safe from damaging gossip."

Foreboding seeped through Phoebe. "And that course is?"

"You must marry Lucas, of course. As soon as possible."

Phoebe closed her eyes, wishing she could shut everything out of her mind as easily. She hated that she possessed so little control over events, and hated even more that her foolish heart clamored to accept the solution so readily offered.

How could she marry him if he did not love her? Her heart told her he might, despite his words to the contrary, though her head told her otherwise. But it was in the heart where love resided, not the head. Love was founded on trust, not logic, and yet logic warned her with absolute clarity that she must answer this question before she could move ahead.

"Phoebe, open your eyes," Aunt Georgie said.

Reluctantly, she obeyed, and met the combined gazes of three very concerned women. They regarded her with so much affection and worry she almost burst into tears.

"Are *you* in love with Lucas?" Aunt Georgie asked.

Phoebe bit her lip, hating to reveal all her insecurities, even to her closest female relatives. "How can I answer that?"

"Honestly, I would think. You're the most forthright person I've ever met, and it's a quality that has served you well and will continue to do so in this situation."

She grimaced. Aunt Georgie was right. Honesty was always the correct course of action, even when courage flagged. "Yes, I love him. But Lucas has been very circumspect in expressing his feelings. How can I give myself into his keeping when he withholds so much?"

Aunt Georgie studied her with a thoughtful air. "From what I understand, Quaker men approach matters of affection more simply and openly than the average aristocratic male. It's no wonder you find men like Lucas so confusing."

Meredith snorted. "Don't expect that to change any time soon."

Phoebe sighed wearily. "You make them sound like some kind of exotic species of animal."

Her aunt unleashed a quick, charming grin. "In some respects, they are. But my point is that men like your uncle, or Lucas or Silverton, have not been raised to express their emotions as directly as the men of your community. I do believe it was one of the things that attracted your mother to your father—that he had such an affectionate and kind nature."

That was certainly true. Her parents' deep and abiding love for each other had shone through in their words and actions. Even her brother, George, as solemn and stiff as he often was, made no secret of the fact that he adored his wife and children.

"Why should I expect anything less from my husband?" Phoebe asked with a show of defiance.

"You shouldn't. I believe Lucas does love you, but that particular emotion has not served him well. He doesn't trust easily, and he sometimes lacks faith in the goodness of others. You must teach him differently."

"How?" she asked, feeling desperate.

Aunt Georgie took her by the shoulders. "By loving him and by being yourself. That's why Lucas wants you in the first place—because of who you are."

Phoebe eyed her aunt doubtfully. She did love Lucas, she could admit that now. But what the family wanted from her seemed somehow dishonest. And she hated that she had to make the most important decision of her life as a result of stupid gossip and a trumped up scandal.

"Could we not wait?" she said. "Perhaps the gossip will die down."

Aunt Georgie gave an impatient jerk of the head. "I assure you, it won't. Whether you realize it or not, Lord Castle called your honor into question. You then disappeared with your supposed fiancé for a considerable length of time. When you reappeared, looking considerably flushed and agitated, you made your exit from Framingham House under the eye of several notorious gossips. Believe me, the scandal will only grow, damaging your reputation and casting Lucas in a very bad light, if you were not to marry. And it will not reflect very well on the rest of us, either."

Stricken by the catalogue of her offenses, Phoebe lapsed into silence. Put like that, the situation sounded very bad.

Still, it felt so wrong to marry a man who might not love her—a man who now more than ever would see her as an obligation and a burden. "I should return to America," she said, feeling wretched. "That way, no one will have anything to gossip about, and Lucas will not be forced to marry me."

"For heaven's sake, Phoebe," Meredith exclaimed. "No one is forcing Lucas to marry you. As if anyone ever could! He *wants* to marry you. We can all see that perfectly well, even if you can't."

Phoebe bristled. "Regardless, I do believe my opinion is the one that matters. Besides, I am not sure we would even suit. After all, he is a soldier, and I was raised to reject everything that life represents. Our philosophies and beliefs are a world apart."

"Lucas is no longer a soldier, my dear," Aunt Georgie responded in a cool voice. "Besides, he has no need to apologize for defending his country and his honor, nor should you ask that of him. As for your differing philosophies, I do not believe for a moment they represent an insurmountable impediment to a happy marriage. After all, look at your own parents."

Unable to sit a moment longer, Phoebe jumped to her feet. Turning her back on her relatives, she paced to the alcove window and leaned her burning forehead against the cool glass. She took several deep breaths, trying to find a way through the morass of anxiety and self-doubt.

Her aunt moved to stand behind her. "Has Lucas ever treated you with anything but gentleness and consideration?"

Phoebe winced. "Of course not."

"And you don't really wish to return to America, do you?"

Honesty compelled Phoebe to admit the truth. Returning to her brother's home would be a soul-shattering retreat. "No. I wish to remain in England."

Her aunt breathed a sigh of relief. With a touch, Aunt Georgie turned her around, resting her palms on Phoebe's shoulders. "My child, I understand your doubts. I do not share them. Lucas may not yet comprehend his own heart, but I see it clearly. He needs you in his life, and we need you in our lives. You will help him heal and, in doing so, help heal our family. I only ask you to draw on that faith I know you possess in abundance. If you do, all will be well. I promise."

Blinking back tears, Phoebe felt her resistance start to slip. Her own faith at the moment quivered on shifting sands, but she did believe in Aunt Georgie's wisdom and in the affection of her new family. How could she say no to such a plea from the people she now loved so much, especially when her heart yearned for the same thing? To walk away from Lucas would be like cutting out that same heart and flinging it into the ocean.

"Very well," she said in a quiet voice. "If he wishes it, I will marry Lucas."

Her aunt rewarded her with a blinding smile. "You will make us all very happy, my love, especially Lucas. And I think you will make yourself happy, too."

As Aunt Georgie led her back downstairs, Phoebe tried to convince herself she had made the right decision, both in terms of heart and head. She loved Lucas, and she wanted to be with him. More than anything in her life, she wanted this man and she wanted this family. It was everything she had ever dreamed of in those lonely years back in America.

Why, then, now that her dream was finally within her grasp, did it feel so wrong?

Chapter 16

Phoebe jerked awake when the carriage slowed to a walking pace. She peered out the window into the advancing dusk as shadows and gloom crept over the windswept fields and orchards. Denuded trees thrust their spindly limbs up to the gray November sky, and even the stubbled hay fields, normally glowing with golden color in the setting sun, looked drab and lifeless. They passed through the heart of England's garden, yet everything looked dreary, a perfect match to her own mood. She had spent the last few days in a tumult of anticipation, worry, and outright dread, all leading up to one thing.

Her wedding day.

It did not seem possible that only four days had elapsed since Lady Framingham's ball. Events since then had moved as quickly as the rushing tide, sweeping her along before it. Haste was of the essence, everyone had said, and the sooner Phoebe and Lucas were married and on their way to Mistletoe Manor, the better. She had a sneaking suspicion Aunt Georgie and the rest of the family worried she would change her mind if they left her too long to think about it.

And so a special license had been procured, her new clothes had been packed up in a frenzy, and Phoebe had found herself this morning standing beside Lucas in St. George's Church, in

Hanover Square. She could barely recall the details of the ceremony, feeling more an observer than a participant in her own wedding. Only when they recited their vows and Lucas placed a simple gold ring on her finger had she come to full awareness. Then, trembling, she had forced herself to meet his gaze. His careful and kind courtesy of the last few days had vanished, replaced with something akin to triumph.

Confused, she had stared back, trying to understand the light in his eyes. What triumph was there to be found in such a rushed affair, one that had its roots in scandal and disgrace?

Then, her new husband had retreated once more into formality. They had returned to Stanton House for a small wedding breakfast, attended only by their immediate relatives and a few friends, such as Nigel Dash. Lucas *had* held her hand under the table during the toasts, and that had helped. But when it was time to say their good-byes, sadness at leaving her new family rose to choke her, and tears had scalded her eyelids.

Aunt Georgie and Meredith had hugged her, with many assurances that they would see her in only a week. Lucas, impatient to be on his way, had cast a look up at the threatening sky before gently extracting Phoebe from her aunt's embrace. The door to the carriage had slammed shut and the coachman started the horses to trot. Quiet at last, with only her maid to keep her company, a sense of doom as heavy as a sodden blanket had settled over her. Perhaps if Lucas had joined her in the coach the feeling would have passed, but her new husband had decided to ride his huge bay stallion. Since one of his grooms could have ridden the horse instead, the only logical conclusion was that Lucas preferred the company of his horse—in freezing November weather, too—to hers.

Exhausted and lonely, she had finally wedged herself into a corner and fallen asleep, coming awake only a few minutes ago.

Sighing, she rummaged in her reticule for a handkerchief.

Her freezing nose was beginning to drip, which meant she had to find the silly thing or be reduced to wiping her nose on her sleeve. That image almost made her snicker. The new Countess of Merritt wiping her nose on the sleeve of her expensive new pelisse, like a street urchin. It would almost be worth doing it in public some day, just to horrify the snobs of the ton.

Her maid, who had also been dozing, blinked fully awake and reached for a large bag at her feet. "Here, my lady," Maggie said, extracting a linen handkerchief. "I was so busy seeing to your trunks that I right forgot to make sure you was properly supplied for the journey."

With a grateful murmur, Phoebe took it from the cheerful young woman, who had previously been an upstairs maid at Stanton House. It felt extremely odd to have her own lady's maid, but she supposed she would get used to it. No doubt a great deal faster than she would to being a countess. It was unfortunate no one had ever written a book of instructions for that particular job.

After dabbing her nose, Phoebe folded the linen into a square and stowed it in her reticule. She peered out the window again as the carriage came to a full stop. "We have not reached Mistletoe Manor, have we?"

"Don't think so, my lady. I could lower the glass and ask, if you'd like."

A sharp rap on the coach window startled them both. After pressing a hand to her thumping heart, Phoebe scooted across the seat and let down the glass.

Lucas had reined up by the side of the carriage and leaned down to look in at her. At the sight of his tough, handsome features, her heart thumped even harder.

"I'm sorry if I startled you," he said. "Were you sleeping?"

"No," she replied in a nearly breathless voice. "We were just about to put down the glass and ask if there was a problem."

"It's just a flock of sheep crossing the road." His gaze

flicked over her, coming to rest on her face. "Are you cold? There's an inn only five minutes on. We could stop and warm up, if you like."

Her nose must be as red as she had suspected. "Thank you, but I think not. I am eager to reach the manor."

As he studied her, his mouth kicked up in a charming smile. Even in the gathering gloom she could see the build of heat in his eyes. The intensity of his gaze made her want to fidget.

"I'm eager as well, my sweet," he said. "More than you can imagine."

His masculine rumble brought fire rushing to her cheeks, which he seemed to find amusing. Grinning, he slid an affectionate stroke along her jawline before straightening back on his horse. "Put the window up and get under that blanket, Phoebe. I would be most unhappy if you caught a chill on our wedding night. *Most* unhappy."

"Really, Lucas," she huffed, but he had already spurred his horse ahead. She shoved the glass back up as the carriage started forward.

"Goodness, my lady," exclaimed Maggie, vigorously fanning herself. "If you don't mind me saying so, his lordship is such a handsome man. It's a lucky woman you are, and that's for sure."

Phoebe blinked, not quite sure how to respond to such a candid pronouncement. But Lucas *had* been very affectionate, which was certainly an improvement on his cool, self-controlled behavior of the last few days.

Feeling rather better about things, Phoebe listened to Maggie's cheerful prattle, even responding now and again. In less than half an hour, the carriage turned into a long gravel lane—one that had seen better days by the jostling that almost bounced them out of their seats—and eventually came to a halt in front of the lamp-lit entrance of a house.

As they waited for the carriage door to open, Phoebe

checked that her bonnet was straight. A moment later, the footman let down the steps and Lucas handed her out. Feeling both shy and nervous, she gave him a smile, suddenly very grateful to have his protective presence at her side. She was about to enter into a strange new life with unfamiliar duties and responsibilities, including running a household considerably larger than anything she was used to.

Lucas bent to whisper in her ear. "Courage, Phoebe. I promise all will be well."

Taking a deep breath, she nodded her reply and raised her eyes to the front of the house. The entrance blazed with light, and a number of servants clustered in the open doorway of Mistletoe Manor. The house itself, a massive shadow in the deepening dusk, loomed over them with ill-defined shapes reaching into the sky. She would have to wait for full daylight for a true picture of the building. For now, she simply had the impression of a brick sprawl, with many chimneys and a few shadowed towers.

Lucas urged her forward, his gloved hand warmly resting at the base of her spine. A rotund woman with a broad smile came bustling down the steps to greet them. "Lord Merritt, welcome home."

"My dear, allow me to introduce you to Mistletoe Manor's housekeeper," Lucas said in a voice as dry as the champagne served at their wedding breakfast. "This is Mrs. Christmas. Mrs. *Honor* Christmas."

Phoebe froze, wondering if Lucas was jesting. *Honor Christmas at Mistletoe Manor?* When she cut a quick glance to his face, his long-suffering expression told her he was not.

"Mrs. . . . Mrs. Christmas," Phoebe stammered. "It's an . . . honor to meet you."

She repressed a groan at her idiotic response. She had a sinking feeling she might have already failed her first test as a countess by unintentionally insulting their housekeeper.

Thankfully, Mrs. Christmas seemed immune to insult.

"Lord love you, my lady," she said with a chuckle. "There's no need to feel one bit uncomfortable with my name. Christmases have been serving the Merritts of Mistletoe Manor since the time of the Jacobite kings, and right proud of the tradition we are. With any luck, there will be many more generations of Christmases to come."

"Indeed," interjected Lucas in a sardonic voice. "But I would suggest we introduce her ladyship to the rest of the servants inside, lest we expire of a chill before the holiday comes to the manor."

Mrs. Christmas's round face scrunched up with comic dismay. "Right you are, my lord. Forgive me, your ladyship, but a woman of my size rarely feels the cold." She punctuated her comment by laughing heartily, her large form shaking with mirth. The woman was so irrepressibly cheerful that Phoebe wanted to join in the laughter. She likely would have, but Lucas looked increasingly impatient.

He took her arm to guide her inside. As they passed under the portico, she glanced up at him and mouthed *Mrs. Christmas?* She expected him to smile, but he just rolled his eyes, looking aggravated. She did not understand why, because on first glance the housekeeper appeared a cheerful, kind soul.

They stepped into a large, timbered hall that looked ancient, at least to Phoebe's eyes. A giant fireplace, large enough to roast an entire cow, was set into the back wall, and there were a few groupings of old-fashioned-looking furniture that seemed inadequate and rather shabby in the cavernous space. Several branches of candles stood on some side tables and a fire crackled on the hearth, but her instant impression was of a dim, shadowy room, the long passage of centuries stamped irrevocably on the walls.

For all that, it seemed clean and tidy.

"My lady, allow me to introduce you to the rest of the staff," Lucas said.

Intent on hiding her nerves, Phoebe forced a smile as she

faced a line of people stretching down the length of the hall. First up was a gaunt little man dressed neatly in black.

"This is our butler," Lucas said. "Mr. Christmas."

When Phoebe's jaw dropped, the butler sighed and gave a morose bow, as if he could not be more pained by the situation. "Your ladyship, welcome to Mistletoe Manor," he intoned in a gloomy voice.

Phoebe turned to her husband. "Really?" she asked in a faint voice.

This time his mouth twitched suspiciously.

Mrs. Christmas let out another peal of laughter. "To be sure, my lady, he is. That be my cousin, Solomon Christmas, and very aptly named he is, too, since he's the most solemn man I've ever met. Doesn't seem right for a Christmas, now does it?"

Dumbfounded, Phoebe stared at her new housekeeper. Were all the servants so forward? She had never noticed anything like that at Stanton House, but she began to wonder.

She glanced at Lucas for support, but the evil glint in his eye told her not to expect any from that quarter. The wretched man had finally begun to enjoy himself, and at her expense.

"I am certain Mr. Christmas is just as he ought to be," Phoebe said, sounding anything but certain. "Thank you for such a kind welcome."

"You're welcome, my lady," the butler replied, every bit as gloomy as he had been a moment ago. Mrs. Christmas gave another hearty laugh and Phoebe began to wonder if she had wandered into a madhouse, albeit a harmless one.

Fortunately, Lucas intervened and introduced the rest of the servants—maids, footmen, most of the kitchen staff, the head gardener, and the head groom. An astounding number of them carried the last name of Christmas, and they all appeared inordinately proud of it.

Except for the butler, who she suspected was perpetually glum. The rest obviously coexisted as one large, happy family, devoting their lives to the welfare of the manor and the Merritt family.

Devoted, but also quite lacking in discipline. The younger ones, especially, whispered behind their hands, and made no bones about carrying on merry conversations with each other and cheerfully commenting on the earl's "pretty lady." She also thought she heard a few approving if innocent comments from the men. A sideways peek at Lucas's long-suffering expression confirmed her suspicions.

By the time she reached the end of the line, Phoebe was biting the inside of her cheeks to hold back a semihysterical laugh. No wonder Lucas had looked so pained when Robert teased him about the manor. The entire staff might have been transported from one of the holiday pantomimes her mother used to describe, and that was not something that would appeal to a man like Lucas. He was a soldier, and soldiers liked order and organization. On first impression, those qualities appeared lacking in their new home.

Phoebe exhaled a tiny sigh of relief as Lucas introduced her to his valet, Mr. Popham. Lucas had told her that Popham had served him in the army as his batman, and was a competent man with a good deal of common sense. From the few vague statements her husband had made to her about Mistletoe Manor in the last few days—deliberately vague, she now suspected—he relied heavily on Popham in dealing with the estate's many problems.

Now those problems were hers, too. No matter her doubts about the marriage, it was time to take up the responsibilities that had been thrust upon her. In that way, at least, she could be of use to Lucas, rather than adding to his burdens.

"Thank—" she bit back an errant *thee*, "*you* for your kind welcome, and for your work on behalf of my husband and the earl before him, my grandfather. It gives me great pleasure to finally come to Mistletoe Manor, which Grandfather so loved and which will now be my beloved home, too."

Her speech won her several approving nods and murmurs, boosting her courage. "I would ask for your patience and help over the next few weeks as I become familiar with you and with the workings of this great house. I have much to learn, and I will be relying on all of you for your assistance."

She glanced up at Lucas. His expression was a trifle stern, as it often was, but his eyes smiled and even, she hoped, held a bit of pride. Taking a deep breath, she reached over and took his hand. Immediately, his fingers closed around hers, and a tentative joy stole through her. "I am very happy to be among you," she said. "With your support, I am confident we will restore Mistletoe Manor to full prosperity and beauty."

The staff erupted into a round of cheers. No doubt their behavior would be frowned upon in so correct an establishment as Stanton House, but Phoebe could not bring herself to fault them. As she smiled at the happy little mob in the hall, Lucas tugged her a few inches closer.

"Well done, my lady," he murmured in her ear. "You'll have them eating out of your hand in no time, exactly like your grandfather. God knows I haven't mastered the trick yet."

His praise dispelled the last of her gloom. "Thank you, Lucas. I will try to do my best."

"I have no doubt of that, sweetheart." He cast a quick glance around the hall, then turned his gaze back to her. "And now," he purred in a seductive voice, "perhaps you would like to see the rest of the house. Starting, I think, with the bedroom."

Chapter 17

Phoebe had almost fainted when Lucas suggested they tour the bedrooms first. The thought of facing her wedding night before unpacking—even before dinner—unnerved her as nothing else had done that day. But, thankfully, he had only been teasing. When she had stammered out a jumbled excuse, Lucas had rolled his eyes before escorting her upstairs to her suite. Once there, he had left her alone to settle in.

That had been something of a shock. After his smoldering glances and suggestive remarks in the hall, Lucas's transformation back into the coolly polite aristocrat had left her confused. One moment he studied her with a warm, eager regard. The next, he treated her much as he would any other member of the Stanton family, a truly disconcerting notion for a bride on her wedding night.

As she sat in front of the old and battered dressing table in her bedroom brushing out her hair, she reluctantly acknowledged that Lucas had treated her with more affection before their precipitous engagement and marriage. Since that fateful night at the ball, he had retreated behind a courteous but rather distant facade that did nothing to ease her doubts about their future together.

She grimaced at her reflection in the smoky glass. Her new

husband was sometimes as obscure as a cipher, and trying to puzzle him out struck her as a waste of time. Only by living with him would she find the answers she sought. She would pray that they would grow happily into their life as man and wife, finding common purpose in restoring Mistletoe Manor and eventually creating a family. Perhaps then he would learn to love her, and she would be able to cast aside her doubts and fears.

But first she had to get through tonight, and that thought hollowed out her stomach. Part of her longed to be back in his arms, experiencing the thrilling sensation of his touch, but she dreaded the encounter, too. She knew only of the essential details of marital relations, and she worried she would disappoint him. Tonight was not just her wedding night—it would be the cornerstone of their marriage and of their dealings with each other. How well it went would set the tone for much to come. They were alone here at Mistletoe Manor, with no other friends and family to occupy them or deflect blame or disappointment. She and Lucas would find their way to each other, relying only on themselves, or founder on a sea of awkwardness, regret, and lost opportunities.

Putting down her hairbrush, Phoebe silently vowed she would not let that happen. She *would* make Lucas happy. If only she was not so ridiculously innocent when it came to—

The old clock on the mantelpiece whirred and then chimed out the late hour in a rusty tone. Where was Lucas? After their first dinner together as husband and wife—ridiculously separated by the immense length of the dining room table—he had repaired to his study for a brandy. But if she had to wait for him much longer, she would likely expire from a fatal case of nerves. With her stomach twisted in knots and her palms damp, his lingering over his brandy was conducive to neither her confidence nor her patience. As much as she worried over what was to transpire, she wanted to get on with it and hoped her nerves would settle once Lucas began to kiss her. She did quite like the kissing they had done that night at Lady Framingham's, and she hoped to like it even more now as his wife.

To give herself something to do with her fidgety hands, she began to weave her hair into a tight braid until Maggie's horrified exclamation stopped her. "No, my lady! Don't be pulling it back so tightly. You're like to yank half your hairs out of your head."

The maid bustled over from straightening up the old press cupboard in the corner and pushed her hands away, quickly undoing the braid. Smiling over Phoebe's shoulder, she took a hank from the top, wove it into a loose, attractive braid, and let the rest tumble over her back and shoulders.

"But I always put my hair up for bed," Phoebe protested. "And wear a cap."

"Not tonight, my lady. You have beautiful hair, and men like to see their ladies wear it down like this. As for your cap—" She grabbed Phoebe's white sleeping cap and whisked it away under her apron. "His lordship won't be wanting his bride to be looking like some old granny now, will he?"

Then Maggie gave her a broad wink, which had Phoebe biting down on her lip to hold back a horrified laugh. She would have to do something about the girl's carefree regard for bedroom matters, as soon as she mustered up the nerve and the appropriate words to address the subject.

Not right now, though. Dealing with her husband was enough for one night. "Oh, very well," she said. "I'll keep it down for tonight."

She leaned forward, peering into the mirror. Her eyes seemed almost feverish and her cheeks were flushed, but Maggie was right. The tumble of dark, curling locks around her face and shoulders suited her, and Phoebe possessed enough vanity to wish to look pretty for her new husband. She just hoped she looked as enticing as Esme Newton, the only other woman Lucas had ever wanted to marry.

Fortunately, before she could worry that idea to the bone,

a quiet knock sounded on the connecting door from Lucas's suite. "Enter," she called, wincing at the break in her voice.

The door opened and Lucas strolled in. He had removed his coat and waistcoat, and was clad only in an open-necked shirt and trousers. In one hand he deftly balanced two crystal tumblers of amber liquid. Brandy, she assumed. Phoebe usually turned her nose up at strong spirits, but tonight she was more than prepared to make an exception.

On legs that trembled, she rose to greet him, managing a shy smile.

"Good evening, my love," Lucas said in that husky voice she was beginning to recognize. It did nothing to still the tremors in her legs—or in her stomach, for that matter. Gazing at his strong, broad-shouldered body did the oddest things to her insides. Not unpleasant things, but certainly unsettling and unfamiliar.

Maggie bobbed a curtsy even as she gave Phoebe a knowing little smile. "Will you be needing anything else, my lady?"

"No, Maggie. You may go."

The maid threw her another wink so broad Phoebe almost gasped, then whisked herself out of the room. Mortified, Phoebe met her husband's ironic gaze. "I do apologize for Maggie's behavior," she sighed. "I cannot imagine why she is so interested in our private intimacies."

Lucas gave a little snort as he strolled up to her. "She's not the only servant in this house to remark upon it. I must say, their manners do seem to harken back to the older generation. I'm surprised they didn't insist on attending the bedding, like some damn medieval ceremony." He shook his head, looking baffled. "And they all seem to blurt out whatever they're thinking and to hell with the fact that I'm supposedly their lord and master. It's remarkably unnerving, though I must say your grandfather never seemed to mind it."

Phoebe gratefully took the glass he offered, wondering at the glimpse into Grandfather's life.

"Perhaps in his loneliness he found their manners a comfort," she said. "I understand he was quite reclusive, especially after the death of my uncle."

"He was reclusive indeed," Lucas replied absently as he wandered over to one of the mullioned windows. The housekeeper had left it open a crack to air out the room, but now a cold wind stirred the thick, faded drapes and swirled with a nasty bite around Phoebe's bare ankles. He seized the handle, wrestled with it, and finally managed to yank the window shut. It closed with an unexpected bang, and a little shower of plaster dust filtered down from somewhere above the window.

Lucas scowled up at the ceiling before throwing her a rueful glance. "I'm sorry to have brought you to such a ramshackle house, Phoebe. I'm sure it was not what you expected."

"I do not mind at all," she said truthfully. "I was just a bit surprised."

What little she had seen of the manor was spotless, but it was clear that something had been amiss for a long time. Carpets were faded and threadbare, furniture was worn, and in some of the rooms she had spied the wallpaper peeling back, exposing mildew and damp. The neglect spoke volumes about her grandfather's state of mind in the years preceding his death, and that saddened her.

With a heavy sigh, Lucas sat down on a low armchair in front of the chimneypiece. "Still, I could have wished for a better homecoming for my bride."

Falling into a brown study, he stared into the flames.

Putting down her glass, Phoebe pulled her wrapper tight against the chill and came to him, gingerly sitting on the creaky footstool at his feet. "I knew there were some problems, but why did you not tell me conditions were so bad?"

He reached to gently stroke her hair, the wry smile returning to his lips. His touch soothed her, even as tingles of awareness shivered through her body.

"I didn't want to scare you off. If you knew how bad it was, you might have run screaming back to America."

"Lucas, you know very well I was not raised in the lap of luxury, and I am certainly not afraid of hard work. In fact, I welcome it."

She hesitated, then carefully placed her hands on his knee. "If I can help you restore the manor and the estate to order, then I will be less of a burden to you."

His body seemed to turn to stone under her fingers. His face did, too, although his eyes blazed with a dangerous heat. Then, so quickly she barely saw the movement, his arms lashed out and circled her waist. Alarmed, she squeaked out a protest when he swept her up in a rush and plunked her onto his lap. She grabbed the front of his shirt to steady herself.

Warm, calloused hands captured her face as he brought her close. Her heart stuttered as he studied her with an intense, heavy-lidded stare.

"Phoebe, you are not a burden to me, and you are forbidden to say that again. Do you understand?"

Butterflies danced in her stomach, but the raw sexuality in his eyes set off another kind of fluttering lower down—one that eagerly anticipated his touch. That was odd, since he was clearly annoyed with her, but she suspected another emotion—the one that made her quiver—also drove him.

She found herself unable to resist temptation's dark urgings. She flicked her tongue out, dampening lips gone suddenly dry. His gaze fastened on her mouth.

"And what will you do if I do not obey you?" she challenged in a breathless voice.

One hand left her face to slide down her spine to her rump. Through the delicate cambric of her night rail and wrapper, his hand felt huge and hot and wonderful. She squeaked again when it slipped underneath, settling her more comfortably in his lap.

When he removed it a moment later, her eyes widened in

startled amazement. Something else nudged her bottom, and it also felt huge and hot and . . . wonderful, too.

When she wriggled against it, he drew in a sharp breath. He held her steady as he dipped his head, his mouth brushing over hers in a moist, teasing press of lips. Phoebe clutched at him, sighing with pleasure, but he broke the kiss all too soon.

"I will show you, Wife, what happens when you don't obey my commands. Especially in the bedroom."

Underneath her fingertips, his heart thumped with a strong, rapid beat. Hers did, too, as he came back to nuzzle her mouth with tempting kisses, his hand stroking along her jaw. Down that hand went, over her neck, her collarbone, and finally settling on her breast. He cupped it, fondling the nipple, and she thought her heart really just might beat out of her chest.

With a helpless shudder, she curled into his teasing fingers. His other hand spanned her back, supporting her. He held her steady as he played with her breast, gently rubbing and tweaking the nipple until it contracted into a hard, aching bead. When he grasped it with the tips of his fingers, pulling gently, she felt an answering tug in the deepest part of her body. And between her legs, in that hidden, intimate place, she felt a hot slick of moisture.

Clutching the edges of Lucas's shirt, Phoebe broke away from the kiss. She stared at him, panting and disoriented by the rush of sensation. He stared back, his gaze hot and slumberous, and that look made her shiver again.

"What is it, love?" he asked in a deep, low voice.

Carefully, she spread her fingers across his chest, taking comfort in the solid strength of him. She was hot and muddled, excited and scared, not knowing whether she wanted to wrap herself around him or run away. "I feel rather strange. My body . . ." she trailed off, unable to express what she felt.

The hand stroking her back reassured her. The seductive smile he gave her did anything but. "What you feel is natural, Phoebe. Your body is getting ready to accept mine."

She bit her lip. He seemed to like that, if the flare of heat in his eyes was any indication.

"How . . . how is it getting ready?" she asked.

It might be an indelicate question, but she truly wanted to know. This morning, as she changed in preparation for the journey to Kent, Meredith had spoken to her about what would happen on the wedding night. Phoebe had formed a general idea, of course, but Meredith's frank, calmly delivered description left her gaping at the details, too embarrassed to ask the questions that might have cleared up her resulting confusion.

"I know this is all very disconcerting," Meredith had said in a soothing voice, "but you mustn't worry too much. Lucas will do everything he can to make you comfortable." Then her cousin had given her a sly grin. "Well, more than comfortable, actually. Just trust that he will take care of you, and everything will be fine."

It was the trust part Phoebe was having trouble with.

She had ducked her head when she muttered her question to him, but he tipped her chin up so he could inspect her face. "Do you really not know?" he asked, his brows arching. "Did no one ever tell you?"

"Lucas," she said between clenched teeth, "my mother died when I was fourteen, and my father a few years after. Who do you think would have explained the precise mechanics to me—my brother, George?"

A quick grin flashed across his face. When she scowled at him, he dropped an apologetic kiss on her lips. "I'm sorry, Phoebe. I should have realized the problem. Well, you may have noticed that a man's . . . ah . . . appendage tends to grow quite a bit larger when . . . stimulated."

His stilted explanation had her rolling her eyes. "I am quite sure you do not usually refer to it as an *appendage*. That sounds quite distasteful."

He laughed. "You're right about that."

"Just tell me what you call it, please. In simple language."

"Well, I suppose I would call it my cock," he said in a rather strangled voice.

"Your *cock*," she said, rolling it around on her tongue. She wriggled again, just to test if what he said was true.

It was. It had grown even bigger than it had been just a moment ago.

"Jesus, Phoebe," he gasped, looking pained. "Sit still before you cripple me."

She peered into his glazed eyes. "Did I hurt you, Lucas? I am so sorry."

He closed his eyelids, as if gathering himself. His cheekbones were flushed a dark bronze, and he seemed to be clenching his teeth. "Not precisely, my dear. But it would be best if you not move around too much at this juncture, or we might find our evening coming to a rather ignominious end."

She frowned. What did he mean by that?

And just like that, her courage deserted her. She had too many questions, too many fears, and this was all too sudden and overwhelming for her to absorb. In so many ways she hardly knew the man who was now her husband, and the idea of turning both her physical and emotional self over to him had her at sea.

"Perhaps we should not do this," she said. "It has been a very long day, and you must be exhausted." She started to slide off his lap, but he caught her, holding her in place.

"No, my love," he said in a gentler voice. "You're not going anywhere." He studied her with a sharply perceptive gaze that made her want to squirm.

"Lucas," she started, her voice trembling.

"Phoebe, are you afraid of me?"

"N . . . no. Not of you, exactly. It is all this," she said lamely. She waved her arm in a circle, as if that explained everything.

"Of sex?"

She winced, too humiliated to admit it.

He wrapped his arms around her, cuddling her close. Grateful to escape that penetrating gaze, she huddled against him with her head down. He held her like that, waiting for her to recover her voice.

"I know it seems silly of me," she said, her voice muffled in his shirt. "But I do not really know thee very well. Nor thee, me."

He let out a husky laugh that vibrated through his body and into hers. "Love, I know you very well. I know you are a sweet, kind person and a beautiful woman." He nudged her upright, forcing her to look at him. "And I've wanted you from almost the first moment I met you. That has not changed, I can assure you."

The devilment in his gaze made every part of her body tingle. Still, she found that hard to believe, especially since she had been a pale, sick-looking creature those first few days after they met.

"Truly? Even looking like an old, sick crow?"

He smiled. "You could never look like a crow. Phoebe, love, would you like me to show you how much I want you?"

His gentle request for permission began to unravel the coil of fear in her gut. And left her feeling rather foolish. After all, Lucas was her husband, and she had vowed to honor and cherish him, body and soul. She loved him, too. To withhold herself seemed somehow sinful. As if she was closing herself off from him and from the sacred promises she had made before God.

She gave him a tentative smile. "Yes. I would like that."

His sea smoke eyes seemed to lighten and a mischievous grin tugged at his mouth. "Thank God. Stand up, love, and let's get this robe off so I can properly show you how much you tempt me."

Blushing, she clambered off his lap. Lucas sat up and spread his legs, gently tugging her to stand between them. She could not help glancing down, caught by how large the bulge pressing against the fall of his breeches appeared to be.

He gave a deep chuckle, and she yanked her gaze back up to his face.

"Do you remember what it's called?" he asked with a wicked grin.

Phoebe rolled her eyes, refusing to be bested by him. "It is called your cock."

He tugged her closer, gently gripping her legs with the inside of his muscled thighs. "Very good. I predict you'll be an able pupil."

Then he unbuttoned her wrapper at the throat and down over her chest. When he eased it open, he let his fingers brush her nipples. They tingled to life once again, drawing into rigid points that thrust through the thin material of her night rail.

Lucas pushed the wrapper off her shoulders to the floor, then cupped her breasts with his hands. The sight of his long, tanned fingers shaping her through the delicate white fabric brought a whimper to her throat.

"I very much like these," he murmured. "So plump, with beautiful, rosy tips." He pulled the fabric taut so they could both see the dark outline of her nipples through the fabric. She drew in a shaky breath as the stiff points throbbed with anticipation.

As if he read her mind, he leaned forward and flicked his tongue over one nipple. Sensation arced through her, and she rose up on her toes. "Lucas," she choked out, grasping his shoulders.

"Mmm. So sensitive. I suspected as much."

Then, so slowly it made her heart pound, his fingers moved up to her neck to undo the laces of her night rail. When her breathing grew shallow, his gaze came up to look at her. His eyes held an understanding she did not expect from so tough and formidable a man.

Leaning in, he pressed a brief, tender kiss on her lips. "Relax, sweetheart. I'll take care of you. I promise."

She nodded, trying to smile back. She must have failed rather miserably, because his fingers stilled.

"Do you trust me, Phoebe?" He voiced the question calmly, without any irritation. He exuded confidence, and the sense that when he made a promise, he would hold to it. If he promised to take care of her, then he would.

Her body relaxed under his hands. "Yes, Lucas. I do trust you."

He rewarded her with a slow, seductive smile that devastated her senses. His gaze fell once more to his hands as they finished untying her bodice. Carefully, he eased the garment down her shoulders and arms, over her breasts, finally pushing the bunched material around her waist. His calloused hands caressed her skin, and he touched her with a reverence that brought a sting of tears to her eyes.

"Like cream and silk," he murmured. "I've been waiting to touch you . . . to feel you under my hands."

She watched, fascinated, as his hands trailed over her shoulders, tracing the lines of her body, raising goose bumps in their wake.

"And these," he murmured, tracing a finger over the swell of her breast. "So full, so soft." He touched her nipple with one finger, rubbing gently. It contracted into a hard, aching point. She moaned as the goose bumps on her skin turned into shivers of delight.

His gaze, scorching hot, lifted to meet hers. "How could I not want these, Phoebe? Your breasts are so damn pretty I could feast on them for hours."

Her mouth dropped open. *Feast on them?* Her knees turned to mush, and she had to grab his shoulders to remain upright.

A husky laugh rumbled up from his throat, and then he returned his attention to her breasts. Capturing them in his big hands, he kneaded until her flesh felt heavy, becoming more sensitive the longer he played with them.

And play he did, especially with her nipples. He gently pulled on them with the tips of his fingers, then brushed his calloused palms across them, over and over again. They burned with sensation, and a pleasure so sharp it almost pained her. With each brush, each gentle twist, her nipples grew harder, rosier, and so hot she longed for more. But more of what?

More of Lucas, a voice whispered in her head.

She drew in a shuddering sob and her breasts quivered, rising and falling with her panting breath. He growled, dipping his head to plant a kiss and then a lick on the white swell of one breast, just above the nipple. The wet heat of his tongue made her knees buckle, and he had to hold her upright between his thighs.

"Lucas," she moaned, investing his name with a desperate plea.

His eyes almost closed as he inhaled the scent of her skin, then brushed his bristle-roughened cheek against her nipple. That sent a bolt of sensation soaring through her, piercing her to the core. Her inner muscles seemed to spasm, throbbing with a liquid heat. "Oh, my," she gasped, her eyes opening wide.

His gaze, heavy-lidded and predatory, flicked upward.

"Do you like that?" he asked. His voice was so deep, so husky, it made everything in her flame hotter. "Do you like it when I do this?" His fingers captured both nipples, and he gently tugged them into aching points.

"Yes," she sobbed, clutching at his shoulders. The muscles under her fingers felt like bands of iron.

"Do you want more?" he growled.

Desire rolled through her, beating thickly in her veins. She did want more, more of whatever it was he could give her. It was more than wanting. It was a need that charged her with a restless energy only he could assuage. "Yes," she panted. "Please, Lucas. I need more."

He made a deep, masculine noise and his hand clamped across her bottom, nudging her forward. Then his mouth came on her, swift and sure, and she suddenly understood what he meant by *feasting*. Sucking hard on her nipple one moment, licking across it with a hot stroke of the tongue the next. One hand gripped her bottom to hold her firmly in place, but his other hand was busy, too, kneading one breast while his mouth devoured the other.

Phoebe writhed under the lash of his tongue, snared by sensation. She felt undone, not herself, and exposed in every way possible. But even as she clutched at the edges of reason, she sensed he would keep his vow. Lucas would keep her safe in his strong arms, as she gave in to the feelings rushing through her.

He swirled his tongue over her nipple, then gave a hard suck, one so intensely pleasurable it wrenched a thin shriek from her throat. She froze, aghast at herself.

Lucas blinked and looked up at her. When he took in her expression, he let out a hoarse chuckle.

"Sweetheart, it's fine. You're supposed to make noise when you enjoy it."

She stared at him doubtfully, still holding his broad shoulders in a death grip. "But now everyone will know exactly what we are doing."

"They would have deduced that in any event. It is our wedding night, after all."

She groaned and closed her eyes. "You must think I am a complete hen-wit."

His hands came to her waist, stroking her. "I think you're the most beautiful woman I've ever met."

The genuine admiration in his voice made her smile, even though she did not yet open her eyes.

"Truly?"

He gave a dramatic sigh, and she raised her eyelids to catch his grin.

"I suppose you need more convincing, don't you?" he asked.

She touched his cheek, and he turned to kiss her palm. Love for him, so strong it took her breath, pulsed through her, as did a flash of understanding that she wanted him more now than she had ever wanted anything.

Needing a moment to recover from the breath-stealing emotion, Phoebe tilted her head, pretending to give the question serious consideration. His eyes, warm with amusement and understanding, glittered back at her.

"Yes, I believe I do. In fact," she said as a reckless excitement coursed through her, "as your wife, I insist upon it."

He bared his teeth in a wolfish smile. "My precious lady, I am yours to command."

Chapter 18

Phoebe stared back at him, her beautiful eyes wide with conflicting emotions. Lucas saw a touching mix of eagerness and vulnerability, along with a large dollop of uncertainty in those sherry-colored depths. It was a heady combination, one that brought forth in him an answering mix of tenderness and lust. He had vowed to be careful with her, but his gut clenched and his muscles burned with the effort to hold himself back.

The fact that she stood between his legs, naked to the waist, didn't help his self-control. Phoebe's beautiful body, awakening to passion, would try any man's discipline. And now she asked for more.

He was happy to comply.

The hardest part—aside from his cock—would be controlling his own rampaging need to get her flat on her back, her legs wrapped around him as he drove into her, slaking what had to be the most insane lust a man had ever felt. But he wouldn't do that to her. Both delicate and innocent, Phoebe had been raised to know very little about relations between men and women. More than anything, he wanted to make her first sexual experience one of complete pleasure and trust.

Looking at her now, with her dewy skin and nipples stiff with arousal, he had every confidence she would prove a quick study. And Lucas would certainly enjoy tutoring her in the lessons of love—of the physical kind, that is. That he was more than willing to give.

She tilted her head, obviously wondering at his silence. Smiling to reassure her, he dusted the tip of his finger across one rosy nipple. She bit her lip, drawing in a breath that lifted the soft globes in a perfect quiver. Christ, she had the prettiest breasts he had ever seen—white and full and topped with berry red nipples. They'd tasted sweet and ripe like berries, too, and he couldn't wait to sample them again.

"Look at you, Phoebe," he breathed as desire pounded through his veins. "So lovely. I can hardly wait to be inside you."

Her mouth rounded into a surprised little circle. "I . . . I want that, too, Lucas," she replied in a hesitant voice.

He gave a soft laugh. His little love was doing her best to please him, but he didn't think she was quite ready for that yet. He had every intention of pleasuring her first, making her body shake with passion as she came for him for the first time. "Soon, love," he murmured. "Just keep holding on to me. Whatever happens, don't let go."

She raised a questioning eyebrow but firmly pressed her fingers into his shoulders. She squared her own slender shoulders, obviously preparing for whatever he had in mind. The slight movement lifted her breasts high. Lust prowled through him at the sight, and he knew a time would come when he would spend long minutes playing with her luscious tits, making her climax from that alone.

But not tonight. Tonight was for claiming her as his wife.

Gently, he slid the endearingly plain night rail from her waist and let it pool around her feet. Her breath hitched and a blush raced from chest to throat, and up to pink her cheeks. Every masculine instinct he possessed purred with satisfaction, supremely pleased with her innocence. His rational mind knew how ridiculous that was, but nothing about Phoebe made him feel rational.

He took in her narrow waist, her smooth stomach, and the delicious flare of her hips. His Phoebe was slender, but she had a woman's curves nonetheless. As he let his gaze travel down to the nest of curls between her legs, dark and silky as mink, he reached around to palm her pretty bottom, luxuriating in the curves that were now his to enjoy.

She sucked on her full lower lip, and his erection pressed in a heavy ache against the fall of his breeches. Soon he would relieve that ache in her virginal heat, but for now he would very much enjoy preparing her tight passage to receive him.

He slid his other hand to her bottom, kneading the firm little globes with a slow, rhythmic pressure. She took a tiny step closer to him, her eyelids fluttering with pleasure. Her movement brought her breasts close to his mouth. Unable to resist, he sucked one of the hard little points into his mouth. He gently closed his teeth around it, giving her the slightest of nips. She gasped, fingernails digging into his shirt. That pleased him, too. Phoebe would do that to him when they were both naked, he was sure, and he would take a great satisfaction in the marking.

He held her in a firm grip as he leisurely tongued and teased her, slowly driving her wild. She trembled in his grasp and hot little whimpers rose from her throat. Her nipple was stiff and hard in his mouth, and yet as silky and smooth as a pearl. He'd never felt or tasted anything better, and the temptation to linger was acute.

But with a last, hard suck, he pulled his mouth free. Phoebe moaned and swayed on her feet. Her head tilted back and her thick hair streamed over her shoulders, a shiny river of ebony in the glow of the firelight. She was a perfect image of a woman abandoning herself to seduction and passion.

And yet her essential innocence still shimmered in the air about her. Lucas would never mistake her burgeoning passion for wantonness. Phoebe's passion was as pure as the woman herself, and just as true. In her innocence and trust she hid nothing from him, and it captured his heart in a way he had no longer thought possible. That seemed something of a miracle, and not one he necessarily welcomed.

He steadied her, reining his own turbulent feelings under control. He had no desire to muddy the already complex waters of their relationship with unreliable emotions. Not tonight, anyway, and never, if at all possible. With her, he wanted simplicity, not the tortured needs and obsessions that too often came with what other men called love.

Her eyelids fluttered open. "Why are you stopping?"

He let out a husky laugh. "I have no intention of stopping."

Wrapping his hand around her neck, he pulled her down for a soft kiss. "Ready?" he growled against her mouth.

A pleasure-laden sigh breathed out from between her lips. "Oh, yes. I am very ready for more, Lucas."

Then her eyes flew open as she heard her own words. She winced, but when he grinned she let out an embarrassed laugh. "Honestly. Thee makes me say the most ridiculous things."

He gently pushed her upright, carefully positioning her between his knees. "Not ridiculous, love. Enticing." Then he slipped his hands between her silky-smooth thighs and nudged her to open them. "Slide your feet wider," he urged.

She blushed as red as fire, but obeyed him. If he wasn't mistaken, a very small but eager smile played around the corners of her mouth.

Gently, he stroked circles on her inner thighs, building her anticipation. With each pass he stroked higher, moving ever closer to her tempting folds. When delicate tremors began to shiver through her muscles, he moved one hand back to her bottom to support her. Phoebe reacted so strongly to his touch that he feared she might collapse in a heap on the floor when he finally delved deep.

After a few leisurely moments of playing with her that way, he finally brushed one hand up between the outer folds of her already-drenched flesh. When she startled, clutching at his shoulders, it gave him the perfect excuse to kiss the succulent breast bobbing in front of his face. As he sucked a nipple back into his mouth, he also gently slipped his hand between her soft folds. When his fingertip connected with the hard little bud hidden there, she jerked up on her toes, as if a bolt of lightning had charged through her body.

"Lucas!"

He tilted his head back to look into her eyes. They were opened wide, the pupils dilated, as a hectic flush swept over her cheekbones. She gazed down at him, seemingly shocked by the sensations storming through her body. Her wondering expression, so innocent and yet so sensual, drove a shaft of heat straight to his groin. Jesus, he might yet come simply from looking at her.

"Do you like that?" he rumbled, drawing a languid stroke through her damp heat.

She gasped and her eyelids grew heavy. "I . . . I think so."

Lucas found the tight little bud again and gently rubbed it. She unconsciously clamped her thighs around his hand. "No, love," he murmured as he again urged her legs apart. "You'll feel more if you keep yourself open to me."

She exhaled on a quivering sob, but without any more urging planted her feet wider apart. Her compliance kicked up his pulse, driving his own needs up another urgent notch. With a shaking hand, he stroked her, dragging his fingers back and forth over the tight knot hidden in her drenched curls.

Phoebe's eyelids fluttered shut and she began to move against his hand. With his other hand, he cupped her bottom, and then increased the rhythm, pushing the heel of his palm against her hard bud. She jerked and cried out again, but he held her firmly in his grasp, not yet ready to let her come.

"L . . . Lucas," she stuttered. "Please!"

Her hands slid from his shoulders to his biceps and she squeezed him in a tight grasp. As she rode his hand, her lush tits quivered in front of his face. He wanted to tongue and suck on them to his heart's content but, more than that, he wanted to see her beautiful face when she climaxed.

"What, Phoebe?" he growled. "What do you want?"

"I . . . I want more. Touch me harder," she panted out in a desperate voice.

He let out a harsh laugh, barely recognizing it as his own. Palming her in a hard grip, he held her still as he slipped two fingers into her hot, wet sheath. Her muscles contracted around his fingers and she tried to rise up again on her toes.

"Oh, oh," she gasped, squeezing her eyes shut.

He toyed with her like that for several moments, even though the sight of her was driving him into a state of agonized lust. But it was all too beautiful to end just yet. Her body quivered with her approaching climax, and her skin dewed with passion. Her slick, hot flesh seemed to melt around his hand as he played with her drenched softness. Now, as he pumped two fingers into her sheath, she tried to press against him, blindly seeking relief.

It was time.

Suddenly, he removed his hand and her eyes flew open. It took her a moment to focus, but then she stared at him, confused.

"Lucas," she wailed, sounding aggrieved. "Why are you stopping?"

"Because I want you to look at me during the next part. Keep your eyes open, my love."

She bit her lip and tilted her hips into his hand. The contact of his palm against her hard little bud brought a fresh gasp to her lips and her eyelids started to flutter closed.

"Keep them open, Phoebe," he commanded.

She pulled in a deep breath and fixed her gaze on him. Her eyes shone with a newfound sensual knowledge and her lips curved into a hot little smile.

"Whatever you say, Lucas," she breathed.

His cock jerked with greedy anticipation, and he gave a soft laugh. Once more he slipped his fingers inside her wet passage, thrusting them deep inside. As he pumped, he rubbed the heel of his hand against her bud. She moved against him, and this time he let her control the movement.

As he watched her, his body flamed with an agonizing need. Her glistening pink flesh seemed to open around his hand, swelling with excitement. Her breath hitched in her throat, and he knew she hovered on the brink.

Gripping her rump tight, he pumped two fingers as his thumb pressed against her. Phoebe grabbed his shoulders, arched her back, and flew into her climax. Her passage contracted around his fingers and a shudder raced through her body as she found her relief. Holding her tight, Lucas clenched his teeth, fighting to keep his own response under control. He had every intention of being inside her when he came, not disgracing himself on his wedding night.

He brought her down gently, softly cupping her mound as her release shuddered through her. After several long moments she finally calmed, and he could feel the tension in her limbs give way to a trembling relaxation. When her knees began to collapse, he hooked an arm under them and lifted her into his lap.

As Lucas cradled her, she subsided against him with a long, drawn-out sigh. His cock was on fire and he thought his head might explode, but he had never felt more than he did at this moment, holding his wife fast in his arms. She nestled against him, one dainty hand clutching his shirt while the other rested limply against her breasts. Her cheeks were flushed and a little smile curled her lips. She looked sated, and very content.

He pressed a kiss to her damp temple. "Did you like that, sweetheart?"

She let out a fluttering sigh. "Truly, Lucas, that was extraordinary. You should have told me about this before we started. I would not have been nearly as nervous as I was."

He shook his head in disbelief. Holding her satiny body close, he stood. She squeaked a bit at that, but settled soon enough. "It's not really something a man cares to discuss with his fiancée," he said dryly.

"Hmm. Well, perhaps he should," she replied in a thoughtful voice. "It might make for a great deal less confusion and anxiety. At least on the bride's part."

He strode with her to the bed. "I'll be sure to mention that to any young men who happen to ask me for advice on appropriate conduct for their wedding night."

She huffed. "Now you are teasing me."

Laughing, he dropped her onto the bed, where she landed on the large pile of pillows. She bounced a bit, scrambled up, and scowled at him.

"How rude," she scolded, even though he could see she was trying not to laugh.

Leaning against the bedpost, he took a moment to study her. She looked utterly tempting, naked against the white sheets and wine-colored coverlet. Her skin glowed with a pearly sheen, her dark hair flowed onto the pillow, and he could even see the pink, sweet flesh peeking out from behind the curls at the apex of her thighs.

And the best thing was the smile on her lips and the happy gleam in her eyes. But as they stared at each other her gaze shimmered from laughter to intense longing and, God help him, a love as naked and beautiful as her body.

His heart clutched with a devastating emotion he hadn't felt in a very long time.

"Phoebe," he rasped from a suddenly dry throat, "I can't wait any longer."

She tilted her head and gave him a puzzled smile. "I cannot imagine why you should."

That's all it took. In seconds, he ripped off his clothes and came down on her, pressing her slim body into the mattress. As her arms twined around him, he plunged his tongue into her mouth, drinking in the sweetest kiss he had ever known. His head roared and lust pounded through his body and brain, so acute he could have sworn the pounding was outside his head instead of in it.

Suddenly, Phoebe put her small fists on his shoulders and shoved with all her might as she pulled away from the kiss.

"Lucas," she hissed. "Stop!"

He shook his head impatiently, swooping back down to her mouth again, but she inserted a hand between them and the kiss landed on her palm.

"Lucas, stop. It sounds like someone is at the door."

He froze, finally understanding that the pounding was indeed coming from outside his head—on the front door, from the sound of it. And whoever was doing it was in one hell of a hurry. The bloody fool was using a stick, thudding repeatedly against the sturdy oaken door.

He groaned and dropped his head on the pillow, trying to ignore the throbbing urgency in his body. "Hell and damnation. I'll kill him. Whoever is pounding on my door—on my wedding night—I'll kill him."

Chapter 19

Propped up on his elbows, Lucas stared down at her, every muscle rigid with disbelief and frustration. Phoebe pushed on his brawny chest again as she tried to wriggle out from under him. Lying trapped and naked under a large man on the brink of losing his temper struck her as a very bad idea.

The heavy pounding on the front door drove away the last remnants of her sensual daze. Lucas had unleashed unknown, delicious forces in her body. He had done it gently and skillfully and, she was certain, with tender affection. But his tenderness had now fled, falling victim to the untimely interruption of their lovemaking.

The rapid change made her nervous. "Lucas, please get off me," she said breathlessly.

He blinked, staring down at her as if she were a stranger. Then he grimaced. "Forgive me. I didn't mean to frighten you."

"I understand, but I would still be grateful to get up."

Grumbling, he rolled to the side, then sat up on the edge of the bed. She scrambled under the sheets, which prompted another irritated look from her husband. "Phoebe, no one is going to burst in on us."

She pulled the sheets up to her neck. "I happen to be cold," she responded with dignity.

Lucas surged to his feet, looking more disgruntled by the minute. Not surprising, although she wished he would stop glowering at her. The interruption was hardly her fault.

The pounding in the hall finally stopped, but a moment later the sound of raised voices replaced it. Yanking on his clothes, Lucas stalked for the door.

"What are you going to do?" she blurted out.

He cast a disbelieving look in her direction. "I'm going to see who is trying to pound my door down. You stay here. I'll be back as soon as I get rid of the damn fool who had the nerve to ruin my wedding night."

The door slammed behind him, sending a hollow boom echoing through the room.

Oh, dear. Phoebe threw back the bedding and rushed to gather her clothes from the floor, shivering as she pulled her night rail over her head. The fire had burned down to embers, and in the fitful light of the candles, the room was cold and dreary, and seemed as shabby and out of sorts as she felt.

She hastily pulled on her wrapper and grabbed her slippers. As she crossed in front of her dressing table, she caught a glance at her reflection. Stumbling to a halt, she stared at herself. She looked exactly like a woman who had just been tumbled, hardly a presentable image.

Quickly, she wove her hair into a haphazard braid and then dug a heavy woolen shawl out of one of her trunks. Casting it over herself, she took another quick glance in the mirror. Although not likely to impress anyone, at least she looked respectably covered. Given the clamor of voices now issuing from downstairs, she could not afford to waste another second.

She threw open the heavy door and made her way quickly down the dark corridor. In her haste, she had forgotten to take a candle. A small branch stood on a table at the end of the hallway, barely penetrating the frigid gloom of the upper house. The angry voices down in the entrance hall, however, reached her with alarming clarity.

When she reached the top of the old staircase she pulled up short. The scene below could only be described as mayhem. The servants—most in their nightclothes—milled around the hall, talking in loud, excited voices. Several men in hats and greatcoats stood inside the massive front doors, glaring at the manor's inhabitants. One of the men, obviously the leader, was speaking to a furious-looking Lucas.

Phoebe's stomach churned when she saw that the intruders carried guns. They stood behind their leader, clearly agitated and unsettled by the volatile atmosphere swirling around them.

Her heart in her throat, she rushed down the steps and into the milling knot of servants. Several turned to her, all talking over each other and so loudly she could barely fathom a word.

Maggie, dressed in a bright red wrapper and with her night-cap hanging off her head, appeared by her side. "Oh, my lady, smugglers, right here at Mistletoe Manor. I swear I shall die of fright," she cried with dramatic relish.

Phoebe gaped at her. "These men are smugglers? They dare to come to the manor?"

Maggie's vigorous head shake sent her cap sliding farther south, revealing a head full of papers.

"No, my lady. That fellow speaking with his lordship is the excise officer, and those are his men. They were chasing a gang of smugglers who came right onto the estate." She gave an exaggerated shudder. "Who'd have thought we'd find such dreadful happenings down here in the country. And on our first night, too!"

Phoebe cast a quick glance around the hall. Unlike Maggie, the rest of the servants looked far from entertained. In fact, they seemed in various stages of worry and fright, and a few of the younger girls appeared to be on the verge of tears.

And both Mrs. Christmas and Mr. Christmas stood right behind Lucas, casting anxious, apprehensive glances between him and the excise officer.

As Phoebe gently pushed her way through the servants,

trying to reassure them with a quiet word, she sensed a genuine degree of alarm in the hall, and not just because law officers had come banging on the door in the middle of the night. No, something felt off-kilter, for lack of a better term. Fear had come in the night to Mistletoe Manor. She could see it in the white faces of the servants, and in the grim, suspicious looks of the excise men.

She finally made her way to stand quietly behind Lucas. He noticed her only when the man he was speaking to broke off to stare at her. When Lucas glanced over his shoulder, meeting her gaze, his eyes narrowed and his mouth flattened into a thin line. "I thought I told you to stay upstairs."

Phoebe repressed the urge to bristle at his tone of voice. "Since every other person in the manor saw fit to come down, I thought it only proper I join them," she replied mildly.

Lucas swore. "Christ, this is all I need. Isn't there one person in this damned place who will listen to me?"

His words stung, but she managed to preserve her temper. Her husband was upset and frustrated, and emotional displays on her part would only worsen matters. Somehow, she needed to deflect the anger swirling around before it manifested into something even uglier.

"My lord," she said in a clear, carrying tone, "perhaps you would be so kind as to introduce me to this gentleman. I wish to understand how we can help him."

Lucas pressed his lips shut and, for an awful second, she thought he would refuse. Then he gave a terse nod. "This is Mr. Harper, the customs officer for the district. Mr. Harper, this is my wife, Lady Merritt."

Mr. Harper, who had the look about him of a sensible man, gave her a neat bow. "Your ladyship, please forgive the intrusion. I deeply regret it, but it was necessary."

"The matter must be of great import if you deemed it necessary to disrupt our peace so late at night," Phoebe replied in a pleasant voice.

The man cast a quick, regretful glance over her attire. "Forgive me. I was not aware his lordship had returned from London when I disturbed your rest."

"That hardly seems a good excuse for you to pound the manor's door down," Phoebe said carefully, ensuring her nerves did not tip her into *plain speech*. "I will take your word for it but I must insist your men lower their weapons. You are in the hall of an English lord, not on a battlefield."

Mr. Harper hesitated, casting a swift glance around the hall as if expecting one of the servants to pull out a pistol at any moment.

Lucas raised an imperious eyebrow. "You heard Lady Merritt, Mr. Harper. I can vouch for your men's safety, no matter how unruly the crowd," he said, sarcasm inflecting his words.

Mr. Harper had the grace to flush, and quietly ordered his men to stow their weapons. As he did, Phoebe turned to her housekeeper. "Mrs. Christmas, please send the servants back to their beds. Their service is not required."

Mrs. Christmas opened her mouth and then shut it, looking mutinous as she crossed her arms across her ample chest.

Phoebe frowned. "Is there some difficulty?"

"Only that it's like to be a miracle if we're not all killed in our beds, what with all the shooting going on," she said.

Startled, Phoebe grabbed Lucas by the shirtsleeve.

"People were shooting at each other? Was anyone hurt?"

He cast her another impatient glance. "Everyone, including you, should go up to bed. I will deal with this situation."

Phoebe propped her hands on her hips, causing her shawl to slide off her shoulders. That had the unfortunate effect of bringing Mr. Harper's gaze—and his men's—right back to her and her unfortunate state of undress. With a sharp intake of breath, Lucas stepped in front of her. His rigid posture sent out an unmistakable warning to every man in the hall.

Groaning, Phoebe snatched up her shawl and wrapped it closely about her chest. Embarrassment stained her cheeks with heat, but that would not deter her. Stepping up to Lucas, she touched his arm. "Please tell me if anyone has been hurt."

"I have no idea," he snapped.

A mournful voice piped up from the small knot of excise men. "I was shot in the arm, my lady," a man said. "Hurts like the devil, too."

Mr. Harper cast an annoyed glance behind him. "It's just a graze, Williams. I'll have someone ride for the surgeon once we're finished with the search."

This time Phoebe did bristle. "A man has been shot and you expect him to just stand there and bleed onto my floor? That is hardly the behavior of a Christian, sir."

"Phoebe," Lucas growled, "stay out of this."

She ignored him, glancing at the housekeeper and butler standing beside her. "Mr. Christmas, we must tend to this man's wounds. Please have a fire lit in the—" She hesitated, suddenly aware of how little she knew about the house.

"I would suggest the study, my lady," Mr. Christmas said morosely.

"Very good. Please light the fire in the study and light several branches of candles as well."

Lucas heaved a tired sigh, as if giving up any hope for the rest of the night. She understood his frustration, but there was little she could do about it until order was restored, wounds tended, and Mr. Harper and his men sent on their way.

Quickly, she gave Mrs. Christmas a few orders. The housekeeper nodded grudgingly and disappeared behind the door leading to the kitchen. Phoebe turned back to the wounded man, a big, burly fellow who gave her a shy, snaggletoothed smile. He, at least, seemed harmless enough.

"Mr., ah, Williams, was it? Please come into the study."

The man stepped forward but Mr. Harper held up a restraining hand.

"My lord," he said, "I must ask you again to allow us to

search the premises, particularly the cellars. I'm certain the smugglers have taken refuge in one of the manor's buildings."

"That's a serious charge to make," Lucas replied in a hard voice. "What's your proof, man?"

His ruthless tone sent a shiver trickling down Phoebe's spine, but she had to give Mr. Harper credit. He did not back down before Lucas, who towered formidably over him.

"Because there was no other way they could give us the slip, my lord. We surprised them, right enough. They dropped their load and ran, but we were hard on their tails. Then, within sight of this house, they disappeared. Vanished into thin air."

Mr. Harper cast another suspicious glance around the hall. "It's the only reasonable explanation. There has to be a tunnel or hidden cellar around here somewhere."

While Lucas stood frowning over that, Mr. Christmas hurried back into the hall, moving with a fair degree of alacrity. "The study is ready, Lady Merritt," he said, slightly out of breath.

Mr. Harper looked ready to further pursue his demands, but Lucas waved him to silence. "Enough, Harper. I have no intention of letting you rummage through my house at this late hour. It's bad enough that my wife has to spend her wedding night tending to bullet wounds," he said, casting Phoebe an irritated glance. "I'll be damned if I'll add a search for smugglers on top of it."

He glanced at the knot of excise men, then back to the officer. "Harper, my butler will take your men down to the kitchen where they can warm up. They are not, however, to leave that room. Do you understand?"

Mr. Harper clearly heard the warning and nodded his reluctant assent.

"Good," Lucas said. "You may come into the study with me while my wife tends to your man's wounds. I'd like a better explanation of what's going on than what I've gotten so far." He glanced down at Phoebe. "Does that meet with your approval, my lady?" he asked in a sardonic voice.

She blushed. "Yes, my lord. Thank you."

He took her hand and pulled her toward the study, not bothering to see if the others obeyed him. Of course they would. When Lucas spoke in *that* tone of voice, everyone obeyed him. He stalked across the hall and Phoebe almost had to skip to keep up. Inside, she sighed. He obviously had his temper now firmly under control, but that did not fool her. His cooperation was razor thin, and would surely come with a price.

He ushered her into the study, one of several rooms Phoebe had not yet seen. It was a handsome space, although obviously not refurbished in some years. But the walls, painted a pale leaf green, created a comfortable backdrop for the heavy, masculine furniture. A large desk stood before an alcove window—a small collection of globes on its polished surface—and two heavy cabinets, filled with curios, flanked the fireplace. Books lined several rows of inset shelves, and comfortable armchairs were scattered about in casual seating arrangements. It had an air of peace to it, reminding Phoebe of the cozy serenity of Uncle Arthur's library in Stanton House.

Lucas drew her over to the fireplace, now blazing with crackling, welcome heat. He leaned in close. "All right, Madam Wife," he murmured. "Do what you need to do and then go back upstairs. This ridiculous scene has gone on long enough."

She pressed her lips tight, annoyed by his patronizing tone. He gazed down at her. Anger leached from his eyes, but frustration rapidly took its place. A stark weariness etched itself on his rugged features, and the sharp words poised on her tongue vanished. "Yes, Lucas. I will be as quick as I can," she said softly.

His mouth twitched with a faint smile, but his eyes remained somber and watchful. Then he motioned the injured man forward to the fire and stepped away to speak to Mr. Harper. Oddly, Phoebe had the sense he was abandoning her.

She shook off the uncomfortable feeling as she and Mrs. Christmas helped Mr. Williams out of his greatcoat—the housekeeper grumbling all the while—and got him to sit in one of the wing chairs in front of the fireplace. The old leather crackled ominously as the man lowered his bulk onto the seat.

He gave Phoebe an apologetic smile as she helped him roll up his sleeve.

"It's ever so kind of you to help, my lady. It's a devil of a cold night to be getting shot."

"You wouldn't be getting shot in the first place if you'd stayed indoors instead of chasing phantoms in the dark, now would you?" snapped Mrs. Christmas.

Phoebe glanced at her, surprised at the animosity in the housekeeper's voice. It seemed completely out of character.

"Phantoms don't shoot pistols and drop casks of French brandy in the middle of a field," interjected Mr. Harper. The housekeeper's face turned red. Mr. Christmas, again moving with surprising alacrity, intervened.

"Here are some extra cloths, my lady," he said, thrusting some clean toweling into her hand.

Phoebe took them, not failing to notice the slight shake of the head the butler gave his cousin. Mrs. Christmas folded her lips in on themselves, as if swallowing her words. No one else but Phoebe seemed to notice the odd silence exchanged between the cousins. Lucas and Mr. Harper had already moved off to a corner, beginning a quiet but intense discussion.

Mentally shrugging, Phoebe turned her attention back to Mr. Williams. Lucas had the right of it. The sooner the excise men were gone from the manor, the better. The servants were hiding something—whether the smugglers themselves or just knowledge of events, she did not know. But a search tonight could only lead to more problems and possibly more violence.

She absolutely refused to begin her married life with the spilling of blood in her own house.

Fortunately, Mr. Williams had only received a graze on his

forearm. Phoebe took just a few minutes to clean the wound and put on some healing salve provided by Mrs. Christmas, and a wrapping.

"That's capital, my lady." The big man beamed at her. "I doubt a surgeon could do it any better. When I heard the guns go off, I thought I was a goner for sure."

She leveled him with a disapproving stare. "Who shot first, Mr. Williams? The smugglers or Mr. Harper's men?"

"Ah . . . we did, my lady."

"And did thee personally engage in this exchange of fire?" she asked, unable to tamp down her anger.

Mr. Williams threw a startled glance at Mrs. Christmas, but the housekeeper maintained a grim silence. Then he cast a worried look over at his superior officer—still occupied with Lucas—before answering.

"I only fired off a warning shot, my lady. Not like I wanted to hit anyone. Not really."

She shook out his coat. Hastily, he lumbered to his feet.

"Those who liveth by the sword will die by the sword, Mr. Williams," she said. "I suggest you take that counsel to heart before it is too late."

"Yes, my lady. I'll try to remember that." Then, with garbled thanks, he took his coat and fled the room.

Lucas looked up from his conversation. "All finished? Good. Now please return to your bedroom."

She shook her head. "Not until you tell me what happened tonight."

"There's not much to tell," he said impatiently. "There are some old smuggling routes across the estate. They'd fallen into disuse, but Mr. Harper tells me that a local gang has been using them again."

Phoebe frowned. "You mean men from this area?"

Mr. Harper nodded. "Yes, my lady. I'm convinced that some of the local villagers are involved."

"Why would they do such a thing?" she asked.

"Because there's little work for them, my lady," Mrs. Christmas broke in hotly. "Hardly enough to keep body and soul together, much less feed a family. Especially after the war and the soldiers coming home."

"That may be the case," Lucas said in stern voice, "but those days are over. Mistletoe Manor will be restored to order, and any honest man who wants a job will find one here."

"And what about the dishonest men?" Mr. Harper asked in a challenging voice.

Lucas's face turned to stone. "If I find them on my land, you can be sure I will turn them over to the law."

Mr. Harper nodded. "Very good, my lord. But I caution you, these men are dangerous."

"They will find me a great deal more dangerous. I will not allow smugglers on my land. Ever."

Phoebe's stomach tightened at the implied violence of her husband's words. Beside her, Mrs. Christmas made a quiet sound of distress. She reached out to give the housekeeper's hand a reassuring touch.

"My lord," Phoebe said, "is it really necessary to make such threats? Surely this problem can be resolved in a peaceful manner."

"I never make threats," he answered calmly. Then he turned to the excise officer. "We're finished here for tonight, Harper. My household has been disrupted enough."

Mr. Harper started to argue again, but Lucas held up his hand. "Yes, I understand you want to search the grounds, but any smugglers who might have taken refuge in my cellars or these supposed tunnels must certainly be long gone. I will come to your office tomorrow, and we can discuss the situation further."

He glanced Phoebe's way. "You've upset my wife quite enough for one night."

Mr. Harper cast her an apologetic smile. "Forgive me, my lady. His lordship is correct. We won't disturb you any longer."

Lucas had upset her more than anyone, but Phoebe could hardly say that in front of the customs officer or the servants. Instead, she murmured a quiet thank-you and followed the men out into the hall. Lucas and Mr. Harper exchanged a few more words, and then the officer and his men departed. As the big oak doors slammed shut, Lucas shot the bolts. He turned around, leaning against the doors as he eyed her.

He looked as unhappy as she imagined a man could look on his wedding night. "And now, Madam Wife, if you've finished managing everything quite to your satisfaction, can we please go back to bed?"

Chapter 20

From just inside the door of her bedroom, Phoebe watched her husband stalk over to the bed and begin undressing. Anger tensed his muscular frame. His actions, normally a study in masculine grace, were hurried and jerky. As she pondered the least upsetting way to continue a discussion he obviously did not want to have, Lucas yanked his shirt over his head. Her mind blanked and her heart stuttered.

His body left her both awestruck and unsettled, with its broad shoulders and chest, muscled arms, and taut stomach. Lucas would impress anyone with his clothes on. Without them, he was like nothing she had ever seen. Not that she made a habit of staring at half-naked men, but she suspected few could compete with her husband's raw power and masculinity.

But, dear Lord, the scars. Pale, cruel lines scored his skin—one across his right bicep, another down the left forearm, a wicked one cutting from one side of his ribs to his waist, and the fourth . . . not a cut from a blade, but a faded and puckered bunching of skin, the evil remnant of a bullet that had obviously pierced his shoulder. She could not help but see his old wounds as an obscene reminder of human wickedness and of man's sins against God.

Lucas tossed the shirt in the general direction of a chair

before turning to see her standing frozen by the door. He raised a brow.

"What's wrong?"

She cleared her throat. "You . . . you have so many scars."

He glanced down at himself and shrugged. "Many battles, many years," he replied as he started working on the fall of his trousers. "I was fortunate to survive and return with my limbs intact. Other men weren't so lucky."

Phoebe swallowed against a rush of nausea. The idea of Lucas lying injured on a battlefield, blood pouring from his wounds, made her stomach churn. She closed her eyes and took a deep breath, willing her insides to settle. If she thought about that image much longer, she would have to race to the basin and empty her stomach.

"Phoebe, come here." Her husband's soothing voice forced her eyes open. He studied her, his expression grave but no longer angry. Then he held out his hand. "Sweetheart, you'll catch cold if you stand there in the draft. Come to bed and get warm."

The tenderness in his voice brought a rush of tears to her eyes, and longing twisted her insides. After all the trials of the day, she could think of nothing better than to hurry straight into the shelter of his arms, and take everything he would give her. But she knew such shelter would only be temporary, disappearing with the dawn and leaving their problems unresolved.

And that included the most immediate issue—whether Lucas intended to use violent means to deal with the smugglers crossing Merritt lands.

She walked slowly to the fire, turning her back to it. It gave little warmth, since the embers had burned low, but she had to keep her distance from Lucas, and that big, tempting bed, the bed where he would surely get her naked and mindless with passion in no time at all. "I wish to speak with you first, Lucas."

His eyes closed and he groaned. "Please tell me you're joking."

"I am not."

He dropped down onto the mattress, rubbing a hand over his face. "Christ, can tonight get any worse? Why do women always want to talk, especially in the middle of the night?"

She frowned, annoyed he would lump her in with other women, but decided it might be best to ignore the implication. "I am sorry, Lucas. I know you are tired, but this cannot wait until morning."

"I'm not tired, I'm frustrated." He gave her a hard stare. "*Very* frustrated, if you get my meaning."

She decided to ignore that, too. "I do, but I need to know what you intend to do about the smugglers. I do not want another repeat of tonight's incident."

He snorted. "Oh, really?"

"Yes," she replied tightly. "Mistletoe Manor cannot be turned into a battleground between those excise men and the smugglers. Anyone could get hurt, including our servants."

"Believe me," he retorted, "I want that as little as you do. But if the smuggling isn't stopped, I guarantee someone will get hurt. Since we agree we don't want his majesty's agents trooping across our land again, then it's up to me to put an end to it."

Silence fell as she chewed on her lip, weighing the consequences of sharing her suspicions.

"Come on, Phoebe," Lucas said. "Out with it."

She met his watchful gaze, still worried how he might react. An impatient energy invested the air around him, but he held himself still, waiting for her to speak. She realized the importance of the moment, one that could build trust between them or go horribly awry. "I . . . I think the servants know something about the smuggling," she finally said.

His lips twitched. "Why do you think so?"

"Because there can be no other explanation for their odd

behavior. Mrs. Christmas in particular was very upset." She frowned, trying to piece it together in her head.

Lucas leaned back on his elbows, watching her with open curiosity. "Well?" he prompted.

"I suspect the smugglers were hiding in the cellars the entire time Mr. Harper and his men were here."

He let out a crack of laughter and pushed himself off the bed.

"Of course they were hiding in the cellars, goose. Why do you think I wouldn't let Harper search the house? The last thing we needed was a pitched battle between smugglers— half of whom are probably from our own village—and the only honest group of excise men in the district. No, love. That was not how I wanted to end an already trying day."

In a few long strides he was across the room and standing in front of her. All she could do was gape at him. "You knew all along?" she choked out.

He grinned, not bothering to dignify her silly question with an answer. Instead, he picked her up, teased her mouth with a light kiss, and carried her to the bed. His strength and easy mastery of her body sorely tempted her to yield to their mutual desire.

Not yet.

She tensed as he deposited her onto the disordered welter of pillows and bedclothes. "Why did you not tell me right away?" she asked.

He cast her a smoldering look clearly intended to bring the heat rushing back to her body. "As you can well imagine, I had other things on my mind," he said in a growly voice.

Phoebe's heart accelerated under his knowing gaze. Her annoyingly seductive husband was trying to distract her, but she would not be deterred. He had alleviated her anxiety to some degree, but she knew him well enough to suspect that he only deferred the outcome. "Yes, but—"

His temper finally snapped. "Oh, hell, Phoebe. Must we really finish this discussion tonight? Haven't you had enough?"

His tone caught her like a freezing blast, obliterating the sensual heat between them. She pushed herself up onto the pillows and pulled her wrapper tightly around her. "Yes, I believe we must finish it," she replied, trying to keep the hurt from her voice.

He sat sideways to her on the bed, staring straight ahead. His commanding profile seemed carved from rock, except where a muscle pulsed at his temple. The silence drew out as he struggled to bring his frustration under control.

Then he turned to face her. "Very well, then. What do you wish to know?"

"What do you intend to do about the smugglers?"

"I'll ride into Maidstone tomorrow to meet with Harper. I need to find out the lay of the land—how big the gang is, what they're running and when, where they come ashore."

"Why do you need to know those things?"

"They will tell me how likely the smugglers are to use Merritt land in the future. Several old routes run from Seasalter to Faversham, and I wouldn't be surprised if there are even some tunnels right here on the estate. Some Merritts in the past were all too happy to turn a blind eye to smuggling—or even aided and abetted—but I don't think your grandfather was one of them. Still, he was sick these last few years, and I suspect he rather lost a handle on things."

She nodded slowly. Already she could sense his mind racing to formulate a plan. That came as no surprise. Lucas was accustomed to action, and to facing problems head-on.

"Once you have that information, what will you do?"

"Put an end to the problem."

The ruthless intent in his voice jolted her. "Ah, how exactly will you do that?"

"By employing whatever means are necessary. I will not allow smuggling on my lands, Phoebe, make no mistake about that. It's a dangerous business, and I won't have my wife or my people put at risk over a bloody run of French cognac. Christ! I didn't spend years fighting the French to turn a blind eye to this sort of thing now."

She understood his logic, but the likely result of that logic filled her with apprehension. "Will you . . . ?" she swallowed. "Will you . . . ?" She could not say the words.

He sighed and a terrible weariness tugged at the hard lines of his face. "Kill them? Not if I don't have to. I'd prefer to hand them over to Harper to deal with."

She eased out her breath. That was something, at least. But capturing a band of desperate smugglers actually sounded harder than killing them. And if they *were* truly desperate . . . well. She did not want to think about that, either, or what might happen to Lucas.

"Assuming you do catch them," she said carefully, "what is likely to happen to them?"

"It depends. They could be thrown in jail, or even deported or hanged, depending on a number of factors."

He sounded so unconcerned that she flinched. She reached over to grab his sleeve. "Lucas, how can you be so cold about that? You said yourself that those men are likely to be local villagers, perhaps even related to the people of your hall. Knowing so little about the situation, how can you even think to turn them over to be hanged or deported? I do not believe you are capable of such cruelty."

He made an impatient, frustrated sound and shook off her hand. Standing, he turned to face her. He towered above her, over six feet of muscled, angry man. She had to resist the impulse to shrink into the pillows.

"It's not cruelty. It's command. This is my land, Phoebe, and my manor house. I didn't ask for the earldom or the estate, not a goddamned bit of it. I never wanted the responsibility, but it's mine now. And I'll be hanged if I'll let this place fall back into the wrack and ruin left by your grandfather. I *will* have order on my lands, and I'll do whatever is necessary to achieve it."

She peered up at him, unnerved and at a loss as to how to respond.

Unaware of the effect he was having on her—at least she hoped so—he carried on. Not shouting, but his hard voice chilled her nonetheless. "Furthermore, I expect my countess to support me on this, Quaker beliefs or no. This is the real world, Phoebe, and there are bad men in it, men who would kill you or anyone else on this estate if you got in their way. Yes, I know it troubles you, but I will not be held back from doing what I must by your quaint, childish notions about the world."

The shock of his words hit her dead-on. She gasped and put her hands to her throat.

His eyes widened. "Christ. Phoebe, I didn't mean—"

He bit off whatever he was going to say, leaning down to her. Shaking her head, she held up a hand to ward him off. "I may be naive, Lucas, but you still think like a man at war. You forget you are no longer a soldier."

His gaze flickered away from her as he straightened up. "Sometimes I wish to hell I still was," he said in a bitter voice.

Her heart broke. For him, for her, and for their marriage.

He drew in a deep breath, and with it came the hard shell of the arrogant aristocrat. "Are we through with this discussion now?" he asked in a coldly polite voice.

She managed to nod.

"Good. Then please move over so I can get back in bed."

Phoebe had to push through disbelief and heartache to find her voice. "No, Lucas. I would ask that you return to your own room tonight."

His hand, reaching for the coverlet, froze. Color washed across his cheekbones. "What?"

"You heard me," she said, her voice firming. It might kill her to say the words, but she knew she had to. "I have no wish to sleep with you when you are filled with so much anger and hatred. Nor do I feel it my duty as your wife to do so. My responsibilities to God and my beliefs outweigh my marital obligations to you."

His eyes seemed to flame at her, his expression stark. Then he turned on his heel and stalked from the room.

A clattering sound pulled her awake. Phoebe's eyes flew open and she bolted upright, her heart thudding and her mind groping to remember where she was. Her gaze flitted from one corner of the room to the other, finally landing on Maggie pulling back the heavy drapes that hung over the window recesses of her bedroom.

Groaning, Phoebe fell back against the pillows. She hated that feeling, awakening in a panic in unfamiliar surroundings. Sometimes it felt more like a nightmare, swimming up from the depths with her heart pounding and her body trembling, trying to gain her bearings. She had experienced similar episodes on the ship's crossing from America, although they had faded the last few weeks at Stanton House. But now they were back, and on her first morning in her new home. That was a very gloomy thought, as was the knowledge that she began her first full day as a married woman alone in bed.

"Good morning, my lady," Maggie trilled in a voice so cheery it made Phoebe cringe. With a cheeky grin, the girl brought her a cup of tea, obviously no worse for wear after last night's adventures in the hall. In contrast, Phoebe felt rather like the bottom of an old shoe.

"Here, my lady. His lordship said to let you sleep in, and then serve you breakfast in bed. He said you were all done up by them goings-on last night." She gave an exaggerated shudder. "Smugglers! Why, it's a miracle none of us were murdered in our beds."

"Yes. I believe you said much the same last night," Phoebe replied in a dampening tone. She had no wish to revisit the dreary events of the previous evening. As far as she was concerned, the smugglers and the excise men could not have done a better job of ruining her wedding night if they had met in secret and planned the entire thing out.

Maggie eyed her uncertainly and then shrugged. Leaving Phoebe to her tea, she moved briskly about the room, straightening up clutter and restoring order. When she picked up Phoebe's wrapper from the floor—where she had tossed it in a fit of frustration after Lucas stormed out of the room— Maggie stifled a giggle, obviously assuming it had landed there during a passionate encounter.

Nothing could be further from the truth, since Lucas had complied with her request to leave with depressing ease. She had half expected him to refuse, and part of her *had* hoped he would stay and have it out with her. But when he simply gave her that blazing look and turned on his heel, she had been stunned. It had taken her a few moments to recover, but then she had jumped out of bed to follow him. But with her hand poised on the handle of his door, she had realized how foolish she would appear, especially after her ultimatum.

Frustrated and discouraged, she had returned to bed, where she had proceeded to burst into tears and cry herself to sleep. Thank God Lucas had not returned to witness her acting like a silly schoolgirl. The evening had degenerated into enough of a farce without adding that humiliation on top of everything else.

She sighed and picked up a piece of toast, then put it down again.

"Is something the matter, my lady?" Maggie asked.

"Ah, no. I suppose I am just feeling a bit tired."

"His lordship said you would be. He seemed quite concerned about it. Said I was to check on you if you slept past ten o'clock."

"Ten o'clock!" Throwing back the covers, she shimmied down off the high mattress to the threadbare carpet. She grabbed her wrapper from the end of the bed, where Maggie had carefully placed it.

"Oh, it's not to be wondered that you slept so late, my lady,"

Maggie said, handing over her slippers with a little smirk. "After all, it *was* your wedding night."

Phoebe scowled, knowing exactly what everyone thought of her late rising. If they only knew the truth.

"And his lordship is so handsome," Maggie went on with a dreamy sort of sigh. "If he was my husband, I don't think I'd let him out of bed for a week."

Phoebe squeezed her eyelids shut, praying for patience. One day soon she would have to deal with Maggie's loose tongue. But not today. She had enough problems to confront this morning, starting with her errant husband. "Has Lord Merritt already had his breakfast?"

"Yes, my lady. His lordship took his phaeton and went to Whitstable. He said not to expect him back until dinner."

"Whitstable? Where is that?"

"It's the nearest port. Mrs. Christmas said his lordship was going to talk to that excise officer, Mr. . . . Mr.—"

"Mr. Harper."

Feeling deflated, Phoebe put on her slippers. Lucas had clearly decided that ridding his lands of smugglers took priority over spending the day with his new wife.

And how could she blame him, after her rejection? At the time, it had seemed very important to stand on principle. But in the cold light of day, she wondered if she had pushed him too far. After all, Lucas was an ex-soldier, used to order and discipline. The idea that lawbreakers could run rampant over the estate, even seeking refuge in the cellars of the house, would of course infuriate him. He would see it as an insult to his dignity as lord of the manor, something he could not tolerate.

Phoebe shook her head. Lucas had the nerve to call *her* quaint, but some of his ideas were positively medieval. Still, part of her understood. He was trying to feel his way through a new life and new responsibilities as much as she was. But while she had longed for change, Lucas resisted it. The estate, the manor, an entire village, and a household of dependents—

he wanted none of it. It was no wonder he struggled to contain his resentment.

But wanted or not, those responsibilities now belonged to him. And to her. As his wife and countess she was duty-bound to assist him, helping him face and resolve the many challenges that he encountered.

She pondered quietly for a few minutes, and then headed to the washbasin set behind the magnificent but faded Chinese screen in the corner of the bedroom. "Maggie, put out my warmest gown and my walking boots. And tell Mrs. Christmas I wish to speak to her right away."

"Yes, my lady. Mrs. Christmas is waiting for you. She has the accounts set out in the breakfast room, and she says whenever you want to go over the house, she's at your disposal."

Phoebe stepped behind the screen, swiftly pulled off her nightclothes, and began to wash. "Not this morning. I wish to speak to her for a few minutes, and then I will be walking into the village."

Maggie peered around the corner of the screen, frowning. "You will, my lady?"

"Yes. I have something very important I must do."

As she scrubbed her face and hands, Phoebe calculated how best to approach the problem of Lucas and the smugglers. She was his wife and, whether he wished it or not, she *would* help him carry out his responsibilities. That did not mean, however, that she had any intention of allowing him to turn those men—no matter how misguided they were—over for deportation or worse. She would find another way, but first she needed more information and a sense of how serious the smuggling problem had become.

And she needed someone willing to tell her what she needed to know.

Chapter 21

A gust of wind kicked up the hem of Phoebe's skirts and set the ribbons of her bonnet flapping against her neck. She ducked her head, closing her eyes against the spray of dust that swirled up at her from the uneven surface of the lane. It was barely half a mile from Mistletoe Manor to the local village, but the December weather had her silently thanking Aunt Georgie for the gift of her new pelisse. The cherry red wool fabric not only lifted her spirits, it protected her from the biting chill of the dreary, overcast day.

Mrs. Christmas had urged her to take a carriage into the village, claiming she should make her first visit in style, but Phoebe had refused. She had spent the last seven years of her life in the country and missed her daily walks. Her sedate strolls through the carefully trimmed parks of London had been a poor substitute. She longed to be out in the open air, with the wide, arching sky over her head and the rich soil of the land under her feet. In the country, she could open her heart and spirit to the quiet solitude that whispered of things greater than the tiresome worries of everyday life.

She had also refused Maggie's company. The girl's unending stream of chatter proved a considerable barrier to quiet meditation. And meditate she must, for a number of vexing problems needed solving if she and Lucas stood any chance of starting their marriage on positive footing.

Starting with how she could negotiate a peaceful solution to the smuggling problem.

Phoebe had done her best to get Mrs. Christmas talking about last night's invasion of Mistletoe Manor, but the doughty housekeeper, who seemed a very conversable sort, pursed her lips and confined her answers to reluctant, half-uttered sentences. After several frustrating minutes spent trying to elicit information, Phoebe had capitulated. Mrs. Christmas had no intention of revealing anything, nor could she blame her. After all, it was common knowledge that Lucas had ridden into Whitstable to see Mr. Harper, and everyone in the manor knew what that meant.

Phoebe would have to get the information from other sources. In most villages, that meant the vicar or the local publican, or both. She would start with the vicar since she hardly thought her first visit to the village should commence with the tavern, especially without even a maid along as companion.

Besides, she could also take the opportunity to inquire about the general well-being of the villagers, and of the children in particular. From the few details Lucas had imparted about Apple Hill, the vicar and his wife had taken over the duties of educating the children when the last schoolmaster departed two years ago in a fit over Phoebe's grandfather's refusal to repair the schoolhouse roof.

She picked up her pace, passing by several orchards and the occasional barley field, mowed down to golden stubble after the recent harvest. Despite the barren season, she took pleasure in what she saw. The land rose and fell in gentle swells, and in the distance she saw a large stand of oaks, denuded for the winter but hinting of their reemergent majesty in the spring. The colors were muted under the cloud-driven sky, but she knew the landscape needed only a burst of sunlight to reveal its simple, satisfying glory.

As the lane wheeled in a lazy curve around a copse of trees, she found herself coming into the village. On first impression, Apple Hill seemed more a hamlet than a proper village, but it did have a central green around which stood a number of timbered or brick houses with steep, shingled roofs, and a few stores and a smithy. Several of the timbered houses looked very old and rather sad, as if they had been allowed to sag into regretful neglect. The shops and the local pub hardly looked better, with their brick frontings worn and their shutters and signs in desperate need of fresh paint.

She stopped at the head of the street to consider what she saw. What little cheer she had gained on her pleasant walk evaporated. Lucas had told her the village had fallen on hard times, the victim of both her grandfather's neglect and the deprivations of wartime. Now it seemed practically deserted, giving the impression that if left to its own devices it would fade away under a thick coating of sadness and dust, slipping away until no one remembered it had even existed. No wonder the villagers had turned to a life of crime to support themselves.

Inhaling a deep breath of bracing air, Phoebe refused to be cowed by the size of the task. There was a new lord at the manor, and she knew Lucas would do his best to heal the scars of past neglect, and in doing so he might even heal his own regrets. True, he missed the soldiering life, but his responsibilities as earl should provide him with enough purpose to satisfy the most restless soul.

If Phoebe could prevent him from turning half the village over to be deported or hanged, that is.

She made her way around the green to the church, nodding pleasantly and saying hello to the few locals who passed her on the street. Most were shabbily dressed and all were surprised to see her. She received a few nods in acknowledgment, one or two words of greeting in the soft dialect of Kent, and several gap-toothed stares of astonishment. No one seemed hostile, though, which she had feared might be the case after last night's incident at the manor.

Finally she reached the church, an old building constructed of some kind of gray stone, with an unusual, rather squat tower on the west side. She went past it to the small but tidy vicarage, the tidiest home in the village, so far, and knocked on the front door. But when no one answered after repeated raps, Phoebe retraced her steps to the church. Picking her way up the broken slate walkway—one of the first things she would see repaired—she reached the church porch, pushed open the big oak door, and stepped into the vestibule.

And into cheerful pandemonium.

At the front of the church, a group of children of various ages milled about, obviously in the throes of some kind of rehearsal. Some were barely more than toddlers and were the noisiest of the bunch, shrieking with excited delight at the antics of the older children. It squeezed Phoebe's heart to see them, so thin and pale in their homespun, shabby costumes.

Despite their appearance, they seemed not the least bit unhappy as they raced around the edges of the pews, rehearsed their lines in high, piping voices, or took turns climbing up into the pulpit to pretend to deliver a sermon. Ineffectually presiding over all this mayhem was the vicar, a gangly man gaunt to the point of emaciation, but apparently a cheerful soul who enjoyed the commotion as much as the children.

Phoebe hovered at the back of the church, reluctant to call attention to herself. The appearance of the new countess would surely put an end to their boisterous fun. For a few minutes, she just watched, remembering what it used to be like to feel such uncomplicated joy. Whatever she had to say to the vicar could wait until the children had finished their rehearsal.

She started to creep toward the back pew when the door opened again. A stout woman wearing spectacles bustled in, barely missing a collision with her.

"Oh, goodness," she cried. "You gave me a fright, young lady, and that's the truth."

She leaned closer, peering at Phoebe. The lenses of her spectacles made her pale blue eyes appear huge, like some kind of exotic insect. But those eyes inspected her with a good deal of intelligence and friendly interest. "Gracious me," she exclaimed. "You must be the new countess."

Phoebe murmured her assent and the woman began to drop down into a ponderous curtsy.

"Please, ma'am," Phoebe said, catching her by the elbow. "Do not put yourself out on my account."

The woman creaked back up to her full height, which was not very tall to begin with. In fact, Phoebe would have to say she was almost as tall as she was wide.

"Lady Merritt, if I'd only known you were coming we could have had the children ready for you." She cast a worried look at the altar. "It's always a bit of an uproar when I leave my husband alone with them. I tell him he must be firm, especially with the boys, but he won't listen. Goodness knows what you must be thinking about all this commotion."

She finished with an apologetic smile, although her glance darted anxiously to the front of the church. Why was she so nervous?

Phoebe gave her a reassuring smile. "There is no need to apologize. His lordship and I arrived late in the day yesterday, and I wished to look about the village this morning without making a fuss. I did call at the vicarage first, but no one answered."

"Oh, yes . . . Well, our housemaid, Sarah, must have been out and about, although I can't imagine where." She cast another apprehensive glance around the church, as if looking for something she did not want to see. Then she seemed to recollect herself.

"Well, you're here now and that's a blessing," she said in a hearty voice. "It's been one mishap after the other today in the village, or I'd have been here to meet you. Oh, and I'm Mrs. Knaggs, my lady. The vicar's wife, as you've already guessed."

Phoebe had to work to keep the surprise from her face. *Mrs. Knaggs?* Did every person who lived in the vicinity of Mistletoe Manor have a name out of a fairy tale?

"I am very pleased to meet you, Mrs. Knaggs," she managed, "and I do wish to speak with you about conditions in the village, and how Lord Merritt and I might be able to improve things. Especially for the children."

The shadow in the woman's eyes seemed to dissipate, and a warm smile crossed her features. "I shall be happy to help you in any way I can. Our people have suffered mightily these last few years, and much needs to be done to restore the village. We have been praying for a generous lord and lady to help us."

Phoebe was touched by the fugitive hope in the woman's gaze, and by the sincerity in her voice. "You shall have that help, but first I do need to talk to the vicar about something quite pressing. I was hoping to steal a moment of his time this afternoon."

Mrs. Knaggs hesitated, then nodded. "Of course, my lady. I believe we're done rehearsing. If you can call it that," she added with a laugh. "Come up to the altar and I'll introduce you to my husband."

"What are the children rehearsing?" Phoebe asked as they walked up the aisle.

"*The Second Shepherd's Play*." Mrs. Knaggs paused halfway up the aisle, speaking in a low, confidential voice. Not that it was necessary, given the din reverberating off the raftered ceiling. "There hasn't been much celebrating the last few years. The old earl's son died, and then the poor man fell sick himself for those last few years. Such a tragedy."

The older woman sighed, and once again trouble looked to weigh her down. Then she shook it off, giving Phoebe a broad smile. "But we're so happy to have you with us, especially for the Christmas Season. Mr. Knaggs thought it would be appropriate to have the children put on a pageant for the new lord and lady. I do hope that wasn't too forward of him."

Phoebe smiled, pleased she and Lucas could do something to make the children happy. "It is a splendid notion. When and where will you hold the performance?"

"In the old days, the pageant was held on Christmas Day. The entire village would spend the afternoon at Mistletoe Manor with the earl and his family. There would be quite the most generous feast you could imagine, and afterward the children would put on the play. Then there would be music and games, and the children would be given presents by the old lord. But it's been several years since any of that happened."

Mrs. Knaggs's face furrowed with sadness as she reflected on the glories of Christmas past, as if those days were gone forever.

"Then that is exactly what we will do this year," Phoebe said, putting out a quick hand to touch the woman's sleeve. "It sounds perfect for our first Christmas at Mistletoe Manor."

Mrs. Knaggs clasped her hands across her ample bosom. "Oh, my lady! Are you sure his lordship wouldn't mind?"

"He will be delighted," Phoebe said, mentally wincing. She really had no idea how Lucas would react, especially after last night's troubles. But if restoring the old Christmas traditions gave the villagers something to look forward to, she would convince him it must be done.

"Splendid, my lady! The villagers will be thrilled." Mrs. Knaggs bustled up the aisle and set to restoring order amidst the chaos. After pulling two quarreling boys apart, she held them at arm's length as she introduced Phoebe to her husband.

Mr. Knaggs bowed over her hand. "It is a great pleasure to meet you, Lady Merritt."

Up close, the vicar appeared even thinner, the look accentuated by the hollows under his cheekbones and his large, bushy eyebrows. Standing next to his wife, the effect was comical. Phoebe had heard only a few nursery rhymes in her childhood, but she did remember one about a man named Jack

Spratt. If memory served, Mr. and Mrs. Knaggs would have made excellent models for an illustrated version of the story.

He folded his bony hands across his waistcoat and gave her a beatific smile, one so honest and charming it warmed Phoebe from the inside out. "How can I be of service, Lady Merritt?"

She glanced around. Under Mrs. Knaggs's direction, the din had subsided to a tolerable level, and the children had been lined up in a neat row. All of them, even down to the smallest one with a grubby thumb stuck in her mouth, studied Phoebe with avid curiosity. "Perhaps you might introduce me to the children, Mr. Knaggs," she said. "Then I would like to chat with you."

With evident affection, the vicar introduced each child by name. Under his kind and encouraging regard, the little ones returned her greetings with shy grins and softly spoken hellos.

"And what role might you be playing?" she asked one of the older boys, wrapped in a faded brown cloak that all but swallowed up his gawky frame. He had a sharp, clever face and big brown eyes, and something in his gaze reminded her of her youngest nephew back in America.

"I'm Joseph, my lady," he said. He reached behind and pulled a shy girl with a blue cloth on her head up beside him. "And this is my wife, Mary. We be the parents of baby Jesus."

The girl blushed and ducked her head, retreating quickly behind the boy.

"We can't really have baby Jesus here for rehearsal," the boy continued in a long-suffering tone. "He's got colic, Mrs. Martin says—that's his real mum, the butcher's wife—and he's like to spit up all over us if we're not careful."

He wrinkled his nose, as if all too aware of the hazards of a colicky baby. Then he gave Phoebe a gap-toothed smile that had her simultaneously biting back laughter and longing to see her own nieces and nephews again.

"Young Sam is Ned Weston's boy," Mr. Knaggs added. "And quite the best scholar we have in school."

Phoebe smiled at him. "How wonderful! I am sure your parents must be very proud."

The light in the boy's eyes vanished, as if smothered by a blanket. "I don't have a mother anymore. And my pa says I have no use for book learning, especially since there's so much work to be done around the Ivy."

"Mr. Weston is our publican at the Holly and the Ivy," Mr. Knaggs murmured from beside her. "Mrs. Weston died of consumption just this past spring."

"Oh," Phoebe whispered. She cleared her throat. "I am very sorry, Sam. My mother also died when I was young. It is a difficult burden to carry."

Sam shrugged, as if it was not a great matter, but she could see the sheen of tears in his eyes. Her heart ached for the brave little boy.

"It's been hard, but I helps my papa around the pub, and—" He clamped his lips shut at the same time as Mr. Knaggs let out a quiet hiss from between his teeth. Some kind of silent communication that seemed like a warning passed between man and boy.

"Mr. Knaggs," his wife sharply interjected, "I think you've taken up quite enough of her ladyship's time with the children. It's time for their dinners now. Their mothers will be looking for them."

"Now, my dear," the vicar admonished in a gentle voice, "there's no need to nag. The children will be home in ample time for their dinners. And there will be little enough for them to eat, in any event," he ended on a mutter.

"I never nag, as you well know. I only suggest. My lady," she said, addressing Phoebe, "if you would be so kind as to tell my husband when you would like to tour the village and the school, I will be more than happy to accompany you."

"I will be sure to do so," Phoebe answered politely, knowing full well she had just been handled. Rather expertly, too.

But there was little point in objecting, and she might have better success extracting information from Mr. Knaggs in the absence of his redoubtable wife. Though they were clearly hiding secrets, she suspected the mild-mannered cleric might not be very good at keeping them.

Phoebe stood at the head of the aisle and smiled at the children as they scampered off in Mrs. Knaggs's ample wake. Sam Weston took up the rear. When he reached the vestibule, he turned and gave her a little wave. Her heart contracting once more with that quiet ache, Phoebe waved back. Then the door slammed shut behind him and the old stone building seemed to breathe out a sigh of relief as peace settled about them.

"Lady Merritt, there's no need for you to stand," said the vicar. "Please do be seated."

With a murmur of thanks, Phoebe slid into the first pew. Mr. Knaggs settled beside her, clasped his hands in his lap, and gave her a kind but wary smile. "And now, my lady, please tell me how I may be of service to you."

Phoebe looked him directly in the eye. "Mr. Knaggs, you can be of great service by telling me everything you know about the smuggling ring that is operating in this village, including those who might be involved. And then I want you to tell me what needs to be done to put a stop to it without anyone getting hurt."

The vicar's mouth fell open like a sagging drawer. It was in that moment Phoebe realized *everyone* in Apple Hill was likely involved in the smuggling ring in some way.

Including even the kindly Mr. Knaggs.

Chapter 22

Phoebe stood outside the door to her husband's study, hesitating. Lucas had been avoiding her for several days now. Ever since their argument on their wedding night, he had made certain they were never alone, only sharing meals with her in the semiformal splendor of their decrepit dining room, and only deigning to speak with her if she had some specific question about the household. Scrupulously polite, he treated her with a careful respect, but in subtle ways he made it clear he preferred to keep his distance.

His conduct was even more striking at night, when he invariably failed to join her in the bedroom. That was her fault but she had never expected a genuine estrangement to develop, never expected they would not discuss the problem that hung like a pall of smoke over their marriage. Countless times in the last week, after staring for hours at the faded canopy of her bed, Phoebe had jumped up and stalked to the connecting door between her dressing room and his bedroom, intending to barge in and force Lucas to acknowledge her.

And countless times she had lost her nerve, retreating to her cold, virginal bed.

If only they had finished what they had started on their wedding night she might have been able to work up the courage to confront him. But after the terrible things they had said to each other, she did not know if Lucas even wished her in his bed. The idea that he might not want her—and as every day passed that eventuality seemed more likely—made her nauseous. Add in the unresolved issue of the smugglers, and the chill between them rivaled the December wind seeping under the door of the great hall and swirling around her ankles.

Phoebe sighed, resting her forehead on the door. How *did* one address such a situation? She hated that she could find no way around it, especially since Lucas refused to talk about the smuggling problem in the village. To her mind, it was her husband's job to protect the people of their village, not turn them over to coldhearted officers of the law for an uncertain fate. Unfortunately, it would not be easy to solve the problem since most everyone in Apple Hill was involved.

Under her prodding, Mr. Knaggs had finally revealed the tale. Desperate to feed their families, a good portion of the men in the village had turned to smuggling. Those who did not—such as Mr. Knaggs—either turned a blind eye or did what they could to throw dust in the eyes of the excise officers. But Mr. Harper was relentless in his pursuit, and the situation was growing more dangerous by the day.

Even worse, some of the children were being pulled into the ring by their parents. Mr. Knaggs had stewed over that problem for months, and been almost pathetically grateful to confess his concerns to her. Outraged, Phoebe had insisted he reveal which parents were putting their children at risk, but he refused, saying he was duty-bound to protect his flock. She *was* tempted to march home and tell Lucas immediately, but she had already given her word to Mr. Knaggs she would not.

Naturally, she informed the vicar that the smuggling must stop. Lucas would eventually restore Apple Hill to prosperity and the locals could then return to a life of law-abiding tranquility, but that would never happen if the people did not invest their trust in the new lord. The fastest way to lose that trust was to turn even one man from the village over to the law.

She had also tried to discuss the matter in a roundabout way with her husband, but her inquiries about his meeting with Mr. Harper had run into the stubborn wall of his iron will. "You are to stay out of this, Phoebe," he had ordered. "You don't know a damn thing about it and you'll only get in the way. And likely get yourself into trouble, too, which will annoy me profoundly when I have to rescue you."

She had bristled as he must have known she would. One thing led to another and before she knew it, they were in the middle of a full-blown argument. When Phoebe refused to comply with his demands, Lucas had read her a lecture on disobedient wives. That had the effect of sending her storming out of the room and slamming the door. Not quite the actions of a dutiful Quaker or wife, but she could not entirely blame herself for her unfortunate reaction.

And who could she go to for advice about stubborn, hardheaded husbands? Meredith and the rest of the family would be arriving at Belfield Abbey in a few days, but Phoebe cringed at the idea of relating her problems to Meredith because she would probably tell Aunt Georgie, who would tell the General, who would no doubt demand a public airing of the problem. And *that* would lead to no good for anyone, especially Lucas.

No, Phoebe had to act on her own, before matters got any worse.

After one quick rap on the door, she slipped into her husband's study. The book-lined, cluttered room seemed to welcome her. The study glowed with the light and warmth of a roaring fire and several branches of candles scattered on tabletops and on the burnished walnut desk. The furniture might be old and the carpet faded, but Mrs. Christmas had the maids polish the exposed floorboards until they gleamed, and scrub, dust, or clean every object not nailed down. Despite the evident deterioration of the last few years, the abiding affection held by the servants for Mistletoe Manor and the Merritt family shone forth.

Lucas propped his elbows on the desktop as he frowned at

a massive ledger. By his expression, whatever he was studying displeased him. Lately, she rarely saw him with anything but a stern or unhappy expression on his rugged features. Her heart squeezed with sympathy and a longing to relieve him of at least some of his burdens.

He glanced up, surprise lifting his brows. A swift but obscure emotion rippled across his features, but then his usual polite mask slipped back into place. "Phoebe, I wasn't expecting you. Is anything wrong?"

She gave him a tentative smile. "No, but I do wish to speak to you. Would you like me to come back later?"

He grimaced. "Frankly, I welcome the interruption. It's taking me days to straighten out these damn books. For some reason that eludes me, your grandfather let go his last estate manager. He took over the books himself, although Mr. Christmas did inform me that he was occasionally dragooned into service as record keeper."

"I take it my grandfather had not a strong head for numbers."

"That would be a colossal understatement, my dear," Lucas responded dryly.

Phoebe had to repress the urge to defend her grandfather. Even though she had never met the old earl in person, she held him in great esteem. But Lucas needed her loyalty now and, if he would accept it, her love. "Have you made any progress in finding a new estate manager?" she asked as she settled into the wing chair in front of his desk.

Lucas eyed her, his expression slightly puzzled. Then he gave a slight shrug. "I interviewed three more candidates today. One is a possibility, although he's young and inexperienced." The faintest of smiles touched his lips. "But I'm just desperate enough to hire him. God knows, I can't keep relying on Christmas or Popham to do the job. Popham has been overseeing the most urgent of the repairs on the estate, and he told me today that if he had to deal with one more complaining tenant or leaking roof he would quit on the spot."

"Oh, dear! I hope not," Phoebe exclaimed, worried how Lucas would react to that.

He laughed. It sounded rather rusty, but she welcomed it. "Actually, you'd have to drag the man away from my side. But he's never spent much time in the country. He doesn't know one type of grain from another, or have a clue how to mend a fence or fix a roof."

He leaned back in his chair, his smile fading into caution as he studied her. Nervously, Phoebe clenched her hands, praying for wisdom and patience. After all, men like Lucas did not easily reveal themselves to others, and especially to women.

"What did you want to ask me?" he asked.

"I have several questions, actually. The first is, what would you like to do for Christmas?"

He arched his brows. "Why do we have to do anything? Besides go to church, that is." He gave her a sardonic smile. "I'm assuming you do want to go to church."

"Yes, of course," she said, refusing to be baited. "But we must also plan celebrations for the servants and the villagers—"

He cut her off with a dismissive wave. "I expect they'll have their own celebrations. Why would we need to do anything out of the ordinary, since most of them will be with their families? The servants will have Boxing Day to themselves, and I expect you'll want to give them the usual gifts. As for the alms for the poor, I'll give an ample amount to Mr. Knaggs for distribution. Other than that, I don't see the need to do anything else."

Phoebe stared at him. Could he truly be that unaware of his responsibilities? "Lucas, you are lord of an estate called Mistletoe Manor. Half your servants and many of the people in the village go by the name of *Christmas*, for heaven's sake.

Surely you realize there are expectations and traditions to be upheld. Already the preparations are under way. The puddings have been stirred and put up, and—"

"Phoebe," he said, impatiently interrupting again, "you're a Quaker. You don't even celebrate Christmas."

She crossed her arms, giving him a stern look, but he likely missed it since his gaze followed her motion, fixing on her breasts and remaining there. Instantly, a hot, shivery reaction flashed through her body. Annoyed he could elicit so ready a response, she resisted the urge to squirm in her seat.

"My lord," she said firmly, "I would prefer you look at my face when you speak with me, not to other parts of my anatomy, no matter how attractive you might find them."

His gaze snapped up to her face and he choked back a laugh. "I have no idea what you're talking about, my dear wife."

His eyes gleamed with mischief and a burgeoning sensuality. It took every ounce of discipline on her part to resist the siren lure of her husband's powerful masculinity. She *did* want that from him, but not just yet. Not until they reached an understanding in other areas of their life. "Yes, well. To address your concern, Lucas, although it is true that my father's family did not celebrate Christmas, that does not mean I do not wish to do so myself. In fact, I find the prospect quite exciting."

Lucas rolled his eyes.

"And as I said," she continued, ignoring his annoying reaction, "there are certain traditions here at the manor, many of which have been lost in recent years. It would mean a great deal to the locals if we restored them. It would be a wonderful way to show we are now truly a part of their lives, and that we share their concerns and their hopes."

That prompted a snort from her husband, but she carried on doggedly.

"To that end, I have been thinking of what we should do on Christmas Day."

"Nothing?" he asked hopefully.

She narrowed her eyes at him. "In the past, the earls of Merritt opened the manor to the tenants and villagers. Food and drink was provided for all, and there was music and games for . . ."

She stumbled over her words, surprised by the grim look on her husband's face. "You would not have to do anything," she said defensively. "Mrs. Christmas has been taking care of this for years, and knows exactly what is to be done. All that would be required of you is to preside over the day's festivities. And not scowl at everyone like a grumpy old bear with a thorn stuck in his paw," she could not help finishing in a snippy tone.

"Is that all?" he asked dryly.

She sighed. "Lucas, did you never celebrate Christmas? Do you not have any fond memories of the occasion?"

He shrugged. "As a child, yes. But not in the military. There were years when a celebration of any kind seemed wrong, or at least beside the point."

"But you are not in the military now."

"So you keep telling me."

When she let out a frustrated sigh, he rose and came round to the front of the desk, leaning against it. He was so tall she had to tilt her head back to meet his gaze.

"Phoebe," he said, gently nudging her shoe with his booted foot, "do you know how much it would cost to provide that sort of entertainment?"

Her stomach jumped. "Are you saying we cannot afford to do this?"

Another faint smile lifted his lips. "*Goose.* Of course we can afford it. That's not the point."

"Then what is?"

He began a restless prowl around the room. "I think sometimes you don't realize what bad shape the manor and the home farms are in. I'm not poor by any means, but I don't possess anything like the wealth that someone such as Silverton has."

She watched him as he paced, not missing the shadow of bitterness that crossed his face when he mentioned his cousin's name.

He came to a halt in front of the fireplace. "I'm pouring all my resources into the manor and the estate, trying to bring them back to life." Staring down at the flames, he fell into a brown study that she felt loath to interrupt.

Finally, he glanced up, looking stern and determined. "I *will* bring it back, Phoebe. The place deserves that, and I believe the estate can be prosperous again. But it's going to bleed me dry until it does, and I don't want to waste a penny on something as frivolous as a Christmas party."

She nodded, her insides twisting with sympathy. Lucas took everyone's burdens upon himself, never asking for or expecting help. She wondered if in some strange way he did it to punish himself. But for what? The pain he had caused his cousin and the Stanton family? Surely Lucas realized it was time to forgive himself, and forgive Silverton, too.

Rising, she joined him by the fireplace. Perhaps he did not want her help, but she would give him no choice. "I am sorry you think I do not understand the complexities of restoring the estate," she said earnestly. "But you must not regard such things as celebrations as wasted time or money. They are not."

Steeling herself against rejection, she reached out and slipped her hand into his. He tensed for a moment, and then his warm hand engulfed her fingers. "You know better than anyone how difficult life has been for the people of the village," she said quietly. "For too long they have suffered without hope. Under those circumstances, how can it possibly be a waste to lift their spirits and cheer their hearts? People need more than hard work and food on the table to be whole, Lucas. They need fellowship and good cheer in their lives, too."

If anyone understood such a lesson, she did. For too many

years in her brother's household, she had been lonely and without joy. But the Stantons had changed that for her. Lucas had changed that.

He gripped her hand, staring down at her, but his eyes seemed to look through her to something very far away. She tugged on his fingers to recapture his attention.

His lips twisted in a self-mocking smile. "I suppose that's what Christmas is all about, Lord help me. All right, my sweet. You shall have your Christmas party. I suppose my pockets are still deep enough to stand the strain." His smile slid from mockery to mischief. "And you *are* a Quaker, so I don't expect you'll pull me too far into dun territory."

His capitulation caught her by surprise. "I will do my best not to bankrupt us, although I make no promises," she said. On impulse, she went up on her toes and brushed a kiss along the rugged angle of his jaw. "Thank you, my lord. I know everyone will be very excited. Especially the children. They have been preparing for weeks."

He looked startled by her gesture, but recovered quickly. "What children are you talking about?"

"The vicar has been preparing the village children for their Christmas pageant. I already invited them up to the manor to put it on for us."

He winced, looking truly pained. "God help us all. There's nothing more gruesome than amateur theatricals. Madam Wife, what were you thinking?"

"Lucas, I do not think—"

He shook his head. "It's fine, really. I doubt I could hold back any of these festivities even if I wanted to. I'll leave it up to you and Mrs. Christmas to handle all the details." He squeezed her hand gently, then dropped it, giving her a smile both kind and dismissive. "If you'll forgive me," he said, going back to his desk, "I have quite a bit more work to do."

"Oh." She tried to keep the disappointment from her voice.

"I do not wish to keep you from your work, but I have another question."

He raised his gaze back up from the ledger with mock alarm. "You are turning into a regular pickpocket. What now?"

"I have no intention of picking your pockets," she replied in a dignified voice. "I have received a letter from Meredith, inviting us to a party at Belfield Abbey two days before Christmas. She suggests we come in the afternoon and stay until the next morning."

The icy expression in her husband's eyes dropped the temperature of the room by several degrees. Her stomach dropped as well, but she pushed on. "I know it is not comfortable for you, but I would like very much to see the family again. And I know Aunt Georgie and Uncle Arthur wish to see you."

He studied her in a silence broken only by the crackle of the fire. It was hard not to fidget under his perceptive gaze. "It's been hard on you these last few weeks," he said.

Not wanting to lie, she simply shrugged.

He grimaced and muttered something under his breath before he finally replied. "I suppose I can put up with Silverton for one night if it makes you happy."

"Thank you," she whispered.

He nodded and returned to his books, but when she kept her place he glanced up. "Is there something else?"

This time, she heard the undisguised impatience. Her courage almost deserted her, but she had only one more hurdle to clear. Unfortunately, it was the biggest one. "I wish to speak to you about the smugglers."

He raked a frustrated hand through his hair, making the thick locks stand straight up before they tumbled across his brow. "We discussed this, Phoebe. You are not to get involved."

She held her hands up, palms out. "I am not trying to interfere, but I cannot help but worry. Both about you and the villagers. You must realize they fell into smuggling because of the wretched conditions in the village. Some people were actually starving, Lucas. What were they to do?"

"You think I don't know that? It has been a bloody nightmare for just about everyone, which is one of the reasons why I'm emptying my pockets to get this estate back in working order."

"I know. And that is wonderful, but in the meantime—"

"In the meantime I have already let it be known that any man who seeks an honest day's wage can find it at the manor, no questions asked. I'm not a hard-hearted bastard, no matter what you might think about me." He flung the last words at her like a challenge.

"I have never thought that," she answered quietly. "I never would."

The fire crackled and leapt like a merry, mad thing, filling the silence that fell again. That silence seemed a solid, breathing creature, growing the distance between them.

"Then you also know I can't let the smuggling continue," he finally said in a rough voice. "It's too dangerous. Someone is going to get killed if I don't put a stop to it."

She thought of Samuel Weston, and the other children who might be at risk, and could only nod in agreement. "I understand. I only ask that when the time comes, you exercise as much compassion as you can. For all our sakes." She was surprised to feel tears pricking her eyes. "You must return to your work, so I will bid you good night."

Phoebe started for the door, struggling to keep her emotions at bay. She should be satisfied, since he had given her more than she had expected, but the idea of another night in her lonely bed left her weary and chilled to the bone. Right now, she needed Lucas more than ever, but she was not to have him.

"Phoebe." His deep voice pulled her up short, and she turned slowly to face him. He now lounged in his chair in a careless sprawl, looking big and powerful, and more than a little dangerous.

"Yes?" she whispered, barely hearing herself over the thumping of her heart.

"Where are you going?"

"Ah . . . up to my chambers."

His eyes turned smoky gray with desire. "Not yet," he said. Then he extended his hand. "My sweet, come here."

Chapter 23

Phoebe remained frozen by the door, her big, dark eyes filled with a combination of yearning and apprehension. She clearly wanted him as much as he wanted her, enough so she had bearded him in his den and refused to back down, even though he'd sure as hell been less than welcoming. Her determination to bridge their estrangement sent triumph and no small measure of relief surging through his veins.

Living this close to Phoebe and yet not being able to touch her had been a special kind of torture—worse than some of the hellish conditions Lucas had faced in the military. But she'd drawn the line on their wedding night, using her naive moral beliefs to reduce him to little more than an exaggerated fairy-tale villain. It had practically killed him to walk away, but he would never take her against her will, or use her own innocent passion to overcome her objections.

He knew he could have seduced her. But his pride wouldn't stand for it, and he knew on some level it would damage her as well. His lesser angels *had* urged him to use her sexual inexperience against her, but the price would have been far too high, the wound to her spirit far too great.

And so he had kept his distance this last week, both physically and emotionally. But as the days crept by and his frustrations with the estate grew along with his sexual hunger, he'd begun to question the point of it. They'd argued over a bunch of inept smugglers, for Christ's sake. A damn group of idiots who didn't have the sense to realize they risked their own safety and that of their families by making ever more dangerous runs while the legal noose pulled tighter by the day. His visit to Harper had confirmed that. The excise officer and his men were closing in on the local gang, and it was only a matter of time until they were apprehended.

Lucas could choose to ignore the whole business, of course, as the previous earl had done and as many estate owners continued to do. Phoebe, with her tender heart, obviously wanted him to do just that. He wasn't too proud to admit that late at night, when his sexual frustration reached unmanageable proportions, he was tempted to give in to her.

More than once his feet had hit the floor and he had stalked to the connecting doors between their rooms, ready to accede to her wishes. It wasn't merely the desire to feel her perfect body wrapped around his, although that image affected him powerfully. It was his growing need for her gentle understanding at the end of another wretched day spent trying to resurrect something meaningful from this wreck of an estate. He longed for that as a man on the battlefield longed for peace and respite. It was one of the reasons he'd married her, for the pleasure and consolation of her generous, kind nature.

But he couldn't capitulate, not even to please his new wife. To do so would violate everything he believed in, both as an officer and a gentleman. Phoebe had to learn and learn quickly that he would be lord in his own manor. She, along with everyone else, had to realize his word was now law. Not for any foolish exercise of power, but because the safety and well-being of those in the village and the manor now rested squarely on his shoulders.

Thankfully, Phoebe had finally come to him, sweet and nervous and yet determined to make the first difficult step in breaching the barriers between them. Her actions touched him more than he cared to admit, and he respected what it must have cost her. In return, he was willing to let her have her silly Christmas party and her abbey visit—as annoying and distracting as those two events were going to be—if it meant they could put the blasted estrangement to rest.

And if it meant he could finally have his lush little wife in his bed, where she belonged.

He smiled at her, waiting patiently for her to come to him. She had backbone, his Phoebe, but she was still an innocent. Her desire was as soft and fragile as new petals on a blooming rose. At this point, his lust for her was so overpowering it might scare the hell out of her if he let it become fully evident.

When she still didn't move, he lifted an inquiring eyebrow. "Phoebe?"

A fugitive smile trembled on her lips and she took a deep breath. Her breasts, tightly encased by her modest dress, strained in full, pretty mounds against the fabric. He didn't think it was his imagination that her nipples were faintly outlined beneath her bodice. His mouth watered with the idea of tasting them.

Finally, she came to him, hesitant but graceful. When she rounded the desk and stopped before him, her brow slightly furrowed, he didn't say a word. Instead, he took her hand and tugged her into his lap.

Gasping, she tumbled across his thighs and clutched his shoulders to steady herself. Her pretty bottom made contact with his stiffening cock, and he had to bite back a groan.

"Lucas, what in heaven's name are you doing?" Her voice was high with nerves.

With one hand he tipped her chin up. Then he leaned in, inhaling her clean, feminine scent, before he laved the throbbing pulse at the base of her neck. She let out a strangled moan and dug her fingers into his coat.

"I'm getting ready to make love to my wife," he murmured.

Her body went rigid in his arms. Frowning, he lifted his head to study her. Had he read her wrong? He could have sworn she wanted this as much as he did.

Yet she clung to him, staring back with naked longing in her eyes. And something else he couldn't quite put his finger on.

He nuzzled her soft cheek. "Don't you want us to be together as man and wife, Phoebe? Isn't that why you came in here?"

She worried her plump lower lip, the small motion sending a flash of heat to his groin. Between that and the pressure of her sweet arse, he had to clamp down hard on the impulse to grind up into her.

"Y . . . yes. I mean, no. I mean . . . yes, I do not wish us to be estranged, but I did not specifically come to ask for *this*."

That last word was accompanied by a fluttering of one small hand from her chest to his, meant to encompass all that was implied in their present situation.

His modest little Quaker. He bit back a smile, contenting himself with a gentle brush of his lips across her mouth. Her eyelids drifted down and her fingers once more dug into his shoulders. This time he did smile. "But you do want this, don't you?"

"Yes," she breathed against his mouth.

"That's all I was waiting for." He wrapped his arms around her and surged to his feet, holding her high against his chest. Dodging around his desk, careful not to thump her into anything, he strode toward the door.

Her eyes went round with astonishment. "Lucas! What are you doing?"

"I'm taking my wife upstairs to bed."

As he hoped, that brought a charming blush to her cheeks. "I am quite capable of walking to my bedroom. You really should put me down."

He juggled her a bit as he opened the door. "Right now I can't think of a single reason why I should."

In fact, it had taken all his willpower not to sit her on his lap, shove her dress up, and take her right there in the uncertain privacy of his library. He had no intention of putting her down until it was on her bed, with the damn door to her rooms locked behind them.

"Because one of the servants might—" She cut off her sentence with a groan as their butler appeared at the top of the stairs, making his evening round to check all the windows and doors.

"Good evening, my lord," Christmas intoned in his usual lugubrious manner. "My lady, I do hope you are not unwell."

Phoebe went as stiff as a board in his arms. Giving her an evil grin, Lucas gazed down at her, waiting for her to answer the question. She flashed him a scowl, then promptly wiped it from her features before addressing the butler. "I am perfectly well, Mr. Christmas. Thank you for your kind inquiry. His lordship is simply helping me up to my chambers."

"How kind of his lordship," the butler responded. Not even the unusual sight of the master carrying the mistress to bed was enough to lighten the death knell quality of the old fellow's voice.

Christmas gave them a dignified nod and passed by, acting for all the world as if nothing was amiss. Phoebe smiled and nodded back, although she was rigid with indignation in her husband's arms. Lucas almost burst into laughter but he managed to choke it down, not wanting to provoke her any further. If he did, she might kick him out of her room, and that would surely drive him completely insane.

As he strode down the hall, enjoying the warm little package she made in his arms, Phoebe crossed her arms over her chest and glared at him. "You, sir, are a perfect beast. God only knows what the poor man thinks of us."

"I do. He thinks whatever we pay him to think."

She rolled her eyes, but a smile twitched the edges of her mouth. He loved that quality in her—so dignified and modest, and yet possessed of an unpredictable sense of humor and so much passion. Sometimes, it manifested itself in surprising displays of temper, like that night at the Framingham ball. Yet at other times, like tonight, a little imp peeked out from behind that proper facade. It fascinated him to the point of obsession, and God help him if she ever discovered that.

When they stopped in front of her bedroom door, she reached out to turn the knob herself. As he carried her in, Maggie popped out of Phoebe's dressing room, a bundle of clothes draped over her arm. She took one look at them and came rushing forward.

"Oh, my lady," she gasped as she fluttered uselessly around them. "Whatever is wrong? Are you ill?"

Lucas let out a long-suffering sigh, while his wife looked at him and raised a challenging eyebrow. Fair enough. He'd made her handle the butler. "Nothing's wrong, Maggie. I'm simply helping her ladyship get ready for bed. Run along now. You won't be needed."

Maggie's round eyes got even rounder as understanding dawned. She only half tried to stifle a giggle as she bobbed them a curtsy. "Of course, my lord. Whatever you say. Shall I tell Popham he won't be needed either?"

"Yes. Thank you."

Maggie backed out of the room, gently closing the door. But through the panels they heard the girl call out, "Oh, Mr. Popham. No need to wait up. His lordship will be sleeping in my lady's bed tonight. And about time, too, I might add."

Fortunately, they were spared Popham's reply.

Phoebe groaned and thunked her head against his chest.

"I don't like to criticize, my love," Lucas said in a musing tone, "but it strikes me that your maid is a titch too forward in her manners."

"Then she fits in very well with the rest of the servants at Mistletoe Manor, does she not?" Phoebe responded dryly.

He laughed. "Yes, we've been extraordinarily lucky in that

respect, haven't we?" He strode to the bed, then dropped her into the soft welter of stacked pillows and bedclothes.

She bounced once and then collapsed with a giggle onto the pillows. When she recovered her breath, she smiled up at him. "I am not sure how lucky it is to have a houseful of servants discussing our intimate relations on a regular basis," she said, wrinkling her adorable nose.

He gazed at her, all a-tumble, her skirts hiked up around her thighs, exposing her pretty legs in their simple white stockings. His groin tightened and every muscle in his body went hard.

"I don't know about you, sweetheart," he murmured, tracing his hand from her ankle up to the knee. She shivered under his hand, and he smiled. "But right now I'm feeling very lucky indeed."

Phoebe peered at her handsome, imposing husband. As he braced one hand against the bedpost and smiled down at her, the hot gleam in his eye had her stomach jumping with nerves and anticipation. She had wanted him—wanted this—so much, but now that the moment had arrived she had no idea what to say or do. When he made her laugh, it seemed so much easier. But the prospect of Lucas finally taking her to bed was anything but a laughing matter.

His head tilted as he assessed her. "You're feeling anxious again, aren't you?"

She nodded, her throat so dry she would likely croak if she tried to utter a word.

With a smile easing the lines of his strong features, he sat down beside her. "You weren't anxious the other night, were you? Not once we got started."

"No," she said. And her voice sounded *exactly* like a frog's croak.

He laughed softly. "Then trust me and all will be well."

That was the crux of the matter. Trust. She had trusted him enough to make that first approach downstairs in his study, and he had not failed her. But this was the final bridge to cross. Once done, there would be no more keeping her distance from him, physically or emotionally.

As he waited patiently for her to respond, he began pulling the pins from her hair. He worked methodically, as if nothing could be more interesting than playing lady's maid. His manner, more than anything, reassured her. Lucas would take care of her, as he took care of everything and everyone in his life.

"I do trust you," she whispered.

"Good." He slipped his hands under her shoulders and helped her sit up. Then he moved behind and began unbuttoning her dress. As each button came free, he parted her dress and planted a kiss on her back. Even through her stays and chemise, the press of his lips along her spine made her shudder.

"What a lot of silly buttons you have, Lady Merritt," he said as he methodically worked his way down.

"Do not blame me. Blame that ridiculous modiste Aunt Georgie and Meredith dragged me to."

"I find I'm quite enjoying unwrapping my wife. It's rather like finding an early present several days before Christmas."

While he worked, Phoebe had been undoing the buttons at her wrists. Her hands trembled so much she only managed to free one wrist before he finished with the back of her dress.

He moved around to help, and his deft fingers made quick work of her cuffs. Then, as he leaned over to kiss her, slipping his tongue between her lips for a quick taste, he eased the dress off her shoulders. A moment later he had it down to her hips, and she lifted her bottom to help him remove it completely. Without looking, he tossed it behind him in the general direction of the chair in front of her dressing table. It missed, landing in a heap on the floor.

"Lucas," she exclaimed. "That is no way to treat a very expensive dress."

He was already at work on her stays. "I thought you didn't like it."

She rolled her eyes. "I never said that."

"Don't worry," he said in a distracted voice as he pulled the garment from her body, "I'll buy you a new one. As many as you like, with hundreds of buttons for me to undo."

She smiled at his teasing, but shivered a moment later when his big hands came right to her breasts, kneading the plump mounds for a few seconds before scraping his calloused palms across the rapidly stiffening points. Phoebe bit her lip, stifling a moan.

He gave a rough laugh. "Don't hold it in on my account, love. I like it when you make noise."

She eyed him doubtfully. "You do?"

Lucas planted his hands on either side of her hips, and bent over to tongue her nipple through the thin fabric of her chemise. It contracted into a hard bead under the rough pressure of his tongue. An exquisite sensation arrowed from the tip of her breast to the crux of her thighs, and she fell back on her elbows as a moan forced its way from between her lips. Lucas hummed his satisfaction deep in his throat as he continued to suck and tease one nipple and then the other.

Soon the fabric of her chemise was wet from his mouth, the tips of her breasts thrusting against the transparent linen in stiff points. Lucas teased them relentlessly, sucking them between his lips, and flicking them with his tongue. All the while, she could not help but arch up to him as little whimpers issued from her mouth.

After several minutes of that delicious torture, he pulled back. His cheekbones had flushed a dark bronze and his eyes glowed with lust, but a mischievous smile played around his lips. "See?" he rumbled in a deep voice. "I do like it. It increases your pleasure, too, doesn't it? Don't hold back, Phoebe. Say what you want and move as much as you want."

She stared up at him, feeling a little dizzy with all the

sensation. He was right. Making noise *did* seem to increase her pleasure, although she had no idea why.

He smiled at the expression on her face. "Don't try to figure it out. Just let it happen. It will feel that much better if you do."

She gave him a dubious nod, then ran her gaze over his broad-shouldered frame. A frame that was impeccably clothed in evening garb, while she lay undressed before him. The contrast rather excited her, although it was not strictly fair.

"Lucas."

"Yes, love?"

"Do you not think it rather odd of me to be lying here half naked, while you stand there fully clothed?"

He gave her another of those hot-eyed, assessing stares. "Not in the slightest, but I take your point. Let me remedy that."

Quickly divesting himself of his coat, waistcoat, and cravat, he tossed them into the rapidly growing pile of clothes on the floor. Phoebe made a clucking noise with her tongue. "I had no idea my husband was so untidy."

He perched on the edge of the bed and began to pull off his boots. He had to struggle a bit but he managed, all while casting a devilish grin over his shoulder as he did so. "That's what wives are for, aren't they? To clean up after their men."

"Not this wife," she said in a sugary tone. "I have other things to do."

The boots thudded to the floor and he stood. "Is that so? Pray tell, what would those other things be?" Then he pulled his shirt over his head, revealing his magnificently hard torso and muscular arms.

Phoebe's entire body went boneless with anticipation. Fighting a delicious lethargy, she struggled into a sitting position. "Well," she whispered, reaching out to trace a finger along the narrow scar that cut across his rib cage, "right now I have to make love to my husband."

His eyes flared with desire, and she could see the bulge of

his erection swell against the fall of his breeches. With hands not quite steady, he grasped the hem of her chemise and eased it up her body. The nubby linen caught on her nipples, teasing the sensitive points, and she moaned again. A dark laugh emerged from her husband's throat, echoing her pleasure. After he pulled the garment from her, he gently pushed her back onto the pillows. She lay there, trembling, clad only in her garters and stockings.

Lucas stood over her, his features harsh with the intensity of his desire. The gleam in his eyes made her pulses jump—in her throat, low in her belly, and behind her knees. And as his gaze roamed over her, stopping at her nest of feminine curls, a pulse throbbed there, too. Hot, wet, and heavy.

"Christ," he said in a strained voice. "You're the most beautiful thing I've ever seen. I don't deserve you, Phoebe."

Her throat tightened with a sudden rush of longing, and of love. "Thank you," she managed to whisper. "It is very kind of you to say so."

Her silly response pulled a startled crack of laughter from his lips. "Kindness is the last emotion I'm feeling right now."

Planting his hands on the inside of her thighs, he nudged her legs wide. She peered up at him doubtfully. "Do you want me to take off my stockings, Lucas?"

He shook his head. "Not on your life, my sweet."

After making that odd statement, he came up on the bed and settled between her spread thighs. His smoldering gaze fell on that part of her body usually hidden but now spread wide for his pleasure. Phoebe flushed with heat, trepidation, and an excitement that made her squirm. She could feel the rush of it spread through her body, coalescing in a throbbing ache deep in her womb.

She stirred restlessly beneath him, and Lucas's big hands clamped on her thighs, holding her still.

"And now," he said in a voice so dark and rough it almost made her swoon, "I intend to play with my wife."

Chapter 24

Phoebe stared up into her husband's face. Consummating a marriage seemed a serious business to her, but he made it sound more like a game than anything else. What her body felt now—raw, disturbingly carnal sensations—was far removed from any kind of game she could imagine.

And it took some getting used to, lying naked and spread before one's husband like a heathen sacrifice. It was both mortifying and exciting, and the exciting part urged her to do outrageous things, like lay back, open her knees wide, and . . . wriggle her bottom, which struck her as quite odd. She could imagine doing other things, too, although even imagining them made her flush with embarrassment. They struck her as wicked and yet so intensely desirable, which generally fit any definition of sin she had ever heard of. But Lucas *was* her husband and this was the marriage bed, so how could anything they did here be sinful?

She wished she could ask him about it, but shyness overcame her.

As if he read her thoughts, Lucas smiled and murmured soothing words to her. Then his calloused palms slid up the insides of her thighs and a delicious heat rippled from his hands to settle deep in her soft, hidden folds. As he stroked her, his fingers inching ever closer to the curls between her thighs, sensation raced across her skin and her body released a soft flood of moisture.

Phoebe jerked with surprise and involuntarily tried to close her legs. She could not, of course, not with Lucas sitting between them. But the idea that he could see everything that was happening *down there* made her blush from head to heels. "Lucas," she said in a strangled voice, "perhaps we should get under the covers."

His gaze had been fixed intently on the secret place between her legs—not so secret now—but his head came up when she spoke.

"Don't be embarrassed, love. Your body is doing exactly what it's supposed to do, and I want to see all of it."

She frowned. "Why?"

"Because it's beautiful. You're beautiful."

"If you say so," she answered doubtfully. Perhaps she could partly understand, since she was deriving a great deal of pleasure from viewing her husband's magnificent body.

Obviously finished with explanations, Lucas returned his attention to his hands and what they were doing to her. Slowly, stroking her as if she were a kitten, they moved up her thighs to finally reach her damp heat. Shivers raced in the wake of his fingers, making her weak and light-headed. She was tempted to collapse onto the pillows, but something compelled her to keep watching. It fascinated her, the harsh, desirous look on his face, and that made all the sensations racing through her body wildly exciting.

Gently, his fingers stroked her, finding and then parting her soft folds. Phoebe moaned, raw need awakening in a throbbing rush of desire. Unable to stop herself, her legs fell wide, opening everything to his touch and sight.

"That's it." His voice came out in a rasp. "I want to see every part of your luscious body."

She sank back on her elbows, eyelids heavy, and watched

her husband. Now she understood the word *play*, because that is exactly what he did. His fingers traced through her wet curls, rubbing, stroking, and eventually finding that delicious point of sensitivity. When his blunt fingertips brushed against the little knot of flesh, she cried and arched up, pushing her mound against the palm of his hand. It felt as if an arrow of liquid heat shot straight to her womb, then gathered at the base of her spine.

"Yes, darling. That's it," he urged. Up on his knees now, his big body loomed over her. A faint sheen of perspiration slicked his shoulders and chest, and the hard lines of his features looked carved from granite. "Just let yourself feel everything." He circled the hard nub with his teasing fingertips as he murmured to her in a deep, entrancing voice. "Let your body go where it will."

She had no choice. Phoebe had never felt so out of control, as if something shivered under the surface of her skin, waiting to explode. She had experienced something of that on her wedding night, but this was stronger, wilder, as if that previous interlude had unleashed a sensation—no, an emotion, yearning to escape. It required only her husband's touch to call it forth to freedom.

His hands danced magic over her flesh until she twisted beneath him in a mad craving for release from the sensual torment. And yet she could not help spreading her legs even wider, silently begging him to give her more.

"God, Phoebe," he groaned. "You're so hot. So wet. I can't wait to bury my cock deep inside you."

Her eyes, almost closed, flew open. His words made her stomach clench with wanting, and she shifted restlessly beneath him.

"Lucas, please," she begged, "I want . . . I want . . ."

She wanted what he gave her the other night, but had no words for it. She stared up into his eyes, stormy gray with desire, and silently pleaded with him.

He gave a husky laugh. "All right, love. I'll give you what you want. Then I'll take everything I want."

His dark promise made her shiver.

"Look at me when you come, Phoebe," he whispered. "Look at what I'm doing to you."

Helpless to do anything else, she watched him part her folds with exquisite delicacy, and then slowly push a finger into her tight passage. She gasped as her body clenched around him with tiny spasms. Gently, he stretched her, then inserted another finger. It burned a bit, but the shivery little contractions grew as he slowly pumped in and out, dragging his fingers through her slick folds and then pushing them back into her soft passage. Each time, he deliberately rubbed over the hidden bud, assailing her body with more hunger, more need.

Phoebe writhed against the tangled sheets, arching up to press into his tormenting fingers. With a rough laugh, Lucas reached up one hand to capture her breast. He rolled the stiff tip between his fingertips, then gave it a gentle pinch. She cried out as a storm of sensation rushed through her.

"Lucas," she wailed in a ragged voice.

As she sobbed, straining for release, he once more pumped his fingers deep inside as his thumb pressed down against the hard nub of her sex. Her womb contracted in a deep spasm, sending luxurious ripples through her tight inner muscles. Her flesh clamped around him and she cried out, arching her hips up into his hand, straining to increase the wild pleasure. For several moments she seemed to hang suspended, arousal slamming through her with a rapturous heat.

Then the hard, driving pleasure began to fade, easing into little shudders that leached the strength from her limbs. Phoebe fell back onto the pillows, gulping in air as her heart gradually stuttered into its normal rhythm.

As she lay panting, trying to catch her breath, Lucas slid his fingers from her passage. Without his touch, without the feel of him inside her, she felt empty and already aching for more. How could she possibly feel that way? She could barely move a limb or even lift her head. And yet, she still wanted more from Lucas.

She wanted *him*.

With a great force of effort, she managed to prop herself up on her elbows. Lucas had moved back to sit quietly on his heels, watching her with a dark, captivating gaze. Her heart gave an erratic thump and, unexpectedly, tears stung her eyes. She wanted him so much that her throat grew tight with emotion.

"What are you doing all the way down there?" she whispered.

A wicked smile lifted the corners of his mouth, and he came to his knees and began a slow prowl up her body. He stopped at her breasts for a few minutes, leisurely tasting her. He went from one to the other, plumping and kneading the full mounds as he sucked her tight peaks into rigid, aching points. Dragging his tongue slowly across her nipples, he soon had her writhing and panting again, and aching for the feel of him inside her.

Finally, he left her breasts and kissed his way up her neck to hover over her mouth. She languidly draped her arms over his broad shoulders, loving the way his tough, muscled body pressed her down into the mattress. As much as it excited her, it also made her feel protected and loved.

"Did you like what I did to you?" Lucas whispered as he nibbled around the edges of her mouth.

She drew her nails from his neck across the bridge of his shoulders, relishing the way his muscles jumped under her fingertips. He pulled in a deep breath, and against her chest she felt the rapid pounding of his heart.

"What do you think?" she said, craning up to capture his mouth.

He swooped to meet her, taking her lips, her tongue, all of her in a kiss so passionate it tumbled her insides with excitement. Growling low in his throat—and she felt the rumble vibrating all through her body—his tongue swept into her mouth, swirling and tasting in a hot dance of possession. She clung to him, pouring her soul into the kiss. All the loneliness and yearning of her life was obliterated by the taste of his mouth, the weight of his body, and the energy that sparked between them.

He broke away, his breath almost as shattered and panting as hers. His eyes were as turbulent as a storm at sea. "I need you, Phoebe. Now."

His primitive rasp made her body clench with anticipation. She stared at him, her mind dazed by passion. The time for games was past. What they did now would seal her fate and bind her to him forever.

Swallowing convulsively, she gave him a shaky nod as she instinctively drew her knees up to his lean hips. Then she wrapped her fingers around his biceps, holding on tight.

The hard lines of his face softened as he gazed down on her. He leaned down and brushed a soft kiss on her lips. "So sweet," he whispered. "Never worry, love. I'll always take care of you."

She blinked away sudden tears as a smile trembled on her lips. Never had she loved anyone as much as she loved him in this tender, earth-shattering moment.

Reaching down, he nudged her leg up higher on his hip. She pressed into him, but still he denied her—denied them—completion. Instead, he slid his thick, silken length back and forth against her wet little bud. Delicious tensions once more coiled low in her belly and in her womb. She wrapped her arms around his neck, pleading with him in broken, foolish words.

Finally, she felt the muscles in his arms bunch under her hands. He shifted, and the tip of his erection nudged into her slick entrance. Slowly, he rocked into her, parting her melting flesh with a steady slide. There was a sudden, sharp burn as he stretched her, and she went rigid in his arms.

Clenching his teeth, he rested his damp forehead against hers. His body, so bronzed in the light of the fire, held a damp sheen that glowed. They panted, chest to chest, skin to skin, a moment frozen in time. After long, breathless seconds, the burn faded and an aching fullness took its place. Phoebe blew out a little puff of air and lifted one hand up to stroke her husband's cheek.

He lifted his head. "Better now?"

She wriggled beneath his weight, testing it. Lucas made a strangled noise and his pupils seemed to dilate.

Phoebe smiled. "Yes, much better. In fact, I think I rather like it."

Lucas clenched his teeth. "I'm so glad, because I'm at the end of my rope."

She giggled, but when he began to move, the laughter died in her throat. The sensation of having Lucas inside her, stroking her so intimately with his body, overwhelmed her. Arousal once again fired all her nerves. The steady rhythm, the flexing of his hips, twisted her insides with a tight, acute sensation that soon had her rising to meet his thrusts.

He rose over her, ruthless and dominating. She arched her back, thrusting her breasts up in wanton pleasure. When she rubbed her nipples into the hard vault of his chest, he actually growled, pressing her down into the bedding. His body seemed to cloak her, and she grew dizzy with the contrast between his unyielding muscles and her soft curves. Whimpering, she twisted beneath him, overcome by his effortless masculine strength. She loved how he made her feel—how this act of loving made her feel—vulnerable, sensual, and feminine.

And a wife. *His* wife.

As that idea took hold, she slid her arms around his back, gripping him close. He slipped one hand under her bottom and tilted her, increasing the depth of his penetration.

"Lucas," she gasped.

He let out a rough laugh as he withdrew almost completely from her body, then pushed back with a hard flex of hips that threw her over the edge. Fire raced through her veins and devastating pleasure seized her body. When Lucas gave a ragged groan, surging into her one last time, she wrapped her arms around him and clutched with a desperate strength.

"Oh, God," she cried. "Lucas, I love you!"

His entire body went rigid in her arms, then he slowly collapsed onto her. For a few moments he lay on top of her, crushing her into the mattress, then he rolled to his side, bringing her with him.

Gradually, Phoebe returned to earth, and with it returned sanity. The seconds crawled by in silence, stretching into minutes, and still Lucas said nothing. Her head rested on his chest, his crisp hair tickling her cheek as one of his hands slowly stroked down her back. It should have been the perfect moment, the culmination of everything she longed for, and yet doubt once more crept into her heart.

Emotionally undone by the intensity of their lovemaking, Phoebe had blurted out her love. And Lucas had said not a word. As the minutes ticked by, she could not help sensing he had somehow withdrawn from her.

Not physically. But emotionally, she could almost swear to hearing the steady rebuilding of the wall that had stood between them. She held as still as she could, waiting and praying she was wrong.

Finally, he stirred, gently nudging her leg with his foot.

"Are you awake, Phoebe?"

"Yes."

He turned, rolling her onto her back. Propping himself up on one elbow, he gazed down at her as he stroked back the damp hair clinging to her brow. As she stared back, studying him in the fading light of the fire and the single branch of candles on her dressing table, her heart sank. He bore the expression of a man completely in control of himself, not one who had just flung himself wholeheartedly into passion's delight. And in his eyes she saw a retreat behind that discouraging high wall, the one he tended with his quiet determination to keep everyone at bay, including her.

"Are you all right?" he asked. "I didn't hurt you, did I?"

"No, I am well," she responded automatically. "How are you?"

Drat. That was *not* the question she wanted to ask him.

He dropped a quick kiss on her lips before sitting up. "Exhausted." He threw her a wry grin. "You wore me out, my sweet. As much as I'd like to spend the rest of the night making love to you, it's very late and I have an early meeting with more candidates for the estate manager position."

Not looking exhausted at all, he strode across to her dressing table, giving her a very interesting view of his muscular backside. He snuffed out the candles on her dressing table and then crouched down to bank the fire. Shadow and light played over his muscles, accentuating the lean power of his naked form.

"You must be tired, too," he said, glancing back over his shoulder. "I'd be a brute to keep you awake any longer. I know how much you have to do to get the house ready for the Christmas party, and that's without taking account of our overnight trip to the abbey."

Phoebe narrowed her eyes at him. Uncharacteristically, her husband was suddenly very near to babbling, apparently trying to deflect any attempts at conversation about what had just happened between them, including that she had confessed to loving him.

Chores completed, he quickly returned to bed. Pulling her into his arms, he arranged her so that she faced away from him, with her backside snuggled up against him. He gave a contented sigh and draped an arm over her chest. "Go to sleep now, sweetheart," he murmured. "We both have a long day ahead of us."

"Lucas—"

"Shh," he murmured as he stroked her arm. "Time for sleep."

A very short time later he slept, his steady breathing stirring her hair. She lay quietly, far from slumber, as she reflected on an astounding fact—when dealing with matters of the heart, her fearless warrior husband turned tail and headed for the hills.

Chapter 25

Lucas stared at the *Morning Chronicle*, pretending to read, just as he was pretending to eat his breakfast. Mr. Christmas was pretending to wait on him, mostly by resetting the silverware and tidying up the sideboard, hanging about as if he expected something to happen. When Lucas continued to ignore him, the butler released a melodramatic sigh and slipped out, leaving him to eat his breakfast in the magnificence of the manor's formal dining room.

He sighed out his own exasperation as he studied the cavernous room. Perhaps Phoebe could arrange to convert one of the drawing rooms into a family dining parlor. If he had to eat one more solitary meal in moth-eaten Jacobean splendor, he would become demented. The damn room was freezing, too, as Phoebe could attest. His poor wife usually came to dinner wrapped in at least one woolen shawl and she still shivered her way through every repast.

His wife.

The wife he'd left asleep in her bed while he crept out early this morning, unable to decide what to do with her. Their explosively sensual encounter had left him stunned, and while he'd been trying to recover his wits she'd blurted out her impossibly naive admission of love. It had caught him completely flat-footed and unable to respond. He felt many things for his wife—tender, affectionate things—but love wasn't one of them. He'd been in love before and it felt nothing like this. Love consumed a man, burning him up from the inside out. It turned him into a snarling, obsessive beast who would betray his oldest friend in order to possess the woman he loved. He would lie, cheat, and sell his soul to gain her, destroying whatever stood in his way.

Lucas knew love, and what he felt for Phoebe bore no resemblance to the ugly emotion that he'd fallen prey to so long ago.

Still, he could have done better than simply rolling over and going to sleep. He might not love Phoebe the way he had loved Esme—thank God—but he would cherish her, protect her, and shower her with as much affection as his cynical heart possessed. He would do everything he could to make her happy. He would do it for her sake and for the added benefit that making her happy made *him* happy, too. It might not be everything Phoebe wanted, but he'd do his best. She deserved it. She deserved—

"Lucas?"

He jerked, dropping his paper into the remains of his breakfast. His wife had slipped into the room as silently as a ghost, appearing a few feet away. But unlike a ghost, Phoebe shone with life and color, from the glossy black locks curling around her face to the faint blush pinking her clear complexion to the pretty green gown that lovingly hugged her figure.

But more than that, the light in her eyes shone forth with a compelling mix of honesty, determination, and vulnerability. When she looked at him like that, it never failed to bring out every protective instinct he possessed. His chest suddenly tightened with urgent need, but he beat it down and dredged up a smile as he rose to his feet. "I beg your pardon, Phoebe. I didn't hear you come in."

She returned his smile with a tentative one of her own. "I am sorry to have interrupted your reading."

He pulled out the first chair to the right of him. They had decided after their first meal that it was ridiculous to be shouting at each other from opposite ends of the long table. Since then, she had always made a point of sitting next to him, and he looked forward to those quiet, intimate meals in their absurd dining room as one of his favorite parts of the day.

"You didn't." He pushed in her chair, dropping a kiss on the top of her head as she sat. "Did you sleep well, my love? You stirred not a bit when I got up this morning."

She quickly glanced up. Some emotion, perhaps surprise, flickered in her eyes, then disappeared.

"Very well. I must have been more tired than I thought."

Lucas went to the sideboard, inspecting the various offerings. "It's no wonder, given how hard you've been working," he said, loading up her plate. "Both at the manor and in the village. Mr. Knaggs informed me yesterday that you and his wife have been making great strides in reorganizing the school."

He returned to the table with eggs, several rashers of bacon, kippers, and toast. When he set the plate in front of her, she gave him a comical look of dismay. "Lucas, I cannot possibly eat all this food."

He sat in his chair. "You can and you will. You're wearing yourself to the bone, and I'm not happy about it. We have plenty of servants to do the work around here. I want you to use them more."

She picked up her fork, staring at her loaded plate as if wondering where to begin. "I will, but there is so much to be accomplished to ready the manor for Christmas. I cannot afford to laze about like a fine London lady."

He snorted. "You're the farthest thing from lazy I know." He leaned over and gently grasped her chin. "And I will be most unhappy if you wear yourself out so much that you don't have time for me. I have plans for you, as I think you found out last night."

Blushing, she plunked down her fork and gave him an adorable scowl. "Really, Lucas. I hardly think it proper—"

The door clicked open and Christmas entered, bearing a carafe. Phoebe bit back whatever little scold she had been about to deliver in favor of gracing the butler with a sweet smile.

"Good morning, Lady Merritt," Christmas said. "May I pour you a cup of coffee?" The man managed to make the simple request sound like an invitation to a hanging.

"Yes, thank you."

While the butler poured her coffee, Lucas took the opportunity to change the subject. As much as he enjoyed teasing her about last night's activities, it might be best to avoid the topic. Knowing Phoebe, she might use it as an opening to question him about his feelings. "Well, Madam Wife," he said in a hearty voice, "what plans have you for today?"

She peered at him, her fork halfway to her mouth. From the look in her eyes she knew exactly what he was doing, but he held her gaze, refusing to back down. She shrugged, then took a bite of her food, taking her time before answering. "Mrs. Knaggs and some of the children are coming to the manor, to help me gather the greenery for decorations. We are also going to search for an appropriate Yule log for the fireplace in the entrance hall."

Lucas frowned. "Surely you intend to take some of the servants with you. I don't want you wandering around the estate by yourself, Phoebe."

Especially with those damned smugglers hanging about. The likelihood of daylight runs was small, but not unheard of. Harper suspected the gang had done them at least twice in the last several months. They weren't as likely to attempt one now that the manor was occupied, but the idea of Phoebe and a bunch of children wandering about the woods by themselves worried him.

She gave him a reassuring smile. "Mr. Christmas has arranged for two of the gardeners and William, who is one of the stronger footmen, to accompany us."

Lucas glanced at the butler for confirmation. Christmas let out another lugubrious sigh. "Everything has been arranged, my lord."

The man couldn't have sounded more depressed if he was planning his own funeral. As much as the relentless cheer of Mrs. Christmas and the other servants sometimes tried Lucas's patience, he was beginning to find the butler's permanent air of doom rather irritating.

Phoebe pulled a small watch from the slit in her gown and checked the time. "Mrs. Knaggs and the children should be here shortly. I must get ready."

Lucas rose and pulled out her chair. "Make sure you dress warmly, and wear your sturdiest boots. It's very cold today. We even got an inch of snow overnight."

She glanced up at him, her eyes brightening and her gorgeous pink mouth curving in a delighted smile. He felt the pull of that smile deep in his gut, and he had to exercise a considerable amount of willpower not to draw her into his arms and smother her in kisses.

"How wonderful," she exclaimed. "That will truly make it seem like Christmas."

"It's little more than a dusting, and it will likely melt as soon as the sun comes out. I wouldn't get your hopes up that it will last."

She wrinkled her nose. "What a shame. Still, I am quite looking forward to the outing. The children are, too, I am sure."

"Especially the part where they come back to the manor to be stuffed with tea and cakes," Lucas commented.

As they walked into the hall, Phoebe threw him an uncertain look. "You do not mind, do you? I will make sure they do not disturb you."

He frowned. "Of course I don't mind. I'm not an ogre, Phoebe. I don't begrudge the children a few simple pleasures."

"I never thought you would," she replied in a quiet voice. "But I know how busy you are. A houseful of rioting children would hardly be conducive to work. I will keep them confined to the kitchen, where I am sure they will be very happy to stay."

That made perfect sense, but it still annoyed him that she thought it necessary to tiptoe around him. "A little noise won't bother me, I assure you."

She nodded and crossed to the stairs, then stopped and turned back to him. "Would you   " Her voice trailed off as she hesitated.

He gave her an encouraging smile. "Yes, love?"

"Would you like to join us today? I am sure the children would be delighted if you did." She smiled shyly.

He suspected the opposite would be true, but it touched him that she so obviously wanted to include him. He couldn't imagine a more tedious way to spend a morning, but if it pleased her it would be worth the sacrifice, especially after the ham-fisted way he dealt with her last night. He tilted his head, pretending to consider it.

As he expected, she began to fidget. "If it is too much trouble—"

"Not at all. I have another interview this morning, and then I'll join you." The outing would probably do him good. He'd been spending too much time cooped up in his study, anyway, and he'd enjoy spending some time with her. Maybe if he was lucky he could even spirit her away for a little dalliance.

More to the point, he couldn't shake that nagging sense of worry when he envisioned her wandering about the woods, with only a few servants for protection. With smugglers on the loose. Until they were brought to heel, no one on the estate or in the village would truly be safe.

Chapter 26

Phoebe flattened herself against the door as the unruly pack charged past, tumbling into the kitchen garden. Their reedy, childish voices rose to an excited din as they dashed between the neat rows bisecting the snow-covered beds. Before she could stop them, three boys ran around the corner of the manor, shrieking as they chased each other right under the window of Lucas's study.

She sighed. Lucas hardly needed a noisy game of tag disrupting his work. She knew better than anyone the burdens that weighed on him, and the last thing she wished to do was test his admittedly formidable patience any more than she had to.

Not that he had been anything but affectionate this morning, although she sensed the emotional distance between them. She was coming to learn that while her husband easily manifested displays of physical affection, he shied away from declarations of love—either in the giving or the receiving. Whether that resulted from his reluctance to let go the wounds of the past, or from the fact that he did not love her, Phoebe could not tell.

"Goodness! Such a noise," exclaimed Mrs. Knaggs as she

bustled out from the kitchen passage. "I'll round up those naughty boys, my lady, if you wish to wait here in the garden."

Phoebe nodded her approval before turning her attention to the four girls dancing around her, all talking at once as they vied for her attention. The boys ignored the girls, of course, too excited to do anything but tromp up and down between the vegetable beds, seeing who could make the biggest footprints in the snow. Today was a rare treat for them. An outing devoted solely to fun, ending in the manor's kitchen with a feast of tea, scones, gingerbread, and even, Cook had promised, a piece of plum cake for everyone.

She ran an assessing gaze over the little ones, worried they might yet suffer from the cold. The children had arrived at the manor a tattered, poorly dressed lot, and Phoebe had felt compelled to voice her concern to the vicar's wife.

"I know," Mrs. Knaggs had replied with a grimace. "But you mustn't think their parents fare any better. Worse, in fact. I thought twice about letting some of them come today, especially with the snow, but I knew their little hearts would be crushed if I kept them back."

Phoebe understood, but she could not allow the children to go out in the bitter cold so poorly dressed. She had dashed upstairs, calling for Maggie, and the two of them had quickly rummaged through her wardrobe for extra gloves, a muff, and several of her thickest wool shawls. Then she had dashed into Lucas's room and bullied Mr. Popham into relinquishing a number of her husband's warmest scarves. The valet had been stunned, clutching the expensive lengths of soft wool to his horrified breast, but Phoebe eventually prevailed.

After swaddling the children in the mismatched collection of warm clothing—naturally, some of the boys had protested vociferously—she finished the job with extra pairs of gloves donated by some of the household staff. The results were comical, since the children resembled nothing so much as unkempt spindles of yarn, but at least the poor mites would be able to keep warm. And with the exception of Mr. Popham, all the servants had gotten into the spirit of giving, eager to contribute and chatting gaily as they helped the children prepare for their adventure.

"Well, Lady Merritt," puffed Mrs. Knaggs as she steamed around the corner of the manor, her charges in tow, "I think we're ready."

Phoebe glanced out to the manor's broad lawn, where two groundskeepers patiently waited with the necessary tools and the cart to carry the greens they would collect, along with the Yule log. Will, the footman, came rushing out of the back door to join them.

"All set?" Phoebe asked him.

"Yes, my lady. And very happy to be here. The old earl was much too sick the last few years for any such festive goings-on. We had nary a sprig of greenery about the place. Everyone is right looking forward to seeing the old place tricked out as it used to be, and that's a fact." He beamed at her. "Especially the mistletoe. Everyone sorely missed that."

"Why the mistletoe in particular?" Phoebe asked as they tromped off in the direction of the apple orchards, the children gamboling behind them like clumsy lambs following their shepherds.

Will threw her a startled look. "My lady, surely you know what to do if you're caught standing under a sprig of mistletoe."

Phoebe shook her head. She had no idea.

The young man's face reddened as he cleared his throat. "Ah, well . . ." He trailed off, casting a helpless glance at Mrs. Knaggs.

The woman nodded. "Nothing to be shy about, Will. Even the vicar has been known to catch me under the mistletoe."

Mrs. Knaggs smiled at Phoebe's mystified glance. "If a young man catches a girl under the mistletoe, the girl must give him a kiss," she explained. "For each kiss the man collects a berry, and when all the berries are gone, then the privilege is revoked." Her eyes twinkled. "If there's a lot of mistletoe hanging in the house, there can be quite a lot of kissing."

Phoebe opened her mouth, then shut it, not sure how to respond. Mrs. Knaggs laughed. "I know it sounds shocking, but it's harmless fun. It's tradition and, after all, you do live in Mistletoe Manor. You have a reputation to uphold."

"Oh, yes. I . . . I am sure we do," Phoebe replied faintly. As if anyone at Mistletoe Manor needed any encouragement with *that* sort of thing, if their interest in the intimate relations between the master and the mistress was any indication.

Mrs. Knaggs edged closer, dropping her voice to a confidential murmur. "And I'll wager his lordship won't mind catching you under the mistletoe now and again, will he, my lady?" She sighed. "And such a fine, strapping man, too. Lady Merritt, if I wasn't so happily married, I might envy you."

"Ah, thank you," Phoebe replied with a weak smile.

Mrs. Knaggs was as free in her opinions as the servants, which seemed unusual in a vicar's wife. Then again, every adult Phoebe had met since arriving at Mistletoe Manor was remarkably forthright on any number of issues—often to the point of indiscretion. With the exception of the smuggling issue, unfortunately.

When they reached the orchards, Phoebe split the children into groups, one to help each groundskeeper as he gathered up the mistletoe. She watched, fascinated, as the men severed the boughs of the plant from the apple trees, which served as hosts.

"I did not realize the plant grew directly from the branches and trunks of the trees," she said to Mrs. Knaggs.

"Oh, yes. The mistletoe plant loves apple trees. And since Kent is full of them, now you know how both the manor and the village got their names."

"The plant depends on the tree for sustenance, just as

the village and the manor are inextricably linked." Phoebe smiled. "I like that image very much."

The vicar's wife gave her a thoughtful nod. "That's always been the way, as far back as anyone can remember. And like the manor and the village, when the mistletoe is neglected it can overwhelm the tree and choke the life out of it. Then both will suffer and die." She hesitated, looking as if she wished to say more, but closed her lips.

Phoebe reached out a quick hand and touched her arm. "I understand, and I assure you the earl does as well. Neither the plant nor the tree will be neglected any longer."

"Mr. Knaggs and I are so relieved, my lady. We've seen many dark days here in the village." The older woman blinked several times as she pulled a large white handkerchief out from her sleeve and loudly blew her nose. Then she gave Phoebe a watery smile. "You and his lordship have brought us hope, and at the best time of year, too. You can see it in the village. Our people finally have something to celebrate this Christmas."

Phoebe glanced around. The children and the men had moved on to the next stand of trees and out of earshot. Since Mrs. Knaggs had conveniently raised the issue about the struggles of the villagers, perhaps she might finally be willing to talk about the smuggling. "Mrs. Knaggs, I wondered—"

"Here now, Becky," Mrs. Knaggs called out loudly. "Don't let the branches hit the ground. Put them right in the cart as soon as the men hand them to you."

The woman gave Phoebe an apologetic grimace. "Sorry to yell, but it's bad luck to let the boughs touch the ground once cut from the tree. I think we'd best go over and help the children."

Phoebe tamped down her frustration and trudged with Mrs. Knaggs to the handcart, now partly stacked with mistletoe. "You do not really believe that kind of superstition, do you?"

"No, but they do," the older woman said, gesturing to the

others. "It won't do to break with tradition, especially when it comes to the mistletoe."

"And the mistletoe should be the last greenery out of the house after Candlemas, ain't that right, Mrs. Knaggs?" asked one of the smaller boys as he struggled with a particularly large bough.

"*Isn't* that right," corrected Mrs. Knaggs. "And yes, Peter. The mistletoe is always the last of the greens to be burned when the celebrations are concluded."

Phoebe eyed the rapidly filling cart. "I believe we have enough mistletoe to build a bonfire. Do we not also need to collect some holly and some other greenery?"

"Yes, my lady," answered Griffin, the senior grounds-keeper. "I be thinkin' we've got ourselves enough mistletoe for this year."

Phoebe nodded her agreement. If they mounted even half the pile resting in the cart, there would be so much kissing going on at the manor she doubted anyone would have time to work.

Although she enjoyed the prospect of Lucas catching her under the mistletoe. Of course, now that their estrangement had ended, she doubted he needed any excuses to kiss her.

They set off for the home wood, following Griffin's lead. "We'll be sure to find a proper Yule log not too far in, my lady," he said. "There were some fierce storms this summer, and a few ash trees came down, along with some branches from the bigger oaks."

She nodded. "The children must stay together in their groups. I do not want anyone wandering off and getting lost, especially in this cold."

Griffin, a burly man in his middle years, with a steady, comfortable manner, smiled at her. "Lord love you, m'lady. There ain't one of these nippers that don't know his way blindfolded through these woods. Most of 'em have been comin' and goin' on manor lands since the day they started walkin'. Not much fear of them gettin' lost."

He paused to study her, rubbing his bristled chin as if deep in thought. "If you don't mind me sayin' so, m'lady, you be the one who stands a fair chance of gettin' lost. Best stick close to me or young Will."

"Very well," Phoebe said. Though Griffin's manner was a bit forward, he was no doubt correct.

They approached the woods across open lawn—sheened a brilliant white with the dusting of snow—and made for the first copse of trees. Trailing behind the others, Phoebe turned to gaze up the wide expanse of gently sloping lawn to Mistletoe Manor, set on the highest point of land for several miles. She had not ever seen the manor from this vantage point, and she paused to take it in.

From this vantage point it seemed magnificent, a noble building with irregular wings and chimneys, and turrets that spoke of its ancient heritage. Diamond-paned windows glistened in the sunshine, and the stone balustrade that surrounded the back terrace of the house gleamed with its coating of snow. The bulky shapes of urns and the occasional statue of an angel or fawn, all coated in white, broke the stately, formal lines of the house. The garden shrubbery and yew hedges—squat and bulky under their thin veil of snow—gave the manor an almost whimsical appearance.

As Phoebe gazed at the old pile, a surge of affection and pride flowed through her veins. Yes, it was cold, drafty, and starting to crumble around them, but it was beautiful, nonetheless. She could be happy here, with the man she had come to love, and who would, God willing, give her the children she longed for. They had a roof over their heads, fertile soil beneath their feet, and loyal, hardworking people to help them. Everything she and Lucas needed to live a peaceful and happy life could be found at Mistletoe Manor.

Of course, whether Lucas saw it that way remained a question. Where she saw blessings, he perceived only burdens and responsibilities. She could only hope that her husband would eventually come to see the riches God had placed before them.

She turned and headed to the woods, striding to catch up with the others. They had all disappeared into the thick stand of oaks, but she easily followed their voices and their trail through the snow. The rough ground, littered with dead leaves and twigs, forced her to pick her way around the windblown shrubs covering the forest floor. Eventually, she came upon a narrow trail, and a few minutes of brisk walking brought her into a small clearing. Mrs. Knaggs and some of the children clustered about Griffin, collecting the evergreen branches he was sawing off the trees.

"There you are, my lady," said Mrs. Knaggs. "We were just about to send out a search party."

A few of the girls ran up to her, tugging on her hands. With a laugh, Phoebe allowed them to pull her into the group. "Where are the others?"

"They've gone off to look for a Yule log. Delia, please do not pull on Lady Merritt's pelisse. You'll stain it." Mrs. Knaggs delivered the scold in the mildest of voices, but the little girl, all big eyes and pink cheeks, started to cry. With a sigh, the vicar's wife began to comfort her. "I do apologize, my lady. The poor dear tends to get overwhelmed with the excitement."

Phoebe smiled and bent down to gently snug the girl's woolen scarf around her neck. "There is no need to apologize. I shall go look for the others, which will give Delia time to recover."

The girl, clearly mortified, pressed her face against Mrs. Knaggs's generous stomach. The vicar's wife rolled her eyes. "Perhaps that would be best," she said in a loud stage whisper.

Biting back a grin, Phoebe took the trail into the woods,

following the footprints. After perhaps two hundred feet, the trail divided. Several tracks of prints ran in both directions, showing the children had split into two groups. For no other reason than the left path cut through a magnificent stand of noble oaks, Phoebe chose it. She set out, following both the footprints and the faint sound of laughing children that drifted through the trees.

The air had a clean bite to it, and for the first time in days the sun had broken through the clouds. It filtered down through the bare branches of the noble canopy of oaks and beeches, sketching rows of shadows on the snow-covered ground. She slowed her pace, enchanted by the signs of life all around her in the forest depths—the cloven prints of a deer, the dainty trails of marks left by birds, and the tidy tracks of a fox, cutting across her path and snaking deep into the woods. Birds flitted and sang in the upper branches. She recognized the blackbirds and the sparrows, and heard the song of the thrush.

Phoebe stopped and drew in a deep breath, reveling in the austere beauty of her surroundings. Raising her face to the pale winter sun, she drank in the solitude, so grateful to be once more in the country after her tumultuous interlude in smoke-filled London. Peace settled over her, and she breathed out a prayer of gratitude to the Maker of all things.

A sharp crack and then a desperate rustling sounded off to the left, jolting her. A fierce growl was followed by a frantic whimpering that signaled some creature was in distress. Phoebe peered through the trees in the direction of the noise, but could see nothing. The whimpering was soon followed by several high-pitched yips that sounded like a dog.

Whatever it was, it needed help. The voices of the children had now faded, so it was clearly up to Phoebe to find the poor animal and render assistance.

She left the trails, pushing through the underbrush, which in this part of the woods seemed to be mostly a kind of trailing thornbush. The branches snagged her skirts, forcing her to stop and untangle them, but she forged steadily on. The yipping had been replaced by more whimpering, which now sounded near at hand.

After a minute, she broke into a small clearing and found the source of the noise—a bedraggled little dog, perhaps some kind of terrier, whose bristly, dust-colored coat was tangled up in a holly bush. As she rushed over to help, he broke into pitiful yelps.

"Oh, dear," she said as she crouched down beside him, "you have gotten yourself into quite a mess."

His ears flattened and his breath came in anxious pants, but she was heartened to see that his tail—full of knots and as tangled up as the rest of him—feathered in a desultory wag. Clearly a stray by the look of him, he seemed distressed rather than vicious.

"Now, Mr. Doggy," she said in a soothing voice, "I would beg that you keep your teeth and claws to yourself. If you stay very still, I think I can get you free."

He whined, but his tail whipped a little harder. She let him sniff her hand, and when he showed no signs of biting her, she set to work. The poor thing cried piteously as she struggled to free him, but he never once bared his teeth or tried to claw her, which spoke of an excellent temperament.

It took several minutes, and by the time she finished, it seemed almost as much fur was left behind on the branches as remained on the dog's scrawny body. Despite the cold, perspiration trickled down Phoebe's spine, and she huffed with relief when she finally had him free.

"There, sir. You are once more at liberty," she murmured as the poor beast frantically licked her gloved hand.

He did not struggle as she took him in her arms and stood, wincing at her protesting muscles. Her skirts were covered in mud and leaves, with wet patches at the knees and hem. The damp had leached into her bones, too, since the winter sun had already begun its decline toward the horizon. The shadows of the trees now stretched across the clearing, and a late-afternoon chill had descended. In the stillness, even the birds had stopped singing, and Phoebe suddenly became aware of the silence.

Actually, the silence felt menacing. With the dog shivering in her arms, she turned in a slow circle, unable to shake the sense that something lurked in the trees.

Nothing.

Shaking her head in self-disgust, she hefted the dog more comfortably in her arms and started to retrace her steps. But before she could reach the path she heard a loud snap and then a gasp, quickly choked off. Whipping around, she saw young Sam Weston at the edge of the clearing, clutching the bridle of a small donkey. Behind him, half hidden in the woods, several men and several more donkeys, all laden with packs, had come to a halt.

One of those men stepped in front of Sam, raised his arm, and pointed a pistol straight at Phoebe.

Chapter 27

Phoebe gaped at the man, her brain addled with shock. She had seen hunting rifles before, but Quakers had little traffic with guns. To stare down the barrel of a pistol pointed directly at her chest seemed impossible. The man brandishing the weapon looked ready to use it, too. Broad shouldered and sturdy, his face was partly covered with a scarf, but his dark eyes glared daggers. The menace visible in his gaze and stance sent a wave of fear crashing over her.

"Pa, don't," yelped Sam. "It's Lady Merritt."

Phoebe practically swallowed her tongue. This man was the village publican? Mr. Weston was one of the few locals she had yet to meet, but she could hardly believe he would actually shoot her. Cautiously, she took a step backward, clutching the stray dog to her chest. As if sensing her fear, he nudged her chin, giving her a small lick.

"That's far enough," snarled Mr. Weston, yanking down his mask. "If you take another step, I might be forced to use this." He waved his pistol in an alarming manner.

Phoebe jerked to a halt. A fierce scowl distorted Mr. Weston's features, but it was the desperation she saw in his gaze that convinced her to remain motionless.

Sam dropped his donkey's bridle and rushed up to his

father. "Pa," he said in a loud whisper, "you can't do that to her. She's a *lady*!"

Without shifting his gaze, Mr. Weston gave Sam a shove. "Shut your gob, boy. I'll take care of this."

Phoebe's temper flared, warring with her fear. How dare the man bully his son!

"It is not necessary to threaten me," she snapped. "I will not run, nor will I cry out for help. The last thing I want is for my husband to discover you on his lands. There would be the devil to pay if he did, I assure you."

Mr. Weston gave a harsh laugh. "And I can assure *you* that we've been paying the devil for years, thanks to men of his *lordship's* ilk. There's nothing you can say or do that'll frighten me, my lady, and that's a fact."

"And what about your son?" she asked. "Are you so willing to risk his life? Mr. Knaggs told me some of you were involving the children in this business, but I could hardly believe it."

He glowered at her, but anger had a good hold on her now. For once she welcomed it, allowing it to sweep away fear and carry her along on a boiling tide. "Thee had no business involving the children, no matter how difficult life has been. It was very poorly done of thee to act in so sinful and reckless a manner, Mr. Weston. Shame on thee."

The publican's jaw sagged for a moment, but then his face flushed red with anger. Shoving the pistol into his belt, he stomped toward her. Phoebe tried not to cringe when he grabbed her arm. She also clamped down on the urge to protest his rough treatment. It would do no good, and would only upset poor Sam more than he already was. The little dog in her arms, however, issued his own form of protest, snarling and baring his teeth at her captor.

"That's quite the pet you've got there, my lady," he sneered. "Not exactly a lap dog, is he?"

"I found him tangled up in that bush. That is the only reason I was here in the first place. I heard him whimpering."

Startled, he glanced down at her. "Oh. That was kind of you. Especially since he's such a runty-looking beast."

The dog snapped at him and tried to leap from her arms, but Phoebe held him tightly against her chest as Mr. Weston frog-marched her across the clearing.

"Sir, I would ask that you not frighten him," she said in a sharp voice as they reached the others.

"He don't look frightened to me."

Mr. Weston came to a halt by his donkey, holding her fast by the arm. For several long moments they stared at each other. From the disgruntled, rather baffled expression on his face, Phoebe got the impression he did not know what to do with her. The other men in the group were just as uneasy, shifting from one foot to the other and murmuring amongst themselves. She thought she recognized a few of them, although scarves obscured their features.

Suddenly, Mr. Weston appeared to come to a decision. "Sam, take the dog from her ladyship," he ordered.

Phoebe tried to jerk away. "I will not let you hurt him."

He rolled his eyes. "Of course I'm not going to hurt him. What kind of monster do you take me for?"

"The kind that involves his son in dangerous, illegal activities."

Again, she saw that flash of desperation in his eyes. "Do you think I want to do this? There's barely enough blunt in the whole damn village to keep body and soul together, you daft woman. Why the hell do you think we're doing this?"

Phoebe bristled. She did not set much store on titles or formality, but she did not appreciate the label of *daft woman*.

"That is going to change, Mr. Weston. Lord Merritt has promised that any man who wants a job can find one at the manor. That includes you."

"Mucking out stables? No thanks, m'lady. I'll take care of

my boy in my own fashion, without any charity from you or his lordship."

"Yes," she retorted. "I can see you are making a fine job of it."

He jerked slightly, as if she'd slapped him, then his face reddened again. "No thanks to you or your husband," he sneered. "Or the old earl, either. Now give Sam the dog and let's get on with it."

Phoebe tilted her chin. "I have no idea what you want to *get on* with, but I have already made it clear that threats are unnecessary. I will not turn you over to the authorities, nor will I reveal your identity to my husband."

"Pa, listen to her," pleaded Sam.

"Aye, Ned," piped in a man who sounded suspiciously like the local blacksmith. "My missus says the lady is a good 'un. Let 'er go and let's get out of 'ere."

That intervention was all it took, and suddenly everyone was arguing with everyone else. Sam tugged on his father's arm, pleading with him to let her go, and the dog set up a barrage of excited snarls and yips. Mr. Weston seemed to be arguing with all of them, even as he kept a grip on her arm. Phoebe was convinced they must be the noisiest smuggling ring in England.

A familiar, lugubrious voice cut through the din.

"Ned Weston, you will unhand her ladyship now."

A shocked silence fell over the glade as everyone spun to stare at Mr. Christmas, who had snuck right up on them. Not that such a feat had been difficult to manage, since they had been making such a din an elephant could have paraded by and they would not have noticed.

Much to Phoebe's surprise, Mr. Weston dropped her arm. "Thank you," she said automatically. Then she peered at Mr. Christmas, attired in a dark greatcoat and sturdy boots, and looking for all the world like—

"Mr. Christmas, not you, too," she groaned.

Mr. Weston snorted. "That Friday face, one of us? Not likely. But he's always skulking around when we're making a run across the manor's lands, just to make sure we don't get up to anything. Acts like we're common criminals, he does."

"You *are* criminals," Phoebe said. Then she switched her attention to the butler. "You knew about these smuggling runs?"

After he nodded, she studied him for a few moments, while the men all exchanged uneasy glances.

"And you wanted to make sure no one got hurt," Phoebe said. "Is that correct?"

"Yes, my lady," Mr. Christmas answered mournfully. "To that end, I would suggest Mr. Weston and his men move along. Lord Merritt is on his way to join you and the children, and I fear he will be upon us soon. I shudder to think how he might react if he were to discover you thus."

That image made Phoebe shudder, too. "You are absolutely right. Mr. Weston, you and your men would be wise to depart immediately."

The publican looked ready to argue, but she held up her hand. "I have promised not to alert his lordship to your presence, and I intend to keep that promise."

Her stomach twisted at the idea of withholding the truth from Lucas, but right now she had no choice. If he discovered the smugglers were making runs across manor lands—and that Mr. Weston had threatened her—Lucas would hand the entire gang over to the law for deportation or execution. That would blight too many lives to count, especially those of the children. Phoebe simply refused to carry the burden of such a dreadful outcome.

Mr. Weston rubbed his face, frustrated and, she thought, worried. He glanced down at Sam, who clutched his father's arm in a nervous grip.

Phoebe shifted the dog and reached out to rest a hand on Sam's shoulder. "Mr. Weston," she said in a gentle voice, "you must trust me. I would never do anything to hurt the people of Apple Hill, including you and your men, or your families. But my husband has a different notion of justice. So, you must leave now, or face the consequences. I fear they would not be pretty."

"Pa, let's go," urged Sam.

Mr. Weston hesitated, then nodded as the other men started to melt into the woods. He gave Sam a little nudge. "Go along, boy. I'll be right behind you."

Sam threw Phoebe a grateful smile, slipping away with his donkey to leave her, Mr. Weston, and Mr. Christmas in a wary circle, staring at each other.

"I have your word you won't tell?" Mr. Weston asked her.

"You do."

His mouth loosened in a grudging smile. "You ain't what I expected, my lady."

"Thank you. I think."

He let out a gruff chuckle and touched the brim of his cap before heading after his son.

"Mr. Weston," she called after him. He paused in the shadow of the trees. "You cannot evade my husband or Mr. Harper's men for much longer," she said. "The smuggling must stop, before Sam or anyone else is hurt."

Silent and still, holding the donkey's bridle, he stared back with a somber expression on his face. For the first time, she noticed how careworn he appeared. A man with too many burdens. "We'll see, my lady."

He faded into the forest, and all was still once more. Except for the presence of Mr. Christmas, Phoebe could almost imagine the entire episode had been a dream.

"My lady," said the butler, casting an anxious glance over his shoulder, "you must return to the others."

Phoebe nodded as she rearranged the dog more comfortably in her arms, then she and Mr. Christmas crossed the clearing, heading for the trail. "I will not ask how you knew about the smuggling run," she said to him. "I do not think I want to know."

"That would be for the best, my lady." He eyed the dog in her arms. "Is your ladyship bringing the animal to the manor?"

"Of course I am! Did you think I would leave him out here to fend for himself?"

"No, madam. I simply wondered——"

"Phoebe! Where are you?" Her husband's call sounded alarmingly close, and they both froze in place.

"My lady," Mr. Christmas said quickly, "if you don't mind, I'll take another route back to the house."

She nodded. "Fine. But next time you hear anything at all about the smugglers, you must tell me. We cannot let this happen again."

He gave her a courtly bow, exactly as if he were ushering her into dinner, and then faded into the woods as expertly as the smugglers. Phoebe gave a ghost of a laugh. Mr. Christmas must surely be the oddest butler in the land.

"Christ, Phoebe! There you are."

She whipped around, biting back a startled shriek. Only a few hundred feet away, Lucas stalked toward her along the trail. She cast a quick glance through the woods, but Mr. Christmas had vanished.

"Why did you go off like this?" Lucas asked in a stern tone as he came up to her. He looked so big and strong, and so worried, she could not help tumbling thankfully into his arms. Only when he held her close did she fully realize how frightened she had been. She shuddered with relief, leaning into the comforting hardness of his brawny chest.

"Are you all right, my love?" he asked urgently.

"Yes. I . . . I just lost my way."

He squeezed her a little tighter, and the dog, nestled under her arm, yelped.

"What the——"

"Lucas, be careful," Phoebe exclaimed as she pulled away.

"Do not hurt the poor thing." She stroked the dog's ears, soothing him. "I heard him crying in distress. That is why I left the trail."

He raised his eyebrows as he studied the bedraggled bundle in her arms. The animal gave a pathetic whimper, feathering his tail.

"Good God. He looks like a drowned rat. What do you intend to do with him?"

She scowled. "Take him home, of course, and give him a bath and something to eat. The poor thing obviously has not had a decent meal in days."

Lucas cast his gaze toward the heavens, obviously seeking patience. "You're not intending to keep him, are you?"

She and the dog gazed up at him, both doing their best to look pitiful. "I would like very much to keep him. I never had a dog."

He sighed. "I'm not sure he really counts as a dog, but I have a feeling you won't give me much choice in the matter."

"I would never try to force him or anything else on you," she said with dignity.

"Really? You must tell me all about that sometime. All right, hand him over. He's sopping wet and he's already made a mess of your pelisse."

"The stains will come out," she said, happy to hand him over. Her arms were beginning to ache, and all the strains of the day weighed heavily on her.

Lucas tucked the dog under his arm, and the little fellow settled quite comfortably. In fact, he looked ready to drop off to sleep. As they headed back to the main trail, Phoebe did her best to show no sign that a man had just pointed a gun in her face. That task was proving remarkably difficult, since her instincts were prodding her to reveal the truth to her husband.

"I thought I heard voices back there, just before I saw you," Lucas said. "Were you talking to someone?"

Panic seized her, and she almost stumbled. His free hand

shot out to grasp her elbow. "Careful, Phoebe. You don't want to take a tumble." He gazed at her, frowning. "Was someone else there?"

"N . . . no, of course not. I was simply talking to the dog. He was very upset and I kept trying to soothe him. You would not fathom how badly he was tangled in the brambles, Lucas. It is a wonder I was able to free him at all."

Her voice ended on a suspicious quaver. Keeping such a terrible secret, especially from her husband, made her cringe with shame. But she had promised Mr. Weston, and she would keep that promise. She could not bear the thought of Sam losing his remaining parent, and she needed to protect the villagers involved in the ring. And protect Lucas, too, who would go charging full bore after the smugglers if she told him the truth. The idea of what might transpire then made her ill.

"Phoebe, what's the matter?"

"Nothing," she said brightly. "How are the children? Did they find a proper Yule log?"

She could feel his eyes burning into her. Pinning on a smile, she forced herself to meet his gaze. That did nothing to bolster her courage, since he studied her with a suspicious frown. He looked ready to say something—and that made her heart clutch—but then he seemed to give a mental shrug.

"Yes, they have. A right proper one, as Griffin would say. Speaking of the children, I noticed that a few of the boys were wrapped up in familiar-looking scarves, and if I'm not mistaken at least three of the girls were wearing your shawls, including the one lined with Norwich silk that Annabel gave to you as a wedding present. Did the children make an unauthorized visit to our dressing rooms?" her husband asked sardonically.

This time she did wince. "I had to give them warm clothing, Lucas. They would have been too cold otherwise. You do not really mind, do you?"

"Would you care if I did mind?"

Guilt lanced through her. "Lucas, I—"

He gave her a brief hug. "It's all right. I only felt a small pang of regret that you picked my best scarves to use. Popham, however, may never recover from the shock."

Phoebe sighed. "I will find a way to make it up to him."

"I'm sure you will. Now let's get you home and out of that wet clothing. I don't want you catching a chill."

As they emerged from beneath the canopy of oaks onto the broad expanse of the manor's lawn, Phoebe resisted the temptation to cast a glance over her shoulder. For now, at least, the forest would keep her secrets.

Chapter 28

Phoebe sneaked a glance at her husband's profile, half cast in shadow by the fading daylight filtering through the carriage window. The distance from Mistletoe Manor to Belfield Abbey measured a scant ten miles, but for most of the journey an awkward silence prevailed between them. There had been several such awkward silences since yesterday, the product of her guilty conscience and her inability to lie to her husband. For the hundredth time, she cursed the chain of events that had thrown her into contact with the smugglers.

She had managed to avoid a private discussion with Lucas for most of yesterday by taking refuge in the children's company. But by the time they met for dinner, she could barely look him in the eye. Her guilt seemed to cleave her tongue to the roof of her mouth, and she had eventually fled to the doubtful security of her bedroom, ready to crawl out of her skin with shame. Lucas had come to her bedroom later and pointedly asked if something was bothering her. Praying that she was not making a mistake, she answered in the negative. She had then forestalled any more questions by going up on tiptoe, wrapping her arms about him, and planting an enthusiastic kiss on his skeptical-looking mouth. He had initially seemed a bit startled, but soon got into the spirit. In a trice, he had divested her of her clothing and there had been no more talk for the rest of the night.

But his demeanor the next morning was cool, a sure sign he suspected something was amiss. As she had gone about her morning tasks, organizing and helping the servants to decorate the house with the greens they had collected, she had wracked her brain for a solution to her problems, with the smugglers and with Lucas. As for the first problem, she had concluded Mr. Knaggs was her best hope. With his help, she would confront Mr. Weston and attempt to persuade him to give up his dangerous activities. If he would not, she would have little choice but to tell Lucas. Mayhem would likely ensue, but she could not allow Mr. Weston to continue to put his son's and other lives in danger.

As to her second problem, she could only hope addressing the first problem would resolve the issues with Lucas. She could not keep lying to him forever. That was no way to build trust in a marriage, especially when the male partner in that marriage had once suffered betrayal at the hands of a faithless woman.

"What troubles you, love?"

Phoebe jerked, startled by Lucas's deep voice cutting the heavy silence. He had canted his body to stretch his long legs across the floor of the carriage as he studied her with a thoughtful tilt to his head.

"Why . . . why would you ask that?"

"You just sighed. Rather tragically, I thought, as if the whole world were against you."

Phoebe swallowed. She had best find a timely solution to the whole mess or she would probably blurt out the truth, if for no other reason than she did not possess the internal fortitude to keep lying to her husband. That was a good thing, but right now it felt dreadfully inconvenient.

"I am a bit tired," she hedged. True enough. After Lucas

had made love to her, she had been unable to sleep. It counted as something of a miracle she had been able to rise so early this morning, all things considered. "There is much to accomplish before Christmas Day. I want everything to be perfect when we open the manor to the villagers, the tenant farmers, and their families."

He snorted. "It will take more than a few days to make Mistletoe Manor anybody's idea of perfection. But I'll remind you again that I don't want you wearing yourself out. I'm sure whatever you do for the locals will be just fine."

"I want it to be more than *just fine*, Lucas," she said earnestly. "I want this to be a truly wonderful Christmas no one will forget."

"I'm damned sure my purse will remember."

She had no idea how to respond to that salvo, so she kept silent. She had hoped Lucas would graciously accept the wisdom of opening the house to all comers on Christmas Day, as her grandfather used to do, and as his ancestors had done for generations.

Perhaps not.

She gave him a placating smile, which he did not return. Instead, he eyed her with a narrow gaze. "Phoebe, you do realize you can tell me anything, don't you?" he asked abruptly. "I will always listen carefully to whatever you have to say to me."

She mentally winced. It was not the listening part she worried about, it was what he would do after he heard.

She forced herself to answer calmly. "Of course I do. And I promise that whenever I have something to tell you, I will."

The stiffening of his shoulders signaled how little he liked her reply, but it was the best she could do for now. "Are we almost to the abbey?" she blurted out before he could say anything else.

A muscle in his jaw pulsed, but he allowed the deflection. "If you look out the window, you can see it on the rise of the hill."

She breathed a sigh of relief, grateful that for all his commanding ways her husband had the grace not to push her. His patience, unfortunately, made her own actions seem all the worse. Clamping down hard on her guilt, she leaned across him to peek out the window. He gently wrapped an arm around her waist to support her against the jostling of the carriage, his other hand brushing a stray lock of hair back from her neck. Her heart throbbed as she silently acknowledged that Lucas would always take care of her, no matter what.

She cast him a grateful smile, then looked out the window. The sight that met her eyes drew a gasp from her lips. "What a magnificent building," she breathed. "Like something out of a fairy tale."

"Isn't it just," he replied sardonically.

Of course. Belfield Abbey was Silverton's domain, and Lucas could not help but compare it to Mistletoe Manor. And not very favorably, she knew.

She eyed him. "You are not going to make a scene, are you?" she asked in a wary voice.

He snorted. "After the way we almost demolished Annabel's dining room last Easter, I think Aunt Georgie would murder us both if Silverton and I got into another argument."

"Thank God," she said, perhaps a tad too enthusiastically.

He laughed, and the tension between them eased. "I promise to be as meek as a church mouse, my love."

Phoebe was too busy looking at the massive edifice that loomed at the end of the drive to respond to his teasing. Indeed, she thought it looked more like a castle than her idea of an abbey, with its peaked roofs, high turrets, and scores of windows gleaming with the reflected fire of the setting sun. Lucas had told her portions of Belfield Abbey had been built under the early Tudor kings, and that the estate had been held by a marquess of Silverton for over two hundred years. That fact did not impress her nearly as much as the majesty of the building itself, with its graceful towers, and chimneys reaching up into the darkening sky.

Their carriage bowled smoothly up a tree-lined drive that wove through spacious parkland, finally drawing to a halt under an imposing portico. A liveried footman stepped forward to let down the carriage steps, and a moment later Lucas handed her out onto a well-maintained sweep in front of marble steps. He quickly ushered her through the high front doors into a hall at least twice the size of the one at Mistletoe Manor. Every bit of wood, marble, brass, and silver had been polished to a high gleam.

She glanced at her husband. His jaw had squared with tension and his eyes had cooled to resemble flint. Cousin Stephen's domain spoke of wealth, elegance, and a power that made Mistletoe Manor seem small and rather shabby in comparison.

Well, the manor *was* still shabby, but it was hardly fair to compare the two estates. But the look on Lucas's face indicated he was doing exactly that.

She sighed. The infamous Esme Newton was obviously the root of the problem between Lucas and Cousin Stephen, but there were clearly other points of resentment, at least for her husband.

Meredith appeared from the back of the hall, festive in a cherry red gown trimmed in white velvet ribbons. With her tall, elegant figure and her glossy black hair piled on her head, she was stunning.

"I'm so happy to see you both," she exclaimed. She held out her arms and took Phoebe in a warm, enthusiastic embrace.

"You look simply lovely," she murmured in Phoebe's ear. "Marriage obviously agrees with you."

At a loss to devise an appropriate reply, Phoebe settled for giving her cousin a fierce hug. Meredith returned it, then drew back and ran a swift, perceptive glance over Phoebe. A tiny frown appeared between her brows, but when she turned to Lucas her face showed nothing but kindness and cheer.

"And you are looking very dashing, Lucas. How goes the battle at the manor?"

He took her hand and leaned in to kiss her cheek. "I'll let you know once I'm winning."

Meredith laughed. "You must tell me all about it later. The others are in the drawing room, but I know you will wish to go to your rooms and freshen up. Dinner is in an hour. Lucas, you needn't look at me like that. Of course it's ridiculously early, but you know the General. He insists that there's no point being in the country if you can't keep early hours."

Lucas had been regarding her with an ironic eye. "Gay to dissipation as always, I see. You must forgive me for forgetting my flannel waistcoat and arthritis liniment. Perhaps I can borrow Silverton's."

"You could if he had any," she retorted. "But truly, it won't be as bad as all that. We do have some entertainment planned, including a visit from the Waits." Her eyes twinkled. "And don't forget the poetry recitation. The General has been practicing all morning."

Lucas gave an exaggerated groan. "God. It gets worse every year."

"I have no idea what either of you are talking about," Phoebe interjected. "Who are the Waits? And why is Uncle Arthur reciting poetry?"

"My love, you are about to be inducted into the Stanton family Christmas traditions," Lucas said. "Guaranteed to strike terror in the hearts of stout men." He leaned down, pretending to whisper. "It's not too late to escape. Say the word and I'll have the carriage brought round at once."

Meredith swatted him on the arm. "You beast! Stop your nonsense or you'll frighten the poor girl. Now, let me show you to your rooms. If you're late, then you *will* put the General in a mood, and then we'll all want to run away."

Lucas grasped Phoebe's hand and they followed Meredith up the central staircase to the first floor. They strolled through a grand corridor lined with marble busts on graceful pedestals, and enormous portraits that reached almost from the ceiling down to the floor. Everything at Belfield Abbey seemed to be larger than life, and Phoebe could not help being awed by its magnificence. But it made her feel rather small and insignificant, and she could not help feeling a twinge of longing for Mistletoe Manor. The manor might be drafty and run-down, but in the short time she had lived there she had come to love it. Somehow it suited her, and it felt like home.

"Here is your suite of rooms. I do hope you like them," Meredith said. She opened a pair of doors and stepped aside, waving them in before her.

Phoebe smiled as she glanced around. After the rather alarming magnificence of the rest of the house, she could not help but be delighted. The suite was spacious but not overly large, and was decorated in cheerful shades of yellow and pale green. The furniture looked overstuffed and comfortable, covered in a pretty cotton fabric patterned with cream and yellow stripes. Crystal bowls of gorgeous red roses adorned the polished tabletops, and a roaring fire in the large marble chimneypiece warmed the room.

She turned to Meredith. "It's very beautiful. Where did you find roses at this time of year?"

Meredith's eyes gleamed with happy pride. "They're from our succession-houses, which are the best in the country as Silverton is very fond of telling me."

Phoebe sensed Lucas stiffen beside her. The manor had succession-houses, too, but they had fallen into disrepair. He had told her it would take a great deal of money to restore them.

"Then I shall be sure to ask Cousin Stephen all about them," she said politely.

"You will make him very happy if you do. Now, I beg you

both to hurry. Lucas, your dressing room is through there."
She pointed to a door to the right of the fireplace.

After Meredith took herself off, Lucas excused himself to
change. Worried, Phoebe watched him go. Though he was
trying not to show it, he was battling to keep his rising resentment in check. Perhaps it had been a mistake to come to the
abbey after all, but now she had to make the best of it, and
hope the two men would have the good sense to act like reasonable adults.

With a quiet knock on the door, Maggie let herself in.
Phoebe quickly washed and dressed, then sat for Maggie to
dress her hair. While the maid was putting the finishing touches
to her coiffure, Lucas prowled into the room, devastatingly
handsome in the black and white evening attire that set off his
lean, muscular build to perfection. Phoebe almost wished they
could remain right where they were, snuggled up in the sinfully
luxurious four-poster bed that dominated the room. A mere few
days ago she had still been a virgin, but she could easily imagine becoming utterly addicted to her husband's lovemaking.

He studied her, his eyes heating with appreciation. "You
look beautiful, my sweet. I believe you are more than ready
to face the collected might of the Stanton family and their
noble guests."

She gave him a grateful smile and stood, letting him take
her hand to lead her out of their suite.

"I hope you know your way to the drawing room," she said
as they strolled down the long corridor. "I should be lost if I
had to find it myself."

"Yes, it's quite the pile," he said in a cynical voice. "What
do you think of it so far?"

"It is very impressive, of course, but I prefer our home."

He threw her a startled glance, then seemed to chew on the
notion for a few moments. "I think I agree with you, which
surprises the hell out of me."

"Lucas! You must watch your language. You know how Uncle Arthur scolds whenever you swear."

"I think you can match him very well in the scolding department, Madame Wife."

She protested, but he simply laughed, keeping up his teasing until they descended the staircase to the entrance hall. As they reached the bottom step, one of the doors off the hall opened and a young woman carrying a swaddled baby emerged. Both petite and voluptuous, she was one of the most beautiful women Phoebe had ever seen. Her auburn hair glowed with a fiery hue, and her complexion was as rich as cream. She glanced up, her green eyes filling with pleasure as she spied Lucas.

"It's the Earl of Merritt, arrived at last," she said in a warm voice. "I see marriage has yet to mend your bad habits, my friend."

Lucas smiled, obviously delighted to see her. "Ah, Mrs. Blackmore! I didn't realize you would be here for the holiday, although I can't blame you for wanting to escape the wilds of Yorkshire. My dear ma'am, how do you bear it?"

The beauty scowled with mock fierceness. "Lucas, do not call me *ma'am*. You make me sound like an old hag."

He laughed, then gave her a kiss on the cheek when she offered it. "No one could ever accuse you of that," he said. "Trust me."

Phoebe stood quietly, wondering if her husband had forgotten her. He seemed so taken with the other woman, who, despite the fact that she juggled a baby on her shoulder, exuded a sensuality no man could possibly ignore.

The woman gave her a disarming smile. "And you must be Lady Merritt. I'm very pleased to meet the woman finally able to bring Lucas Stanton to heel. Dozens have tried, but only you succeeded." She tilted her head, studying Phoebe. "And I can see why. You're absolutely gorgeous."

Phoebe's mouth dropped open. "Ah, thank you, ma . . .

madam. It is very kind of you to say so." The woman's frankness was disconcerting, to say the least.

"Don't worry, Phoebe. You'll get used to her soon enough," Lucas said with a wry grin. "And now, let me formally introduce you to Mrs. John Blackmore, known to her friends as Bathsheba. You must remember that I told you about Dr. Blackmore, her husband."

Phoebe blinked, surprised that such a stunning beauty had married a country physician. Of course she had heard all about Dr. Blackmore from Meredith, and how he had delivered her twins. Phoebe knew from the harrowing story that the babies and probably Meredith would have died without the doctor's dramatic intervention.

"It is a great pleasure to meet you, Mrs. Blackmore," Phoebe said, giving her a slight curtsy.

"You mustn't curtsy to me, my dear. You are a countess and I'm simply the wife of a country doctor," she said with an easy smile.

"But you were a countess, were you not?" asked Phoebe. She had assumed that once a countess, always a countess. The arcane social conventions of the aristocracy never failed to trip her up.

"Once," she replied cheerfully. "But those days are over, thank God. Now I live in the back of beyond—as Lucas so kindly pointed out—and do my feeble best to help my husband with his work."

"You do a great deal more than that, I hear," Lucas said in an admiring voice. Mrs. Blackmore shrugged away his praise.

Phoebe reached out to gently stroke the baby cradled in her arms. "And is this your child, Mrs. Blackmore?"

The woman carefully pushed back the cambric and lace cap obscuring the baby's face. "This little monster? No. I'm happy to say he's the son and heir of Lord Silverton. I thought I would rescue his mother by taking him back to the nurse."

She immediately offset her flippant remarks by kissing

the baby and cuddling him close. The infant gave a sleepy, contented sigh and nestled closer.

Phoebe smiled. "Of course. Now I recognize him. He's a lovely boy."

"Tell that to his mother when he's feeling colicky," she said. "Which seems to be a great deal of the time. My husband claims little Stephen should grow out of it very soon, but I have my doubts."

Lucas pointed to Mrs. Blackmore's shoulder. "Speaking of colic, you look a little worse for wear. Is that what I think it is?"

She glanced down at her dress. "Sadly, yes. Viscount Thornbury just disgraced himself all over my gown. Once I deposit him in the nursery I'll be changing forthwith." She wrinkled her pretty nose. "Take it from me, there is *nothing* worse than baby vomit for ruining one's clothes. If you wish to avoid a sartorial accident, I suggest you stay clear of this little one."

Lucas laughed again, and even Phoebe had to smile. She thought she might grow to like Bathsheba Blackmore, for her plain manner of speech if nothing else. But she was not so sure she liked the way her husband studied the other woman with so warm an expression.

Mrs. Blackmore tucked the blanket around the sleeping child. "Run along, my dears. The others are waiting for you in the drawing room. I'll see you at dinner."

With a gracious nod, Mrs. Blackmore disappeared up the stairs. Lucas stared after her, a little smile playing around the edges of his mouth. "The most beautiful and witty woman in the ton, and now she spends her time soothing colicky babies and tending to her husband's medical practice. It's extraordinary."

A shaft of jealousy stung Phoebe, sharp and cold. Her husband obviously thought *Bathsheba* was extraordinary, and he made no bones about stating it.

"You like her very much," she ventured, striving to keep her voice neutral.

He glanced at her. "She's easy to like. At least now she is. And once you get to know her, I'm sure you'll like her, too. She can be very blunt, and I would think you'd appreciate that quality."

Phoebe opened her mouth, then closed it, not sure if Lucas meant to compliment or insult her. She did not think it was the latter, but the encounter with Mrs. Blackmore—whom she suspected had been one of Lucas's flirts—had left her rattled. Compared to the sophisticated beauty, Phoebe could not but feel awkward and shy. She had not felt like that since leaving London and the fishbowl of the ton, but her husband's evident appreciation of Mrs. Blackmore brought all her inconvenient insecurities charging to the surface. She had not expected to feel that way, not once they were married, and her confidence slipped another notch.

"Phoebe, what's wrong?"

She glanced up to meet her husband's frown. Was he concerned, or was he merely impatient with her lack of social polish? She could not tell. "Nothing."

He narrowed his eyes.

"Well," she amended, "perhaps I am a little tired." And suddenly she was. Tired of lying, tired of wondering if Lucas would ever love her, tired of wondering if she would ever truly feel like his wife.

His gaze softened and he raised her hand, pressing a kiss on the tender skin of her wrist. She shivered, her body responding to his lightest touch.

"I know, love. You've been much too busy with all this Christmas nonsense. You need to sit and have a sherry and stay quiet for a bit. All this gallivanting about is obviously too much for you."

She repressed a sigh. If it were only that simple, she would be a happy woman.

Chapter 29

Phoebe's gaze wandered the length of the table, sumptuously decorated with silver bowls of Christmas greenery and plump oranges, offset by handsome crystal vases filled with red roses. At the center of the table stood a remarkable flower basket composed entirely of sugar, so lifelike she could swear she caught a hint of scent. Everywhere in the abbey she saw the joy and beauty of Christmas, and most especially in the happy expressions of the family and friends gathered together in the elegant dining room.

Emotion tightened her throat, and she sent up a silent prayer of thanks to God for leading her to the Stanton family and to this time and place. Aunt Georgie and Uncle Arthur, Annabel and Robert, and all the rest had greeted her with genuine affection. To be gifted with a loving and kind family was truly the greatest of blessings.

Except for the blessing of a loving husband who did *not* make a habit of flirting with every pretty woman who crossed his path.

From the moment Bathsheba Blackmore returned to the drawing room, Lucas had attached himself to her side. Phoebe suspected he had done so to avoid Cousin Stephen, who had greeted him with a cool manner that made her heart sink. After that, Lucas had given his cousin a wide berth, resisting all attempts by Aunt Georgie to draw him into the family circle. He had sat with Bathsheba on an elegant settee in the corner, and the two had kept up a lively conversation until they were called in to dinner.

Unfortunate luck had also placed Lucas and Bathsheba next to each other at dinner, which had more the feel of an intimate family gathering than a formal occasion. And none seemed to enjoy the evening more than those two, who chatted and laughed throughout the long repast, exchanging gossip about mutual acquaintances in London. Phoebe tried to be happy that her husband was finally enjoying himself, but his actions reminded her too much of his flirtatious behavior the night of Lady Framingham's ball.

She tore her gaze away to stare at the roasted pheasant in front of her, concentrating on its artful display on a bed of its own feathers. Her anxiety was ridiculous. She was seated in splendid comfort, enjoying a wonderful meal in celebration of the Lord's nativity. She had everything she had ever wished for. A family who accepted her with open arms, a home to call her own, and a husband who might not be madly in love with her but who—

Lucas's husky laugh cut through her thoughts, pulling her gaze back across the table. He and Bathsheba had their heads close together again—his burnished gold to her flame—as they shared a joke. He leaned an elbow on the table as he talked in an animated fashion, more at ease than Phoebe had seen him in weeks. Unlike her, the former countess certainly had a knack for making a man comfortable and happy. Perhaps Phoebe should ask her for advice on how to manage husbands. Once she got over the horridly uncharitable impulse to throttle the woman, she might do just that.

"They make quite a striking pair, don't they?" Dr. Blackmore's cultured voice interrupted the downward spiral of her thoughts.

Phoebe blinked, and then dredged up a smile, turning slightly to address him. "They do. One might even think they belonged together."

She winced. Would she never learn to control her wayward tongue? For all the wrong reasons she was grateful her brother, George, could no longer see and hear her. He would be ashamed of her conduct, and rightfully so.

"I . . . I am sorry," she stammered. "I do not know why—"

"You mustn't apologize," he said with a kind smile. "I understand completely." He flicked a glance across at his wife, a wry expression shaping his noble features. "Believe me. I know exactly how you're feeling."

Puzzled, she put down her fork and stared at him. "And it does not bother you?"

"That my wife so easily charms other men? No. Not anymore. It's second nature to her. I might as well ask her to stop breathing."

"But it used to bother you?"

He grinned, his unusual silver eyes filling with warmth. Dr. Blackmore was a truly handsome man, but even more attractive was his kind and forthright nature, readily apparent from the moment she had met him in the drawing room. "You have no idea, my lady. When I first met Bathsheba, I didn't know whether to throttle her or kiss her."

Phoebe choked back a startled laugh.

He nodded sagely. "I see you know exactly what I'm talking about."

Her brief spurt of amusement faded, and she could not hold back a sigh. "It is very wrong of me to be jealous. But I cannot seem to help it."

"It's human nature, although in your case I would think you have nothing to worry about. But don't fall into the habit. It's a sickness, and nothing will poison a relationship more quickly."

"How do you avoid it?" she asked, genuinely curious.

He smiled. "Bathsheba and I have no secrets from each other. I know her as well as I know myself, and vice versa. It's almost impossible to be jealous under those circumstances."

Oh, Lord. Secrets. No wonder she felt so awful.

"And I trust her," Dr. Blackmore continued. "When you trust the person you love, you trust her no matter what. You accept everything about her, even her less attractive qualities. Because without those qualities, she would not be who she is. My wife is the sum of all her parts, and I would not change a single detail about her."

A sad little yearning twisted in Phoebe's heart. What would it be like to love like that, with total trust and devotion?

"And you never succumb to doubt?" she asked softly.

He gazed thoughtfully across the table at his wife, still deep in conversation with Lucas. "No. Never."

His deep voice rang with quiet conviction and bone-deep satisfaction. As if he had called to her, Bathsheba switched her attention from Lucas to her husband. Her expression of social enjoyment fell away, replaced by one so intensely loving—so *private*—that Phoebe had to shift her gaze. She pushed food around her plate, trying not to wish so desperately that Lucas would someday look at her with that same intensity.

When she looked up, the moment had passed and Bathsheba was once again talking to Lucas. Dr. Blackmore raised an eyebrow at Phoebe as if to say, *see?*

She had to laugh. "Yes, I do take your point. You are indeed a fortunate man to be so loved. I congratulate you."

"I am. And I expect you are equally fortunate, Lady Merritt, if I am any judge of the matter."

Phoebe had no idea how he could draw such a conclusion, but it would be rude to voice the thought when he clearly meant to be kind.

"Thank you," she said politely. "I am indeed fortunate in the love of my family."

Dr. Blackmore frowned and started to say something, but a rumbling noise from the other side of the table interrupted them as Uncle Arthur cleared his throat in a portentous fashion. He had risen to his feet, obviously preparing to make some kind of pronouncement.

Phoebe glanced at Lucas, who widened his eyes at her in mock alarm. When she swallowed a giggle he gave her a wink and a sly grin, and the knot in her chest eased by several degrees.

"Ahem," Uncle Arthur began. "On behalf of my nephew, the Marquess of Silverton, I would like to welcome all of you to the abbey. For those of you who are spending Christmas with us for the first time, I bid you a special welcome and good cheer."

He paused to lift his wineglass and everyone—the Stantons, their guests, and a few local families from the neighborhood— lifted theirs in return, followed by a few hearty cheers.

"Some of you may not know," her uncle continued, "but we have a long-standing family tradition of reciting a special poem on Christmas Day."

Robert, seated on the other side of Phoebe, leaned close. "Actually, we don't," he said in a penetrating stage whisper. "But Grandfather read this poem in *Gentleman's Magazine* a few years ago, and decided it would make a good family tradition. No one has the faintest clue why."

"Hush," Phoebe hissed softly as her uncle glared at them.

"As I was saying," Uncle Arthur said in a slightly aggrieved voice, "I always recite this poem on Christmas Day. But since Phoebe and Lucas will be celebrating the Lord's birth in their own home, I thought it proper we break with tradition this year, and hold the recitation tonight."

Phoebe smiled at him, touched by his thoughtfulness. Reciting poetry at dinner seemed a rather odd thing to do, but she appreciated the gesture nonetheless. Unfortunately, she chose that moment to look at Lucas, who was clearly struggling not to laugh. A giggle again made its way up her throat, but she forced it down, giving her husband a severe frown.

Uncle Arthur grasped the bottom of his waistcoat and assumed a dramatic pose. An expectant hush fell around the table, although she could also sense Robert quivering with repressed laughter.

"This piece was written by Robert Southey on Christmas Day," Uncle Arthur began.

> *"How many hearts are happy at this hour*
> *In England! Brightly o'er the cheerful hall*
> *Flares the heaped hearth, and friends and kindred meet,*
> *And the glad mother round her festive board*
> *Beholds her children, separated long."*

As the dignified old man recited the poem, Phoebe let her gaze drift around the table. Everyone had turned to watch her uncle, and every face held a smile. Poetry readings at dinner might be considered rather quaint, but there was no doubting the goodwill and cheer around the holiday table this night.

Uncle Arthur proceeded dramatically through the verses, rising to a crescendo.

> *"As o'er the house, all gay with evergreens,*
> *From friend to friend with joyful speed I ran,*
> *Bidding a Merry Christmas to them all."*

He ended with a flourish. Everyone broke into enthusiastic applause and even Lucas joined in, looking genuinely appreciative. The old man acknowledged their acclaim with a dignified bow and resumed his seat.

"Thank you, General," Cousin Stephen said from the head of the table. He rose, and they all came to their feet.

"In honor of another family tradition," he said, "I'll ask the men to dispense with their usual after-dinner brandy and join my wife and me in the great hall. I do believe Meredith has a treat in store for us."

Phoebe could not fail to detect the note of sarcasm in his voice.

"I certainly do," Meredith said. "And I know you will all enjoy it." She smiled down the length of the table at her husband. "Or else."

They all laughed, and in the general commotion of rising from the table and getting organized, Phoebe found herself once more with Lucas. He drew her hand through his arm and led her to the great hall. "Did you enjoy dinner, Phoebe?"

Only parts of it, thanks to his flirtatious behavior, but she would face another trip across the Atlantic before admitting it. "I certainly enjoyed my conversation with Dr. Blackmore. He is a most interesting and kind man."

"Yes, he is. I'm glad you enjoyed his company."

She peered up at him. He still looked relaxed and at ease. Clearly, he had not suffered any pangs of jealously to see her conversing so intently with the doctor. That meant he either trusted her completely, or could not be bothered to care.

"And you clearly enjoyed talking to Mrs. Blackmore," she said. "Have you been friends with her for many years?"

"Bathsheba? Lord, no. I only met her this past summer."

Her heart sank. If they had been old friends, she might have understood the nature of his attentions to her. She was trying very hard not to be jealous, but her husband made it a challenge.

"What's wrong, Phoebe?"

"What? Oh, nothing."

He tilted his head, a concerned frown marking his brow. "Do you wish to retire? I'll take you upstairs if you do."

She wanted to sigh, but then he might think she suffered from the vapors, or something equally annoying. "No, thank you. I am just wondering what will happen next. Do you know?"

He glanced at a door in the back of the hall. "I'm assuming it's the . . . yes, the wassail bowl. Here comes the butler with it now."

From a partly concealed door the butler emerged, and behind him two liveried footmen carried an enormous and elaborately worked silver bowl, which they carefully set on a table decorated with evergreen branches and swags of ivy. Cousin Stephen stepped up to the table, and Meredith joined him a moment later.

"Dear friends," he began. "My lady and I welcome you to our hall tonight, and wish you good cheer at this festive time of year. This wassail bowl, so symbolic of the generosity of the Season, is from an old family recipe. I prepared it myself before dinner, and I can assure you that a cup of it will chase away all worries and cares, and bring glad hearts to all who drink it."

"Yes, very glad, as I discovered during my first Christmas at the abbey," Meredith said in a rueful voice. "Until the next morning, when I felt anything but. It is a *very* strong recipe."

Everyone laughed. Silverton tipped up Meredith's chin and gave her a quick kiss. That elicited more laughter and a few good-natured jests.

Phoebe glanced at Lucas. His easy manner had disappeared, and he studied his cousin with a grim expression, suddenly looking like he would rather be anywhere else. Obviously, the sight of Cousin Stephen's prosperous contentment grated on him; no doubt he was comparing it to his own problems at Mistletoe Manor and in his marriage.

She repressed the impulse to rub her forehead with frustration. She did not know which was worse, a flirtatious Lucas or a resentful Lucas. Not for the first time this evening, she almost wished they had stayed at home.

Cousin Stephen began ladling out the wassail. The guests crowded around the table, each taking a cup.

"Here you go, Phoebe," said Robert, handing her one. "You wouldn't believe it, but in the old days everyone had to drink directly out of the wassail bowl." He glanced over at one of the guests, an elderly gentleman who seemed to be wearing half his dinner on his cravat. "Take Sir Mortimer, for example. Could you imagine having to drink out of the bowl after he's had a go of it?" He gave a dramatic shudder.

Annabel elbowed him in the ribs. "That's disgusting, Robert. And you know poor Sir Mortimer has terrible eyesight. I'm sure he doesn't mean to keep dropping his food down his front."

"Just be grateful *you* didn't have to sit across from him," Robert parried. "Almost put me off my feed."

"Nothing puts you off your feed," said Lucas. "Your stomach is a bottomless pit. How you manage to remain so thin is a miracle of nature."

"No such thing," Robert protested.

Annabel laughingly agreed, and the young couple fell into a good-natured argument. Smiling, Phoebe raised her cup and took a cautious sip. Both sweet and highly spiced, the brew was strong enough to burn a trail of delicious fire down her throat.

"Careful," Lucas murmured. "Wassail is very potent. If you drink too much I'll have to carry you up to bed." He brought his mouth close to her ear. "And then I'd be forced to have my way with you. Over and over again."

The shock of his words heated the air around them. Their eyes met, and his flared with desire. A coil of yearning twisted low in her belly and, suddenly, she, too, wished more than anything they could be alone.

Then she remembered how annoyed she was with him. She pinched his arm. "Lucas, behave yourself!"

He responded with a sardonic smile. "Hush, my love. You wouldn't want anyone to know what we're talking about, and that blush on your face is a dead giveaway."

The sound of voices from outside the hall saved her the trouble of answering. Breathing a sigh of relief, she turned her back on Lucas to see the butler opening the front door. A chorus of singing voices drifted into the hall, along with a rush of frigid air.

> *"Wassail, Wassail, all over the town!*
> *Our bread it is white and our ale it is brown;*
> *Our bowl is made of the maple tree,*
> *With the wassailing bowl, I'll drink to thee."*

"At last," Meredith exclaimed.

A group of men and women, warmly dressed, clustered into the hall, each wearing a silver chain around the neck. Phoebe glanced behind her to ask Lucas about the visitors, but he was gone—back to the other side of the hall, where he again was speaking with Bathsheba.

She ground her teeth. Her husband was fast becoming the most frustrating man she had ever met.

"Have you ever heard the Waits sing before?" Annabel asked her. "They're really quite wonderful."

Deciding to ignore Lucas for now, she smiled at Annabel. "No, I have not. Who are they?"

"They're organized groups from the village, who go from house to house to perform Christmas carols and share the wassail bowl. It's a very ancient tradition."

Phoebe blinked. The drive from the abbey gates to the house must be two miles long. "You mean they walked all the way from the nearest village?"

"No, silly! Meredith arranged for it. She had carriages pick them up."

Phoebe studied the merry group, who were eagerly accepting cups of wassail from Meredith. Cousin Stephen stood behind her with a long-suffering expression on his face.

"Why do I sense that Cousin Stephen is not thrilled?"

Annabel laughed. "A few years ago some of the men were quite drunk by the time they reached the abbey. They caused a bit of a scene."

"A bit!" Robert hooted. "One of them fell right into the bowl and sent it crashing to the floor, and then another one cast up his accounts, narrowly missing Grandfather's toes. As you can imagine, Silverton was not pleased, especially since it was Meredith's first Christmas as marchioness."

Phoebe laughed at the expression on his face.

Annabel wrinkled her nose. "It sounds comical now, but Silverton was furious and swore he would never let any Waits step foot in the house again. Fortunately, Meredith was finally able to convince him to relent. And Silverton *does* understand the importance of keeping up the local traditions, however reluctantly he might do so."

Phoebe shook her head. "Why do men have such a problem with Christmas traditions? It all seems wonderful to me, and it makes everyone so happy."

"I don't," Robert protested. "I love Christmas. Especially the food and the presents, and I quite like the singing, too."

Annabel went up on tiptoe and kissed her husband's cheek. "It's one of the reasons I love you."

Phoebe repressed a sigh. She was delighted her cousins were all so happily married, but right now their contentment felt like a rebuke. Especially since *her* husband had chosen to stand as far away from her as he could, obviously preferring the company of another woman.

Except he was no longer enjoying Bathsheba's company. She had rejoined Dr. Blackmore, while Lucas now stood by the staircase, clearly brooding and appearing . . . lonely.

She hesitated, wondering if she should go to him, but then the Waits began to sing. Reluctantly, she turned back to listen.

"Come, let us join with Angels now,
Glory to God on high,
Peace upon Earth, Goodwill to men,
Amen, Amen, say I."

She listened, letting the rich voices and the beautiful words wash over her. Her worries leached away, replaced by gratitude and an almost prayerful sense of awareness of how fortunate she was to be in this magnificent place, and with her new family.

"The Christ he come to do us Good,
To Christ art thee yet come?
A burthene'd, weary, thirsty soul,
A lost sheep to bring home."

She cast her gaze behind her, searching for Lucas, wanting to share the precious moment with him. But the space where he had stood was empty.

Chapter 30

Lucas poured himself a brandy from the drinks trolley, casting a glance over his shoulder as the door to the drawing room opened. Family members strolled in, having had their fill of the wassail bowl, the singing, and all the other mawkish amusements celebrated during the Christmas Season. As a boy, he had reveled in the singing, the games, and the good cheer. Now all that simply served as a reminder of how cynical he had become.

He replaced the decanter as Phoebe drifted toward him, her big eyes wary. His military career had made him impatient of frivolity, but that didn't excuse the way he'd abandoned her. Still, if forced to spend another minute in that damn hall watching Silverton play lord of the manor, he might have snapped someone's head off. Irrational, yes, but Silverton's perpetually charmed life always felt like a rebuke, illustrating by effortless example the ways Lucas had failed in so many aspects of his life.

Starting with his wife. Poor Phoebe didn't deserve to be saddled with his problems, and he probably counted as a selfish bastard by manipulating her into marriage.

She approached, her gaze now full of worry and concern. That made his gut clench, and his desire to protect her warred with his need to keep her at a safe distance. Phoebe's open and generous heart made them both too vulnerable. Her because he would surely disappoint her, and him because her willingness to love made him vulnerable in a way he wished never to be again.

Especially since he was damn certain she must be keeping something from him. Her recent behavior had been wholly unlike the Phoebe he had come to know, and that bothered him more than he cared to admit.

"I missed you in the hall," she said tentatively. "I hope you are not unwell."

Perversely, even when he most wished to keep his distance from everyone, including her, he longed for her voice and company. She soothed him, much like an experienced groom could quiet a skittish stallion. That bothered him, too, because it spoke of a dependence that weakened him.

He managed a smile. "I apologize for abandoning you, but I'm not keen on all this Christmas business. As you know," he finished, all too aware he sounded like a mutton-head.

She nodded. "I understand. I am sorry to have dragged you here, but I am so very grateful to have the chance to spend some time with the family." She gazed up at him, not a shred of judgment in her expression. "Thank you, Lucas. It was very kind of you to bring me to the abbey."

He exhaled a sigh. "Phoebe, I truly wouldn't mind if you ripped up at me. I'm sure I deserve it."

She blinked in surprise, then her eyes filled with unexpected amusement. "If that would please you, I will be happy to oblige once we return to our room. I daresay by the time I am finished, you will regret that suggestion." She wagged her finger at him. "I can be quite terrifying, you know."

He laughed. How could he not when he had a wife who constantly surprised him? "Then I shall look forward to it. Thank you, love. I certainly don't deserve your consideration."

"No one would disagree with that," Silverton's voice interjected from behind them.

Lucas swung around to meet his cousin's challenging gaze. Irritation flared, but he managed to hold back a retort. Not for Silverton's sake, but for Phoebe's. Lucas had inflicted enough trouble on her for one evening, and he'd be damned if he'd make a scene in front of her.

Not unless his cousin forced him to.

"Cousin Stephen," Phoebe said, stepping between them, "what a lovely scene in the hall. As you know, this is my first real Christmas and I am thoroughly enjoying it."

Silverton unleashed a charming smile. "I'm so glad." He flicked a glance at Lucas. "How unfortunate your husband can't say the same."

Before Lucas could respond, Phoebe's chin went up in an aggressive tilt. "I am sure that is not the case. Lucas has been most helpful with the Christmas preparations at Mistletoe Manor. In fact, he told me just this morning how much he is looking forward to our own celebrations. He is convinced they will quite exceed the festivities at the abbey."

Lucas had to choke down a laugh. He would have been shocked that his sweet little Quaker had told a bold-faced lie, but he was too busy enjoying her impassioned defense.

Silverton's jaw dropped for a brief moment, but he quickly recovered. "I stand corrected, Cousin. Please forgive me."

She returned him a dignified nod, then switched her attention to Lucas. "Aunt Georgie wishes you to sit with her. She says she has been missing you greatly these last few weeks."

As Phoebe practically dragged him off, he couldn't help throwing Silverton a taunting grin. His cousin narrowed his gaze, but Phoebe tugged him away before anything could happen.

"Behave yourself, Lucas, or else," she threatened in a low voice.

He widened his eyes at her. "I have no idea what you're talking about."

She shook her head, muttering imprecations under her breath.

His mood improved another notch. Clearly, he had been a terrible influence on her. He couldn't wait to get her alone so he could spend more time corrupting her morals.

His aunt, seated on a sofa before the fire, greeted him with a gentle smile. "Ah, Lucas. We are so honored you have decided to grace us with your presence, despite your well-known boredom with these occasions. We must count ourselves grateful you have put away your scruples in order to visit with us."

Christ. The royal *we* had come into play. Obviously, it was time to bow and scrape. "I don't know how you've tolerated me all these years," Lucas said in a contrite voice. "Since I'm such a very bad seed."

She laughed and patted the seat next to her. "You've been horrible, but I forgive you. Phoebe, come sit next to your husband. We'll have a nice chat while we're waiting for tea."

Once they'd all settled themselves, Aunt Georgie let out a comfortable sigh. "I'm sorry the other guests had to leave early, but I must confess I'm relieved to have only a family party tonight. Well, except for the Blackmores, but one counts them as family."

Lucas glanced around at the elegantly decorated but comfortable space, one of the smaller drawing rooms in the sprawling pile that made up Belfield Abbey. He was torn between pleasure at its refined sense of comfort and annoyance that everything in Silverton's home was always so bloody perfect. He and Phoebe couldn't possibly receive guests at the manor, given that the windows in the large drawing room leaked and the new furniture for the family parlor had yet to arrive.

And he could hardly invite anyone to sit on chairs that had been found to conceal more than one rodent's nest. Not to mention the dismaying state of most of the chimneys, belching smoke back into the house every time the wind came from the north.

"Why did the other guests leave so early?" Phoebe asked.

"It's starting to snow," Aunt Georgie replied. "The roads can turn bad very quickly out here in the country, and the squire's wife thought it best they not linger. The other guests agreed."

Lucas almost groaned. *Snow.* If it came down heavily and they got trapped at the abbey for more than a day, he would likely shoot himself. Or Silverton.

Phoebe's face, however, glowed like a branch of candles. "I love snow. It makes everything look so different, especially the formal gardens. The statues wear white velvet coats and cone hats, and the hedges are iced cakes."

Aunt Georgie smiled at the imagery. "I agree it's lovely, but we're fortunate the snow rarely lingers in Kent. At your uncle's estate in Yorkshire, we can get snowed in for weeks."

"God help us all," Lucas muttered.

His aunt laughed. "You spent more than one winter holiday snowed in with us, and I clearly recall you quite liked it. You and Silverton used to spend hours tramping over the downs and skating on the village pond, or sledding down the hill behind the house. I don't remember you complaining one bit at the time. Oh, wait. One winter, you tumbled down the icy hill and broke your wrist. Then you complained loudly because you were trapped indoors for the rest of the holiday."

A reluctant smile tugged his lips at the distant memories. He'd enjoyed the fun back then, when life was uncomplicated and straightforward.

They chatted for several more minutes while Meredith served tea and the men drank their brandies. No one seemed in the mood for cards or games, preferring conversation instead. Lucas found himself gradually relaxing, even starting to enjoy himself. Bathsheba was her usual witty self—although a loving marriage had obviously taken much of the amusing acid from her conversation—and Robert kept everyone laughing with his ridiculous jokes. Cantankerous Uncle

Arthur was in good humor, and even Silverton had the grace to sit quietly and not ruin things.

And Phoebe was having a grand time as she chatted with her aunt and cousins. For once, it seemed they might get through a holiday without any kidnappings or poisoning, or without him and Silverton tearing up the dining room.

"I say, Lucas," piped up Robert. "I hear you've got a smuggling problem down your way. Damned impertinent of the blackguards to use manor lands, if you ask me."

"Language, Robert," Aunt Georgie admonished.

Uncle Arthur, dozing in a comfortable wingback chair, came to full alert. "What's this? Smugglers on the manor's lands? Not that I should be surprised, given the way Merritt ignored the problem. Ridiculous, turning a blind eye to it like he did. But he insisted it was better to leave it alone than confront the gangs. Some claptrap about protecting the locals. Personally, I always believed he allowed them free passage because they kept him well-supplied with French brandy. Bloody fool."

"Language, Arthur," Aunt Georgie said in a long-suffering voice.

"What's that? Oh, sorry, my dear. Well, out with it, boy," he demanded of Lucas. "Are the smugglers still at it?"

So much for a pleasant evening in the Stanton family bosom. Lucas dodged the question. "Robert, how did you come to hear about this?"

Robert blinked. "Oh, Meredith told Belle, and Belle told me. Can't keep a thing like that a secret, old man. Not in this family."

Out of the corner of his eye, Lucas caught Phoebe and Meredith exchanging a guilty look. Obviously, his interfering wife had written to his equally interfering cousin, who hadn't been able to keep the news from her sister. Now he'd have the entire family weighing in on his problem, which was exactly what he'd been trying to avoid. "It's nothing I can't deal with.

I should have the matter resolved to my satisfaction within a few weeks."

Next to him, Phoebe made a little squeaking noise and went as stiff as a board. Understanding suddenly lit up his brain.

Oh, good Christ. Could that be what she'd been hiding from him? Something to do with the smugglers? He might have known she couldn't keep her inquisitive little nose out of it.

"How bad is the smuggling?" Silverton asked.

Perfect. His cousin had clearly deduced he wanted to cut off the conversation, so naturally he had to prod.

"It's nothing I can't handle," he grated out again.

"That's not what Meredith said, old chap," Robert insisted in his usual, ham-fisted manner. "Something about excise officers bursting into the house in the middle of the night, pistols at the ready. Sounds rather worrisome to me."

"Robert, you're exaggerating," Meredith said with annoyance.

Storm clouds began to gather over Uncle Arthur's head. "Lucas, what the devil is going on? Is Phoebe in danger from this business? Sounds to me like you should keep her here at the abbey until you track these blackguards down. It would not be well done to put your wife in danger, my lad. Not well done at all."

Lucas clenched his fist, trying to keep his temper under control.

"Oh, no," Phoebe broke in earnestly before he could respond to his uncle. "I am sure the problem is not nearly as alarming as it sounds. It is just that life has been wretched for the people in the district. Now that Lucas is restoring the manor and estate to prosperity, I am sure the problem will fade away on its own soon enough."

Lucas gave her a disbelieving stare. She looked flushed and guilty, but she didn't drop her gaze.

"I doubt it will be that easy," he said.

"It won't be," said Uncle Arthur. "Smugglers are like rats. You have to poison them or flush them out of the nest, by any means necessary. You'll never get rid of them if you don't."

Aunt Georgie's mouth rounded with horror. "Arthur! That is positively uncivilized."

The old man grimaced. "Just a euphemism, m'dear. You understand."

"Grandfather's right," Robert said. "You can't let those criminals get away with it. Why, look what happened to the Blackmores and me last summer with that bounder O'Neill. He almost killed all of us."

A thug *had* attacked Blackmore, Bathsheba, and Robert five months ago, the night Meredith gave birth to her twins. But that situation bore no resemblance to what Lucas faced.

Bathsheba pointed that out a moment later. "O'Neill was a madman, not a smuggler. There's quite a difference."

"Mrs. Blackmore, your tolerance amazes me. What difference does it make? They're all criminals in my book," huffed the General.

"Uncle Arthur, these men are not criminals," Phoebe said in a tight voice. "They are poor, struggling every day to feed their families. It is up to us as lord and lady of Mistletoe Manor to assist them, not resort to violence against them." She turned pleading eyes on Lucas. "Isn't that right, Lucas?"

He practically had to pry his clenched teeth apart. "Phoebe, I told you, we are not having this discussion, here or anywhere else."

She flushed, but her jaw set in a stubborn line.

"Quite right, Nephew," Uncle Arthur chimed in. "This business is best left to men. Don't bother your pretty little head over it, Phoebe. Leave everything to Lucas."

That resulted in the all too predictable and contentious response from the ladies until Phoebe's voice cut through the tumult. "I *will* be involved, because I refuse to allow Lucas or anyone else to turn those unfortunate men over to a harsh and unfeeling justice."

Lucas thought his head might explode, and when Silverton decided to open his mouth it almost did. "I have to agree with Phoebe," his cousin said. He relaxed in his chair, the very picture of a wealthy, self-satisfied lord. Lucas wanted to plant a facer on his aristocratic chin.

"Things have been very bad in Kent since the end of the war," Silverton continued. "So, it's no wonder the smuggling has intensified. But with the return of prosperity to Mistletoe Manor, and with a judicious blind eye, I suspect you'll see the gangs die out by themselves. I believe that would be the wisest course of action, rather than an intemperate rush to justice."

"When I want your damned opinion I'll ask for it," Lucas grated out as his self-control finally snapped. "Until then, keep out of it. What the hell do you know about it, anyway? It's not as if you have any smuggling on abbey lands."

Phoebe groaned and even Uncle Arthur looked affronted. Lucas didn't care. He only had eyes for his cousin.

And his cousin was currently rising to his feet, blue eyes shading dark with anger. "For the sake of the family, I will put up with much from you, Lucas. But I will not allow you to use insulting language in my house. Apologize to the ladies and to me, or I assure you that you'll come to regret it."

Hell. Lucas already regretted his outburst, but it was too late to back down now. He would not be intimidated by Silverton or anybody else. When he rose, Phoebe grabbed his sleeve, but he shook off her hand. "Is that so? And how do you intend to put your threat into action?"

Bathsheba and Blackmore exchanged exasperated glances and Annabel dropped her head into her hands. "Not again," she moaned.

"Cheer up," Robert said to his wife. "At least it won't be our furniture that's destroyed this time."

It might come to that, since Silverton was still glaring at him with murderous fury, and Lucas imagined he looked much the same. But beneath the anger he felt a weariness tugging at his soul. How in God's name had they let this happen again?

"I forbid either of you to say another word." Aunt Georgie's frigid voice sliced through the escalating tension. She came slowly to her feet, as angry as Lucas had ever seen her. "I am disgusted with both of you," she snapped, "as is every other member of the family. You are grown men, blessed with good health, fortune, and wives who love you. And yet all you can do whenever you meet is fight like spoiled children. For what? Over the memory of a woman utterly unworthy of either of you? Lucas, will you not look at your wife and realize how lucky you are?"

Phoebe, who had risen, made a distressed noise in her throat. Startled, Lucas peered at her. Her face had paled, and tears glittered on the end of her lashes. The next instant, she blinked them away, regarding him with an expectant gaze, clearly waiting for him to make a decision.

The right decision. And gazing deeply into her beautiful eyes, he finally understood what that entailed.

But Aunt Georgie wasn't finished. She turned her guns on Silverton. "And you, Stephen. You are the head of this family. Shame on you for acting in so selfish a fashion. Time and again, you have wasted the opportunity to forgive the actions of youthful folly."

Silverton winced, his shoulders edging up around his ears. Lucas understood. His aunt had reduced them to the level of disobedient schoolboys with a few choice words, and they richly deserved it.

She pointed a finger at each of them in turn. "You and you, come with me now." She spun on her heel and headed out the door.

Lucas and his cousin glared at each other for a moment

before Silverton shrugged and followed Aunt Georgie out of the room. Sighing, Lucas went, too, with Phoebe and Meredith trailing in his wake.

His aunt was waiting across the hall at the door to Silverton's library. She opened it and stepped aside. "The two of you will go in there right now and you will not come out until you have apologized to each other and put this dreadful business behind you. I will keep you in there until Twelfth Night if I must, but you *will* forgive each other."

She scowled at them with hands fisted on her hips, a tiny, elderly woman who would put them over her knee if she could. Somewhere deep in Lucas's chest, a bubble of laughter began to form. When Phoebe and Meredith flanked Aunt Georgie, adopting identical postures, he had to swallow hard to keep the laughter from bursting forth.

"Listen to your aunt, Lucas," Phoebe ordered, looking like an angry kitten.

He glanced at Silverton, recognizing the telltale twitch in his jaw. His cousin was also trying not to laugh as he took in Meredith's imperious glare.

Silverton then glanced at him, and with a slight jerk of the head gestured Lucas into the room. Shrugging, Lucas walked into the library, and Silverton followed. Aunt Georgie slammed the door shut. A moment later, he heard the key rotate in the keyhole, locking them in.

Chapter 31

Silverton strolled across the library to a tall cabinet and retrieved a bottle of what looked to be very old French brandy.

"I think I could use something special," he said. "Join me?"

Lucas gave him a nod, wary of his cousin's casual demeanor. Long ago, he and Silverton had spent countless hours here, in study or in companionable conversation. But now the shared memories of those days, even the room itself, seemed to rebuke him for his role in the long deterioration of what had once been the closest of friendships.

Silverton handed him a generous glass, then headed to a set of leather armchairs in front of the fireplace. Lucas followed, glancing around him. He had never forgotten the quiet beauty of the spacious, elegant room. Its walls were lined floor to ceiling with an unparalleled collection of exquisitely tooled books, and the furniture and art spoke to wealth and taste passed down through several generations. It made Lucas's study at the manor shabby in comparison, but it surprised him to realize he preferred his study's modest yet solid comforts to the grandeur of Silverton's lair.

They sat in silence for a few minutes, sipping the excellent brandy and contemplating the crackling flames in the large grate. Lucas sensed they both knew the time had come to confront their past, but that neither knew how to begin. While a fragile sense of companionship hovered between them, a single misspoken word could plunge them back into enmity and discord.

Finally, Silverton shifted in his seat and let out a weary sigh. "It *was* your fault, you know," he said.

Dammit. Not a good beginning. Even though Silverton's pronouncement held a great deal of truth, Lucas wasn't yet ready to wave the white flag. After all, he was a soldier, and surrender didn't come easy.

"Bugger you," he replied, keeping his voice genial and light.

Silverton narrowed his eyes, but maintained his relaxed sprawl in the chair. He didn't fool Lucas, though. Tension hummed in the air between them.

"The women do have the right of this," Silverton replied after several charged moments. "For the sake of the family, we must put the animosity behind us. It's idiotic and a waste of time and energy." His lips twisted into a wry smile. "I'm not going to ask you to apologize, if that's what you're worried about."

That was probably the best opening Lucas could expect, and it was a fairly magnanimous one at that. Might as well get it over with, because Lord knew he was tired of the bloody awful mess it had become.

"You're right," he admitted. "It was my fault, and we both know it. But you need to know something else if we truly intend to put this behind us. I did love Esme. Quite obsessively, in fact, and I was convinced you didn't. Not until it was too late. And by that point, I couldn't step back or even talk to you about it."

Silverton tilted his head to study him. Lucas saw no anger in those extraordinary light blue eyes, only curiosity and something that might be akin to sympathy.

"Why ever not?"

Lucas forced the difficult words out of his mouth. "I was ashamed, dammit."

"Ashamed of loving Esme?"

"God, no. That came much later."

"Then of what?"

Lucas avoided Silverton's perceptive gaze by staring at the fire. He had repressed his shame for so long, allowing only anger to live within him. But the dreaded emotion now came flooding back, and he couldn't bear to look at the man whose trust and friendship he had betrayed.

But he had to face it. Not only did honor demand it, his wife expected this from him, too. The memory of Phoebe's heart-felt gaze in the drawing room rushed into his mind. She trusted him to do the right thing. God only knew why, but it gave him the courage to put his resentment aside and give Silverton what he deserved.

The truth.

Lucas turned to squarely face his cousin. "I envied you, and that made it impossible for me to beg forgiveness. You had everything I ever wanted, and it all came to you so easily. It always did. Everyone doted on you. And why not? You were Marquess of Silverton, the golden-haired lad who could do no wrong. Compared to you, I always came up short, as my father and Uncle Arthur made a point of reminding me on a regular basis."

The bitter-tasting words made him cringe. Still, he'd been a fool all these years and he would finish this if it killed him. The fact that Silverton was now gaping at him, mouth open, made it a bit easier.

"It wasn't that I wanted everything you had," Lucas explained. "God knows, I led a life of privilege and never had cause to complain. What I envied was the respect everyone handed you on a gold platter."

Silverton was slowly shaking his head at him, like he was a damned fool.

Lucas spread his hands. "All right, it was stupid. But that was how I felt. And when Esme chose me, it restored the balance somehow. But then when she rejected me for you, it told me I could never measure up. No matter what I did, I would never be anything but a shadow of the Marquess of Silverton."

Silverton slumped back in his chair, his expression pained. "My God, Lucas. You *were* an idiot to believe that, but so was I. If it wasn't so pathetic, I would be laughing at our stupidity."

Lucas frowned. It was hardly the reaction he was expecting. "What are you talking about?"

A rueful smile touched his cousin's lips. "I'd always been jealous of *you*. You had the freedom I wanted. You could do whatever you wanted, be whomever you wanted. But from my earliest days I had nothing but duty and responsibility drummed into my head. The estates, the family, and all the people I had to watch over —I was never allowed to forget, even for a moment."

He raised an arm in an encompassing gesture. "All this, for example. I can't tell you how often it has seemed a millstone around my neck."

Now it was Lucas's turn to gape. "You're the Marquess of Silverton. Who the hell wouldn't want to be in your boots?"

"Believe me, I'm well aware of my good fortune. But it's a burden, too, at least if you're a man who takes his duties as seriously as I do. Now it's the same for you. After all these years, I suspect you finally understand."

Lucas let that sink in. He did feel different, now that he had a wife, and the manor and its people to look after. The army had carried its own set of duties and concerns, but its success hadn't rested on his shoulders alone. In civilian life, he had people depending on him for everything, and to fail them would blight their lives. For his cousin, with his huge estates, the demands were even greater.

"You possessed the freedom I craved," continued Silverton, "or at least I thought you did. And when Esme obviously preferred you, only wanting my name for the wealth and status it carried . . . well, it had the unfortunate result of confirming everything I believed. That *you* were the lucky one, someone who was judged on his own merit rather than on his title or the size of his purse."

Lucas choked out a disbelieving laugh. "Good Christ, you're right. We *are* idiots."

Silverton shrugged and rose to his feet. He grabbed the brandy bottle and replenished their glasses. "We were young. Worse mistakes came later, when we were old enough to know better. Truly, Lucas, the best thing to do is put all that foolishness behind us. It serves no purpose to lament what might have been. It's only the future that matters, and the people who love us."

Lucas's throat tightened with emotion. He stood and offered his hand. "Thank you, Cousin," he said gruffly.

They shook, and for an awful moment Lucas was afraid Silverton would hug him.

His cousin rolled his eyes. "Don't be more of an idiot than you already are."

Lucas grinned and they tapped their glasses, offering a silent toast. After they drank, Silverton put down his glass and gave him an easy, charming smile. It was the first genuine smile Silverton had directed at him in years. God, it felt good.

"Are we ready to rejoin the ladies?" Silverton asked.

"Perhaps we should torture them a bit longer," Lucas said in jest.

Silverton smiled. "We could break a few glasses, I suppose."

"It's tempting, but I'm not that brave. I fear Phoebe and Meredith would come storming in to box our ears."

They walked to the door together, and Silverton called out, "Meredith, we've kissed and made up. You can let us out."

"I don't believe you," she yelled through the door. "You haven't been in there long enough. And it's been too quiet. You obviously didn't even talk about it."

The two men stared at each other in disbelief.

"Good Christ. How long do they expect us to talk about this rubbish?" Lucas asked.

Silverton let out a sigh. "You've been away from women for too long." He glanced at the longcase clock by the door. "They obviously insist that we either start yelling at each other, or spend at least another half hour in here."

"Perhaps we should just break down the door," Lucas said dryly.

"No need, Cousin. We'll take the other way out of here."

Lucas glanced over at the French doors out to the terrace and lifted an eyebrow.

Silverton smiled. "Exactly."

They slipped out into the cold, wind-whipped night. The snowfall had ended, laying down little more than a dusting of white over the terrace stones. Crunching down the wide steps to the lawn, they skirted the east wing and came around to a small side entrance to the abbey. Silverton stopped and turned to look back over the broad expanse of lawn and the home woods, stretching into the distance under a sky rapidly clearing of clouds. A frigid half-moon rolled through the endless, inky vault, its beams painting a canvas of shadows and pale crystal on the snow-covered landscape.

Lucas stepped up beside him, gazing out over the grounds of Belfield Abbey. A fugitive peace stole over him, settling deep in his bones. He recognized that it came not only from the quiet of a winter's eve, but from an acceptance of the past—mistakes and all—and from looking forward to what lay before him. A few times these last few weeks he had felt something similar, but only in Phoebe's company.

If he wasn't such a cynic, he might even call it hope.

Silverton spoke quietly. "It was worth it, Lucas."

"What?"

"Esme. The fight between us."

Startled, Lucas stared at him. "How do you figure that?"

His cousin kept his gaze fixed on the sky, as if the answers to all life's questions were writ large in the stars. "I would never have married Meredith, nor had the twins. I would never have understood the real worth of life or what was truly important to me. I'm sorry for what happened between us, but I can't regret any of it." He clapped Lucas on the shoulder. "And neither should you, with the wife you've got. The woman obviously adores you."

Lucas snorted. "When she's not reading me a lecture."

"That's a wife's privilege. And I know you, Lucas. You're completely mad for her, and rightly so."

Well, he was *something* for Phoebe. But before he could acknowledge what it was, there remained a few matters that needed resolution—starting with her owning up to her secrets.

Silverton gave him a sly grin. "What's the matter? Cat got your tongue?"

"Oh, sod off," Lucas growled.

His cousin laughed and led the way into the house. Although happy to abandon their long-standing feud, Lucas had no intention of discussing Phoebe, or his marriage, with Silverton or with anyone else.

Not until he figured it out for himself.

Chapter 32

Balancing the tea tray on one arm, Phoebe eased open the door to her husband's study. Her new pet, ensconced in a basket by the fire, tumbled out to greet her. Yipping with excitement, the dog frisked around her skirts, almost tripping her.

"Hush," she scolded. "Behave yourself, Holly, or I'll put you out in the hall."

The ragtag rescue from the woods gave her a doggie smile and trotted beside her as she carried the tray over to the desk. Lucas put down his book and stood to help her.

"I told you that animal would be trouble," he said. "And whatever gave you the demented idea to call him *Holly*? I trust you noticed he's a male."

Phoebe smiled at the dog. Though hardly handsome, with his dust-colored coat and floppy ears, he had a sweet, loyal temperament. Lucas had rolled his eyes when she insisted on keeping him, but had finally said to consider him an early Christmas present.

"Holly is a perfectly appropriate name," she replied. "After all, I found him tangled up in a holly bush. Everyone else likes the name, too. Mrs. Christmas said it fit right in at Mistletoe Manor."

"She would."

Phoebe wrinkled her nose at him as she fixed his tea, then sank into a chair to enjoy her own cup. Her feet hurt and her back ached from all the work of the last few days, but she was enjoying every minute of her first official Christmas holiday.

"I presume the festivities are still going on in the servant's hall?" Lucas asked.

"Yes. Quite vigorously, I might add."

Lucas grinned. "Ah, that explains the charming blush on your cheeks. Who did you stumble across? Maggie and one of the footmen?"

Phoebe sighed. "How did you know? She and Philip were in the pantry when I went to fetch the tea tray, kissing under a sprig of mistletoe. Thank goodness, Christmas only comes once a year. I was not entirely aware how enthusiastically the younger servants would observe that particular tradition."

"They're not the only ones," her husband purred.

The sensual gleam in his eye—and the memory of what had put it there—brought heat rushing to her cheeks. Earlier that afternoon, Lucas had pulled her into a window alcove in the east corridor that Mrs. Christmas had decorated with a large bough of mistletoe. Standing directly under the hanging cluster of berries, he had drawn her into a scandalous kiss. Things had quickly escalated, and he had soon reached out a hand to pull the drape over the alcove opening. Phoebe had put up a weak protest, but within seconds her husband had one hand up her skirt and the other hand down her bodice. If one of the servants had not come clattering up the stairs at that moment, goodness only knows what might have happened next.

"Perhaps we should not put up quite so much mistletoe next year," she said pensively.

"There does seem to be an alarming amount of it around the manor. I'd say you outdid yourself with the decorations."

Phoebe glanced around the study, which nearly resembled

a forested bower. Swags of evergreen and ivy, interwoven with cuttings of holly, draped the mantelpiece. More ivy twined the bookshelves and up the bookcase ladder, and she had encircled the lamps with wreaths of evergreen dotted with small apples. More mistletoe, tied up with red and green satin ribbon, hung from every window frame. The rest of the house, including the bedrooms, had received much the same treatment. Even the entrance hall, where they had entertained the villagers today, was smothered in greenery, with gigantic garlands of fragrant laurel framing the great fireplace and twined around the columns of the old oak staircase.

She sighed. "Too much?"

Lucas smiled and shook his head. "It's perfect. You did a splendid job of upholding the old traditions. If the servants and villagers didn't already adore you, they will after today."

She blushed again, but this time it was his praise that warmed her. "Thank you. But I had no idea it would require so much work. I will be better prepared next year."

But despite the hard work, she had loved it, from the moment Lucas and the footmen dragged the gigantic Yule log into the hall last night, through the church service this morning, with its beautifully sung carols, to the merry feast in the afternoon with the villagers and farm tenants. She had found the large boar's head fairly alarming, but the villagers had roared their approval when the two strongest footmen carried it into the hall, resplendent on a silver platter.

Her favorite part, however, had been the children's rendition of *The Second Shepherd's Play*. There had been a few mistakes and some bungled lines, but also a great deal of merriment and enthusiastic applause from the audience. At the play's conclusion, young Sam Weston had stepped forward to recite the stanzas of an old Christmas hymn. All had fallen silent, as the words rang out in his clear voice.

"Come, let us join with Angels now,
Glory to God on high,
Peace upon Earth, Goodwill to men,
Amen, Amen, Amen, say I."

Tears had filled Phoebe's eyes, both for the beauty of the hymn and for the lack of peace in Sam's life. Mr. Weston had not come for the festivities, which was not surprising given her ill-fated encounter with him in the woods. Sam had pretended not to be troubled by his father's absence, but Phoebe had noticed the lad casting his gaze about the hall, clearly expecting and hoping his father would appear.

"What's the matter, Phoebe?"

Startled, she glanced up to find Lucas studying her. "Oh, I was just thinking about poor Sam Weston. I do wish Mr. Weston had come today. He was noticeable by his absence."

Not the whole truth, but close enough. Still, she hated keeping secrets from him, no matter how necessary.

He eyed her thoughtfully, and a whisper of unease drifted through her. "I imagine he was at the tavern, as usual," he finally said.

"You mean the tavern was open on Christmas Day? That's dreadful!" The idea scandalized her.

"At least Sam has a father who works to keep a roof over his head."

Lucas did not know the half of it, but the thought of what he would do when he found out made her stomach clench.

"Besides," he continued, "Sam and the other children had you to watch over them. And give them presents. Very generous presents."

She winced at his dry tone. Perhaps she had been a tad overgenerous, but the children had been so thrilled—board games and tin soldiers for the boys, and dolls and puzzles for the girls. She had objected to the soldiers, but Lucas had insisted. "You do not really mind, do you? It made them so happy."

He smiled. "One can never have too many presents, I always say. Which reminds me. I have another one for you."

She stared at him, disconcerted. "Lucas, you have already given me too much. All the books and my new fur tippet, and that lovely silk workbox. Not to mention Holly, the best present of all."

At the sound of his name, the dog thumped his tail.

Lucas snorted. "That seems more like a piece of bad luck than a present."

"Oh, but—"

"No," he said, holding out his hand. "Come here and get your real present."

Obediently, she went round the desk and stood by his chair. When he tugged her down into his lap, she gave a little laugh, very aware of his hard thighs under her bottom. And something else that was hard, too.

"Is that my present?" she asked shyly, putting her arms around his neck.

He nibbled beneath her ear, sending shivers racing across her skin. "That part comes later. For now . . ."

Leaving off, he opened a drawer in his desk and pulled out a black velvet bag tied with a red satin ribbon. Her stomach dropped. The bag reminded her of the jewels he had tried to force on her on the night of the Framingham ball. The memory was not pleasant.

"Go ahead and open it," he urged.

She slowly untied the ribbon and tipped the contents into her hand. A gasp escaped her lips as a string of shimmering pearls fell into her palm, glowing with a pale, simple beauty.

"Your mother's," he said, cuddling her against him. "A gift from the old earl on her eighteenth birthday. I understand she left most of her jewels here when she married your father."

Phoebe swallowed, overcome with emotion. "She would have had nowhere to wear them."

But as she fingered the smooth orbs, she knew her mother

would have cherished those pearls. She could scarcely imagine how difficult it must have been to leave them—and everything else—behind. Her mother had sacrificed so much for her father.

For love.

Blinking back a rush of tears, she raised her eyes to meet her husband's gaze. He studied her, his features, as always, a bit stern. But his sea gray eyes smiled at her.

"Thank you, Lucas," she whispered.

He took the strand from her shaking fingers and fastened it around her neck. She touched the pearls, loving the silky feel against her skin.

"Merry Christmas," he said, brushing his mouth over her lips. "It's been a very successful holiday, don't you think? Silverton and I have stopped trying to kill each other, and the restoration of the manor is moving forward. And a very large part of all that is because of you."

He kissed her again, lingering on her mouth. "You deserve these pearls, my sweet, along with everything else I can give you. No man could ask for a better wife."

His affectionate words triggered a wave of guilt that almost overwhelmed her. Would he still feel that way if he knew she was hiding so many secrets? Worse than that, she had lied—to the man she loved. Although her motive had largely been to protect him, he would no doubt see it as a betrayal of his trust, and by his exacting code of honor, it surely was.

He tilted her chin up, forcing her to meet his somber gaze. "I know something's wrong, Phoebe," he said quietly. "I've known it for the last few days. I haven't wanted to press you, but as your husband I have a right to know what troubles you."

Startled, Phoebe choked down a gasp, dismayed at how easily he had read her thoughts. Then again, she had always been a terrible liar, and the secrets had been a dead weight on her soul.

She eyed him, longing to tell him but afraid how he might react. Not afraid for herself, but for the men of the village.

And for him. Who knew what could happen if he decided to confront the smugglers?

His gaze probed, but his quiet smile encouraged her. "You must trust me, my dear. Whatever it is, I'll listen and try to understand."

A thousand conflicting emotions tumbled through her, but he patiently waited her out. She studied his calm face, searching for clues, trying to see her way. They often disagreed about important things, but she never doubted that Lucas was a good man. And he *had* reconciled with Cousin Stephen, relinquishing years of animosity because his family asked it of him. With her love and support, perhaps he might now be ready to make peace with the smugglers, too. Or at least show them mercy.

Regardless, she could not hold the secret inside any longer, not without doing damage to herself, and especially to her relationship with Lucas.

Taking a deep breath, she placed a hand on his chest. "Yes, I have been holding something back." Her voice quavered a bit, and she stopped.

Lucas stroked her cheek. "It's all right. Go on."

Although tempted to look anywhere but at him, she forced herself to meet his gaze.

"The day I found Holly in the woods, I encountered something else, too."

"Yes?"

"I came upon the smuggling gang."

His face went momentarily blank, but quickly his features seemed to turn to stone. "You mean you actually saw them making a run? On Merritt lands?"

"Ah, well, a bit more than that, actually."

His wintery gaze froze her tongue to the roof of her mouth.

"Phoebe, stop beating around the bush and explain exactly what happened."

She longed for a sip of tea to wet her parched lips, but she doubted Lucas would let her get up to do that. His body had tensed, and though his grip was gentle, it was also unyielding.

"Well, I spoke to them," she said in a weak voice.

His pupils dilated. "Christ!"

She flinched. "There is no need to swear, or to raise your voice, Lucas. I can hear you very well."

"Phoebe, why in God's name would you talk to a band of criminals? You could have been hurt!"

Crossing her arms over her chest, she sat ramrod straight, not an easy thing to do while perched on his thighs. "I did not have a choice," she snapped. "I was in a clearing, freeing Holly from the bush, when they came upon me. There was no chance to run or hide. In fact, if I had tried to run, things might have gone much worse."

He closed his eyes and inhaled several deep breaths. When he opened them he appeared calmer, although his grip on her remained firm. "Very well. I can accept that circumstances left you no choice. What did you discuss?"

She cast up a prayer of thanks that Lucas did not insist on a detailed accounting of events, especially since Mr. Weston *had* pointed a gun at her. But still she hesitated. If she told him what they had discussed, she would divulge who was leading the smugglers. And given that her husband did not currently seem in a forgiving mood, that was a bad idea. Especially for poor Sam Weston, whose father would be the first man hauled off to prison.

"Phoebe," Lucas growled in warning.

"I told them you would not countenance their activities any longer, and that they must give up their ways."

He snorted. "I bet that went over very well."

"Some of the men may have listened," she said with offended dignity.

"I'm sure. How many were there, exactly?"

She made a vague gesture. "It was hard to tell. Most were hidden in the woods."

He narrowed his gaze. "Why do I have the feeling you're deliberately leaving things out?"

"It all happened very quickly, and I was frightened. It is hard to remember details."

His grip tightened. "You were frightened? Did they threaten you?"

"Not really," she hedged, annoyed she had revealed even that bit of information.

He swore under his breath and his grip on her tightened a fraction. "You are such a terrible liar. Did they have guns?"

Desperate, she clutched the lapel of his coat. She could not lie to him again, even knowing how he would likely react. "Yes, but they did me no harm, I swear. Please, Lucas, just let it go. I am sure the smuggling will die out on its own, now that the local men can get jobs on the estate and in the village."

"Hell, Phoebe! They came onto my property with guns and threatened my wife. Do you really think I'm going to stand by and let that happen?"

His harsh, unforgiving tones lashed at her. "What are you more concerned about? That they threatened me, or dared to violate the sacred boundaries of your kingdom?"

She tried to struggle off his lap, but he held her fast. Taking her face between his hands, he forced her to look at him. "Phoebe, it scares me to death that something might have happened to you," he grated out. "You have no idea how dangerous those criminals can be. If anything ever happened to you—" He bit off the words and averted his gaze. Anger curved his features into harsh angles, but Phoebe sensed his fear.

"Lucas," she said softly, turning his face back to look at her. "You saw me right after it happened. You know I was completely unharmed."

He took her hands and placed them in her lap. "And

while we're on that subject, why didn't you tell me about this encounter immediately? Why hide something like this from your husband? Something so vital?"

His eyes had frosted over again, but something else lurked behind the anger. She saw pain, and the fear of trust betrayed. For Lucas, there was no greater sin.

"They had guns," she explained patiently.

His mouth pulled into something close to a sneer. "Thank you for assuming I would shoot them all on the spot. Your confidence in me is sorely deficient, Madam Wife."

Her temper flared. "No, you stupid man. I was afraid they would shoot you."

He gave an incredulous snort. "That's ridiculous. You're not supposed to be protecting me. *I'm* supposed to be protecting *you*."

Angry, she struggled to free herself again. This time he let her go, although he had to lash out a hand to keep her from tumbling to the floor. Once she regained her balance, she wrenched her arm from his grasp. "Excuse me for thinking a man and his wife should try to help and protect *each other*," she stormed. "I will not make that mistake twice."

He surged to his feet, eyes blazing with a furious intent. "Please spare me a lecture on domestic philosophy. Just tell me if you recognized any of the men. Now."

Phoebe propped her hands on her hips and glared up at him. Lucas in a fury made a very intimidating picture, but she knew he would never lift a hand to her—or to any woman—and dark looks alone could not force her to reveal her knowledge, given the actions likely to ensue. He might not think he required her help and protection. *She* knew better.

He also propped his hands on his hips, his voice going lethally soft. "Phoebe, I insist you tell me if you recognized those men. It is your duty to me, as my wife and countess."

She pressed her lips firmly together and shook her head. She struggled to remain calm, but inside her emotions roiled and her heart ached with the chasm of mistrust yawning between them. But what other choice did he give her?

"Phoebe, I swear to God—"

Her control finally snapped. "I will not allow violence between thee and these men," she shouted. "I will not allow it!"

Holly, snoozing in his basket by the fire, came awake with a startled yip. He rushed from his basket and skidded around the desk.

Lucas drew himself up, every inch the soldier. "That's not up to you. I will be master in my house, Phoebe, and that's a lesson you'd best learn right now."

Holly, upset by the harsh tone of his new master's voice, growled and backed up against Phoebe's skirts. She scooped him up in her arms. "For shame, Lucas," she scolded. "You are scaring the dog."

Her husband stared at her in disbelief. "I wasn't the one who started yelling. And why is the blasted dog in here anyway, instead of out in the hall? Isn't there anything or anyone in this damned house who can act normally?"

Since it had been Lucas's suggestion to place Holly's basket in his study, Phoebe could only gape at him. Holly, however, responded with a volley of high-pitched barks. Phoebe tried to shush him, but to no avail.

"Oh, Christ," Lucas muttered. He took the dog from her arms and marched over to retrieve Holly's basket.

Phoebe started after him. "What are you doing?"

He pointed at her. "You, stay. I'm not done with you."

"Lucas! Do not talk to me like a dog."

She peered after him, worrying about Holly. Lucas opened the door to the hall and placed the basket just outside the study. But when he gently deposited the dog back in his cozy nest, he stroked his fuzzy head and, with a soothing murmur, admonished him to go back to sleep. Despite her anger, Phoebe could not hold back a smile.

"What are you smiling about?" Lucas growled as he closed the door behind him.

She wiped her face clean. "Certainly not you."

He strode back to the desk. "I should think not. I find your defiance most disturbing. Even more so, you lied to me. That is not the behavior I expect of my wife. My *Quaker* wife. That you of all people could act this way defies belief."

She froze, stunned by his criticism. If she closed her eyes, she might be listening to another one of her half brother's endless series of disapproving lectures.

Shaking off her paralysis, she struggled to bring her emotions under control. But all semblance of control slipped from her grasp, overwhelmed by a wave of hurt and shame. And anger, an anger that prompted her to strike back. "I am sorry to be such a disappointment, but your behavior is hardly exemplary, Lucas. Despite your reconciliation with Silverton, I was most distressed by your conduct at Belfield Abbey."

He had been starting to look as if he regretted his harsh accusation, but her words had him scowling again. "I already apologized to you for being out of sorts at the abbey."

"That is not what I was referring to," she said in a tight voice.

"Then what?"

His eyes glittered with a narrow intensity that should have warned her to hold her peace. But the anger and hurt seemed to push the words from her tongue, whether she wished to speak them or not. "It is thee flirting. I know thee does not love me, but that is no excuse to treat me with such disrespect."

His eyes opened wide. "Me, flirt?" He sounded mystified.

"Do not try to deny it."

Silence, then understanding dawned in his stormy gaze. "You think I was flirting with Bathsheba Blackmore?"

"You were!"

He shook his head. "I cannot believe this." With no warning, he shot out an arm to sweep the piles of journals and papers from his desk, sending them crashing to the floor. Then he grabbed her around the waist, lifted her, and gently plopped her on the polished surface. Gasping, she grabbed the edge of the desk to steady herself.

"Lucas, what are thee—you doing?"

He pointed at her again. "Stay right there."

"I repeat, I am not a dog," she huffed.

He strode to the door and locked it. "I know exactly what you are. You're my wife, and I'm going to show you precisely what that means."

He turned, his eyes blazing with a harsh, blatant desire that stole the breath from her body. The air seemed to vibrate around him, parting in waves as he stalked back to her. Even as her breath caught with trepidation, her limbs grew heavy and weak, already craving his touch. When he pushed her skirts up to her thighs and stepped in close, crowding her, she did nothing to resist. Her body was obviously no longer under her control, since she widened her legs to accommodate him and clutched his broad shoulders in a desperate grip.

"What is thee doing?" she whispered.

"I am showing *thee* that Phoebe Stanton is the only woman I will ever want. And by the time I'm through, you'll never doubt it again."

Chapter 33

Phoebe might have pushed Lucas too far. But his rebuke had stung, and her buried insecurities had burst forth in a shocking display of jealousy. She should feel ashamed of her childish outburst, but her husband's eyes blazed with such passionate hunger that any apology died on her tongue.

His big hands reached around and slipped under her bottom. When he slid her to the edge of the desk and then molded his rock-hard body to her most sensitive part, she let out a squeak of protest. Through the fabric of his breeches, she could feel the aggressive thrust of his erection. Her precarious position forced her to clasp her knees around his lean hips for support.

Despite their battle of words, there was no mistaking what Lucas wanted from her right now.

He swooped down and took her mouth in a punishing kiss, ravaging her with a hot, delicious slide of lips and tongue. She moaned, clutching at his arms as she tried to deny the fierce longing surging through her veins. But just as suddenly as he claimed possession, he broke away. He glanced at her flushed face, then down at her mouth, his expression brooding.

"I . . . I do not understand," she stammered. "How can you want to do this when we have been fighting?"

His laugh sounded more like a groan. "Ask me later."

There was likely no explaining it, she decided, since she wanted him as badly as he wanted her, and her anger had not abated one whit.

Even as his hands stroked the inside of her thighs, brushing so close to her sex that it made her shiver, she saw bitterness in his dark gaze and in the sternly cut angles of his face. Sadness and regret twisted within her, knowing he saw her lies not as a means to protect him, but as a betrayal of his trust. His first love had betrayed him those long years ago, and Phoebe worried that his heart might now be damaged beyond repair.

His hands moved in sensual patterns over the sensitive skin of her thighs, moving ever closer to her dampening flesh. Phoebe cupped his cheek, bringing his attention back up. His eyes blazed with a need so starkly evident it clawed away the lingering remnants of her own pain.

"I am truly sorry, Lucas," she whispered.

His gaze narrowed with suspicion, even as his long, clever fingers brushed through her curls and across her sex with a light, teasing motion. She bit her lower lip, forcing back a moan.

"For disobeying me?" he growled.

She shook her head, stroking the hard line of his jaw, now rough with the bristle of his night beard. "No. I am sorry you had to marry a woman you do not love. It was selfish of me to allow you to do so."

His anger seemed to bleed away. He pressed an affectionate kiss to her brow, then a tender one across her lips. She swallowed hard, her throat growing tight with the taste of his regret.

"Phoebe," he sighed. "None of this is your fault. Well, lying to me was your fault, but at least I understand why you did it. But the other—" He fell silent for a moment, although his hands continued their gentle play, stroking her with a soothing caress.

"I'm a soldier," he finally said. "Words don't come easily to me. I wish—"

She grabbed the edges of his waistcoat and pulled him closer, silencing him with her mouth. She did not want to hear about his regrets and unfulfilled desires, or the loving part of him that Esme Newton had destroyed forever. If she could not have his heart, then she would take what he could offer, praying with every corner of her soul it would be enough.

Her impulsive gesture unleashed a fire in him. Lucas may not ever come to love her, but he clearly wanted her with a warrior's fierce passion, and with a hunger that left her breathless and aching with a need only he could assuage.

As he ravished her mouth, he pulled her close, nudging the ridge of his erection into the cradle of her thighs. She melted in his arms, pulling her knees back to open herself to the seductive thrust of his hips. He groaned against her lips and started to pull back, but she curled her hands around the back of his neck, holding fast as she eagerly tasted his mouth. She poured all her tangled, treacherous emotions into her kiss, possessing him with a silken glide of lips and tongues that tasted both forbidden and sweet. Desire curled low in her belly, and she could not help rocking against the shaft that pressed against her.

Lucas surrounded her, looming tall as his hands roamed her body. His kisses teased away her pain, igniting a heat that rolled through her body like flaming brandy. When he nudged once more into the vee of her thighs, his shaft against her aching flesh, she broke away from his mouth with a strangled cry.

"Christ, Phoebe," Lucas panted.

She clutched his arms and slid her trembling legs down to dangle over the edge of the desk. "We should go upstairs," she managed in a strangled voice.

"The hell with that," he muttered as he attacked the fastenings of her bodice. "I might not make it up to the bedroom."

Her eyes widened as he yanked her dress down past her shoulders, trapping her arms. "We cannot do this in the study. The servants might come in."

His clever fingers were already busy with the lacings at her back. "Why do you think I locked the door?" Under the bronze of his tan, his cheekbones were flushed, and his eyes were heavy with a sensuality that set off a quiver low in her belly. It frightened her to think how vulnerable he made her, even knowing he would never feel for her as she felt for him.

He hummed with satisfaction as her stays loosened around her breasts. "Don't worry," he added. "The servants are busy with their own pleasure." He glanced up, mischief gleaming in his eyes. "As you already discovered."

She blushed at the reminder of what Maggie and Philip had been doing in the pantry.

"And I'm certainly not one to be outdone by the servants, my love," he said with a grin. Carefully, he worked her stays and chemise down to her waist, exposing her breasts to the air. Without the warmth of her garments, her nipples, already half stiff with desire, contracted into tight points.

Lucas took a small step back to look at her. "God, Phoebe," he said in a reverent voice. "You're the most beautiful woman I've ever seen."

She looked down at herself and felt the heat rise up her throat to her face. She was naked to the waist, her breasts gleaming white in the candlelight, the tips hard and flushed pink. Her arms still trapped in the lowered sleeves of her gown, she gripped the edge of the desk for support. Her legs were spread wide, skirts tumbled around her thighs, but that apparently did not satisfy her husband. He pushed the fabric up to her hips, uncovering her completely. The silky nest of curls between her thighs glistened with moisture, and she wanted to squirm, both embarrassed and excited by her wanton position.

"That's perfect," Lucas said with a deep rumble.

"Oh, really?" she muttered, feigning offended dignity. "I cannot even move."

"Yes, I have you right where I want you."

He reached out to palm her breasts, his thumbs scraping lightly over the nipples. Sensation darted from their tips to settle with a quiver between her thighs. Biting back a moan, she let her eyelids begin to fall.

Lucas let out a soft laugh. "Oh, no you don't, sweet wife. I want you to watch what I do to you."

The dark promise in his words brought a soft rush of moisture from the depths of her body. "You are very wicked," she whispered.

He murmured deep in his throat as he teased and gently rolled the stiff points between his fingertips. "I'm about to get a lot more wicked."

She gasped as he tugged and tormented her nipples into tight, burning peaks. And torment was the only word, a delicious torment that had her writhing with frustration. Just when she was about to beg, he bent his head and fastened his mouth to first one nipple, then the next. She choked back a strangled cry, wobbling on the edge of the desk as a luxurious spasm rippled deep in her womb. His hands settled low on her spine, holding her steady as he rimmed her nipple with his tongue.

Phoebe was devastated by the sight of his head at her breast, and by the sensations storming her body. The rasp of his tongue across her nipple, the feel of his hard body between her thighs was too much. Her head swam with a dizzy passion. "Lucas," she panted. "Please . . . please . . ."

She was barely conscious of what she pleaded for, but he knew. He always knew. With a last, tender nuzzle, he lifted his head. His features were stark, but his heavy-lidded, passionate gaze held tenderness, too. He cradled her gently as he finished undressing her. In a moment, she sat open before him, clad only in her stockings and garters, and one shoe—the other having fallen to the floor.

He smiled a distinctly masculine, evil grin. "Just when I thought it couldn't get any better."

She was about to scold him when he interrupted her. "No, wait. I know."

Her eyes popped wide when he pushed her thighs apart, exposing her completely to his roving gaze.

"There. That's better," he purred.

She choked, caught between disbelief and laughter. "You are truly most wicked, Husband."

He simply shrugged his shoulders. "Guilty as charged, Wife."

Then he was on his knees before her and those wide shoulders were pushing her thighs even farther apart. Before she could utter a word his hands snaked under her naked bottom, tilting her up. With a hot rush, his mouth fastened on that most sensitive part of her with a masterful kiss. This time she did cry out, falling back on her elbows as sensation pulsed in a hot, heavy throb.

Phoebe's breath came in shattered sobs, her emotional control unraveling under his sensual assault. They had made love many times, but never like this. If he had told her of this first, asked her permission, she would have refused. But he'd taken her by surprise and breeched her defenses.

Her body asserted its desires. She rested on her elbows and spread her thighs wide, inviting Lucas to pleasure her.

And pleasure her, he did. His fingers gently parted her drenched folds so he could reach everything. He sucked and kissed, slicking his tongue over aching flesh again and again, as sensation gathered in her womb, first as tight little contractions, but then in long pulses of pleasure that built and built. She was spread out before him—naked, vulnerable, and open. He controlled her, dominated her—big, handsome, utterly masculine, and . . . fully clothed.

Phoebe blinked several times. Suddenly, it was too much. She needed him inside her. *Part* of her, not *apart* from her, made too vulnerable by this unfamiliar act.

Not when he controlled so much and she so little. She struggled up and grabbed his shoulders. "Lucas, st . . . stop."

His head came up right away and she trembled at his hard expression, his features tight with lust. His voice came out in a dark rasp. "What is it?"

"I want . . . I want . . ." She could not find the words. She only managed to run her shaking fingers through his thick tumble of hair.

His gaze grew tender. "What do you want, my love?"

She took a deep, steadying breath. "I want you. Only you."

He surged to his feet, his fingers pulling at the fall of his breeches. She reached out to help him, and in a moment he was free. Lucas stepped close between her thighs, fitting the broad tip of his staff to the snug opening of her body. He nudged gently inside, then took her in a slow but relentless slide. She clutched at his back, digging her fingers into the fabric of his coat as she sobbed with relief when he was lodged deep within her.

"You have me, Phoebe," he said in a voice heavy with emotion. "You will always have me."

She tilted her head back to look at him. "Do you promise?"

He smiled gently as he stroked the damp hair back from her brow. "I promise."

She pulled his head down, feathering a kiss across his lips. "I love you," she whispered. It was reckless and foolish to admit it, but her heart refused to be silenced.

Lucas murmured his satisfaction, kissing her as he began to move. She gasped as he gave a hard nudge, kindling an erotic burn in the deepest part of her. Her heart raced with excitement and she arched her back, grinding her pelvis into him. Then she exploded, the spasms rippling out from her womb with a power that wrenched a cry from her throat. He rode her through her climax until he shuddered and convulsed inside her.

Clutching her within the shelter of his embrace, he kept her safe while her senses returned and the world began to right itself. When her breathing had returned to normal, Lucas carefully pulled out. Then he cradled her against his chest and silence fell around them, thick and peaceful, broken only by the crackling of the fire.

Phoebe rested against him, listening to the steady thump of his heart. Once again, she had told her husband she loved him. And once again, she had been met with silence.

Chapter 34

Lucas stamped his feet as he thrust his gloved hands toward the heat of the bonfire, watching the roaring flames cast leaping shadows through the grove of apple trees. On Epiphany Eve, as lord of the manor the duty had fallen to him to light the huge pile of wood and kindling that had been stacked by his groundskeepers. The male servants, the farm tenants, and most of the men from the village had gathered in the orchard, as was the custom this night across the length and breadth of all the counties. Some would discharge guns or blow horns in the ancient tradition to frighten away evil spirits and promote the health and vigor of the trees across England's fair lands.

And they would drink and tell stories as they tended the fires through the night, strengthening the bonds between the men of the village and the fields through the age-old custom that spanned generations. Of all the traditions of the Season, this one made the most sense to Lucas. It brought men together, from the lowest day laborer to the lord of the manor. On this January night, they united in a profound desire for peace and prosperity throughout the coming year. They stood together in the biting cold, shivering under the vast, starry vault that stretched over their heads. Only the warmth of fire and the bonds of their mutual fealty kept danger at bay. It joined them in an ancient pact of survival, fellowship, and good cheer.

Lucas had never participated in the tradition as an adult, and damned if he didn't feel like an outsider. He recognized most of the men, and all had greeted him with smiles and tips of the hat. But in many subtle ways their actions indicated wariness, even mistrust. That bothered him more than he cared to admit. After years commanding soldiers, he was used to earning the troops' respect—swiftly and unconditionally. But he was quickly learning that his particular brand of leadership, one forged in battle, did not necessarily carry over into his new life as Earl of Merritt.

And try as he might, he had yet to acquire the knack of easy conversation with the men of the village or his tenant farms, a fact all too evident in the way they kept a polite distance from him. He wasn't fool enough to think that aloofness signified respect for the lord of the manor.

Mr. Knaggs joined him by the fire, extracting something from inside his greatcoat. "Lord Merritt, can I interest you in something a bit stronger than mulled ale to keep the cold at bay?" he asked with a twinkle.

Lucas couldn't help smiling. "You shock me, Vicar. Whatever would your wife say if she saw you promoting public drunkenness?"

The cleric's eyes widened in mock alarm. "This is purely medicinal, my lord. We can't have you succumbing to a chill. I'm sure her ladyship would be most distressed if that were to happen."

Lucas held back a grimace. *A chill* definitely described the state of affairs between Phoebe and him. Since their fight on Christmas night, they had been living in a state that reminded him of a shaky armed truce.

After that spectacular bout of lovemaking on his desk, he had assumed they'd made up. But he'd quickly discovered otherwise. Phoebe, professing love for him one minute, had retreated behind a facade of dignity the next. Her reserve only broke whenever he tried to compel her to reveal the names of the smugglers she had encountered in the forest. She staunchly refused each time, and that had resulted in more than one sharp exchange of words and wills. For a Quaker, Phoebe had proven to be a capable fighter. Unfortunately, their battles always ended in frustration and disappointment for them both.

And refusing to express his feelings for her didn't help the situation, either. His world was beginning to revolve around Phoebe in ways he never could have imagined. That, frankly, worried the hell out of him, making it well nigh impossible to force any kind of declaration past his lips.

"You seem troubled, my lord," Mr. Knaggs said quietly.

Startled, Lucas frowned. "How so?"

The cleric glanced around, assessing their distance from the other men.

"Your heavy sigh," he replied, obviously satisfied they would not be overheard. "And I cannot help but notice you seem . . . withdrawn."

Knaggs might look like a weather-beaten scarecrow, but his eyes gleamed with intelligence and perceptiveness. And he had an air of patient empathy that no doubt served him well in the village, especially during the hard years of the war. Lucas had never had much use for the clerical cast, but he was beginning to understand why the people of Apple Hill held their vicar in such high regard.

Not that he would confide his deep concerns about Phoebe with anyone. Besides, he knew the source of his worries. It wasn't just about the smugglers, no matter how much he wanted to believe that. It was about their marriage—it was about *him*, and his inability to sort through his tangled emotions.

Mr. Knaggs gave him a verbal nudge. "Lord Merritt, if you ever need my help, I hope you won't hesitate to ask. You and your lady are the very heart of this community. All of us will do whatever we can to assist you."

Lucas breathed out a cynical snort, casting a glance at the men who so carefully kept their distance. Just like his wife. No matter how he tried, he couldn't seem to breach the barriers that separated him from so many aspects of his new life.

"I'd like to believe what you say about the community is true, Mr. Knaggs, but circumstances tell me otherwise. I've got smugglers on my land, probably aided and abetted by my own servants, and I doubt there's a single villager who would trust me to deal with the problem as I see fit."

The cleric simply handed over his battered flask. With a wry smile, Lucas took a swig, welcoming the burn of rum down his throat and into his stomach. If only it could warm the part of him that struggled against the bone-chilling cold of loneliness and frustration.

"They're not the easiest lot to get along with, I'll grant you," said Mr. Knaggs. "But these last years have been hard ones indeed." He gestured with his flask to a man huddling with a small group on the other side of the bonfire. "There's Mr. Wilson, the butcher. A wife and three daughters, but only one son. And what did the silly boy do? Ran off to join the army, looking for adventure. He was killed at Waterloo and poor Wilson hasn't been the same since. His oldest girl tries to help him now, but butchering is hard business for a woman."

"I didn't know that about the boy," Lucas said softly, looking at the burly man with graying hair and a gentle face. Lucas had lived through the epic carnage of Waterloo, but many of his men had not.

The vicar nodded. "And then there's Markwith, over there with young Billy."

Lucas swung his gaze toward the short, gap-toothed fellow sharing a laugh with one of the grooms from the manor stables. "Markwith is one of my tenant farmers."

"And a good one, too. But he lost two of his children to the fever last winter. Thank the good Lord, he and his wife have three others, but something like that weighs heavy on a man's soul."

Lucas shook his head, increasingly disgusted with himself. He'd spoken to Markwith a number of times, finding him to be a plain-speaking and capable man. But he'd had no idea the man had suffered such a devastating loss. Then again, in his determination to wrestle order back to his ramshackle estate, he'd focused solely on what pertained to business. He'd treated everything and everyone as a problem to be bludgeoned into line, ignoring what was most important—the people.

His people.

"And you know Ned Weston, the innkeeper," Mr. Knaggs went on in his gentle, inexorable voice. "And his son, Sam."

Lucas transferred his attention to Weston and his son, seated on a log by the fire. The boy gazed up at his father, his eyes round and solemn, as the man swapped tales with his neighbors.

"Yes, I met the lad on Christmas Day." He remembered him—too thin and pale, but smart as a whip. Phoebe had taken a shine to Sam, and had made a point of drawing him to Lucas's attention. "But Ned Weston wasn't there. And I don't recall seeing the boy's mother, either."

"That's because she died six months ago, my lord. In child-birth, and the baby with her."

Lucas rubbed his forehead. "I'm sorry. I didn't know." But Phoebe obviously had. He understood that now.

"Weston and his son have only each other," Mr. Knaggs said. "And I fear Ned doesn't understand the boy. He loves Sam, but he pushes him too hard. It's the anger, you see. Ned is far from over his wife's death. Can you imagine, my lord, losing your wife and child that way?"

He couldn't. The mere thought of losing sweet, beautiful

Phoebe in that kind of tragic circumstance felt like a dagger blow to the heart.

Ned Weston glanced down at his son and, with a smile, slung an arm around the boy's shoulders. Sam's gaunt little face lit up as he gazed at his father with childish adoration.

Lucas felt his throat tighten. "How's the boy doing?"

Knaggs hesitated, then spoke quietly. "Sam is trying very hard to be the man his father wants him to be."

Lucas heard something more in the man's voice, something important that needed to be told.

But then Knaggs gave his head a little shake and averted his gaze. Lucas felt a stab of disappointment, but he couldn't really blame the man. Trust had to be earned. It had been the first lesson he'd learned in the military, but he'd somehow forgotten it these last few months.

"The men of Apple Hill are good, decent people," said the vicar, "trying to care for their families in the best way they know how."

His gaze swung back, and Lucas read a plea in them. "But those men need help, Lord Merritt. They have struggled on their own for too long. They can no longer do it alone."

Lucas had heard those words before—from Phoebe, from Uncle Arthur, from Silverton. Hell, he'd even said the same himself. But he'd never really accepted what they meant.

He let his gaze roam around the clearing, taking in the men in their shabby clothing, their faces careworn but still cheerful with the kinship they found on this cold Twelfth Night Eve. And he finally understood what he had to do.

Chapter 35

Phoebe swallowed hard as she ordered her stomach back to its proper place. For the last three days she had battled nausea. Finally, it had gotten the best of her.

"Let me take that away," Meredith said, removing the basin from Phoebe's hands and handing it to Maggie.

"I am sorry to be such a bother," Phoebe said in a thin voice. "And on your first visit, too."

"Don't be silly," Bathsheba gently reprimanded as she put a hand to Phoebe's forehead. "You don't feel feverish, but I'll have John see you as soon as the men return from gallivanting about the estate."

Phoebe shook her head. "I feel certain a cup of tea will set everything to rights." She leaned an elbow onto her dressing table, resting her perspiring forehead in the palm of her hand.

Meredith pulled up a chair to sit beside her. "Bathsheba's right. You haven't looked well since we arrived this morning."

Phoebe opened one eye. "Something I ate, I suspect. But although it is not very pleasant for you, I am so happy you were able to come for our Twelfth Night party." She managed a weak smile for Bathsheba. "And you and your husband as well. It is so kind of you to visit."

Though disappointed Aunt Georgie and the rest of the

party from Belfield Abbey had already returned to London, Phoebe was grateful that Meredith, Cousin Stephen, and the Blackmores had been able to come for the end of the holiday festivities.

"We were happy to, but I have the feeling Lucas was a little put out when we descended on you, babies and all," Meredith said with a grin.

Phoebe winced. Lucas had *not* been happy about receiving guests, claiming the manor was still barely habitable. But she had insisted. With the increasing strain between the two of them, she had been desperate to see her family. Even though she and Lucas may have temporarily given up their verbal sparring, things remained far from settled. The only time they truly got along was at night, when Lucas came to her bed. No matter how angry she was with him, she could not find the strength to deny him. But every morning when he left, with so much left unsaid, her heart broke a little bit more.

"He does not mean to be inhospitable," she explained. "He still worries that the house is not fit for guests."

Phoebe could not really disagree. Despite the valiant efforts of the staff, Mistletoe Manor was a far cry from the beauty and comfort of Belfield Abbey. "But I do hope the bedrooms are comfortable," she added. "The fireplaces tend to smoke when there is a north wind."

"Who cares if there's a little smoke?" Bathsheba said in a cheery voice. "As long as there's a good fire in the grate, that's all I care about."

Phoebe eyed the stylish former countess, currently wrapped in not one but two heavy wool shawls. She certainly did not blame the poor woman since bracing drafts tended to blow through the leaky frames of the manor's ancient windows.

Meredith patted her back. "Everything's perfectly fine. But I'm concerned about you. How long have you been feeling ill?"

Phoebe thought back over the previous few days. "I have

been feeling a bit out of sorts for the last week or so. But my stomach has only truly been unsettled these last three days."

"Is it upset all the time?" Bathsheba asked.

"It comes and goes, usually when I smell something that bothers me. I noticed it this morning at breakfast, when Mr. Christmas came in with a plate of kippers." She frowned. "That is rather odd because the smell of kippers never bothered me before."

Meredith and Bathsheba exchanged a glance.

"What?" Phoebe demanded.

"As Meredith said, I'm sure you're fine. But John should definitely examine you." Bathsheba cocked her head toward the door of Phoebe's bedroom. "And if I'm not mistaken, all that tromping downstairs sounds like the menfolk have returned."

Over Phoebe's halfhearted protests, Bathsheba left to fetch her husband. Perhaps it was not such a bad idea to see Dr. Blackmore. In only a few hours, they would be hosting a dinner party for the local gentry, and then all the villagers and tenant farmers would arrive for the Twelfth Night celebrations. She had so much to do, and a healing draught to settle her stomach would be most welcome.

While they were waiting, Maggie brought in a tea tray. Meredith fixed Phoebe a cup, which she thankfully managed to keep down. Then Bathsheba and Dr. Blackmore entered the room.

"Lady Merritt," the doctor said, "I understand you're not feeling well."

Bathsheba rolled her eyes. "John, you can tell merely by looking at her face the poor woman isn't feeling well. As I told you, she just emptied her stomach—twice."

Dr. Blackmore's mouth twitched. "Thank you, my love. But perhaps it might be best if we let her ladyship tell *me* how she feels."

Bathsheba rolled her eyes again.

"I'll leave you to it," Meredith said, casting an amused

glance at Bathsheba and John. "I must check on the twins, and then I'll go down to the hall and see how the dinner preparations are progressing. You're not to worry about a thing, Phoebe. Bathsheba and I will take care of everything."

She whisked herself out while Dr. Blackmore began his examination. He checked Phoebe's pulse, looked down her throat, and pulled back her eyelids. She could not repress a ripple of anxiety, especially since he looked so serious.

"Don't worry, Phoebe," Bathsheba said, taking her hand in a warm clasp. "Everything will be fine."

Dr. Blackmore smiled at his wife. "I'm sure Bathsheba is correct. She's generally a much better doctor than I am."

"Well, I do tend to be right about most things," she joked.

Phoebe smiled at their banter, feeling slightly relieved.

The doctor asked several odd questions, and then requested he be allowed to examine her. She agreed, but by the end of it her cheeks were red and she was *very* glad Bathsheba had remained to hold her hand.

"One last question, Lady Merritt, and then I won't pester you any longer," said Dr. Blackmore. "When did you last have your courses?"

For a moment, Phoebe did not understand why he asked, then a light began to dawn. "Not since the third week in November, I believe."

Dr. Blackmore glanced at his wife.

"Was I right?" asked Bathsheba, grinning.

"As usual, yes," he said. "Lady Merritt, it's early days yet, but I can say with little doubt that you will be expecting a happy event sometime in the late summer."

Phoebe's mind went blank as she stared at his handsome face.

He smiled. "You're pregnant, my lady. Congratulations."

Bathsheba gave her a quick hug. "I'm so happy for you, and Lucas will be thrilled. What fun it will be to tease him about how quickly and thoroughly he's been domesticated."

Phoebe's wits—and emotions—came flooding back in a rush. "You are quite sure?" she asked, repressing the urge to burst into tears.

She did not know if she wanted to cry because she was so happy, or because she found the idea of having a baby so unsettling, especially since she had no idea how Lucas would react. She did not know if he even liked children, which certainly said something about the state of their relationship. In fact, she had a sneaking suspicion he might view children as another burden on his already long list of burdens. A list that obviously included her.

"I'm sure." Dr. Blackmore inspected her with a thoughtful gaze. "Do you have any questions you'd like to ask?"

She blinked, barely able to take it all in. "Not that I can think of at the moment."

"There's no rush. I can speak to you and your husband when things have settled down. For now, I'll simply advise you not to overexert yourself. Bathsheba and Lady Silverton can certainly handle any last minute duties for the party."

A stab of panic bolted through her. "Is my baby all right?"

He smiled. "Everything is normal, so you're not to worry at all." He stood, promising to return in a few minutes with a draught to settle her stomach.

Still in a daze, Phoebe let Bathsheba coax her into bed for a rest.

"Do you want me to fetch Lucas?" Bathsheba asked.

Phoebe thought about it. "No, I had better rest first, or else he will think I am unwell. I will tell him later, when we have a chance to speak in private."

Bathsheba nodded as if that made perfect sense and went to fetch a fresh cup of tea.

But to Phoebe, nothing made sense. She was pregnant, and she had not a clue what her husband would think of it.

* * *

The rest of the day passed in a blur of activity as they prepared for the festivities. Meredith and Bathsheba took over the last minute details, but Phoebe insisted on helping with the decorations for the hall and the dining room. It had taken most of the afternoon, but the manor looked beautiful, and she could finally begin to relax.

She had not felt the urge to race for the nearest basin or receptacle for over three hours. Dr. Blackmore's preparation had settled her stomach, although it still had an irritating tendency to jump every time she contemplated Lucas's reaction to her pregnancy. With surprisingly little effort, she convinced herself that today was not the right time to break the news to him. She had never thought of herself as a coward, but in this case avoidance seemed the most sensible course of action given all the tumult in the household—not something her husband appreciated at the best of times.

In fact, she would like to avoid that conversation for the next eight months.

"Is something wrong, my lady?" asked Mrs. Christmas, bustling into the hall from below stairs. Her normally cheerful face wrinkled with concern. "You're looking quite pale, if I do say so myself. Why don't you join his lordship in his study for a little rest? I can have one of the girls bring up a tea tray right away."

"No!" Phoebe blurted out.

Mrs. Christmas's eyes rounded with surprise, and Phoebe inwardly winced. "I am perfectly well," she said, forcing a smile. "And I had a cup of tea up in my bedroom."

Several, in fact. Bathsheba had practically poured the entire pot down her throat until she felt ready to float away.

"I think we are almost finished," she continued brightly. "The hall looks lovely, do you not think?"

They both gazed around the vaulted space, and Phoebe enjoyed a surge of satisfied pride. The faded greens from Christmas had been replenished to even greater effect, and crowns of mistletoe and holly hung from the chandeliers. Candles flickered merrily throughout the room, casting an almost magical glow over the manor's faded but noble glories.

And sitting on a raised platform at the head of the room were two ancient and massive oak chairs, resurrected from a dusty corner of the attic to serve as thrones for the lord of Mistletoe Manor and his lady. They were flanked by potted shrubbery and two darling little orange trees Meredith had donated from the abbey's succession-houses. Mistletoe Manor would never challenge Belfield Abbey for luxury or magnificence, but the manor possessed a homier sort of dignity that suited Phoebe perfectly.

Mrs. Christmas gave a satisfied nod. "I've not seen the old house dressed up so splendidly these last five years and more. It does a body good to see it again as it was in the old days. We have you and his lordship to thank for that, Lady Merritt."

"Thank you, Mrs. Christmas. If I can just ask you to put one of the larger wreaths at the base of the silver urn in the dining room, then I think we are ready. I must change for dinner, but I will be down well before the guests start to arrive."

And with any luck, she would be back downstairs before Lucas was finished dressing himself. Once dinner started, there would be no opportunity for them to be alone for the rest of the evening.

The housekeeper nodded, then glanced around, as if checking to make sure none of the servants could overhear. Satisfied, she leaned in close. "If you have any more problems with your stomach, you let me know," she said in a penetrating whisper. "I make an excellent ginger tea, just perfect for ladies in your condition. Much more effective than what the doctor gave you, I'm sure."

Phoebe suppressed a groan. Why would she think for a minute that Maggie would keep her speculations to herself? It would be a wonder if the whole household had not already had a comprehensive discussion about her condition.

"What's the matter with your stomach, Phoebe? Are you ill?"

She bit back a shriek as she whirled at the sound of her husband's voice right behind her. For such a big man, he had an uncanny and sometimes annoying ability to move with silent grace. "Lucas," she gasped. "You startled me. I thought you were in your study."

"I was in the stables," he answered rather abruptly. "What's this I hear about Blackmore examining you? You've been pushing yourself too hard, haven't you? I knew this blasted party would wear you out."

Despite her skittish nerves, the warmth and concern in his eyes soothed her spirit. When he reached up a hand to cup her cheek, she had to blink back sudden tears. He frowned, taking her face between both hands.

"Something *is* wrong. What did Blackmore tell you?"

"Truly, Lucas, nothing is wrong," she hedged. To make matters worse, the housekeeper hovered close by, doing a poor job of holding back a grin.

"Thank you, Mrs. Christmas," Phoebe said in a stern voice. "That will be all."

Apparently, her voice lacked sufficient conviction, because the housekeeper winked at her before steaming off to the dining room. Not for the first time this day, Phoebe seriously considered the medicinal benefits of a large glass of brandy. Unfortunately, she knew her rebellious stomach could not survive it.

Reluctantly, she raised her eyes to meet her husband's suspicious gaze.

"Phoebe, what are you holding back? I want to know what's wrong, and right now."

She gave him a bright smile. "Nothing at all. What do you think of the hall, Lucas? Is it not beautiful?"

He gave a disgusted snort. "You are truly the world's most inept liar." Taking her arm in a gentle grip, he steered her toward his study.

She fought a rising tide of panic. "Lucas, I must get dressed for dinner. The guests will arrive in only an hour."

He nudged her through the door of his study and closed it behind him. "The bloody guests can wait. You're going to tell me what's wrong, this instant."

Towing her to one of the armchairs by the fireplace, he made her sit. Then he took a looming stance over her, arms folded across his broad chest. He looked big, strong, and very intimidating, and it made her heart clutch with love just to look at him.

And more than a dollop of anxiety.

"Cut line, Phoebe," he ordered. "What exactly did Blackmore say?"

She eyed him silently, biting her lip. Sighing, he folded his lean frame to crouch down before her. He took her hands, lifting first one, then the other to kiss her palms.

"Love, I'm not an ogre, and I'm not going to eat you." He flashed a glimpse of strong white teeth. "At least not until after the guests have left."

"Lucas, really!" She ducked her head. Not that his remarks truly embarrassed her, but she was still too nervous to look him in the eye.

He tipped her chin up. "Whatever it is, you might as well tell me now, because you know I'll find out sooner or later."

She could not deny that truth. Swallowing, she tried to find the right words, but her throat closed around them. His faintly smiling mouth reshaped itself into a grim line. "Would you prefer I ask the doctor instead?"

"No," she croaked. "I will tell you. It is just that you will be surprised."

He made an impatient noise. "Phoebe—"

"I might be pregnant."

His eyebrows shot up. "You *might* be pregnant." He looked dumbfounded. "You mean Blackmore isn't certain? Is something wrong?"

She squeezed her eyes shut. "No. He is certain."

He captured her chin. "Phoebe, please open your eyes and look at me."

Cautiously, she obeyed. Still grim, he had even gone pale under the bronzing of his tan. Her stomach took a twist at the knowledge her fears had been justified.

"How long have you known?" he asked in a tight voice.

"I only found out today, when the doctor told me. Before that, I was silly enough to think I was simply suffering a digestive complaint." She forced a smile, hoping he would return it. He did not.

"I am sorry if this is unpleasant news," she said miserably. Her throat ached so badly it was a wonder she could even speak.

He blinked, obviously startled. "No. It's not that. I'm . . ."

"Surprised?"

"You might say that." He rose to his feet and quietly stared down at her. "Does Blackmore believe you're healthy enough to bear children?"

She swallowed past the lump in her throat. "He said there is no need to worry. He also said he would be happy to answer any questions we might have."

"Good. That's good. We're fortunate he was here, and that he thinks everything is . . . good." He winced and clamped his lips shut, obviously aware he was starting to babble.

With a sigh, Phoebe came to her feet. "I apologize if this is a shock. It was not how I intended you to find out. I realize it might seem another complication in our lives, but—"

"Where the devil would you get an idea like that?" he exclaimed, scowling at her.

Startled, she took a step back. "Because you—"

A knock sounded on the door, and then it opened. Cousin Stephen strode into the room, took one look at them, and came up short. "Forgive me for interrupting. I had a question for you, Lucas, but I will speak to you later."

"You are not interrupting, Cousin," Phoebe said with relief. "I must go upstairs to change."

Lucas muttered a very shocking word, which brought a hot blush to her cheeks and had Silverton throwing a sharp glance his way.

"Phoebe, we need to finish this," Lucas said in a low voice.

"Later," she said, slipping past him. "The guests will be here soon, and I must still visit the kitchens."

"No, wait," he growled.

She ignored him, fleeing the room as if a pack of hounds were snapping at her heels.

Chapter 36

Phoebe had barely managed to force down two bites of the lavish meal served to their guests. Her queasiness had returned—probably more a result of her conversation with Lucas than from the state of her health. She had barely spoken to him since their ill-fated conversation. Racing to dress, she had hurried down to the kitchen to check on the last minute preparations for dinner. The servants regarded her as more hindrance than help, but she could not bear another private conversation with her husband. Her emotions were too unsettled, and she feared bursting into tears at the slightest provocation from him. That would do neither of them, nor the baby, any good.

Her hand stole to the flat of her stomach, settling over the spot where she imagined her child to be growing. No matter what Lucas thought right now, their baby was a miracle. She could only pray that with God's grace and a great deal of patience on her part, admittedly not her strong suit, her stubborn husband would come to welcome the child. If not, life at the manor would be dreary indeed. Bad enough to have a husband who could not love his wife, far worse to have a father who could not love his own children.

The sound of high-pitched giggles and shrieks brought her

attention back to the hall. The villagers had arrived some time ago, and the festivities and games were in full swing. The servants had pushed back the tables in the dining room to allow for dancing, and the hall had been given over to games. Blindman's Bluff was in full swing and seemed mostly an excuse for the boys to chase the girls, or to raise a ruckus by tripping over the furniture. The rafters rang with joyous pandemonium, and everywhere Phoebe looked she saw smiling faces and heard eager voices in cheerful conversation. Whatever else might come of this Twelfth Night, it would appear that Lord and Lady Merritt had provided their people a much-needed respite from their daily cares.

She nodded to Mr. Christmas, who bowed and disappeared behind the door below stairs. Then she stretched up on tiptoe to look for her husband, only to feel a big hand settle low on her back.

"I hope it's me you're looking for."

She blew out an exasperated breath. "Lucas, you really must stop sneaking up on me. You gave me a terrible start."

His arched a brow. "I would never be so undignified as to sneak. In any case, I could march a regiment up behind you and you couldn't hear it over this din."

She grimaced. "It is rather loud, is it not? I am sorry if you find it annoying, but it seems the guests are enjoying themselves."

He took her hand and twined their fingers. "You think I'm an ogre, don't you? Poor Phoebe. Stuck with a beast for a husband."

She looked down at their clasped hands. "No," she whispered. "I do not think that at all."

He bent low, his thick, silky hair brushing her cheek. "What's that, love? I didn't hear you."

She turned as he lifted his head and stared directly into his eyes. The tenderness in his expression brought a little ball up into her throat. "I said, I do not think you are an ogre at all."

"Good, because I wanted to tell you—"

She touched her fingers to his lips. "Not now. It is time for the King's Cake and choosing the Lord of Misrule. We can speak later."

A flash of frustration crossed his features, but he nodded. She tugged his hand and they weaved their way through the crowd, heading for the dais. It took several minutes, as villagers wished them good cheer and warm thanks for the evening's entertainment. Phoebe was too flustered to say more than a few words, but Lucas responded with easy charm, seeming to enjoy himself. When his hand settled once more low on her back, cradling her gently as they strolled, her tension eased.

They reached the dais just as the door in the back of the hall swung open. Mr. Christmas emerged with great ceremony, two brawny footmen staggering behind him under the load of an enormous King's Cake. The confectionary edifice was always the centerpiece of the Twelfth Night celebrations, and Mrs. Christmas claimed that Cook's was the finest in the entire county.

The cake's thick icing gleamed with a brilliant white in the blaze of the candles, and whimsical sugar figurines dotted the polished, two-tiered surface. The round base was elaborately trimmed with sugar flowers in a rainbow of pretty pastels, while a credible representation of the village church and a few of the local shops topped the cake off.

"Good Lord," Lucas exclaimed. "Is that the village square on top of that monstrosity?"

"Yes," Phoebe said proudly. "It was Cook's idea. She did a splendid job, do you not think?"

Her husband laughed. "Actually, yes. It's got everything but the village drunk."

"Really, Lucas," she responded primly. "Come along. It is time to take your seat on the Lord of Misrule's throne."

He frowned. "Why do you think I'm going to be Lord of

Misrule? That's a damned big cake, and there's only one little bean baked into it. Anyone could find it and be appointed lord."

She glanced over at Mrs. Christmas, who was cutting the first slice. "We decided to do things a bit differently this year. Given certain, ah, mishaps in the past, everyone will be handed slips of paper with their cake. He who receives the slip with the appropriate mark will be designated Lord of Misrule."

"Hmm. I suppose someone got drunk and almost choked on the bean one year."

She widened her eyes. "How did you know that?"

"It's a fairly frequent occurrence. It happened to Robert once, and he wasn't even in his cups. Almost went to his grave because of the damn thing. He's only still with us thanks to his grandfather. The General slapped him on the back so hard he nearly knocked the poor lad into the next room."

Phoebe had to laugh at the image. "Well, we want to avoid that sort of thing. Mrs. Christmas came up with the slips as a substitute."

"Yes, but that still doesn't explain why you think I'll—"

Lucas broke off as Mrs. Christmas trundled toward them, carrying a plate. He directed a baleful look Phoebe's way. "Tell me you are not doing this."

She gave him a beatific smile in response.

He groaned. "On top of everything else, I must now be Lord of Misrule?"

"I am afraid so."

Surprisingly, his mouth twitched into a smile. "Well, I suppose it does make a bizarre sort of sense, given how everything tends to go to hell in a handcart around here."

Mrs. Christmas handed Lucas his plate and slip of paper with a dramatic flourish. Lucas inspected the slip with great solemnity, then gave the housekeeper a courtly bow in return. The guests cheered and whistled.

"Well, there's one consolation," he said, raising his voice over the din. "I get to pick you as my queen."

"I am afraid not," Phoebe said with mock regret. "Look."

He followed her pointing finger to where Mrs. Christmas was bestowing a plate of cake on Mrs. Knaggs.

Lucas gaped. "You're not serious! The vicar's wife as Queen of Misrule?"

Phoebe struggled to maintain a straight face. "We thought Mrs. Knaggs would be the perfect choice to assist you in your kingly duties."

"Lecture me, you mean. She's going to nag me about her pet projects all night."

She clucked her tongue sympathetically. "Poor Lucas. How awful for you."

He gave a grudging laugh. "You're killing me, Madam Wife."

"Perhaps later. We do not want any dead bodies littering the hall."

He bit back whatever retort he was about to deliver as Mrs. Knaggs came sailing up. The good woman beamed her excitement at being chosen, and Phoebe was pleased to see Lucas welcome her up on the dais in a gracious manner.

Once the king and queen were seated, the merriment resumed. Mrs. Christmas distributed the rest of the cake, and glasses of wassail and punch were replenished. As part of his duties, Lucas was called on to organize more games, and was kept busy supervising rounds of Forfeits. Eventually, a footman appeared with a large pewter bowl of brandied punch with raisins floating on top. He placed it on a table in the middle of the hall and set it aflame, prompting a rousing cheer from the spectators.

"What is that for?" Phoebe asked as she leaned against the arm of Lucas's throne.

"It's snapdragons. You try to snatch the raisins from the flaming punch without getting burned. It requires a quick eye and a steady hand."

And a great deal of merriment, by the looks of it, as the guests laughingly egged each other on. Phoebe had to admit it looked like fun, if a bit risky.

"Perhaps I should try," she said, starting to step down from the dais.

Lucas's hand shot out, gently pulling her back to his side. "No, sweetheart. No burns for you."

She stared down at him, caught by the affectionate expression in his eyes. His long fingers wrapped around her wrist, feeling rough and warm against her skin. She swallowed, her throat going dry. His simple touch made her tingle from head to toe.

Instinctively, she started to lean into him. His eyes flared with heat and he tilted his head up, as if ready to take her kiss. And she almost *did* kiss him, completely forgetting where she was, until a gentle touch on her elbow jerked her back to awareness. "My lady, forgive the interruption."

Mr. Christmas had suddenly appeared by the dais, tense and alert as his gaze darted around the hall and then back to her.

She frowned. "Is there a problem, Mr. Christmas?"

"A small one, I'm afraid, my lady. In the kitchen."

"I will come right away."

As he nodded and disappeared, Phoebe turned to Lucas and made her excuses. Turning her hand over, he raised her palm to his mouth and gave it a lingering kiss that ended with a little bite.

Goodness. She actually felt a bit faint, and she did not think it came from the heat of the room.

"Don't be long," he murmured in a seductive voice.

She nodded and scurried off, thoroughly confused. Even though Lucas had not reacted as she'd hoped to the news of her pregnancy, he did seem content tonight. For the first time in several days, she started to feel a glimmer of hope.

Phoebe pushed through the swinging door into the kitchen,

before stumbling to a shocked halt. Mr. Weston was seated at the large kitchen worktable, his coarse cotton shirt stained with blood. Little Sam stood behind him, white-faced with fear. She *had* noted their absence earlier in the evening, and had attributed it to Mr. Weston's continuing reluctance to face her. That was obviously not the case.

"Dear God! How did this happen?" she exclaimed.

Mrs. Christmas yanked some towels from a cupboard, stomping over to Mr. Weston and pressing one against the wound to his upper arm. The man flinched and drew in a harsh breath. "The fool got himself shot by the excise men," she snapped. "He and Sam barely escaped."

Phoebe took Sam gently by the shoulders. "Are you hurt?"

The boy shook his head, obviously too frightened to speak. Phoebe cast a quick glance around the kitchen. Several maids and a few of the footmen watched closely in worried silence, but there was no one else.

"Was anyone else involved?" Phoebe asked Mr. Weston.

"Three others, my lady, but they took off into the woods. I'm fair certain they got clean away." He drew in a hissing breath when Mrs. Christmas pressed even harder to staunch the blood.

Phoebe felt sick. "So, you were running goods across Merritt lands again."

He raised a miserable gaze to her face. "Tonight was to be our last run, my lady. I swear it. The cargo had already been promised and half paid for. I didn't have a choice."

"And what about Sam? Did you not have a choice when it came to your son's safety?"

Mr. Weston ducked his head, a glaze of shame coloring his cheeks. "Aye. Taking him was foolish. I won't deny it." He looked back up at her, eyes pleading. "But I'll never put the boy in danger again, I swear. On my wife's grave, I swear it."

Phoebe took a deep breath, willing her anger to subside. The damage was done. Now all she could do was try to contain it. "Mr. Christmas, please fetch Dr. Blackmore. Tell him one of the kitchen maids burned herself."

"Yes, my lady."

"Mrs. Christmas, we will need hot water and more cloths, and send one of the girls up to Dr. Blackmore's bedroom for his bag. And get Sam something hot to drink—some milk or hot chocolate. Oh, and someone give me a pair of scissors."

As the staff scrambled to carry out her instructions, Phoebe took the scissors from a maid and carefully cut away Mr. Weston's sleeve. When the wound was fully exposed, raw and bleeding sluggishly, her gorge rose to her throat. She had to close her eyes and draw in a breath before her stomach settled.

"You're lucky, Ned Weston," said Mrs. Christmas. "A clean shot, through and through."

"Doesn't feel lucky," he ground out.

Dr. Blackmore hurried into the kitchen, frowning as he took in the commotion. "That doesn't look like a burn to me," he said.

Phoebe ignored his dry comment. "Thank goodness. This is Mr. Weston, our local innkeeper. He has met with an, ah, accident."

"Apparently. I will need someone to fetch my bag."

"Here, sir," gasped Maggie, breathless from her run up and down the back staircase.

The doctor went to work, efficiently cleaning and bandaging the wound. Everyone else stood in tense silence, occasionally throwing worried glances at Phoebe.

"That should do," Dr. Blackmore finally said. "You'll need to get the bandage changed every day for the next week, and you'll also need a sling to keep the arm immobile."

Phoebe exhaled a sigh of relief. "Thank you, Doctor." She glanced at the clock on a shelf by the pantry. "I must get back upstairs before I am missed."

The doctor stood. "I'll take you up." He smiled at Phoebe. "I assume you'll want me to keep this quiet."

She hated to draw him into a fabrication, but her options were very limited. "Unfortunately, yes."

"Of course, my lady."

Phoebe was murmuring additional thanks when an awful thought sucked the air from her lungs. "Mr. Weston," she gasped. "Is there any chance the excise men might track you here?"

The publican wet his lips. "I . . . it's surely possible. They've done it before."

"Yes, I remember that occasion," she said in a hollow voice. If the officers found Mr. Weston at Mistletoe Manor, they would arrest him. Sam, too.

It took but a few seconds to reach a decision. "Mr. Christmas, find a fresh shirt and jacket for Mr. Weston. He and Sam must come up to the hall and act as if they have been here all evening."

Dr. Blackmore stopped packing up his case to frown at her. "Do you think that wise, Lady Merritt? Obstructing the law is a tricky business."

Sam clutched the back of his father's chair so hard his fingers blanched white. "Please, my lady. Don't let Pa be arrested. He's all I got!"

Phoebe gave him a reassuring smile. "I will not allow that to happen, Sam. I—"

The door to the kitchen swung open. Lucas stopped cold as he entered, his gaze taking in the scene before him. His eyes grew hard as flint as they settled on Phoebe.

"Well, what have we here?" he asked in a lethally soft voice.

Chapter 37

Phoebe's stomach lurched, and she had to resist the impulse to grab the nearest basin.

Lucas studied her for a moment before flicking his icy gaze to Mr. Weston, grim-faced and pale in his chair. "Is this little tableau the result of a smuggling run across my land, Weston?"

The man looked ready to faint, but managed to come to his feet. "Aye, my lord, and I apologize for it. But as I told your lady, tonight was to be my last run." He swallowed hard. "I'm giving it up, I swear it."

Sam moved to his father's side. "It's the truth, my lord. Honest. Pa promised me this would be the last."

The quaver in the boy's voice closed a fist around Phoebe's heart. She started forward to comfort him, but Lucas shot a hand out. "Stay right where you are, Phoebe."

"But, Lucas—"

"And stay quiet," he said through clenched teeth. "I need to think."

His tone made her bristle, but the situation would not be improved by an argument.

"Weston," Lucas said after a short but fraught silence,

"did you stop to think that Harper would follow your trail to the manor?"

As Mr. Weston opened his mouth to reply, a loud banging sounded from the hall. Someone was pounding on the manor's front door.

Lucas rubbed his forehead. "Christ. Of course they'd end up here."

The entire kitchen froze with apprehension, but Phoebe forced herself to break the silence. "Lucas, what are you going to do?"

He cast her a frustrated glare. "My home is about to be invaded by a group of gun-toting excise officers who are loathed by every person within twenty miles. What do you think I'm going to do?"

Mr. Weston stepped forward. "My lord, I deserve no mercy, and if it was just me I'd go freely enough." He looked down at Sam, standing by his side and quietly sobbing. "I ask for mercy for my boy's sake. He's got naught to look after him but me."

Lucas raked an impatient hand through his hair. "You should have thought of that before, Weston." He glanced at Phoebe. "I've got to get up there to deal with Harper. Please make sure this mess gets cleaned up, and then take Weston and Sam up to the hall."

He pivoted on his heel and strode to the door. When he looked back at them, everyone was still frozen in place. "Get moving," he snapped, then disappeared through the swinging door.

The kitchen erupted into a flurry of action. Within two minutes, the maids had swept the table clean and Mr. Weston was clothed in garb provided by the footmen. As Phoebe took a deep breath, preparing to follow her husband, she felt Sam's hand slip into hers.

"Please, my lady," seemed all he was able to choke out.

She bent down to look him straight in the eye. "Do not

worry, Sam. His lordship and I will not abandon you. But you must be brave and come with me to the hall."

The little boy squared his shoulders. "I ain't frightened, my lady."

"Good." A swift glance reassured her that everything was as it should be. "Mr. Weston, Sam, please follow me."

She hurried through to the corridor, then slowed her pace. It would do no good to arrive breathless. She must appear serene and confident, a truly laughable idea given that her nerves were stretched on a rack of anxiety. Despite her brave words to Sam, she had no idea what Lucas would do. She only knew that if he turned Mr. Weston over to the law she might never be able to forgive him.

And if more blood ended up being shed in the manor tonight, she might never forgive herself. Not for the first time, she flayed herself for making such a hash of things.

She slipped into the hall, glancing behind to see Mr. Weston and Sam melt into the crowd. An unnatural silence had fallen over the packed room, broken only by tense whispers and a low thrum of hostile murmuring.

Swiftly, Phoebe made her way to the front of the room, where Lucas confronted Mr. Harper and his men. She counted at least ten in his small force, all armed and all casting nervous, suspicious glances at the guests. The threat of violence hung in the air like a malevolent fog.

She dodged her way through the crowd, coming to stand beside Lucas. At the same time, Silverton stepped forward, moving to flank Lucas on the other side. Meredith and Bathsheba followed, both staring haughtily down their noses at the excise men. As a strategy of intimidation, one could hardly ask for better than four imperious and clearly annoyed aristocrats.

Lucas glanced at Phoebe and smiled. "Ah, there you are,

my love. I trust you have solved whatever little domestic crisis was occurring below stairs?"

She blinked, surprised by his light tone and easy confidence. One of his dark brows lifted, amused and faintly questioning.

"Oh, yes," she said. "One of the kitchen maids dropped an entire platter of mince pies. The girl fell into hysterics and Cook was quite put out, but I do believe disaster has been averted."

She sounded amazingly calm to her own ears. Perhaps she was a better liar than she gave herself credit for. Not a very consoling thought, but certainly useful in certain circumstances.

"Thank God for small mercies," Lucas said. "As you can see, we have some unexpected guests. Mr. Harper and his men are on the hunt for smugglers. Naturally, he thought a party at Mistletoe Manor the perfect place to find them."

Mr. Harper starched up. "My lord, I have no desire to disturb you, but the blood trail we found in the woods pointed to the manor. I must insist you let us conduct a search."

"You insist?" Lucas replied in a bored but haughty voice. "How extraordinary. One would think the last place a smuggler would run to is a house full of merry people, especially when that house is owned by one who has made it clear he does not countenance illegal activity."

Mr. Harper's suspicious gaze fell on Phoebe. "Mayhap you don't countenance it, my lord, but rumor has it other members of your household do."

Phoebe bit back a gasp as an angry murmur rose from the crowd.

"I would suggest," Lucas said in a voice cold enough to freeze hellfire, "that a sensible man would do well to ignore baseless rumors, Harper. Do I make myself clear?"

"Perfectly, my lord. But as an officer of the law, I must

insist you allow me to carry out my duties and conduct my search."

"You do realize, Mr. Harper," interjected Cousin Stephen, "that as Marquess of Silverton I am a local magistrate. If I feel there is no need to conduct a search, should that not satisfy you?"

"No disrespect intended, my lord," Harper snapped, "but no. It doesn't."

The crowd's muttering grew louder, and the excise men shifted nervously, keeping their pistols at the ready. Phoebe had an awful feeling that disaster might be only seconds away.

Lucas let out a long-suffering sigh. "Very well. Conduct your search if you must, Harper. I'm sure you will find your smugglers hiding in the larder, behind the cheese or the pickles."

Mr. Harper's face turned positively red. "I do not appreciate the jest, Lord Merritt. And be sure I *will* conduct a thorough search"

"Go right ahead. Christmas," Lucas said to the butler, "please accompany Mr. Harper's men to the kitchen and cellars. And see they don't disturb Cook."

Mr. Harper and his men fanned out, some going below stairs and others pushing their way through the hall. When Phoebe saw an officer head toward Mr. Weston, she drew in a sharp breath. Fortunately, Mr. Knaggs bumbled into the man's path, apologizing profusely as he adroitly steered the officer in another direction.

Lucas settled a hand on her back. "Courage, my love," he murmured. "Harper knows he won't find anything. He's just trying to make a point."

He was right. In a few minutes, Mr. Harper's men returned to the front of the hall, assembling behind their disgruntled chief.

"Find anything?" Lucas asked politely.

"No, my lord, which I suspect does not surprise you. But I

swear this won't be the end of it. I intend to track down that gang and bring every last man to account."

"I commend your dedication. Now, sir, I suggest you either put away your pistols and join our celebrations, or be on your way. The ladies cannot be easy as long as your weapons are drawn."

"Thank you, but no," said Harper with offended dignity. "We'll not trouble you any longer."

Mr. Christmas ushered the men out and shut the doors behind them. For a full ten seconds, silence prevailed, then the room erupted into loud cheers. Silverton clapped Lucas on the back, and the men of the village surrounded him, vigorously pumping his hand and thanking him. The women hugged each other, and little Sam threw his arms around his father's waist and burst into tears.

"Well," said Meredith, hugging Phoebe, "you and Lucas certainly know how to throw an interesting party. This is so much more entertaining than fisticuffs over Easter dinner."

"And how lucky you are to have a doctor on hand to treat the wounded," Bathsheba chimed in. "Although I do hope you don't fall into the habit of inviting armed militias to your parties. They tend to make such a mess of the carpets."

Phoebe's head swam and her limbs felt weak with relief. Bathsheba pushed her into a chair. "Sit down before you fall down."

Meredith knelt beside her. "You needn't have worried, Phoebe. Lucas is a good man. He will always do the right thing, even if it's not entirely lawful."

Phoebe stared at her husband, who was now the object of toasts from Mr. Knaggs and some of the other men. He calmly accepted their cheers and then looked at Phoebe. Slowly, his gazed heated.

"I certainly recognize *that* look," Bathsheba said.

"Yes." Meredith sighed happily. "It's so romantic."

"I have no idea what you two are talking about," Phoebe lied, blushing.

"If you don't, you're about to find out," Bathsheba replied. "Here comes your husband."

Lucas strode up to them. "Ladies, if you'll excuse us, I'd like to speak with my wife."

"Go right ahead," said Bathsheba as Lucas lifted Phoebe out of her chair. "I suggest you take her to your study, and make sure to lock the door behind you."

Phoebe glared over her shoulder at Bathsheba and Meredith. Both were snickering as Lucas towed her into his study. Holly, safely ensconced in his basket by the fire, lifted his head and gave them a sleepy yawn by way of greeting. When they ignored him, he grumbled, dug his nose under his paws, and went back to sleep.

Lucas firmly shut the door and locked it.

"You cannot be serious," Phoebe said in disbelief. "We have a houseful of guests!"

"I'll show you serious, Madam Wife."

The grim note had returned to his voice, and her heart sank.

"Lucas, I realize you must be unhappy with me—"

"That's not the word I would use," he growled, pulling her over to one of the ancient leather armchairs by the fire.

Oh, dear. "Ah, what word would thee like to use?" She winced when her slip of the tongue betrayed her jangling nerves.

He sat, then tugged her into his lap. As she tumbled across him, the chair creaked ominously under their combined weights. Her husband sighed. "I suppose we need new furniture in here, too."

"That might be wise."

Despite his gentle touch, she could not yet bring herself to look at him. Perhaps he was not that angry about the smuggling situation—and the interesting ridge nudging her bottom suggested that—but she could not forget how he had reacted earlier this evening to the news she was breeding.

"Phoebe, look at me."

She forced herself to look into his eyes, only to lose her breath at the shadowed intensity of his gaze.

"How are you feeling?" he asked as he stroked her chin.

A chin that quivered at his touch. "I am not entirely certain. It has been a most unusual evening."

"That's one way of putting it."

She winced at his sarcastic tone. "Lucas, I am so very sorry about what happened tonight. I regret I had to place you in a difficult position, and I want to thank you for what you did."

"You didn't think I would protect him, did you?"

She hesitated, wanting to spare his feelings, but she was done with lying to him. "Truthfully, I was not sure what you would do."

His mouth twisted. "All right. I deserve that. It's not like I've done a very good job of winning anyone's trust—either yours or the people of the manor or village."

She placed a quick hand on his chest. "No, I have always trusted you, but we do not always agree on the best way to resolve a problem."

"In other words, I should always listen to you," he said dryly.

"I would never be so arrogant as to suggest such a thing."

When he laughed, she felt a little kick of relief in her chest.

"Well, in this case you were right. No good, and likely a great deal of damage, would have resulted from turning Weston over to the law. Doing the *righteous* thing is not always the *right* thing. That's not an easy lesson for an old soldier to learn." He paused to nuzzle her neck, and a hot little shiver rippled down her spine. "But with your help," he murmured between kisses, "I'm sure I'll evolve into a satisfactory lord of the manor and husband."

She arched her neck to give him better access. "I am sure you will."

Unfortunately, just when things were turning interesting, he pulled back.

"But let's be clear about one thing, Phoebe," he said. "No more lies and no more secrets between us. Understood? I will not tolerate either from my wife."

She stared back, knowing he was absolutely right, which meant she had to ask him the one question she dreaded more than any other. "And you, Lucas. Will you tell me the truth?"

His expression grew guarded. "About what?"

"About our baby."

He frowned. "What truth about the baby? I don't understand."

She gazed down at her hands, her courage failing. How could she bear it if he did not love her enough to love their child?

He tipped up her chin. "What troubles thee, my love?" he asked.

The affectionate mockery brought a mist of tears to her eyes. "I do not know if you want this child. You already have so many burdens to carry. To add another . . ."

She trailed off, disconcerted by the stunned look on his face. He blinked a few times, then shook his head. "Clearly, I am a dreadful husband if I left you in any doubt about that." He captured her face between his hands. "How could I not want any child of ours, Phoebe? What a goose you are to think I would not."

She peered into his eyes, seeking answers. "But you did not seem happy when I told you."

"I was just a bit stunned, that's all. You caught me completely unawares."

"Truly?" she asked, still doubtful.

He gave her a steady look, one that challenged her to believe. "It would be impossible not to want the child when I love the mother as much as I do. Phoebe, I never thought I *could* love anyone as I do you." He gave a ghost of a laugh. "But I do love you, my darling. In opening your generous and honorable heart to me, you taught me how to trust again. You taught me how to forgive, both myself and others. Without you, I would still be a thick-skulled idiot, convinced he could never love another woman again." He kissed her gently on the forehead. "Imagine my surprise to discover how very easy it was, after all."

She clutched at his hands, unable to say a word as her throat went tight.

He unleashed a devilish smile. "Will miracles never cease? Phoebe Stanton silenced at last."

That barb loosened her tongue. "Really, Lucas! You are—"

She never got a chance to tell him exactly what he was, because his mouth swooped down to take hers in a devouring kiss. She wrapped her arms around him, joy sweeping away the last remnants of doubt and anxiety. Phoebe would never be alone again—not as long as Lucas held her in his arms and in his heart.

Their embrace grew more and more heated, until her husband's fingers moved to the front of her bodice, dipping below the lace trim to find the top of her chemise. Phoebe broke away with a gasp. "Lucas, we cannot do this. Our guests are waiting for us."

"Let them wait," he said as he began to unlace her. "This is our home, and if I want to make love to my wife, I will do so." He raised mocking eyebrows at her. "I hope *thee* does not have a problem with that."

She laughed, reaching for his cravat. "Not really."

Lucas was right, of course. In each other's hearts and souls, they had both finally come home.

Author's Note

Readers will note that my heroine occasionally uses what Quakers refer to as *plain speech*, which sounds archaic to our ears. Quakers in the Georgian and Regency periods would have eschewed elaborate or *fancy* forms of address as much as they avoided fancy or richly ornamented clothing. Persons of rank would have been addressed using the familiar *thee* or *thou*, in order to illustrate equality between persons and to encourage direct speech.

By 1817, the year in which my novel takes place, Quakers had replaced *thou* with *thee* as the nominative case form of the second person singular pronoun. That is why Phoebe only uses the word *thee*, and never *thou*. Naturally, any mistakes in her diction are mine!

Readers will also note the number of characters in my book bearing the surname of *Christmas*. Although an unusual name, there are generations of Englishmen and women bearing this name especially, apparently, in Sussex and Essex counties. And on more than one parish or local registry I did indeed find the name, *Honor Christmas*.